W9-CAR-886

Praise for the works of
ORR KELLY,
acknowledged expert on America's
special operations forces

"THIS GUY KNOWS
WHAT HE'S TALKING ABOUT."
Tom Clancy

BRAVE MEN, DARK WATERS:
The Untold Story of the Navy SEALs

"The best work to date on the SEALs."
Publishers Weekly

"Must reading for all special-ops fans.
An objective, well-documented account
of where the Navy SEALs came from
and where they are headed."
The Retired Officer Magazine

FROM *A DARK SKY: THE STORY OF*
U.S. AIR FORCE SPECIAL OPERATIONS

"Orr Kelly has done an admirable job of not just
telling the facts, but bringing the experiences of
Air Force special operations to life."
Lt. Gen. LeRoy J. Manor USAF (Ret.)

"Must reading for anyone interested in a complete
history of Air Force special operations. From
beginning to end, Orr Kelly has written an
important study of the air commandos."
Douglas C. Waller, author of *The Commandos*

SEALS EAGLE FORCE
DESERT THUNDER

ORR KELLY

AVON BOOKS ◆ NEW YORK

This is a work of fiction. Names, characters, places, and incidents either are the product of the author's imagination or are used fictitiously. Any resemblance to actual events, locales, organizations, or persons, living or dead, is entirely coincidental and beyond the intent of either the author or the publisher.

AVON BOOKS, INC.
1350 Avenue of the Americas
New York, New York 10019

Copyright © 1998 by Orr Kelly
Excerpt from *Seals Eagle Force: Terror at Taranaki* copyright © 1999 by Orr Kelly
Published by arrangement with the author
Visit our website at **http://www.AvonBooks.com**
Library of Congress Catalog Card Number: 98-92765
ISBN: 0-380-79114-5

First Avon Books Printing: October 1998

AVON TRADEMARK REG. U.S. PAT. OFF. AND IN OTHER COUNTRIES, MARCA REGISTRADA, HECHO EN U.S.A.

Printed in the U.S.A.

WCD   10   9   8   7   6   5   4   3   2   1

ACKNOWLEDGMENTS

For whatever claims to authenticity this work of fiction may have, I owe a debt of gratitude to my many friends in the SEAL and Air Force Special Operations communities. They generously shared their experiences and their memories with me during research for my earlier histories of naval special warfare and the air commandos. My familiarity with their real-life experiences helped at many points as I wove together this tale from my imagination.

I am especially grateful to M.Sgt. Timothy Hadrych, who coached me by E-mail on the technical capabilities of the Air Force's Pave Low helicopter.

The section of the book dealing with the injury to Denise Bonior required research at both Children's Hospital in Washington, D.C., and the Children's Hospital of the King's Daughters in Norfolk, Virginia.

In Washington, Dr. Daniel Ochsenschlager, medical director of the emergency room at Children's Hospital, and Jeannie Reardon of the hospital staff showed me how a little girl wounded in a drive-by shooting would be treated. But Dr. Ochsenschlager also suggested that it would be more realistic to have a child injured in Virginia Beach taken directly to the Children's Hospital of the King's Daughters.

I followed up by visiting King's Daughters, as the hospital is familiarly known. There I spent much of a day accompanying Dr. Thomas A. Nakagawa, who is in charge of the pediatric intensive care unit, on his rounds. Dr. Nakagawa showed me through the hospital and the emergency room at the adjoining Norfolk General and was most helpful in providing me with background on hospital procedures. I also visited with Kathy Hochmiller, a flight nurse, who told me how the Nightingale helicopter would be used to bring an injured child to the hospital.

The idea for this book came first from the fertile mind of Stephen S. Power, senior editor at Avon Books, and I am grateful to him not only for encouraging me in this venture into fiction but for his painstaking and perceptive editing of the manuscript.

My friend and agent, Mike Hamilburg, did his usual smooth, professional job of working out the details of our contract.

Special thanks, too, to my wife, Mary, who has learned to put up cheerfully with the unorthodox work habits of a writer.

He does not impel his body, like other serpents, by a multiplied flexion, but advances lofty and upright. He kills the shrubs not by contact, but by breathing on them, and splits the rocks, such power of evil is there in him.

—PLINY, ON THE COCKATRICE

THE EAGLE FORCE

Chief Jack Berryman, SEAL, expert with .50-caliber sniper rifle.

Command M. Chief Jeff Bonior, 39, senior SEAL, only black member of the team.

Patricia Collins, 26, team's intelligence expert, widow of Jim Collins, close friend of Chuck Nelson, mother of two children.

S.Sgt. Ray Donovan, Pave Low rear gunner.

M.Sgt. Tim Hutchins, 35, Air Force Special Tactics combat controller.

Maj. Jack Laffer, Pave Low copilot.

Dr. James D. Malcolm, 65, scientific briefer, expert in exotic weapons.

Rex Marker, 22, youngest member of the team, in charge of communications.

Chief Jeremy Merrifield, SEAL, explosives expert.

Cdr. Charles "Chuck" Nelson, 36, SEAL, leader of the team.

Lt. Col. Mark Rattner, 37, Pave Low pilot, second in command of the team.

Chief Mark Raymond, SEAL, machine gunner.

T.Sgt. Tom Shoup, Air Force Special Tactics paramedic.

Chief Ray Pratt, SEAL, explosives expert.

HM3 Bill Wagner, 46, SEAL medic, oldest, most experienced member of the team.

OTHER CHARACTERS

Ben Bernard, 37, known as "Big Dog," former SEAL, foe of Nelson's, head of mercenary commando team.

Dorothy "Dottie" Bonior, Bonior's wife, mother of Beverly, 10; Jeff, Jr., 8; and Denise, 6.

Dick Hoffman, 23, former SEAL, member of Bernard's team, close friend of Rex Marker.

Sergei Kaparov, 44, also known as Abdulkhashim Karimov, Soviet test pilot who defected to the United States with a Backfire bomber.

Adm. Norris McKay, 54, a submariner and chairman of the Joint Chiefs of Staff.

Michelle "Mickey" Moselle, the president's beautiful Eurasian paramour.

Laszlo "Luke" Nash, one-time Hungarian freedom fighter and CIA pilot, now operating behind the scenes to gather wealth, power.

Maynard Walker, 52, president of the United States.

Marcia Carter Walker, 46, Maynard Walker's wife, mother of their son, David, 8.

Sen. Richard Wilson, candidate against President Walker from within his own party.

CHAPTER 1

"GENTLEMEN, I AM DR. JAMES MALCOLM—JIM MALCOLM."

The tall, silver-haired scientist stood at the blackboard at the front of the briefing room with the confident manner of one who had spent most of his career in a college classroom.

"You will be training hard for a very specific mission for the next few weeks here at Site Y." With every syllable, the tone of Malcolm's voice indicated he was a man used to being listened to and taken seriously. "I know it will be a hardship. The living conditions here are, as you are well aware, Spartan. I regret that we have had to block all outgoing telephone calls. And of course there will be no incoming calls because no one knows you are here.

"Up to this point, your training has been general in nature—low-level flight, nighttime insertions, small unit drills. Now you will move into a new phase and it is time to tell you the purpose of this mission.

"Perhaps when I finish, you will understand why you are being put through these hardships. In my opinion, few men have ever been called upon to carry out a mission as important as this one."

Cdr. Charles Nelson glanced over and raised an eyebrow as he caught the eye of Lt. Col. Mark Rattner, sitting on one side of the briefing room with the crews for two Pave Low helicopters. Gathered near Nelson, who sported the gaudy shield of a Navy SEAL on his left breast, were the members of the two platoons of his team—each platoon made up of twelve

SEALs and four Air Force Special Tactics Team members. Rattner, the Air Force officer, was Nelson's deputy.

"Your job," Malcolm continued, "will be to correct a monumental mistake—a mistake that threatens the lives of millions of Americans."

He clicked the remote control switch in his left hand and the projector in the rear of the room flashed on, displaying a satellite picture of an airfield. Cutting diagonally across the picture was a long white line—a single five-mile runway. To one side were a large hangar and a cluster of two-story office or barracks buildings. The complex was ringed by two rows of fencing, but there did not appear to be any guard towers.

"This is where you will be going," Malcolm said. "It is in northern Iraq, just south of the no-fly zone we have been patrolling since Desert Storm."

With the mention of the word "Iraq," a murmur ran through the room. Until this moment, only Nelson and Rattner had known their destination and, roughly, what they would be required to do. The entire planning and training period to this point had been blanketed by a strict need-to-know rule. The time had now come to fill in the other members of the helicopter crew and the SEAL/Special Tactics Team members on the goal of their mission.

Rex Marker broke the silence. At 22, the youngest member of the team, Marker was a SEAL with a genius for electronics. He would be in charge of communications—what little would be permitted—during the mission. A self-confident young man totally lacking in awe of rank or age, Marker never hesitated to speak up.

"Sir," he asked, "you said our job was to correct a mistake. What does that mean?"

Malcolm turned toward him. "Good question, son." Like many civilians, Malcolm had difficulty telling one military rank from another—especially when it came to Navy enlisted men. It was easier and safer to call Marker "son" than to try to decode the insignia on his arm.

"You will all recall how, after the war with Iraq, the United Nations spent years trying to track down evidence of Iraq's attempt to build weapons of mass destruction—nuclear weapons, long-range missiles, chemical and biological materials. The Iraqis resisted every step of the way. But the UN gradually learned that they had been pretty close to making a nuclear weapon and that they already had a stockpile of chemical and biological materials.

"By now, we think we have identified the manufacturing sites and the places where these things are stored and have the problem pretty well under control. That's where we made our mistake. It wasn't a mistake, of course, to deal with these weapons. But we focused entirely on the kinds of weapons that we and other nations have had in our arsenals. Our mistake was in failing to ask ourselves, 'What else is Saddam Hussein up to?'

"Now, we think we know what he is up to—and it is not good news." Malcolm pressed the control and another picture appeared on the screen. "This is what we missed."

The picture, taken from a satellite passing 125 miles overhead, showed a large covered shape sitting in front of a hangar.

Malcolm clicked again. "This is what we think is under that tarp."

On the screen was a drawing of what appeared to be a swing-wing bomber. To Mark Rattner, it looked like an oversized version of the FB-111 fighter-bomber he had flown earlier in his Air Force career.

"If you're not too rusty on your aircraft identification, this is a Soviet-made Blackjack bomber—or at least, that's what it was before the Iraqis began modifying it," Malcolm explained, pointing to the movable wings and the shadows of the two engine pods under each wing.

Rattner, a tall man with a long, lean face who looked more like a surgeon than one of the nation's most skilled combat helicopter pilots, leaned forward for a better look. "Aren't those awfully big engines? I don't remember the Blackjack looking like that."

"Right, Colonel. That's one of its surprises—although not the biggest, unfortunately. My best guess—and I've spent my career working on some of our most advanced aircraft, from the Blackbird to the Stealth—is that they've replaced one of the two engines under each wing with a large ramjet engine.

We did a great deal of work on this kind of propulsion—a kind of cross between a rocket and a jet engine—back in the nineteen fifties and sixties. But we ran into extensive technical problems—and then the money ran out. If the Iraqis have been able to make these engines work as I've always thought this type of engine might, then this plane could have remarkable performance. I'm talking about an altitude of something like thirty miles and a speed of 5,000 miles an hour.

"At that altitude and speed, this plane would be more like a spacecraft than an airplane. We assume they would use the conventional engines for takeoff and climb to something like forty thousand feet. Then the ramjets would take over and kick her up to very high altitudes and very high speed. We're talking about around-the-world in five hours. And once the plane reaches its cruising altitude, there is practically no air resistance. It virtually coasts."

"Dr. Malcolm, that's all very interesting. But it's just one plane. What's so important about it that we have to risk our lives?" Chuck Nelson, the veteran SEAL who would be the on-scene commander, always got nervous when people came up with schemes that could get his people hurt or killed.

"I understand, sir," Malcolm replied. "So let me explain what concerns us about this craft: what we think it's being prepared to carry. We're not sure, but we think the Iraqis have picked up on and perhaps perfected a weapon of mass destruction we did a lot of work on some thirty or forty years ago.

"You gentlemen are too young to remember, but when I was your age, back in the fifties, the Air Force and Navy, especially, spent a lot of money and effort on new weapons. Some of the work we did was remarkably successful. We developed the Polaris submarine and missile system. We built the SR-71 Blackbird, which flies so high and fast it is beyond the reach of antiaircraft weapons or fighter planes. We deployed the Minuteman missile system.

"We also spent a lot of effort on some things that didn't pan out, either because of technical problems or because we didn't want to spend what it would take to make them work. Some of the things we worked on were on the edge of practicality. We did the research, not because we were confident it would succeed, but so that we would understand what was going on if we learned some other nation was taking the same route. The Dynasoar is an example. It was a plane—not unlike what the Iraqis seem to have built—that would rocket into the lower edges of space and then soar for vast distances.

"Some of the things we worked on remain secret to this day. One of my projects—and that's the reason I'm here talking to you—was a truly exotic weapon. Let me try to show you how it would work."

Malcolm took up a piece of chalk and drew a small circle at the top of the blackboard. He labeled it "sun." At the bottom, he drew a slightly curving horizontal line and labeled it "earth's surface." Radiating from the sun, he drew a series of dotted lines, some of them reaching down to the line at the bottom.

"As you know, the earth is being bombarded constantly by energy from the sun—and by particles of energy originating far out in space, even in other galaxies. Much of this constant rain of energy is highly beneficial. Without heat and light from the sun, life on earth would be impossible. But this energy can also be dangerous. The energy that gives us light and heat can also cause sunburn—or cancer."

Malcolm paused, turning to the blackboard again. He drew a small circle and then drew closely spaced parallel dotted lines from the circle to a single spot on the earth.

"We asked ourselves what would happen if we could focus some of this powerful energy at a single spot on the earth's surface."

Rex Marker spoke up again: "It'd be like a magnifying glass. You could start a fire."

Malcolm turned. "Yes . . . but much more than a fire. The concentration of energy we are talking about would simply vaporize whatever it hit. Everything within a quarter of a mile or so of the point where the energy was focused would simply vanish. In an area the width of Manhattan, buildings, bridges, highways, machinery, and people would all disappear as though they had never existed. At the edges, you would find some wreckage and debris, but close to the point where the energy had been focused, all you would find would be a powdery residue.

"Even before the Russians launched their *Sputnik* in 1957, we were thinking about mounting a very large lens out in space. But what if this energy-focusing lens could be mounted on a fast, high-flying plane? It could cut a swath of destruction half a mile wide and thousands of miles long. In half an hour, such a plane, passing over the United States, could devastate a score of our major cities. The loss of life and destruction of property would be by far the worst disaster in this nation's history—perhaps the worst in all history."

The room was totally silent as Malcolm paused and turned away from the blackboard.

"When we succeeded in developing intercontinental ballistic missiles, work on this and other exotic weapons systems was dropped—not because we couldn't make them work, but because it was thought there was no longer any reason to pursue them. Now, gentlemen, we think the Iraqis have pushed on our old research to the point where the weapon may be ready for deployment.

"If our calculations are correct, it is conceivable that they have been able to design an energy-focusing device small enough to be carried by this plane—in other words, something that weighs eighteen tons or less. That's a tough technological challenge and we don't know whether they have succeeded. But we don't want to wait to find out."

Rex Marker broke in. "What do you call this thing, Doctor?"

"We don't know what the Iraqis call it. But I've given it a code name. I call it the *Cockatrice*."

"The crocka-what?" exclaimed one of the SEALs, and a ripple of laughter swept through the room.

Malcolm chuckled. "*Cockatrice*—or, more precisely, *eye of the Cockatrice*. Let me explain. In Greek and Roman literature, there was a mythological beast called a cockatrice. It was supposedly hatched from a hen's egg by serpents. It had the head of a cock and the body of a serpent. Whatever it cast its eye on died and was consumed by flames. One Roman writer, Pliny, said: 'He kills the shrubs not by contact, but by breathing on them, and splits the rocks, such power of evil is there in him.' Isn't that a pretty good description of what we're talking about here?''

A murmur of assent came from the group. Chuck Nelson raised his hand. He was one of those combat commanders whose men would follow him anywhere. But he returned their trust by making sure the odds were always stacked as much as possible in their favor. More than once he had defied superior officers and turned down assignments that would have put his men in needless danger. "That's pretty impressive, sir, but you still haven't answered my question: Why us? We can take that place out with a couple of Tomahawk cruise missiles with hardly any risk at all.''

Malcolm turned and regarded him for a moment. "You're right, of course, Commander. But we want that plane and that weapon. We want to understand what they have done and how they have done it. And we don't want to be caught by surprise again if anyone else tries something like this.''

"Would one of you gentlemen in the rear open the door?'' Malcolm asked. A special tactics man reached over and complied. As the door swung open, a man who looked as though he had parked his horse outside stepped into the room. Of medium height, he appeared to be in his late forties. He was dressed in jeans and a faded plaid shirt. Little clumps of dried cow manure clung to his boots. His face had the same weathered look as his old leather jacket. In his hand he held a ten-gallon cowboy hat.

"Come in, Sergei. Sorry to keep you waiting. Gentlemen, I would like you to meet Sergei Kaparov. He's going to accompany you on your mission, and with your help, he's going to get that plane airborne and fly it and its weapon out to us.''

"Howdy, boys.'' Kaparov gestured with his hat as he walked to the front of the room and took up a position between Malcolm and the blackboard.

Malcolm chuckled. "Sergei has gone native on us. In nineteen eighty-seven, just before the Soviet Union collapsed, Sergei was a colonel in the Soviet Air Force, and probably their most experienced test pilot. He decided for a variety of reasons that it was time to get out. Although it has never been publicized, he was able to defect and deliver an operational Backfire bomber to us. At the time it was their first-line strategic bomber. He's made some friends in our Air Force and has been able to keep his hand in as a pilot. But most of the time, he's a cattle rancher out here in Arizona.

"Sergei was the test pilot on the Blackjack, which is something like our B-1 bomber, and is intimately familiar with its flight characteristics—at least before the Iraqi modifications. We think he is the person best qualified to bring that plane out to us safely."

Malcolm didn't mention that Kaparov's decision to defect to the West had made him a wealthy man. For the U.S. military, the chance to fly and analyze a potential enemy's first-line bomber was almost priceless.

Malcolm looked at his watch. "Let's take a break, gentlemen, and then come back to go through the mission in some detail."

Chuck Nelson rose and stepped forward to shake Kaparov's hand. The other members of the team followed his example and then left the room, talking quietly among themselves.

Rex Marker took Master Chief Jeff Bonior, the only black and the oldest and most experienced SEAL on the team, by the arm as they emerged. "A Russkie! Do you think we can trust the son of a bitch?"

Bonior smiled. "Of course we can trust him, Rex. He's the kind of guy who goes to the highest bidder. And in this case, that's us."

CHAPTER 2

MAYNARD WALKER ALWAYS FELT JUST A LITTLE TWINGE OF guilt when he leaned back in the soft leather of his executive chair, stretched out his long legs, and gently placed his shiny wingtips on the edge of his desk. After all, this was the same desk where John Kennedy had worked, the one that John, Jr. had been photographed crawling under. But the twinge of guilt quickly passed. After all, Maynard Walker was now the president of the United States and *he* could do what *he* wanted in *his* Oval Office with *his* desk.

"So, Mac, you think your guys can pull this off?"

Adm. Norris McKay, the chairman of the Joint Chiefs of Staff, nodded.

"Sir, this is far from an ideal situation. The textbook way to handle something like this is to send in at least a brigade of Army Rangers—five hundred men—and just overwhelm the place. But I know you're not going to send a lot of soldiers into Iraq. Keeping such an operation secret would be virtually impossible. Even if we could maintain security through the operation itself, the details would become public very quickly. We would have questions from every nation in the area, and the press would be all over us."

Walker shook his head. "No, we can't have that. You know the political situation I'm in right now. We have to get our hands on that plane but we can't get ourselves into the situation where we have to explain publicly what we've done and why."

9

In a subconscious gesture, Admiral McKay shifted positions in his chair. As a military man, he was decidedly uncomfortable talking politics. Yet as President Walker had gotten to know him and trust his judgment, he had more and more often used him as a sounding board on matters far removed from the Pentagon's normal business. McKay had the feeling that Walker had few people he could talk to with complete candor in the confidence that his words would not be repeated elsewhere and that the answers he got were not tinged with selfish interest. He supposed all presidents were that way.

Walker stood and turned to look out over the Rose Garden. When he began speaking after a long pause, it was almost as though he were talking to himself.

"We're halfway through June and I've got the convention coming up in less than a month and a half and then the election less than four months later. My record in these last four years has been very good. On my record, I deserve to be reelected—with a solid majority this time, not the plurality I got last time.

"But I've got this loose cannon on the deck—this damn Dick Wilson. I've beaten him in the primaries, but he's still going to come into the convention with enough delegates to force a vote that might even go to a second ballot. And even after I beat him, he's probably going to go off and start his own third party. I just wish I knew where he's getting all the money he's spending. He says it's all coming out of his own pocket, but. . . ."

McKay filled in the pause in the president's monologue. "Yes, I've read a lot of speculation about that."

"Damn it, Mac, we've got to get that plane. But I sure as hell don't need a big flap in the press right now. Things are dicey enough as they are. Do you think your boys can pull this off?"

"As I said, sir, I would prefer to use a much larger military force. But I think it is the best we can do. This team we are going to send in there is one I personally created. I have watched them very carefully as they have developed and matured over the last year and a half, and they are very good.

"When I was chief of naval operations, I became convinced we might need such a small, highly efficient force. We had the Army's Delta Force and the SEALs' hostage rescue outfit, but they've gotten very big. They're ideal for a rescue operation where we're operating in a favorable environment—an airport in a friendly nation, for example. But I concluded they'd gotten too big, and, in a sense, too cumbersome if we needed a force to deal with something like this situation we face now.

"I designated a small SEAL unit down at Little Creek, Virginia—their East Coast headquarters—and got them together with a team from the Air Force Special Operations Command at Fort Walton Beach, Florida. The Air Force has never been very big on special operations, but fortunately their chief of staff had worked with them and he went along with my idea."

"What do you call them? Mob-something?" the president asked.

McKay grinned. "I call them the Eagle Force, although they've been calling themselves MOB-X—something they picked up from a little SEAL history. Back in the late seventies, a similar unit was formed at Little Creek by SEAL Team TWO when they foresaw the need for a special anti-terrorist outfit to deal with hijackings and hostage situations. They called themselves MOB-TWO—a SEAL Team TWO unit that could be quickly mobilized in an emergency. That group was eventually expanded into SEAL Team SIX and made a major anti-terrorist command.

"These guys have trained together often enough so that they know and are comfortable with each other. I think, given the constraints we are operating under, that our best bet is this small commando team. They can get in, do the job, and get out without causing a big stir. With luck, they can handle it without anyone knowing they have been there—except the Iraqis, and they won't tell."

A light flashed on the intercom on Walker's desk. He pushed a button and responded: "Yeah."

"Sir, Mrs. Walker is here and she's preparing to leave on her trip."

"Excuse me a moment, Mac." Walker strode quickly to the door. McKay could see the first lady framed in the doorway.

Marcia Carter Walker would have been a striking woman

even without the help of the personal hairdresser who did her shoulder-length auburn hair each morning and helped with her makeup. Dressed in an off-white linen suit with matching shoes and handbag, small gold earrings, and a gold necklace, she looked both businesslike and very feminine. She was proof that for many women true beauty comes with maturity. She was 48 years old and had never been more attractive.

At her side stood their eight-year-old son, David, dressed in a tan suit and a necktie with broad diagonal blue and red stripes.

The president leaned over and kissed his son on the forehead, at the same time shaking his hand.

"This is going to be a big trip for you, David. Will you take good care of Mommy for me?"

The boy looked up and nodded solemnly.

"I'm going to be lonesome in this big old house," Walker said, turning to his wife and resting his hands on her shoulders. "How long are you going to be gone this time?"

"Only ten days. I have meetings in London and Berlin, and then I'm going to stop in Paris to charm the president. I'll send you a bill for diplomatic services rendered."

Marcia Walker was the first president's wife to continue with her own independent career after becoming first lady. While she performed some of the expected traditional ceremonial functions and carried out an occasional delicate diplomatic mission, she also was the highly successful chief executive of a worldwide talent agency, bringing together large firms and highly skilled managers, scientists and engineers. She was probably the world's most successful headhunter and her fees easily overshadowed the president's salary when they—with a good deal of reluctance on her part—made their joint income tax returns public.

Walker laughed: "No, no, Marcie. Your bill would bust the budget." As he drew her close to him, she turned her head slightly and brushed his cheek lightly with her lips.

"Take care," she said, taking David by the hand and turning away. "See you in ten days."

Walker closed the door and took a seat beside Admiral Mc-Kay.

"It's true, Mac. It does get lonesome here. We agreed when I got into politics that she would continue with her own career. But she does travel a lot—more than most guys' wives. And now she's started to take David along with her." He sighed. "Anyway, as far as this business with the airplane is concerned, let's go ahead with the training and all the preparations. I want to think about this some more, but I want them ready to go if and when I make the decision."

"Yes sir," McKay replied. "I'd like to give them about three more weeks to do a full-scale rehearsal for the operation and then we'll be ready to go. If we're going to go, the ideal time would be the third week of next month. We'll have just enough moon to help them see what they are doing without so much light that they might be spotted."

"So you're giving me a deadline? That would make this just three weeks before the convention—not exactly the time for something to go wrong."

"Not a deadline, sir. I know you have many other things to consider. But if we want to stack the odds as much as possible in our favor, that would be the ideal time to go."

"Okay, Admiral. You've made your point. Before I make the final decision, I'd like to meet with the young man who's going to run this operation. Set that up for me, will you?"

"Commander Nelson—Chuck Nelson. I'm sure you'll be impressed by him. I've watched his career closely—been a kind of sea daddy to him. He's the kind of young officer I hope will stay in the Navy and end up holding my job twenty years from now." McKay stood, sensing that the meeting had already eaten up too much of the president's schedule—to say nothing of the pile of work he had waiting for him at the Pentagon. The drive back across Memorial Bridge through the last stages of the evening rush hour traffic would be the only moments of peace for many hours.

As McKay left the Oval Office, he passed the usual coterie of aides and functionaries waiting for a moment of the president's time. And then, as he strode down the hallway, he glimpsed, through the half-open door of a small meeting room, one of the most extraordinarily beautiful women he had ever seen. Sitting beside her was Cindy Carson, a Secret Service agent McKay had seen several times before.

Michelle Moselle was tall, like her American father. From her Vietnamese mother she had inherited raven black hair and a silky olive complexion. Her eyes had just enough of an Asian cast to add a hint of mystery. With a natural flair for the dramatic, she had found it relatively easy to support herself in modest comfort with a series of minor roles in several movies and a number of soap operas. But she had never quite made the transition to the stardom her beauty seemed to warrant.

Grace McKenzie, who had been the president's trusted *confidential* secretary throughout his career, stepped to the door of the waiting room. "Okay, Cindy, you can go on up now."

Special Agent Carson and Michelle Moselle rose and walked quickly down the hall to a small elevator. It was not the first time Michelle Moselle had taken this route to the family living quarters on the second floor of the White House.

Maynard Walker tried to make it a point to be out of his office by 7 o'clock in the evening. He knew that after every late meeting in the Oval Office, his staff still had hours of work to do to carry out the decisions made during the day. If he couldn't discipline himself to finish his work by a reasonable hour, he knew, then staff morale, and often staff marriages, would begin to crumble. He dealt quickly with those who had been waiting outside his office during his conference with McKay and then announced: "Okay, that's it for today."

Michelle was alone, sipping a cup of tea, in a sitting room adjoining the president's bedroom when he walked in. She put down her cup and rose as he crossed the room.

"Mickey! You don't know how good you look to me." He held her at arm's length and ran his eyes down her body, lingering at the V in her dress that revealed the roundness of her breasts, then on down to where the material of her miniskirt stretched smoothly across her abdomen and around her hips and then to her legs, clad in sheer black.

He drew her to him and kissed her on the lips, holding her close against his body with a hand cupping her buttocks.

Her arms remained at her sides as her body seemed to melt against his. And then he felt her hands gently caressing his thighs.

Walker slowly ended the kiss and leaned back, still holding her firmly against his body. "I think this is going to be a nice evening. Would you like a drink . . . or supper?"

She reached up to loosen his tie and pull it out from around his neck before beginning to unbutton his shirt.

"A drink, yes. Can we have supper a little later?"

Walker released her and strode to a small bar concealed in what appeared to be a chest of drawers. "Martini okay?" The president was one of that new generation that had rediscovered the subtle mixture of gin and vermouth—very little vermouth—and had learned to look forward to the kick in the back of the neck the first sip imparted after a long, hard day.

"Yes, but just a small one, Mr. President."

"Come on, Mickey. I tell you: forget this Mr. President stuff. Just call me Chip." Maynard Walker was not a name that leant itself to nicknames. Since infancy, when he was just as bald as his father, he had been called "Chip"—as in . . . "off the old block."

He handed her a drink and then, with an arm around her waist, guided her to a couch in front of the fireplace. A fire had been laid. Setting down his drink, he struck a match and applied it to the crumpled newspapers. In moments the layers of paper, kindling, and dry oak were converted into a warm blaze.

The president was not an admirer of one of his predecessors, Richard Nixon, but he didn't feel guilty about copying Nixon's habit of having a fire burning in his fireplace while the air conditioning let him forget the hot, humid Washington summer outside his window.

Walker lowered himself onto the couch and drew her toward him, leaning down to kiss her behind the ear, and then let his tongue run down the curve of her neck to the deep cleavage between her breasts. Her dress slipped easily off her shoulder and he reached around to unfasten her bra.

As he caressed her breasts, he felt her fingers loosening his belt and then felt that inimitable sense of freedom as she eased his zipper open.

Their drinks sat forgotten as they slipped to the soft rug in front of the fireplace, in a gentle race to undress each other.

"Chip," she whispered. "Lie on your back and let me admire you." She knelt beside him, running her fingers down his body, carefully caressing him. And then she was crouching over him and suddenly she was surrounding him and he was lost—no, really, found—inside her.

The warmth of the fire bathed their bodies as they lay together, savoring their nakedness.

"Oh, that was so good, Mickey. You are so good for me. You don't know how much being here with you does for me. All day I am surrounded by people wanting decisions or wanting something for themselves. It is so good to just be here with you and forget all that even for a little while."

"I know," she said, rubbing her body gently against his. "You can relax with me."

"You know what happened today?" He rose on an elbow and looked down at her. "This damned fool senator from out west came in and he threatened me. He said I'd lose his state and all the western states if I didn't open up logging in one of our most beautiful old-growth forests. The trouble is—dammit—I need those states. But I don't like to be blackmailed."

"What did you tell him?" she asked.

"Oh, I told him I'd study it," he said. "But he's got me in a tough spot, and I don't like it."

Later, when they were both dressed, Walker picked up the phone. Within minutes, an attendant rolled in a cart containing a plate of sliced beef, ham, and cheese, a bowl of fresh fruit salad, a basket with warm rolls, and glasses of iced tea.

They sat side by side on the couch in front of the fire as they ate their supper. With the practiced skill of a professional politician, Walker soon had Michelle talking animatedly about her life, beginning with her dimly remembered early childhood in Vietnam.

As she spoke, Walker sat back, relaxed. Perhaps without realizing it, he interspersed her narrative with comments of his own about problems he faced daily in the Oval Office.

Finally, pushing the supper cart aside, he picked up the phone: "Please tell Miss Carson she can come on up now."

"I wish we could spend more time together, Mickey. But you wouldn't believe how much work I still have to do this evening—what they call 'bedside reading.' It's quite a game here to see who can get their paper high enough in the pile so I'll read it before it all puts me to sleep."

Cindy Carson guided Michelle on what was by now a familiar route, down in the small elevator to the basement of the White House and through a long tunnel to the nearby Treasury Department building. There they entered a black sedan with non-government District of Columbia license plates.

The Secret Service agent held the wheel with both hands and looked straight ahead, without speaking, as she drove through the quiet nighttime streets of the capital to a six-story apartment building on Q Street Northwest. She pulled smoothly into the semi-circular entranceway and Michelle Moselle slipped quickly out the door.

"Goodnight, Cindy. Thanks," she said.

"Goodnight, Miss Moselle," Cindy replied. Her tone was crisply professional, with no hint of warmth.

As Michelle entered her apartment, she was not surprised to see a young man, neatly dressed in a slim black Brooks Brothers suit, sitting in her favorite chair, an empty coffee cup on the table beside him.

"Good evening, Miss Moselle. You are later than I expected."

She slipped off the light sweater draped over her shoulders and fluffed her hair with both hands. "Time flies when you're having fun."

He reached into the attaché case at the side of the chair and extracted a small tape recorder and a notebook. "Our mutual friend will be most interested to hear about the conversations that may have taken place between the episodes of 'fun.' "

"Oh shit," she said, "all he talked about was cutting down some trees and a lot of stupid politics."

"We'll decide what is stupid. Please tell me everything he

said.'' He clicked on the tape recorder and poised his pen above the notebook.

When he left the apartment, a thick white envelope lay on the table beside his empty coffee cup. Michelle Moselle undressed and took a long, hot shower. Only later did she slit open the envelope and count the hundred-dollar bills it contained.

CHAPTER 3

"I DON'T CARE WHAT YOUR INSTRUCTIONS ARE. EITHER YOU GIVE Mrs. Collins all the intel we need to do this job right, or you'll find your candyass back in Langley so fast it will make your head spin."

Chuck Nelson stood so close to the taller CIA officer that their chests were almost touching. With warm brown eyes under an unruly shock of black hair with just a touch of gray in the closely trimmed sideburns, Nelson's face normally had an open, friendly look that made people like and trust him. He was only five feet eight inches tall, but he was five feet eight inches and 155 pounds of SEAL, and he could be intimidating when he wanted to be. In this case he fully intended to be.

The CIA officer took a step backward. "I'm sorry, Commander. I have very specific instructions about what information I can and cannot provide to you. I am not allowed to tell you the sources of our information."

Nelson moved forward to take up the space the other man had surrendered. The muscles tightened under the faint shadow of the black beard on his face.

"If you think I am going to take my men into a situation where we don't know how good our intel is and where it comes from, then you're no use to us. It may be more than thirty years ago now, but the SEALs learned in Vietnam that relying on bad or outdated intelligence at best is a waste of time, and at worst can get you killed."

Patricia Collins stood to one side, a slight smile of bemuse-

ment on her face. She had known Chuck Nelson for five years
and she had never seen him appear so angry. They had met
when she was dating Jim Collins and he and Nelson were
instructors in the Basic Underwater Demolition/SEALs training course—the notorious BUD/S—at the SEAL headquarters
in Coronado, California. She had just graduated from the Uni-
versity of California at San Diego with a degree in business
administration and had gone to work in the headquarters of
the Naval Special Warfare Command—Specwar. She had
soon begun to specialize in intelligence. Over the next few
years, she had often worked closely with Nelson as she gained
experience and became one of the intelligence analysts most
trusted by the SEALs.

"Mrs. Collins is putting together the intelligence we need
for this op. We will rely on her judgment to help us carry out
our mission successfully and get in and out of there alive.
Now, you just wait outside while I make a phone call, and
then we'll see whether we have to get somebody else in here
who can do what we need." Nelson stepped back and pointed
toward the door. The CIA man left the room as though he
were escaping from a burning airplane.

Nelson turned to Pat Collins and winked. "How'd I do?"
As he'd advanced through the Navy ranks, Nelson had learned
that a carefully controlled display of anger can sometimes
work wonders in getting things done.

"You scared me." Pat Collins did not look as though she
scared easily. At 27, she was in superb physical condition, the
result of early-morning runs along the beach. Her dark brown
hair, ending in a wave just at her shoulder line, framed a face
with high cheekbones, large, luminous blue eyes, and a mouth
that seemed to crinkle at the edges with the beginnings of a
smile. All that marred her beauty were the premature worry
lines at the corners of her eyes.

"I'm afraid we're going to have to call for help. I really
meant it when I told him we're not going in there with bad
intel if we can help it. What they can provide us may not be
perfect, but we want the best they can do, and I want you to
be the judge of how good it is."

Nelson picked up the red phone on his desk. Almost immediately it was answered in Adm. McKay's office in the Pentagon. The voice on the other end sounded like a recording, but wasn't: "Office of the chairman. Chief Petty Officer Tompkins speaking. This is a secure line, sir."

"This is Commander Nelson. Please connect me with Admiral McKay."

Tompkins knew Nelson's name. It was not every commander who could pick up the phone and be put right through to the chairman of the Joint Chiefs of Staff. A moment later, he heard McKay's gravelly voice: "Hello, Chuck. What's the problem?"

Nelson didn't take up time to apologize for bothering the chairman. "Sir, Langley is giving us problems. Their guy out here refuses to provide us with the sources of their intelligence. We don't know how good it is or how old it is."

"Let me talk to him."

Nelson opened the door and beckoned the CIA man into the office. He handed him the red phone.

McKay spoke so forcefully that Nelson did not have to strain to hear his voice.

"This is Admiral McKay, the chairman of the Joint Chiefs. I will call your headquarters and get this business straightened out. You will hear from them in a few minutes. But I want you to know that this is a very high-priority operation and I want you personally to be totally cooperative with Commander Nelson and Mrs. Collins. Anything they want, you give it to them. Is that understood?"

The CIA man had never gotten instructions from anyone as exalted as the chairman of the Joint Chiefs. He swallowed hard and replied, "Yes sir. As soon as I have instructions from my headquarters, I will be totally cooperative."

"Good. Now let me talk to Mr. Nelson. . . ." Once the receiver was passed back, McKay continued: "Chuck, I'll get on Langley right now. Thanks for calling me to straighten this out. Remember, don't hesitate to call if there's anything I can do to make this whole thing go smoothly." The line went dead as McKay hung up.

Nelson turned to the CIA man. "Sorry to be rough on you, but this is very important to us. Why don't you get to work putting together answers to Mrs. Collins's questions so she'll have them as soon as you hear from your people?''

"I'll do that," the CIA man replied, and left.

Nelson turned and took Pat Collins's hands in his. "How are you doing, kid?"

She squeezed his hands in response. "Oh, Chuck, it's still hard. Some days are okay. I'm busy at the office and Jimmie Junior and Ashley keep me busy—and keep me company. But other days I have lots of memories and it's rough. Sometimes the nights are awfully long."

Nelson gazed into her large blue eyes—her most striking feature. "I worry about you. It's just not fair. You know, that night I came to your house with the chaplain was the hardest thing I've ever had to do. And I guess you know I'll feel guilty for the rest of my life. After all, I was Jim's swim buddy. Losing your buddy is something you're just not supposed to do."

"I knew something terrible had happened the moment I saw your face, Chuck. You just looked kind of stricken. It's funny, I found myself—the brand new widow—feeling sorry for you. And I still do. You've got to stop feeling guilty. You know in your mind that it was an accident and there's nothing you could have done to prevent it."

Both of them had often relived that day at Little Creek, where the SEALs share space at the Navy amphibious base at the juncture between the Chesapeake Bay and the Atlantic Ocean. The channel near the base is one of the world's busiest, with a constant stream of Navy and merchant ships plying their way to and from the docks of the Norfolk area.

Collins and Nelson had been assigned to the same East Coast SEAL team after completing their assignment as instructors on the West Coast. On the day Jim Collins died, he and Nelson were engaged in what was planned as a routine underwater navigational training mission. Their assignment was to enter the water near their team headquarters on the western side of the base, swim to a buoy near the center of the channel, continue on to another buoy a short distance away, and then return to their starting point.

Jim Collins, who was the stronger swimmer, took the lead,

holding a large compass board in his hands and propelling himself with the flippers on his feet. Nelson followed a few feet behind, attached to Collins with a short tether so they wouldn't lose contact in the murky water. Both carefully counted the strokes of their legs. That was their only way of measuring the distance they had traveled. Their Draeger breathing devices automatically cleansed the carbon dioxide as they exhaled and returned a steady supply of oxygen to their masks. Unlike the tanks of air used by sports divers, their Draegers left no telltale trail of bubbles to betray their passage.

The swim seemed totally routine to Nelson until they were within about thirty yards of the first buoy. Then they both felt the deep thrumming of the propeller of a large freighter approaching. Instinctively they dived for the bottom of the shallow channel, virtually burrowing into the mud to stay below the propeller churning no more than a few feet above.

As the ship passed over them, Nelson sensed a thump. He pulled on the tether to reach his swim buddy. As he drew him close, he made out a bloody gash in his head. Jim Collins's torn mask dangled down on his shoulder.

Nelson braced his feet on the bottom and pushed for the surface thirty feet above. As they floated on the surface, Nelson could see that the propeller or some part of the freighter had cut deeply into Collins's skull. He was limp and unconscious.

Moments after the two men surfaced, a boat assigned to follow their route pulled alongside and the crewmen quickly lifted Collins to the deck. Nelson pushed his mask to one side and clambered into the boat. He thrust through the knot of men standing helplessly around Collins's inert form and knelt beside his buddy, wondering why the other men were not giving him first aid. Then, examining the terrible gash in his head, he understood there was nothing they could do. Jim Collins was already dead.

"A number of times, I've wished that you hadn't moved back to California," Nelson said. "I felt if you had been closer I might have been able to do something to make life a little easier for you. Anyway, I've thought about you."

"It was best for me to move. San Diego was my home

before I met Jim, and my parents and friends are there. And things have worked out at Specwar. I think they appreciate my work on intelligence, and I know I enjoy the challenge.''

"That's why you're here, Pat. Everyone knows you're the best. And besides, we get to see each other again.'' His face lit up with an infectious grin.

"Oh, yes,'' she replied, smiling back. "A beautiful reunion over a table full of satellite images.''

"I'm afraid that's what it's going to be.'' Nelson, preoccupied with the upcoming mission, was all business. "Now, as soon as you get the stuff from this agency guy, I want you to prepare a briefing for us on the layout of that field in Iraq. We need to know the location and dimensions of each building. We need to know how many people are there, where they are likely to be, and what they will be doing. How many of them are mechanics and engineers, and how many of them are soldiers? What kind of arms do they have? What will be the best time of night to hit them?

"We need all this stuff by oh-eight-hundred, so I'm afraid you're in for a long night. I want to spend tomorrow planning, and then we'll run through the ground part of the operation here tomorrow night. Can you do it?''

"Sure,'' she replied. "But it all depends, of course, on the quality of the intel I get. One thing I'd really like to know is whether they have any humint—and, if so, how current it is.''

Satellites, high-flying aircraft, interception of radio and radar signals all provided valuable intelligence. But in some cases—and this was one of them—there was no substitute for real-time human intelligence, an agent reporting live from the scene of the proposed action.

"That's what they get so antsy about,'' Nelson said. "Let's hope they've got somebody on the ground. We'll get together here in my office at oh-seven-thirty to go over what you have. I'll have coffee on.''

Pat Collins stepped out of the door of the World War II–era wooden building into the blinding heat of the Arizona summer. Inside, a window air conditioner kept the temperature bearable, but outside, there was no protection from the blazing sun. Shielding her eyes, she hurried to her own office in the building next door.

As soon as Admiral McKay had tapped him to organize this special commando unit, Nelson had arranged to take over this air strip where fighter pilots had been trained half a century before. The same hot, very dry climate that made the summers almost unbearable had helped to preserve the old office and barracks buildings. A few weeks' work had been enough to turn them into usable office and living quarters for the unit. The single paved runway and the simple network of taxiways and working areas were still in remarkably good condition. Most important, the base—now named Site Y—was located in a rural area well removed from the two major cities of Tucson and Phoenix. Military activity in this remote area would attract little if any attention. Local residents who asked what was going on were told the field was being reactivated as a "multiservice tactical training facility," which was the truth, but not the whole truth.

At half past seven the next morning, Pat Collins arrived at Nelson's office with a bundle of Vu-grafs under her arm. In surrender to the summer heat, she was dressed like the SEALs in khaki shorts, running shoes, and a loose-fitting T-shirt. Across her chest was the legend "The Quiet Professionals"— the motto of the air commandos.

"Have you sold out to the Air Force already?" Nelson asked.

She looked at him blankly and then glanced down. "Oh, this. The Special Tactics guys gave it to me. You know, it's not a bad motto for your whole operation."

Nelson gave her a look. He enjoyed serving with Air Force personnel. But he had no desire to *be* Air Force personnel.

"What have you got?" Nelson asked, changing the subject and glancing at the bundle under her arm.

"Good news—I hope. It didn't take long for the agency to come through, once Admiral McKay rattled their cage. They say they have an 'asset' on the ground in Iraq who is providing real-time reports on the situation at the base. They've given me a rundown on the security setup. It sounds fairly sloppy to me. There is a fence around the facility, but we see no guard towers. They apparently feel the base is deep enough in their territory that there is not much threat.

"The most interesting thing I learned is that they are about ready for a full-scale test of the plane. That means they are getting closer to the time they might use it against a target. But it also means we may be able to time our attack for a night when the plane will be fueled and prepared for a flight."

Some of the tension around Nelson's eyes and jaw seemed to slacken. "That's great, Pat. I've been worrying that we would have to provide security long enough to get that plane fueled—and I'm not at all sure we could do it. If we know it's already full of fuel, that will make our job a lot easier."

She held up her hands. "Whoa, let's not get too excited. I said, 'good news—I hope.' Maybe I've been in this business so long I'm overly-suspicious. But I still don't know as much about this 'asset' as I'd like to know. I'm not sure if this person is actually at the airbase. Perhaps it's someone in a government agency in Baghdad. His information could be out of date by the time it gets to us. I also don't know what access this person has to what's going on over there. If he's just some passing camel jockey, it's not the kind of thing we want to rely on."

The worry lines immediately reappeared around Nelson's eyes. "I thought they got the word: that's exactly what we need to know. Do I have to call the admiral on them again?"

"No," Pat replied. "Let me work with this fellow a little more. I think he personally has an understanding of what we need and will do his best to get it for us. If I'm still unhappy tomorrow morning, you can make your call."

Nelson glanced at his wristwatch. "Okay, let's go. Give the guys the best briefing you can on the situation they'll find on the ground when we arrive there. We'll do a separate briefing for the air crews tomorrow. And then I want a full-scale run-through of the entire operation by the end of the week. We'll do everything but the carrier takeoff. That would just attract too much attention."

Together they hurried to the team's briefing room next door. The members of the ground team—Navy SEALs and Air Force special tactics men—were already there, sitting as comfortably as they could in student chairs, with notebooks open on the small desktops attached to the chairs. Most of them were dressed as casually as Collins, in T-shirts and shorts.

She quickly doused the lights, pulled down a screen at the front of the room, and began to display a series of pictures and computer-generated drawings of the Iraqi airfield.

"This overhead photo gives you the general layout of the field," she said. "Here you see the large hangar where most of the work on the plane is done. Here, to the south of the main hangar, is the engine test facility. Our information is that engines are tested during much of the night. If a test is being conducted when you arrive, the sound of the test will mask whatever noise you may make."

She clicked another slide onto the screen. "This shows you what we believe are the barracks and ready-room for the base security force. There seems to be room for about fifty soldiers. Parked in front of the building, you can make out four pickup trucks, each with a .30-caliber machine gun mounted in the back. Each is capable of carrying an eight-man squad, including the driver and machine gun crew. The other men are probably armed with AK-47 assault rifles. This building is about fifty meters to the southeast of the large hangar. Adjoining it is another barracks-type building. We believe it is used by the technicians. They are probably only lightly armed, if at all."

Another slide appeared. "This small structure directly behind the hangar, to the east, is very important. It appears to be a small substation controlling the power supply for the base. We assume they have emergency generators located in the hangar and perhaps elsewhere. But if you can knock out the power supply from this building, you will have a period of total darkness that will enhance the effectiveness of your surprise attack. There is one guard at the entrance to this building."

Nelson rose from his seat and turned to two SEALs sitting behind him. "As soon as this briefing is over, Mrs. Collins will give you everything we have on this building. I want you to spend the rest of the day working out your plan. I want you to figure out how you're going to approach the building, what you will need in the way of explosives, and what each of you will do. I'll get together with you this evening before we go through the op. Okay, Pat. Go on.''

The next photo showed the ramp in front of the hangar. Dominating the view was the shrouded image of the plane that was the target for their attack. Parked in a row near the larger plane were four fighter planes—export versions of the Soviet-built MiG-23 Flogger. Next to them were two large Soviet-built Hind helicopters—formidable, heavily armored gunships, each with a four-barrel Gatling-type machine gun in the nose and with rocket pods under each wing.

''We'll take those out with the fifty,'' Nelson interjected. In preparation for just such a mission as this, the SEALs had developed a powerful .50-caliber sniper rifle with a long barrel adapted from the one used on a heavy machine gun. It was accurate at long distances and capable of sending a heavy slug of metal clear through the engine block of an aircraft, disabling it with a single shot. The sniper rifle would be used to put the Iraqi aircraft out of commission so they would not be able to pursue the converted Blackjack bomber or the commando team as it left after the raid.

Mark Rattner raised his hand. ''Pat, what do we know about the surrounding area? Are there any other troops around there that can give us trouble?''

''No, we don't think so, Mark,'' she replied. ''We think the Iraqis deliberately located this operation at an isolated site so it would not attract attention.''

''Any more questions?'' Nelson glanced around the room. ''Okay, get some rest today. We're going to have a busy night.''

That night, half the team took up positions around the buildings of the Arizona base, simulating the defending force at the Iraqi field. The other half gathered in a remote corner of the field, pretending that they had just been delivered by helicopter. Then they ran through the operation, taking control of the field and putting the pilot in a truck used to represent the airplane. Riding small motorcycles, two special tactics men raced across the field to place a "box-and-one"—four infrared lights in a square, with another at the end of the field—to guide the pilot on his takeoff from the dark runway.

At the briefing early the next morning, Nelson was not happy. The whole rehearsal had been sloppy and poorly co-ordinated. Patiently Nelson went back over the entire operation, pointing out flaws in the team's performance.

"Okay," he concluded. "That's what rehearsals are for. This wasn't bad for a first try. Get some rest today and we'll go through it again tonight."

Mark Rattner, the helicopter pilot, was waiting at the rear of the room when the briefing ended. At 37, Rattner was a few months older than Nelson and the oldest member of the team. Although they both held comparable ranks, Nelson was the commander of the entire team and Rattner served as his deputy in charge of the two Pave Low helicopters assigned to the unit. The two men had often worked together and had a smooth working relationship based on their close friendship and the respect each had for the other's competence. Rattner had flown almost everything in the Air Force inventory, from the F-15 Eagle fighter to the FB-111 bomber. His favorite was the Pave Low helicopter used by Air Force special operations—the air commandos.

The two men took chairs at the rear of the briefing room. "How's it going, Mark?" Nelson inquired.

"Oh, we're doing fine," Rattner replied. "After all, this is what we do for a living. There are no big new challenges in this operation. We've been spending most of our time playing 'what-if' games, practicing what to do when things go wrong. We've practiced every kind of problem with the power and rotors. In most of those cases, it's just a matter of trying to get onto the ground safely. The real challenge is to compensate for the loss of electronics. What do you do if your terrain-following radar goes out? What if you lose your inertial guidance? That's what we've been working on."

"Sounds good," Nelson said. "Are you comfortable with

the fuel arrangements? We'll top off from the Combat Shadow tanker just before we cross the border. But from then on, there are no filling stations along the way.''

''It's going to be a little tight, but I don't expect any problems. We'll work our way through the mountains rather than burning a lot of fuel to climb over them.'' Instinctively Rattner simulated their flight path with his right hand. ''And we'll use careful power management to conserve fuel. We'll be okay if we don't take severe battle damage.''

''I want a full-scale rehearsal this weekend,'' Nelson said. ''I want to fly the full distance we'll fly in the real operation through terrain that's as close as we can get to the real thing. We'll go through our scenario on the ground and then practice our withdrawal—matching terrain and distance as much as we can. That way, we'll get to see what effect fatigue will have on both your air crews and our troops.''

''I've already got it plotted out,'' Rattner said. ''There are some good mountain ranges in the southern Rockies, near Albuquerque, that are very much like the terrain we'll be flying through in Iraq.''

''Okay, Mark. We're going to go through our training on the next two nights, and then at the end of the week we'll all do the whole op together.''

The next morning Nelson was in a buoyant mood. The rehearsal the night before had been almost letter-perfect, even with a couple of surprises thrown in by the opposing force. Pat Collins was waiting in his office when he arrived.

''Langley finally came through,'' she told him. ''They say their 'asset' is on the ground at the Iraqi base. They say he's a senior engineer and that he has a burst transmitter that can send a message to a passing satellite. The transmission takes only a second or two.''

Nelson was pleased. ''That's even better than I expected. That means the information we receive is at worst only a few hours old.''

''Right. The only delay should be the time between the

satellite passes," she replied. "The problem is that we can't even hint that we're coming and we can't ask him specific questions. All we can do is hope that the information he sends is what we need."

"Good work, Pat. Keep after them for frequent updates. And then we'll just keep our fingers crossed. I'm going to go check on Sergei."

———————— ★ ————————

Chuck Nelson was one of those fortunate mortals who are not bothered by extremes of heat or cold. In fact, he almost enjoyed the intense heat of the sun on his back as he walked down the dusty desert roadway to a hangar adjoining the field's long runway. In one corner of the hangar, Dr. Jim Malcolm had set up a simulator to help Sergei Kaparov and the special tactics men become familiar with the cockpit of the modified Blackjack bomber they hoped to spirit away from the Iraqi airfield.

Malcolm was leaning on the back of an aircraft seat behind Kaparov and peering at the instrument panel when Nelson entered the room. He looked back over his shoulder. "Oh, good morning, Chuck. We're just running through a simulation. Let me show you what we've done. Sergei, take a break while I fill Commander Nelson in on our simulator. Why don't you climb in, Chuck?"

Nelson slipped into the seat and found himself looking at a large screen that showed both the interior of an airplane cockpit and the view through the windscreen. A throttle control was located on a console near his right hand and a control stick and rudder pedals were mounted on the floor in front of him. Unlike most large aircraft, the Blackjack was fitted with a stick like that found in fighter planes, instead of a wheel and yoke.

"This isn't anywhere near as complex and realistic as those multimillion-dollar simulators the services have now," Malcolm said. "But I think we've done a remarkable job, considering the time limitations and the need for secrecy. Mrs. Collins got for us a good description of the changes the Iraqis are believed to have made in the cockpit. I've got a computer genius on my staff. He fed everything we knew into his computer and then modified a commercial video game to simulate the performance of this aircraft.

"Sergei is, of course, familiar with the Blackjack. With this simulator, he can get up to speed on the changes in the cockpit. He can practice starting the engines, taxiing, taking off, climbing to cruise altitude, and landing."

Nelson rocked the control stick back and forth. It felt almost as though he were controlling a real airplane. "What about the engines?" he asked.

"That's one thing we've had to guess about—and we can just hope our guesses are on the mark," Malcolm replied. "Originally, there was a large pod containing two engines under each wing. We think they have replaced all four engines. Two of them have been replaced with more powerful and more reliable jet engines—perhaps even the same basic General Electric engines used in our own B-1 bomber and F/A-18 strike fighter. The other two engines, we believe, have been replaced with their own ramjet engines.

"Our assumption is that the two jet engines have enough power to get the plane airborne and take it up to high altitude. Then the ramjets will be cut in to boost it into a near-orbital path at something well over 100,000 feet."

"Have you gotten the special tactics guys up to speed on the cockpit?" Nelson asked. "They're going to have to get Sergei into the cockpit and make sure he's all set for the flight."

"Yes, they've spent hours here in the simulator. I've run them through the engine-start and taxi procedure themselves so they're fully familiar with the cockpit and the controls Sergei will be using during that phase. On the actual operation, they'll run through the pre-flight checklist, doing the job normally done by the copilot."

"What about the weapon controls?" Nelson inquired.

"From our understanding of the cockpit, they're all in this panel to the pilot's left. We've pointed that out to Sergei and the Air Force guys and told them not to touch anything in that area. We'll have plenty of time to figure it out after we have our hands on the plane.''

"Okay," Nelson said, climbing out of the seat. "I want Sergei to be ready for a full-scale rehearsal at the end of the week. We'll run through the entire operation and I want to see how he holds up to the strain of a long low-level helicopter flight. We'll be going through some pretty rugged mountains and it could be kind of rough. It's important that we make the rehearsal just as realistic as possible.''

CHAPTER 4

THE DIVER'S FACE WAS ONLY DIMLY VISIBLE BEHIND HIS MASK, IL-luminated by the faint rays of the sun filtering through the murky lake water. The greenish tint of the water added to the eerie look on the man's face. His eyes were round with terror and his mouth was wide open in a frantic hunt for air—but there was no air.

The other diver smiled behind his faceplate. Then he grasped the other man by the webbing that stretched over his chest and kicked quickly to the surface.

As soon as they broke the surface, the first man tore away his mask and sucked in the warm, moist air. Finally catching his breath, he exclaimed: "You son of a bitch! You damn near killed me!"

The other man lifted his mask and laughed. "You SEALs think you're the only ones who can swim." He reached behind the other swimmer and unfastened the clamp he had applied to his air hose, out of reach behind his back. The clamp was as close as they could come in training to what could happen in combat when one swimmer cut the other's air line.

Rolling onto his back, the first swimmer breathed deeply. "Man, that was really scary. I thought I was going to die."

Kicking slowly, the two men swam to a dock extending into the lake from the edge of a grove of pine trees.

Ben Bernard, wearing a pair of khaki shorts, a white T-shirt, and a pair of paratrooper's boots, stood on the dock, his feet spread apart and his hands on his hips, as he watched the two swimmers approach. On the front of his T-shirt was a circular logo. In the center was a stylized artist's rendition of an assault rifle. Around the edge was the legend "GTG Enterprises." To those in the know, GTG stood for "guns-to-go."

"Hey, Big Dog, when are you going to get us some action?" called the swimmer whose hose had been clamped. With his name, it was almost unavoidable that Bernard had been known as "Big Dog" since his first days in Basic Underwater Demolition/SEALs (BUD/S) training.

"It looks to me like you've already got as much action as you can handle, Dick," Bernard replied, without removing the large cigar from his mouth. "You're not supposed to let those Army pricks get behind you."

The two swimmers pulled themselves up onto the dock and sat on the edge with their fins dangling in the water. It was uncomfortably warm as their black wet suits soaked up the heat of the Georgia sun. The temperature of the mountain lake was tepid and they didn't really need the suits. But Bernard insisted that all their training be as realistic as possible—and that meant wearing all their gear, even when it wasn't needed.

"He's pretty good for a dogface, but I'll get him next time," Dick Hoffman replied. Hoffman had put in one tour of duty as a Navy SEAL and then, when Bernard had offered him a place in the new civilian commando unit he was organizing, had jumped at the chance. Even the intensive training of a SEAL team did not provide enough action for Hoffman. Like so many young SEALs, he thirsted for the day he would be able to prove himself in real-life combat against other men.

Bernard had offered that chance. He promised that the team he had put together, picked from among veterans of the SEALs, Army Special Forces, Marine Force Recon, and Air Force Special Tactics, would see plenty of action, fighting as guns-for-hire anywhere in the world. But so far it had been the same-old same-old: more training. It was tough training, tougher and more realistic than the military's safety rules would permit—as realistic as Bernard could make it without getting his men killed. They fought with each other on land and under the water. They jumped from so high that they needed oxygen to breathe and from so low that their chutes barely had a chance to open. But it was still training.

Bernard crouched on the dock, a hand on a shoulder of each man. His grip was like steel, and his shoulders, arms, and thighs bulged with so much muscle they almost seemed disfigured.

"I'm going to get you some action," he told them. "I'm going to be gone for a couple of days. I have to see this guy who has a job for us. When I come back, we should be ready to go."

"Go where?" Hoffman asked.

"Need-to-know. Need-to-know." Bernard spoke in a low-pitched voice that was almost a growl. "I'll tell you where we're going and what we're going to do when you need to know. Until then, you're going to be a mushroom—in the dark, eating shit."

"I can put up with a lot of shit, but this training is getting pretty old," Hoffman replied. "I should have stayed in the Navy and built up time for retirement."

"Retirement, shit. You won't live that long—if you're lucky." Bernard rose and stretched. "I'll be gone for a couple of days. The chief will keep you guys busy."

Members of Bernard's commando unit didn't know where he had gotten the money to set up the team and its training facility. He was one of those men who couldn't balance a checkbook and wouldn't if he could. But somehow the money was there. He had signed a long-term lease on a hundred-acre parcel of land surrounding a small lake in the rugged mountains north of Marietta. The lake was large enough and deep enough to permit underwater training and limited boat operations. In a small clearing in the pine trees stood a barracks, a briefing room, an equipment building, a small secure arsenal, and a mess hall. A short distance from the camp, over a rise in the earth, was the shooting range and a structure lined with automobile tires where the men could practice indoor operations with live ammunition. They were far enough from homes and farms that the frequent sound of explosions didn't bother the neighbors.

A fleet of vans stood ready to move the entire team. So far, they had been used almost entirely for taking the men to a nearby county airport for practice parachute jumps.

Counting the Twin Otter they used as a jump plane, the vans, the real estate, and the pay for the men, it would have been obvious to someone with an accountant's eye that Bernard had somehow come up with at least a few million dollars. Where the money had come from was not something his men worried about.

While his men were transported wherever they had to go in vans, that was not Bernard's style. Late in the morning, he emerged from his cabin wearing a business suit and carrying a briefcase and climbed into his sleek topaz Jaguar XK-8 convertible. The rumor among the men was that he had laid out $74,500 in cash for the car. With a roar of the engine and a screech of tires, he departed in a cloud of red clay dust down the winding road that led from the lake down to Georgia State Route 382.

Driving with the top down, Bernard loved the feel of the warm sun and the wind on his face as he maneuvered his powerful convertible skillfully down the twisting mountain road. His speed seldom dipped even close to the speed limit. His fuzz buster helped protect him from tickets, and there weren't many cops patrolling the roads through the mountains anyway.

As he pulled into the parking lot at the sleepy little airport, he was pleased to see a small executive jet on the apron, and two pilots and a cabin attendant standing near the stair. As he stepped from his car, Bernard noticed one of the pilots climbing into the cabin. Moments later, the right engine roared to life.

Bernard grinned. "This is my kind of traveling," he thought.

As he approached the plane, the pilot stepped forward and extended his hand. "Sir, I'm Dick Carter. I'll be your pilot on this flight. My copilot, Jim Exeter, is in the cabin."

Guiding him toward the plane, Carter introduced the young

woman standing near the doorway. "This is Sandy Mansion. She'll be your cabin attendant. Anything you want, just ask."

Bernard shook hands with her. A striking brunette with a ready smile, she was wearing a trim, tailored navy blue suit that was both businesslike and appealingly feminine.

"Anything?" Bernard asked, taking in the young woman from head to toes.

Sandy Mansion glanced at Carter and raised an eyebrow. He sensed the unspoken question: "One of *those*? This is going to be a *long* flight."

Carter ignored Bernard's comment. "We're ready to take off as soon as you're settled."

Bernard took the steps two at a time and settled himself into a swivel chair by the window. He hated airline seats. The people who designed them had never seen a SEAL. But this seat was perfect, big enough so his legs and shoulders didn't feel cramped, yet firm enough so he didn't feel as though he had fallen into a feather bed.

Sandy Mansion pressed a button to retract the door, which also served as the stairway, and locked the door in place. She checked to make sure that Bernard was properly strapped in and then sat and adjusted her own seatbelt. The plane was already rolling. Bernard smiled. He liked traveling first class and this was even better. In a few moments they were airborne and soaring toward cruising altitude.

"Mr. Bernard." Carter's voice came over the loudspeaker near Bernard's right ear. "We should have a smooth flight most of the way. I'm going to jog around a couple of these summer afternoon thunderheads, but we should avoid most of the turbulence. We'll be flying at about forty thousand feet most of the way. I expect to arrive at Colorado Springs at fifteen-thirty hours, Mountain Daylight Time. If you have any questions, press the button on the armrest and we can hear you through the intercom."

Bernard sensed the delicate fragrance of Sandy's scent before he felt the gentle touch of her hand on his shoulder as she leaned down to speak into his ear. "Can I get you anything to eat or drink, sir? We have sandwiches, soup, and just about anything you'd like to drink."

Bernard turned and smiled. "How about a ham and cheese—provolone—on rye? Lettuce, tomato, dill pickles, and just a little mustard. And I'll have a gin on the rocks. Bring me the drink first."

"Ham and cheese and a gin on the rocks. Will Sapphire be all right?"

Bernard gave her a quick look. These folks have done their homework, he thought. They even know what kind of gin I like.

"Yes," he replied, "Sapphire will be just fine."

Moments later she was back with the drink. As she turned to go, Bernard reached out with his big left hand, grasped her around the waist, and pulled her toward him. Caught off balance, she almost toppled into his lap.

"The sandwich can wait. Why don't we just sit here and talk a little?"

He felt her hand on his leg as she caught her balance and shifted her weight. Then suddenly she drove her extended fingers deep into his crotch, hard. As he bent forward in pain, she raked the back of her hand up across his face. Then she was on her feet facing him, a slight smile on her lips.

"I'll have your sandwich for you in just a moment, sir." She turned, leaving Bernard grimacing with pain, and headed toward the galley.

There she pushed the intercom button. "Dick. God's gift to women is acting up already."

"He's got a reputation for that sort of thing. Don't put up with anything. Let me know if you have any problems."

"Oh, I don't think he'll be a problem. He grabbed me and I gave him a couple of ache-ers. He's up there massaging his groin right now."

"Good girl."

She made the sandwich quickly. When she set the tray on the table in front of Bernard, he didn't even glance at her. He lifted his glass from the tray and grunted: "*Uno más.*" Then he picked up half a sandwich and almost made it disappear with one large bite.

Mixing his second drink, Sandy debated whether to water

the gin and then decided against it. Anyone who drank his gin straight would know the difference.

When he had finished his second drink, he fell sound asleep. He awoke only when the pressure in his ears built up as the plane descended for its landing at Colorado Springs. Looking out the window, Bernard could see the foothills of the Rocky Mountains rising in gentle folds off to the west with the snow-covered peaks looming in a solid rank dominated by the bulk of Pike's Peak. As the plane circled, he could see the land sloping off to the east. If his eyes were sharp enough, he supposed, he could see all the way across Colorado, Kansas, and Missouri to the Mississippi River.

As the plane descended, Bernard was puzzled. Instead of lining up for a landing at the Colorado Springs airport south of the city, they seemed to be headed toward the mountains. Then, as the plane made a final low-altitude turn, he saw a single long, straight runway stretching out in front of them. The tires emitted a single screech as Carter greased the plane in to a landing. He put the engines in reverse thrust, quickly turned off the runway, and stopped in front of a single-story white stucco building. To the sides were three corrugated-metal hangars.

The engines were still turning as Sandy Mansion opened the door and dropped it down to form a stairway. Bernard rose, straightened his tie, picked up his briefcase, and headed toward the door. As he stepped out, he glanced at Sandy. "No hard feelings?"

She grinned. "No hard feelings on my part, sir."

Waiting at the bottom of the steps was a young man wearing a black suit, white shirt, and solid blue tie. Bernard quickly sized him up. His skin was an olive hue, but it was not obvious whether he was Hispanic or Asian. His straight black hair seemed to rule out African-American ancestry. His eyes might have provided an additional clue, but they were hidden behind dark glasses. He was obviously in superb physical condition— the kind of man Bernard might have recruited for his team. Bernard later learned that the security team assembled here was made up of unemployed warriors from all the world's battlefields, from Southeast Asia to Bosnia. A slight bulge under the man's suit jacket near his left armpit told Bernard he was armed.

He extended his hand. "Welcome to the Rock House, Mr. Bernard." "Rock House" was a play on words, connoting the fact that the main building at the compound was made of native stone and echoing the German word for city hall, *Rathaus*. "Please step in here for a moment and then we'll go on up to the château." His voice carried the hint of a foreign accent. Bernard decided it might be Thai.

Inside the small terminal building, out of sight of the airplane crew, the man said, "Sir, we have a practice here of making sure that our guests are not armed. Are you carrying any kind of weapon?"

Bernard almost said no before he noticed the man had picked up a hand-held metal detector. Often Bernard had breezed through airport security checks with the small plastic Glock pistol in a special holster fastened just above his ankle. But this guy was not fooling around. Silently he pulled up his trouser leg to reveal the hidden weapon.

"Thank you, sir. If you'll please remove the weapon and holster, I'll check it here for you. And may I see the inside of your briefcase?"

Bernard opened the case. It held a few business papers, a couple of magazines, a small tape recorder, and a laptop computer.

"If you don't mind, let's just check the briefcase, too."

Bernard shrugged, closed the case, and handed it over.

"Our car is just outside, sir." The man motioned toward the door opposite from the one by which they had entered.

The road curved upward through a forest of aspen and pine until it came to a stop in front of a three-story building of native stone that seemed to be a part of the hillside. The compound was surrounded by a ten-foot-high stone wall topped with razor-sharp concertina wire. The driver spoke briefly into a microphone and a heavy metal gate smoothly swung open as they approached. To his right, Bernard could see the edge of an Olympic-sized swimming pool with a row of cabanas on one side.

They entered the building through a tall door that led into

a marble-floored atrium that rose the full three stories. Window walls on the upper levels filled the entranceway with light. On the walls at the ground level were two large paintings of knights in combat. Bernard didn't know anything about art, but they looked expensive. He vaguely recalled having seen pictures like this once at a museum in Madrid.

His guide showed him into a small waiting room. "If you'll wait here, Mr. Nash will be happy to see you in a few minutes."

Bernard had never seen Nash before and he looked forward to the experience. Up till now, all of their dealings, including the infusion of money that had permitted him to organize his own little army, had been conducted through intermediaries.

Moments later, an inside door opened and an aide beckoned to him.

Bernard stepped into a large, circular office. The lighting was so dim that he had difficulty making out his surroundings. Across the room, backlighted by the glow of sunlight through curtained windows, he perceived the figure of a man seated behind a desk set on a slightly raised platform. Despite the dim lighting, the man wore dark glasses.

"Sit there," the man commanded, gesturing toward a straight-backed chair placed directly in front of his desk. His voice was deep and vibrant, but he spoke so softly that Bernard had to strain to make out the words.

So this is the mysterious Luke Nash, Bernard thought. He wanted to laugh at the stage-setting aura of the office, as if Nash were the Great and Powerful Oz. But with the man staring at him, Bernard simply took the chair and sat with his hands folded, waiting.

"Laszlo 'Luke' Nash" had been born Laszlo Nagy in Budapest in 1936. In 1956, he was one of the brave, foolhardy young men who tried to stand up to the Russian tanks during the Soviet invasion of Hungary. He was also one of the fortunate ones. When resistance collapsed, he managed to escape to the West. In the cities of the West, he and his friends stood out with their long hair combed straight back and with their cheap suits and even cheaper shoes.

He arrived in Munich broke, with little more than the clothes on his back, but carrying a burning hatred of the Soviets. When a friendly Hungarian-speaking American offered him a job, he leapt at the opportunity. Over the next few months, he went through an intensive pilot-training course. Soon he was checked out in both the C-47—the military version of the venerable DC-3 civilian transport plane—and the high-speed A-26 attack bomber.

For the next few years, he flew intermittent missions into the Soviet-occupied countries of Eastern Europe and even deep into the Soviet Union itself. In missions patterned on those of the American Carpetbaggers, who supported resistance forces on the Continent in World War II, Nagy and the other pilots dropped scores of agents behind the Iron Curtain. He was never told what the agents' missions were or what happened to them. He would have been disappointed to learn that most of them were quickly captured, tortured and killed.

In 1960, with a growing bank account, Nagy arrived in New York and went to work as a clerk on Wall Street. He soon changed his name to Nash and began calling himself "Luke" instead of Laszlo. Putting in long hours during the day and attending school at night, he worked hard at mastering the art of arbitrage: buying stocks, bonds, commodities, even currency, in one market, and selling them at a profit in another. With his Continental background, his mastery of English, French, Hungarian, and Russian, plus a quick, computer-like mind for figures, he prospered.

Perhaps because of his experience in the Soviet invasion, Nash had a passion for privacy. From his estate in the mountains above Colorado Springs, he controlled a worldwide trading empire, dealing not only in the old familiar stocks, bonds, commodities, and currency but buying and selling entire corporations or pieces of corporations. And just as he exerted his power from behind the scenes, he had carefully hidden his wealth deep in a bewildering labyrinth of shell companies based in countries whose secrecy laws shielded him from prying eyes.

Luke Nash made it his business to be sure he was never on the list of *Forbes*'s wealthiest men, although, if the editors had known, they'd have placed him near the very top of the list. He was not like other wealthy men, who feed their egos by counting their money in public or by showing off their possessions and their trophy wives. To him, money was nothing more than a means to an end. And the end was power—absolute power.

Still slim and powerfully built, despite his sixty-odd years, he spent a part of each day religiously working to remain in good physical condition. Every evening, wearing brief Speedo trunks, he swam lap after lap in the pool just outside his office window. Because of an eye ailment that made him sensitive to light, he did his swimming after the sun had gone down. He had come to enjoy the feeling of cutting through the darkness like a shark. Sometimes he did his laps, swimming underwater as long as he could hold his breath, just to enhance the sensation.

He also turned his eye problem to his advantage in another way. By having to keep the lighting in his office so dim, he would mildly intimidate those he called before him—if they weren't intimidated already.

In the water, Ben Bernard sometimes fancied himself a shark as well, but here in a suit and wingtips, having to sit still, he understood how a cod must feel when it was about to be devoured. Nash simply sat observing him through his dark glasses. As Bernard's eyes grew accustomed to the light, he could see that Nash's head was entirely bald and shone, almost like a halo, in a ray of light filtering in from the windows behind him. Bernard suspected the ironic effect was deliberate.

When Nash spoke, it was in a low voice that still carried the hint of a Hungarian accent.

"I understand your training is going well, Captain Bernard. Now, I have a mission for you."

Bernard was startled at Nash's use of the Navy rank. Actually, he had never quite become a captain before he left the Navy.

"Yes, sir. My guys are ready to go. In fact, they're getting a little antsy."

"Good. A certain article of mine will soon be delivered to a location in a foreign country. I want you and your men to take charge of security at that location. A larger security force is now being assembled, but you will be in overall command, making sure that my property is fully protected.

"I won't go into details. When you leave my office, one of my aides will brief you on the entire operation. He will make sure that you are provided with all the equipment you need, including aircraft. As before, adequate funds will be made available through your firm's account in the Cayman Islands, south of Florida. Do you have any questions?"

"No sir. I assume your man will be able to tell me everything I need to know."

"That's right." Nash stared at him for a moment and then added, "Captain Bernard, I want to impress on you that I demand perfect execution of my orders—and that I am willing and able to pay for perfection. I am also unforgiving of those who fall short of perfection. Is that understood?"

The threat in Nash's voice was unmistakable. It made Bernard uneasy.

"Yes, sir. I understand perfectly."

"There's one other thing. I think you are familiar with a Navy officer, a Commander Nelson? You may well come in contact with him on this operation."

"Chuck Nelson." The name brought back a flood of memories, most of them unpleasant. "Yes, I know Chuck Nelson very well."

CHAPTER 5

EVEN DURING THOSE FIRST AWFUL MONTHS AT ANNAPOLIS IN THE summer of 1978, it was obvious to the other plebes that Chuck Nelson and Ben Bernard had "grease"—not the bad grease of the obsequious ass-kisser, but the good grease of the born leader.

All new midshipmen existed in a state of constant terror, intimidated by a system that seemed carefully contrived to break them. It was bad enough during the summer, when they outnumbered the upperclassmen at the Naval Academy, but things became much worse when the entire brigade returned for the fall semester. Every upperclassman seemed to have only one thing in mind: to make life miserable for the new arrivals—better yet, to make life so impossible that they would give up and quit.

Nelson and Bernard suffered along with the others. They quickly learned that there were only six acceptable responses to an upperclassman: Yes sir; No sir; Aye, aye, sir; I'll find out, sir; No excuse, sir. The sixth possible response was the correct answer to any ridiculous question asked. But that only led to more questions. Like the others, Nelson and Bernard learned to "shove out," which meant assuming a stiff sitting position—without a chair. And they were subjected to the indignity of the greyhound race, in which the "greyhound" scoots along on all fours with a jock strap over his nose.

But, unlike many of the others, Nelson and Bernard seemed to roll with the punches, even finding a sort of grim humor in the Navy's process of breaking them down so they could then be properly molded into naval officers. Perhaps the difference was that while many of the others understandably thought of themselves as frightened, bewildered plebes, Nelson and Bernard thought of themselves as future admirals.

By the time they were in their second year, the two young men were friends, but it was a restrained friendship. No matter how much they were thrown together, there always seemed to be a barrier of sorts between them, not only formed of their rivalry within the midshipman community, but also reflecting a subtle difference in character. The first sign of a strain in their relationship noticeable to others came early in their junior year.

Bernard had a plebe braced at rigid attention against the wall in one of the cavernous corridors of Bancroft Hall.

With his nose almost touching the other's face, Bernard shouted questions about obscure Navy lore. The answers were all in *Reef Points*, the handbook all newcomers were supposed to master. But it contained almost three hundred pages. No one could know all the answers.

"Where is John Paul Jones buried?"

"What was the name of his ship?

"How many masts did she have?

"How tall were the masts?"

Other plebes skittered past, praying they wouldn't be noticed. As the grilling went on, a small knot of upperclassmen gathered to watch. The firstie, as plebes were called, began to sweat and then to quiver.

"Don't you like it here, mister? Why don't you go home to mama?" Bernard moved even closer.

Nelson was one of those who had stopped to watch. He glanced at his wrist. This had now gone on for ten minutes. He stepped forward.

"Okay, Ben. That's enough."

Bernard stopped his interrogation abruptly, almost as though he had been awakened from some kind of trance. He pivoted on his heel and faced Nelson.

"What did you say?"

"I said that's enough, Ben. Let the kid go." Nelson stepped

forward until he was almost as close to Bernard as Bernard
had been to the plebe.

Bernard blinked and then took a step back. Both hands were
balled into fists and his elbows bent, but he did not raise his
hands. "Who the hell do you think you are, telling me what
to do?"

"Just knock it off." Nelson turned toward the quaking
plebe, standing there wide-eyed, observing the confrontation
between the two upperclassmen. "Okay, get going."

The boy turned and hurried down the corridor as fast as he
could without breaking into a run.

Bernard glanced over his shoulder as the young man rapidly
retreated. Then he turned back to Nelson. "Don't you ever
pull that kind of shit on me again!" Abruptly he wheeled and
strode off down the corridor.

In the following weeks, the two men were cool toward each
other, but gradually they both seemed to have forgotten the
incident, or at least, to have put it out of mind. They worked
out together on the track team and even helped each other
prepare for the seemingly endless tests. Bernard had a good
head for math and he coached Nelson and other friends for
the science and math exams. Nelson was better on English,
history, and philosophy, and he helped the others to prepare
for those courses.

But no amount of study or collaboration made any of them
feel easier about the examination in electrical engineering—
the most difficult and most dreaded course any of the midshipmen encountered during the four years at the academy.
Retired admirals who had sailed the seven seas and fought the
nation's wars looked back on that one exam as the most difficult obstacle in an entire career.

A few days before the exam, which came in the first semester of their junior year, Bernard called Nelson aside.

"Chuck, we've got a little thing going on this exam. We
might be able to get a look at the questions in advance. It'll
cost you two hundred dollars. Can we count you in?"

Nelson looked at him aghast. Part of the Annapolis legend
that every midshipman soon learned was how cheating scan-
dals related to the EE exam had rocked the academy before.

"Ben, I don't want to hear anything about this. I'm going to forget we ever had this conversation. If you have any sense, you'll forget about whatever you have in mind."

That night Nelson couldn't sleep. The words of the academy's Honor Concept kept running through his mind: "I will not lie, cheat, or steal and will let the whole truth be known." Then he would hear the words of an almost equally commanding unwritten rule: "Never bilge a classmate."

By the time dawn finally arrived, Nelson had decided on his course. He did not actually know for a fact that Bernard was involved in a conspiracy to cheat on the EE test. He had, as the Honor Concept required, "counseled" his classmate. Therefore, he reasoned, he had no obligation to report their conversation. He would keep what he heard to himself.

Within days of the examination, rumors began to sweep through Bancroft Hall that something strange had happened: the EE exam curve had an unusual bulge. Normally, the results of the exam would have shown a bell curve with a few of the midshipmen doing very well, a few doing very badly, and most of the others clustered near the middle. But, the rumors said, the curve leaned strangely toward the high end—and a number of those who had done surprisingly well were not among the best students.

When the scores were posted, Bernard was one of those who had aced the exam. He was good at math and science, but was he that good?

One by one, midshipmen who had done better than expected were called in for questioning. Several of them quickly admitted they had cheated. But all they knew, they said, was that copies of the exam were available for $200 apiece. How the exams had been obtained and who the ringleaders were, they didn't know.

Nelson had scored a B on the test—about in line with his academic standing and his performance on earlier tests. It was not until late in the investigation that he was called in.

The officer straightened the papers on his desk and then stared for a moment at Nelson.

"Be seated. I'm going to ask you a few questions. All I want is straightforward answers—the truth. I don't have to warn you that any false or evasive answer could lead to your expulsion from the Academy and the end of whatever future you might have had as a naval officer. Is that understood?''

Nelson nodded: ''Yes sir.''

The first question was straightforward: ''Did you cheat on the EE exam?''

''No sir.''

''Did you have an advance copy of the examination questions?''

''No sir.''

''Did anyone discuss with you the availability of a copy of the questions or offer them to you?''

''No sir.''

''Do you know of anyone who had access to the examination beforehand?''

''No sir.''

''Let me be more specific. I will read you the names of some of your fellow midshipmen. Tell me if you have any reason to believe that any of them had access to the questions in advance.''

The officer read the names of twelve midshipmen. Among the names was that of Ben Bernard.

Nelson listened, then looked the officer in the eye: ''No sir, none of them.''

The officer stared at him for a moment then said: ''That will be all. Thank you.''

The investigation concluded as many of the midshipmen had expected it would: those who confessed they had cheated were expelled from the Academy; the ringleaders were not caught and continued smoothly on, preparing for their careers as officers in the U.S. Navy.

It was not until several months later that Nelson brought up the incident.

He and Bernard had just completed a hard mile run, preparing for a track meet on the following Saturday. As they walked alone around the track, cooling down and catching their breath, Nelson glanced at Bernard. ''Ben, I lied for you. If I had gotten caught, that would have been the end of my career, and I took the chance. But that's the last time. I'm never going to cover for you again.''

"Aw, shit, Chuck. Don't sweat it. That's the way things work in this place. Nothing bad happened.''

"No, not this time. But this is the last time. Remember: Never again!'' Nelson broke into a jog, putting distance between the two of them.

Life was busy at Annapolis—so busy that most midshipmen had little time to pay much attention to what was going on in the world outside their own little routine of drill, athletics, and endless study. But the news that captured the world's attention in the spring of 1980 was too big to ignore: an American attempt to rescue hostages held captive at the American embassy in Teheran had ended in disaster in the Iranian desert in what came to be known as Desert One, for the desert landing spot.

Although they didn't realize it at the time, Desert One would have a profound impact on the Class of 1982. When the young midshipmen entered the Academy in 1978, most of them had one of three career goals in mind: carrier aviation, surface ship command, or submarines. Choosing a career involved a long look into the future. The carriers and the naval aviators had dominated the Navy since they took the leading role from the battleships in World War II. There was still a major place for surface warships, but primarily in support of the carriers. And of course the Navy would always need the stealth provided by submarines. To some of the midshipmen, a career in submarines, despite the discomfort of life underwater and the long patrols, offered one of the most promising career possibilities. Unless a submarine skipper ran into something, he risked few black marks on his record. If one's ambition rose to the level of chief of naval operations, submarines might be the way to go.

Almost none of the midshipmen gave any thought to a career in special operations. Most Navy careerists, especially those from Annapolis, considered the Navy's SEALs a scraggly collection of undisciplined snake-eaters. The farther one stayed from special operations, the smoother one's career path was likely to be.

Desert One changed all that. Many members of Congress were deeply disturbed by the way the rescue force had been patched together because the nation had no team of Air Force, Navy, Army Special Forces, and Marines who trained together and were available for such an operation.

It would be several years before Congress created the new U.S. Special Operations Command, but Chuck Nelson and Ben Bernard were among the first of their classmates to see the new opportunities opening up in special operations.

Both asked for assignment to the SEALs. Over the next several months, both would have occasion to regret their choices. Life at the Academy had been challenging, especially that long plebe year. But BUD/S was infinitely tougher, especially for the newly minted ensigns. As they went through their training at Coronado, California, the officers had to do everything the enlisted men did—swim underwater until they thought their lungs would burst, land a boat on a rocky shore at night, get so cold they thought they were going to die. And then, when the enlisted men finally crashed on their cots, the officers had to do what officers in the Navy do: write reports and prepare plans for the next day's activities.

If, at Annapolis, the most important rule was "Never bilge a classmate," at Coronado the would-be SEALs learned an even more important rule: Never abandon your buddy.

Perhaps fortunately, Bernard and Nelson were never matched up as buddies. Their relationship had been cool ever since the EE exam incident. They had as little to do with each other as possible. But when their assignments cast them together, they did not let their personal feelings get in the way of the professional teamwork life in the SEALs demanded.

When they finished BUD/S, they were still not qualified to pin on the big, bizarre SEAL badge—known as the "Budweiser" because it looked like the brewer's trademark. That ceremony would come only after another six months of on-the-job training in a SEAL team. Bernard and Nelson were assigned to different teams. Nelson went to a team at the East Coast SEALs headquarters at the Little Creek amphibious base in Virginia Beach, Virginia. Bernard remained with a team at Coronado. The traditional rivalry between East and West

Coast teams added just a little more to the tension between the two men.

For both men, those six months were in some ways even worse than anything they had gone through before. Both arrived at their new teams feeling a little cockier than they should have. After all, they were not only Annapolis graduates, but they had made it through Hell Week and everything else they had had to endure during BUD/S. But their new teammates were not impressed. They proceeded to treat them as outsiders and test them in every way they could in a no-holds-barred process known as the ''Red Ass.''

When, after six months that made them both question their career choice, Nelson and Bernard finally pinned on their Budweisers, they felt they had earned them—and then some.

Over the next few years, the two men advanced rapidly in the growing special operations force, Bernard on the West Coast, Nelson on the East. They watched appreciatively as officers a few years their senior became captains and then even admirals. It was not many years before that an ambitious SEAL would have considered himself lucky to become a lieutenant and command a SEAL team.

The two men saw each other only occasionally until the mid-1990s, when they were both assigned to staff positions at the U.S. Special Operations Command at MacDill Air Force Base near Tampa, Florida. While the rest of the U.S. military was shrinking, USSOC had both money and room for advancement for ambitious officers. Both Bernard and Nelson, despite their relative youth, considered themselves in line for promotion to captain.

Bernard actually made the list of those under consideration for promotion—to the surprise of a number of those who knew him. Traditionally, a career Navy officer had been expected to marry a woman who could help advance his career—and to stay married to her no matter what. Bernard had broken sharply with that tradition. His first marriage had ended in divorce, and his second seemed to friends to be on the rocks as well. In the past, that would not have been career enhancing.

But the Navy had changed. With many women pursuing

their own careers, it was not unusual for a Navy wife to avoid the teas and the committee work that wives had once devoted themselves to as a part of advancing their husbands' careers.

In the SEAL community, with the stress of dangerous assignments and long absences, divorce had become more the rule than the exception. Along with the high divorce rate came a certain acceptance of infidelity. Many SEALs, on long assignments away from home, expected their wives to remain faithful but thought their own screwing around was not only permissible but even the macho thing to do.

Bernard was one of the leading practitioners of this double standard. He would have sex with any woman who stayed still long enough.

Such behavior raised few eyebrows in the all-male environment of a SEAL team. But the rules were different—and violations were more likely to be noticed—in a large headquarters like MacDill, with many women serving in the command. Bernard didn't see the red flags. What he saw, watching the parade of pulchritude through the corridors, was opportunity. He thought he had gone to heaven.

Trouble was not long in coming.

On several occasions, he had kidded with Lt. (J.G.) Patsy Fagan and she had seemed friendly. He asked her to meet with him in his office. He met her in the doorway and then swung the door closed. Motioning to a chair in front of the desk, he said: "Sit there, honey."

She glanced at him with a questioning look on her face and then took the chair.

Bernard moved in behind her and placed his hands on her shoulders.

"I've noticed your work," he said. "I think you've got a great future in the Navy. I can help you along—you know, a favorable performance report, a word in the right place."

She sat straight in the chair. "Yes sir, I appreciate that."

He could feel the tension in her body.

"Relax . . . you know, I can be a big help to you." His hands slipped inside the open neck of her summer uniform blouse and moved down toward her breasts.

She rose abruptly from the chair and turned to face him. "Sir, I don't think. . . ."

"Aw, c'mon, Patsy. I can help you a lot if you treat me right." He slipped an arm around her waist and pulled her toward him, pinning her arms against her sides. Her struggles to get free only served to move her body against his. She could feel his arousal.

She prided herself on remaining in good physical condition. But her strength was no match for his. She felt a growing sense of panic as he pushed her toward the floor and pinned her with his body as he groped under her skirt. He pressed his lips against hers and she could feel his tongue inside her mouth even as she tried to clench her teeth shut. She felt his hand leave her thigh and then realized he was pulling down his zipper.

"Oh, God," she thought, "this son of a bitch is going to rape me." With his mouth pressed to hers, she couldn't even scream.

The telephone rang and kept on ringing for what seemed like a long time. Bernard ignored it and returned to trying to pull her pantyhose down with one hand.

Then there was a sharp knock at the door. "Commander Bernard! Sir, the admiral asks that you join him. He said he would like to see you immediately, sir."

Bernard rose to his knees, pulling up his zipper, murmuring, "Shit! Shit! Shit!"

He extended a hand. "Okay, Patsy. Later. Remember, I can be a big help to you."

Brushing back his hair with his fingers and straightening his tie as though nothing had happened, he went out the door and closed it behind him.

Patsy Fagan stood unsteadily in the middle of the room. She straightened her uniform and looked in the mirror. She was surprised to see how, except for the redness in her face, she looked so normal, for a woman who had just been delivered from rape by a chance knock at the door.

Well, she thought, what does little Patsy Fagan do now? Do I forget about it and never get behind a closed door with this guy again? Or do I report it and go through all the my-word-against-his-word hassle?

A few years before, the answer would have been obvious. A woman accusing a senior officer of a rape attempt—not even a rape itself—would have received a skeptical response from the Navy's male hierarchy. There might have been a pretense of an investigation and then the whole thing would have been almost forgotten—forgotten except that she would probably be branded as a troublemaker while the man went blithely along with his career.

But the way that accusations of sexual harassment were treated had changed dramatically in the wake of the Tailhook scandal, in which a group of naval aviators, partying at a Las Vegas hotel, had been accused of groping female visitors and other lewd acts. Now, charges of improper behavior were taken so seriously that men were even afraid to compliment a female colleague on a new dress.

Patsy Fagan took another look at herself in the mirror. She saw a stubborn Irish face looking back at her, eyes flashing with anger. She made up her mind.

Striding purposefully down the hall to Chuck Nelson's office, she knocked and walked in the open door. Closing the door behind her, she said, "Sir, can I talk to you for a few minutes? I need some advice."

Nelson pushed aside the stack of papers he had been working on. The trouble with the Navy was that the higher you advanced in rank, the more paperwork you had to do and the less time you got to spend out on the operations that had attracted you into the service in the first place.

"Sure, Lieutenant. Sit down."

"Sir, I'm not sure what to do." Her face was still red, and her breath came more rapidly than normal. "Let me tell you what happened, and then, if you say so, we'll just forget I ever talked to you."

Nelson leaned forward, a puzzled look on his face. This was more than some little office problem. He nodded.

"A few minutes ago, Commander Bernard asked me into his office. I thought he wanted to talk about that project I've been working on. Instead, he started talking about how he could help me, and he put his hands on me."

"Put his hands on you?"

"Yes, he stood behind me and put his hands on my shoulders, and then he tried to reach under my blouse. When I stood up and turned around, he grabbed me and pushed me down on the floor. He was going to try to rape me."

"Wow!" Nelson leaned back and cupped his chin in his right hand. "What happened?"

"The phone rang for a long time and then someone came and knocked at the door and said the admiral wanted to see him. He got off me and left. I came right down the hall to your office."

"Then there was no rape?"

"No sir. He had his pants unzipped and he was clawing at my pantyhose. But then the knock at the door interrupted him."

"I assume there were no witnesses?"

"I don't think so. The person who knocked at the door didn't come inside."

"Did you scream or call for help?"

"I couldn't. He was all over me. He was trying to get his tongue in my mouth and I could hardly even breathe."

Nelson stared out the window at the palm trees moving gently against the background of the blue Florida sky. Even after this brief conversation, he felt trapped and wished she hadn't come to him. It might be best for her just to forget the incident. But if neither of them made a report and it was later learned that she had told him of a rape attempt immediately after it occurred and he had done nothing about it, that would be the end of his career. But he didn't say that.

"The Navy has no room for that kind of behavior. Now, the question is, what should you do? You came to me in confidence, and it will remain that way. I'm sure you realize that if you make a report, it is going to complicate your life. Your veracity will be questioned, especially since there was no actual rape and there were no witnesses. On the other hand, you may be protecting yourself or some other woman if you do make a report."

"Sir, I'm still mad. Maybe I should make a report before I have time to cool down and talk myself out of it."

"If you're sure . . . ?"

She nodded.

"Okay, that's the gutsy thing to do. I'll call JAG and have them send someone over to take your statement. I'll also give them a statement relating how you came to me immediately after the incident."

The judge advocate general's investigator who arrived at Nelson's office a few moments later was a businesslike but sympathetic young woman. Producing a tape recorder from her briefcase, she listened intently as Lt. Fagan told her story, asking only a few questions.

"Now, Lieutenant, I would like you to go to the infirmary. I will arrange for an examination. Since you say an actual rape did not occur, we may not find much. But from what you say, there could be traces of semen on your body or your clothes and there may be signs of abrasions where he tried to remove your pantyhose. I also want to have your clothing examined. It's possible your skirt picked up fibers from the floor that would tend to corroborate your account. I will also have Commander Bernard's office sealed until we can check his floor, where there may be fibers from your clothing."

Bernard was placed under arrest that very afternoon and then quickly released on his own recognizance.

As word of his arrest spread, several other women came forward to relate similar incidents.

"Listen," his lawyer told him, "we can fight this thing if you want to and probably beat it. But you're not going to make captain. As far as the Navy is concerned, your career is toast, no matter how this turns out. I think your best bet is for me to try to work a plea bargain: they'll drop the charges and you'll resign your commission."

Bernard looked stunned. Since when could a little hanky-panky ruin a guy's career? Finally, he nodded. "Okay, see if you can make the deal."

The military prosecutor didn't hesitate long. He knew it would be difficult to get a conviction in a case where there were no witnesses and little evidence of a crime beyond the alleged victim's word. Even if the other women were willing to testify, the fact that none of them had filed a complaint at the time would weaken the impact of what they had to say.

News of the case involving Bernard had quickly reached the Pentagon. When the secretary of the Navy was briefed, he was livid. Since Tailgate, the Navy had gotten nothing but one black eye after another. The worst blow had been the suicide of the chief of naval operations when questions were raised about whether he had worn decorations to which he was not entitled.

As a young Marine officer, the secretary had served in some of the most bitter fighting of the Vietnam war along the border with North Vietnam in the winter of 1967–1968. After the war, he had returned to law school and then prospered. He had been one of the president's earliest supporters and the secretaryship was his reward. But he thought of the job not so much as a political plum, which it had been for some of his predecessors, as a position from which he could continue to serve his country. He remained fiercely loyal to the Marine Corps and to the Navy.

"Let's get rid of this guy," he told an aide. "But first I want to talk to him. Am I going to be in Florida anytime soon?"

The aide consulted a schedule he held on a clipboard. "Yes, sir. You're scheduled for a speech to the Navy League in Tampa next week."

"Okay, give me half an hour or so at MacDill."

When Bernard entered the room where the secretary was waiting, he kept him standing at attention as he looked him up and down with cold eyes.

"Commander Bernard, I wanted to come down here and tell you personally how disappointed I am in you. A lot of good men have worn that uniform and have given their lives for their country. And what do you do? You disgrace the uniform and inflict pain on everyone who wears it.

"I understand you have submitted your resignation. I just

wish we could send you where you really belong. However ... I will personally sign the papers relieving you of your obligations as a naval officer. You, sir, are a bad apple. All I can say is, good riddance.''

He regarded Bernard, still standing at attention, for a few moments and then snapped: "Dismissed!"

Bernard strode rigidly, almost as though he were marching, out the door, but his pace turned to a kind of swagger as he headed down the hall toward his office. Just as he reached the doorway, he saw Nelson walking toward him. He stopped short and stared.

"You son of a bitch! I'll get you for this."

Nelson continued on past him without a glance.

CHAPTER 6

DOROTHY BONIOR, A TALL, ATHLETIC-LOOKING WOMAN WITH skin the color of burnt chocolate, stood at the sink peeling carrots. Her mother, a heavier woman with her graying hair pulled back and knotted in a bun, sat at the kitchen table carefully spreading white icing on a rich-looking devil's food cake.

"Carrots are not the children's favorite food, but they like them with the brown sugar sauce I make for them," the younger woman said.

"They better eat them or they don't get any of Grandma's special cake," her mother replied. She looked up, studying her daughter as she worked at the sink.

"Dottie, do you ever regret you married a SEAL?"

Her daughter turned and gave her a long look.

"Regrets? No, no regrets, Momma. But it's different. It's a different kind of life than other people lead. Like now. Jeff's gone and I don't even know where he is. I think the SEALs, they have their priorities. The team is number one and the wife and children are number two. That's a strain. Jeff and his people will go off in the middle of the night. His beeper buzzes and he's up and he's off and he doesn't tell me where he's going or what he's going to do or when he's coming back or when he'll even give me a telephone call. It's rough. When that happens, of course, I'm in charge. I have to make all the decisions, get the car fixed, get the plumber. Everything a man would do around the house, I do. And when he comes back, he takes over, of course."

"I've wondered. But you and Jeff just seem to hit it off. It seems to me like a happy marriage."

"Oh, yes, it is. He loves me. He loves the children. He loves his job. But not in that order. We are very compatible and we've learned to live this strange life. So . . . how's the cake coming along? I've almost got dinner ready to go."

Her mother ran the knife around the edges. "All ready for the eating."

"I'll put the chops in the oven. Jeff always says meat should be broiled, not fried. Everything else is about ready. I'll call the kids in a few minutes." The three Bonior children—ten-year-old Beverly, eight-year-old Jeff, Jr., and six-year-old Denise—could be heard playing on a swing set in the front yard.

"Things going good at school, Dottie?"

"Pretty good, Momma. Some of these high school kids are pretty rough—a lot different than when I was in school. Most of them don't get the kind of support at home they should be getting—if they have a home at all. I try to make American history meaningful to them, show them they can have a future in this country. I talk about Jeff and my life. I tell them we both came from . . . we didn't live high on the hog. We both work hard. We're going to send our children to college. That's the way to get ahead in this world. But it's hard . . . these kids are just difficult to deal with. I think I have a good rapport with them. A lot of the teachers can't wait until they get out the door. I think some of them, they're even afraid of these children. I like them. I make some friendships with them."

As she spoke, the sound of speeding cars almost drowned out her words.

"Oh, these kids! I wish they wouldn't drive so fast!"

The Bonior home was in a normally quiet residential neighborhood only a short distance from both the amphibious base where Jeff was stationed and the school where Dorothy taught. But it was also only a few blocks from the busy intersection of Independence and Witch Duck in the heart of Virginia Beach.

Suddenly, the sound of the racing cars was punctuated by a rapid popping sound, not even as loud as a backfire.

Two cars roared past the house, their tires squealing. The sound had just begun to fade when the older Bonior girl, Beverly, shouted: "Mommy! Mommy! Mommy!" Little Jeff began to scream in a high-pitched wail.

The two women stared at each other and ran for the kitchen door.

Beverly was standing by the swing, holding her hands against her face. Jeff stood beside her, screaming. Denise sprawled awkwardly on the ground beneath the swing, her right leg bent at an unnatural angle.

Dorothy Bonior reached her daughter first and knelt over the little body. Blood flowed from a wound in her leg, darkening the tanbark on which she lay. Blood also spread in a growing circle on the right side of her T-shirt—the one with the funny bear that her father had brought back from one of his mysterious trips.

Dorothy reached to take her daughter in her arms, but stopped. Everything seemed to be happening in slow motion. She felt a strange calmness come over her. Somehow, she knew exactly what to do.

"Momma, you call nine-one-one. Tell them a six-year-old child has been shot and is in serious condition.

"Beverly, you go in the kitchen and bring me some clean dish towels. Then you go back upstairs and bring me a blanket."

The older woman and the girl ran to the house.

Only then did Dorothy turn to examine her daughter. She noted that her heart was beating regularly. A good sign. But her breathing was rough and erratic. She was also bleeding badly. The blood flowing from the wound in her leg spurted red with each beat of her heart.

"Oh, good," Dorothy exclaimed, as her daughter handed her a dish towel. She folded the towel and held it tightly against the leg wound to stop the flow of blood.

"Momma, did you call nine-one-one?"

"Yes, they said they'll be here in a few minutes."

"Momma, will you please try to take care of Jeffy?" The little boy had stopped screaming but was still crying uncontrollably. His grandmother gathered him in her arms, patting his head and murmuring, "Everything's all right, Jeffy. Everything is going to be all right." Her own heart ached and she wished she could believe the comforting words coming from her mouth.

In the distance, they could hear the wail of an ambulance siren hurrying from Virginia Beach Station Two—the Davis Corner Volunteer Rescue Squad.

"Beverly, you run down to the corner and show the ambulance men where we are."

The wail of the siren seemed to continue interminably, but it was only a few minutes until the vehicle, its lights flashing eerily, pulled up in front of the house and a man and a woman got out. The man opened the back door and pulled out a stretcher and a body board. The young woman came and leaned over the wounded girl and her mother.

"What is the little girl's name?" she asked.

"Denise."

"Denise, are you all right? Can you hear me?"

The little girl gave no sign of responding. The ambulance attendant pulled back one eyelid and then another and then lifted one limp arm and took her pulse.

She returned to the ambulance and picked up the microphone.

"We've got a six-year-old female subject here with multiple bullet wounds. She is unconscious. We're going to need Nightingale."

She returned to the front yard and leaned over Dorothy.

"Ma'am," she asked, "are you the little girl's mother?"

She looked over her shoulder and nodded.

"I've called the helicopter—the Nightingale. They'll take her to King's Daughters. There's an open area down at the end of the street near the Pembroke Apartments. We'll take her there in the ambulance and the helicopter will take her from there. I hate to move her more than once, but it will be safer for the chopper to land over there."

The two attendants bent over the little girl's slight form. Using a metal instrument like a small shoehorn, with a powerful flashlight built in, one of the attendants slid a tube down the child's throat and attached it to a portable device that immediately took over her breathing, pushing oxygen in and withdrawing carbon dioxide. They then turned to her wounds. One placed a pressure bandage over the wound in her leg. The other cut away her T-shirt and placed a compress over the hole in her abdomen, which was slowly oozing blood. Then one of them inserted a needle in her left arm and began a flow of plasma to replace the blood she had lost.

Her mother stood to one side, watching them work. Now that they had taken over, she found that she was trembling. "Will she be all right?"

The young woman looked up. "Your little girl is very seriously injured, ma'am. But we have her stabilized now and we'll get her to the hospital just as soon as we can. There's a hospital near here, but the helicopter will take her directly to Norfolk General. That's where we take all gunshot cases. Then she'll be moved right next door to King's Daughters. That's a first-rate children's hospital. She couldn't get better care anywhere."

Dorothy Bonior nodded. She realized the ambulance attendant had tried to be as comforting as possible without really answering her question.

"Oh," she thought, "if only Jeff were here." Then she caught herself. Her husband wouldn't be here and she would have to tough this out by herself.

Denise was gently rolled into the ambulance and her mother climbed in beside her.

"Momma," she called. "You take care of Bev and Jeff. I'll call as soon as I know anything."

The red and white twin-engine Nightingale helicopter circled once and then settled onto the grass in an area which had been hastily roped off by police.

The pilot remained at the controls with the rotor turning as the flight nurse and flight paramedic opened the rear doors and pulled out their stretcher. Gently they lifted the body board to which the girl had been strapped and transferred it to their stretcher.

Dorothy Bonior stood near the rear door of the helicopter as her daughter was loaded aboard and fastened in.

"Can I come with her?" she asked.

The flight nurse grasped her arm and leaned close to speak into her ear over the sound of the engines.

"It will be better, ma'am, if a police officer takes you to the hospital. If you came with us, we'd have to give you all the safety instructions and that would waste time."

Mrs. Bonior nodded and blew a kiss toward her daughter.

The flight nurse conferred quickly with the ambulance crew and then climbed aboard the helicopter. The paramedic was already on one of the helicopter's six radios calling Norfolk General.

"KNGA eight-one-two, this is Nightingale. We have a six-year-old gunshot victim. We should arrive in ten minutes."

He continued, passing on details of the child's injuries.

A doctor in the emergency room made notes. He had already ordered an alpha trauma alert, sounding the beepers carried by the members of the hospital's trauma team, alerting them that a patient with serious injuries would arrive shortly.

The flight to the hospital took only six minutes. As soon as the helicopter settled onto its home pad a short distance from the doors to the hospital's emergency department, the nurse and the paramedic pulled their stretcher from the plane and rolled it rapidly toward the door.

The nurse reached up and hit a plate on the wall. As soon as the doors opened automatically, she began shouting her report on the child's condition. From long experience, she knew that once those in the emergency room touched the patient, she would lose their attention.

Inside the emergency room, the child was wheeled into one of a series of large bays so well equipped it could double as an operating room, if needed. The attending physician checked her over, dictating his comments in terse phrases.

"Simple fracture of the right tibia. Arterial bleeding under control.

"Entry wound in the lower right abdomen. Evidence of internal bleeding. No exit wound apparent.

"Patient is unconscious. She has suffered a deep laceration on the right frontal area of the skull. Some swelling apparent."

A white child in similar circumstances might have turned deathly pale. But skin color was not a good indicator of the condition of a child with a dark complexion. The doctor pulled off her left shoe and sock and looked at the bottom of the foot. It was pale, almost white, a sign that she had gone into shock.

"Patient is in hypobulemic shock.

"Heartbeat regular. Pulse elevated. Blood pressure ninety-nine over fifty."

As soon as they were satisfied that her condition was stabilized, she was sent to the CT scan and then through a long corridor across to the Children's Hospital of the King's Daughters and up the elevator to the pediatric intensive care unit on the third floor.

Waiting beside an empty bed was Dr. Jack Kitamura, the physician in charge of the intensive care unit. With him were two nurses, a nurse's aide, a respiratory therapist, a neurosurgeon, a resident, a medical student, and a social worker. They hovered over the girl's tiny frame, talking quietly as they connected her breathing tubes to a ventilator on a stand beside the bed. A large intravenous tube was inserted into a blood vessel in her shoulder. It was big enough for blood to be drawn for tests without sticking her with a needle each time. From the same point, a catheter was inserted into the blood vessel and run down into her chest to keep track of her heart function.

The neurosurgeon leaned over her head. The CT scan did not indicate a fracture, but she had obviously received a severe blow on her head, probably as she fell from the swing.

"I think she just got a bad shaking up, but I want to monitor it carefully," the neurosurgeon told Kitamura. He quickly prepared a small drill to cut through her skull. Then he carefully slipped a wire with a sensor on the end down into the center of her brain to monitor the production of brain fluid.

On the surface of her scalp, he attached a dozen monitors and connected them to a scope at the right side of the bed to monitor her brain's electrical activity.

"Let's put her on pentobarbital for twenty-four hours. That'll keep her in a coma while we see how she's coming along. And let's also give her Dilantin to prevent seizures."

Another doctor had begun examining her leg.

"We're in luck, here," he said. "The bullet broke the bone but didn't shatter it."

He drilled a hole at the knee and inserted a pin. He attached a thin rope to the pin on each side of the knee, then ran the rope through a pulley attached above the bed and down to a weight. The weight would hold the bone in position to heal itself.

As soon as he was satisfied that everything had been done, Kitamura slipped away and went to what was called the "quiet room" just outside the doors to the intensive care unit. Dorothy Bonior was waiting there, along with the police officer who had brought her to the hospital.

"You have a strong little girl there, Mrs. Bonior. We have her stabilized now and I think she's in pretty good shape," the doctor told her.

"She's going to be all right?"

"She's still a very sick child. We're going to have to operate to repair the damage from the bullet wound to her abdomen. When the surgeons finish, we'll have a better idea of her condition.

"Mrs. Bonior, would you like to get in touch with your husband? There's a phone right here."

She laughed a brief, wry laugh. "Welcome to the life of a SEAL's wife. My husband is on a mission. I don't know where he is or what he's doing. All I have is a telephone number to call in an emergency. They may or may not be able to get me in touch with him."

She grew silent for a moment, then picked up the phone and dialed a number that was answered on the first ring in the office of the Joint Chiefs of Staff in the Pentagon. She told the aide who answered who she was and why she had called. He took her number and promised to call back as soon as possible.

It was still early evening at Site Y in Arizona when Chuck Nelson called Jeff Bonior to his office. The big chief was in an enthusiastic mood as he entered the office.

"I think the exercise last night was just about on the mark, skipper. Everybody did their jobs pretty close to perfect."

Nelson was fidgeting with a letter opener, tapping it on his desk. He stared at Bonior for a moment before speaking. "Sit down, Jeff. We have something to talk about."

A puzzled look came over Bonior's face as he tried to fathom what might have happened that had caused his boss and swim buddy to seem so somber.

"Jeff, I uh, uh. . . . I got a call today. Just a few minutes ago. From the chairman's office. Dottie had just called them. She was calling from a hospital in Norfolk. And . . . Jeff, I . . . Your daughter. . . . Denise has been shot."

Bonior half rose from his chair. "Dennie has been . . . what?"

"I don't really know anything more. Apparently there were some people driving by, there was an exchange of gunfire. There were some kids playing out front and your daughter was hit."

"She's going to be all right, isn't she?"

"I really don't know. She's been very seriously hurt. She's in the hospital in Norfolk now. It's supposed to be one of the top children's hospitals in the country. They have the best people for handling this kind of thing."

"This kind of thing? What do you mean?"

"Well . . . she's unconscious. She was shot once in the leg, and another bullet hit her in the abdomen. She also has some kind of head injury. She is very seriously injured."

Bonior sat still, stunned. Neither man spoke. Finally, Bonior broke the silence. "I'd better get back there."

"Well, I don't know whether you can. We have opsec on this operation. We're locked down. We're not supposed to be in touch with anybody. We're especially not supposed to be out away from this base. I've got a call in to the chairman. I want to talk to him about it. Let me see what I can do."

"Well, can I talk to Dottie?"

"Let me see what we can do about that, too. We can probably patch something through without violating opsec. I can't do that myself, either."

They lapsed into silence again. Then the red phone—the direct line to the chairman's office—rang.

"Yes, sir. Chief Bonior is right here with me now."

"Chuck, you tell the chief that I will personally see that his daughter gets the best care possible."

"Sir, I'm sure the chief appreciates that. I'd like to plug him through to his wife so he can talk to her and then get him back there if we can."

"This guy is one of your top people?"

"Oh, yes sir. The best, and a very reliable person. I don't have any qualms about security as far as he's concerned. He'd certainly not talk to anybody about our mission. And if he can get back there to be with his daughter and wife—briefly—I can spare him for a short time. We've just finished our all-up rehearsal. Everything is really in shape. So, if you think it's okay . . ."

"Is he there now?"

"Yes, he's sitting right here."

"Let me talk to him." Nelson handed over the phone. "Chief, I want you to know how deeply sorry we are that this terrible thing has happened. I have put in gear from my office everything that can possibly be done for your daughter. I've already talked to the chief of surgery at our Portsmouth Naval Hospital. He says she should remain at King's Daughters instead of being moved. He has great confidence in the people there.

"Now, as far as you coming back here, I am concerned about opsec. I wouldn't let most people go. I'd just have to say that's the job you've got. But in this case I'll get in touch with the deputy chief of naval operations for air. He has an F/A-18 he uses to hop around the country. I'll have him fly you back here. We'll be back to you within a few minutes."

"Thank you sir. And sir . . . pray for her."

". . . Uh, right, I will. And I'll be back to you in a few minutes."

Bonior hung up the phone and turned to Nelson. "I don't know how to ask this, sir, but would you pray with me?"

"Well, I don't know. I'm not very good at that . . . but, sure, Jeff."

"Why don't we just kneel down here and hold hands and I'll say. . . . Well, first, do you know the Lord's Prayer?"

"Yes. I do."

The two men remained kneeling, their heads bowed. Then Nelson blessed himself and rose. As he did, the phone rang.

The F/A-18 pilot introduced himself and asked to speak to Bonior.

"Chief, I'm estimating arrival at the Tucson airport at about midnight your time. If you'll report to the commercial side of the airport—well, you'll see the Hornet with its big twin tails out there. I'll meet you there and we'll be on our way. We'll land at the Oceana Naval Air Station and they'll have a car there to take you to the hospital."

"Sir, what about talking to my wife?"

"Yeah, we've arranged that. I'm going to get going now, but one of our people here will patch you through. Hold on."

Before the call went through, Bonior heard another voice on the line. "Chief, I must caution you that this is a nonsecure connection. No classified material can be discussed on this line."

Moments later, Bonior heard his wife's voice: "Oh, Jeff, it's so good to talk to you."

"What happened? How is she?"

"She's in intensive care now. She's going into surgery first thing in the morning. The doctor told me he hopes she is going to be all right, but he says she is a very sick little girl right now."

"What about Bev and Jeff?"

"My mother was here from Saint Louis, visiting. We were just getting ready for dinner when this happened. Momma is with the kids, and she can stay as long as we need her."

"Admiral McKay arranged for me to fly back there. They're sending a fighter plane to pick me up, so I should be there early in the morning. What time is the surgery?"

"I think it's at eight o'clock."

"I should be there by then. Chuck and I have been praying for her and I'll continue to pray for her. I'm sure you're in good hands . . . and you hang in there."

Bonior was waiting when the sleek twin-tailed strike fighter taxied up and parked. As an attendant placed a ladder against the side of the plane, the pilot climbed out, carrying a flight suit, a pressure suit, an oxygen mask, and a helmet.

"Hi, Chief, I'm Lieutenant O'Toole. Let's go inside the hangar here while they refuel the bird. You can slip into this stuff while I fill you in on the safety features." The two men walked to a nearby hangar.

"The most important thing is, if anything goes wrong, we'll have to eject. You don't have to do anything. If we have to get out, I'll eject us both. I'll try to give you some warning, but I may not have time. These things move awful fast.

"Now, on takeoff we'll go almost straight up. The traffic controllers like us because we get out of their airspace in a hurry. And the airline pilots don't mind waiting for us because we put on a pretty good show. So as soon as we get you suited up, we'll taxi out and we'll be in the air in a few minutes. I'll give you an ETA at Oceana when we're airborne, but it will be sometime very early in the morning."

For all his years in the Navy, Bonior had never flown in a high performance jet before. He felt a tingle of anxiety as the plane paused at the end of the runway and he felt the power of the engines, eager to be unleashed. And then suddenly they were speeding down the runway and then climbing almost straight up.

"Whooo . . . what a ride!" Bonior exhaled and looked back down at the lights of the airport receding below them.

"That's the best part. Gets your attention, doesn't it? We'll level off at about thirty-five thousand feet and be on our way. There may be a few bumpy places along the way but we're well above most of the weather. If you jack your seat up a little you can get a pretty good view from back there."

A staff car was waiting when they arrived. Bonior quickly shed his flight gear and, within minutes, was speeding down the Highway 44 freeway toward the hospital.

Dorothy was waiting when the elevator stopped at the third floor. They embraced and then she took him by the hand to the intensive care unit.

"She's still sedated," she whispered.

Bonior tried to move as silently as possible as they worked

their way toward their daughter's bed. He gasped when he saw her.

Two tubes protruded from her mouth, one supplying oxygen to her lungs, the other a nasogastric tube to her stomach. Fluid dripped through an intravenous tube from a bottle into her shoulder. Another tube from a catheter ran out from under the covers into a bottle attached on the edge of the bed. A forest of wires seemed to emerge from the top of her head and connect to a blinking monitor. Her right leg was suspended at the knee.

Bonior touched her gently on the cheek and whispered, "How you doing, baby?"

There was no response.

An intensive care nurse joined them. "We're going to be taking her to surgery shortly. I think it would be good if you remained here with her until we take her to the operating room. We're deliberately keeping her in a coma but it might help if you talk to her."

The two parents remained hovering beside the bed until their daughter was wheeled away to the operating room. They found the chapel on the first floor and then had breakfast in the nearby coffee shop.

It was more than three hours later that a doctor clad in green came to talk to them in the quiet room on the third floor.

"Mr. and Mrs. Bonior? I'm Dr. Rogers. We've taken little Denise back to intensive care. She's still unconscious. The nurse will let you know when she begins to wake up."

"Is she going to be all right?" Dorothy asked the question on both their minds.

"Let's sit down over here and I'll fill you in," the doctor said. "As you know, she was very seriously injured. We had a team of doctors working on her.

"The neurosurgeon examined her head injury. No surgery was required there. He thinks her brain was just badly shaken. It will take awhile for the circuits to sort themselves out. But his hope is that it will get better soon if we just leave it alone, let the body heal itself.

"That, basically, is the good news. What causes us most concern is the bullet wound in her abdomen. Here, let me draw you a sketch.'' He found a piece of paper and drew a rough sketch of a child's abdomen and chest.

''The bullet entered down here on the right side of her abdomen. It went upward through her small intestine, part of her stomach, and her duodenum. It nicked one lobe of her liver along the way. Then it went up into her left chest and came to rest somewhere in the soft tissue in the upper part of her chest. It caused her left lung to collapse—what we call a pneumothorax.

''We inserted a drain in her lung and we're supplying oxygen through her mouth. She'll be on a ventilator—basically, we'll be breathing for her—for four days, and then we'll put her on a respirator. That may look ominous when you see her, but her lung should heal itself fairly quickly.

''Most of the time in the operating room was spent trying to trace the course of the bullet through her abdomen. We had to stitch up the holes in her intestine and her stomach as well as the liver. The most difficult part was the perforation in her duodenum—the connection between her stomach and the small bowel.

''We'll keep the nasogastric tube in place for about two weeks, along with the drain from her abdomen. With all those tubes, she won't be able to talk. She won't be able to eat, either, during that time, and we'll be feeding her through a tube. So she'll lose weight and muscle mass. She'll be very weak and it will take her awhile to get her strength back.''

''What about the bullet?'' her father asked.

''The one bullet passed through her leg. The other one ended up in the fleshy part of her chest. We decided to leave it there, at least for now. It shouldn't cause any problems so we thought it was best to avoid any additional surgery.''

''Do you think she's going to be okay?'' her mother asked.

''I don't want to raise your hopes too far. Right now, I'd say she is in very good condition, considering the severity of her injuries. We are fortunate the damage to her head was not worse. That would have been cause for very serious concern. I don't want to alarm you, but you must realize she is not out of the woods yet. She could suffer from an infection. She could begin bleeding uncontrollably. Sometimes patients simply become so weak that their systems shut down. So we'll just have to watch her very carefully and hope for the best."

Denise was beginning to wake up when the nurse called her parents into the intensive care unit. She looked so small and helpless, her tiny body seemingly overwhelmed by tubes and other medical paraphernalia. Her eyes followed the movements of her parents with a glint of recognition.

Her father leaned over and kissed her cheek.

"You're coming along fine, baby. Pretty quick you'll be playing outside again." He patted her arm. "Daddy is going to be away for a while, but Mommy will be here with you. Is that okay?"

Dorothy took her husband's hand and led him out into the corridor.

"You're going to have to get back, aren't you?"

"Yes, I really do. I'm sorry to do this to you, Dottie."

"Well, at least you were able to be here for the surgery and to see her. We can be thankful for that. How soon do you have to leave?"

"Right now, I guess. The pilot is waiting at Oceana. I'll give him a call now and let him know I'm on my way."

She put her arms around him and held him close. "I love you, Jeff. Even if you are a SEAL."

"I love you, too, Dottie. You're the best wife a man ever had."

CHAPTER 7

LIKE MOST SEALs, CHUCK NELSON WAS MOST COMFORTABLE IN a pair of swim trunks and an old T-shirt. The stiffness of his summer white uniform added to his discomfort as the car swung up the curving drive to the "back door" of the White House, on the south side of the mansion facing down over the Ellipse and the Jefferson Monument toward Virginia. Beside him sat Adm. McKay, the chairman of the Joint Chiefs of Staff.

"Nervous, Chuck?" McKay asked.

"Yes, sir!" Nelson replied. "Reminds me of my first parachute jump."

The two men were guided into a small meeting room near the Oval Office. If Nelson had been able to consult a guidebook, he would have seen that it was the room now known as the Roosevelt Room. Some of the older retainers at the White House still called it the Fish Room because of a large fish that had once hung on the wall. It was now used for small meetings or, most often, as a holding cell for visitors waiting to see the president.

"If you'll wait here, gentlemen, the president will be with you in a few minutes," an aide said, closing the door.

"Relax," McKay advised. "We'll just brief him on the mission and answer his questions, and that's it. You'll like him. He has a way of putting people at their ease."

The wait was longer than Nelson expected. President Maynard Walker was constitutionally incapable of staying on schedule, and today was no exception. By the time they finished their briefing for this mission, McKay knew, aides would be scrambling to patch together the remnants of a schedule that was already a shambles. As for his own schedule, McKay knew he was in for a very late night trying to get his desk cleared off.

After a wait of nearly half an hour, there was a quick knock at another door opposite the one they had entered. "The President will see you now," an aide said, holding the door open and motioning across the corridor to the door of the Oval Office.

Carrying the large case containing their briefing materials, Nelson followed McKay into the room, surprisingly bright from the light pouring in through the tall windows overlooking the Rose Garden. President Walker stood leaning back against his desk, facing the window, with a telephone cradled on his shoulder. He turned slightly to motion Nelson and McKay to take seats on the couches arranged by a fireplace opposite the desk.

After another minute, Walker hung up the phone and turned to his guests. "You'd think, when you get to be president, you can decide who you want to talk to on the phone and who you don't want to talk to. I swear, I spend more time on the phone than one of those telephone solicitors who call you at dinner time. It's always Senator-this and Congressman-that, trying to get them to do the right thing. . . or, more likely, trying to keep them from doing the wrong thing," he added with a smile.

Walker strode across the room as his two guests rose and stood at attention. "At ease, gentlemen, at ease! Isn't that the way you say it?"

Walker grasped McKay's hand. "Good to see you, Mac. And this is Commander Nelson?"

Nelson felt the firm handshake of the professional politician as Walker simultaneously took his hand and grasped his shoulder.

Like many in the military, Chuck Nelson considered himself apolitical. He paid his taxes, he registered as an independent, and he voted. But he thought of the politicians in Washington, from the president down to the newest congressman, as members of some alien tribe, more likely to make his life more difficult than to make it easier.

He had a fear that he knew was unreasonable that Walker might come right out and ask who he had voted for in the election four years ago. Would he have the courage to tell the truth—that he had voted for his opponent?

Like many politicians of his generation, Walker had not evaded the draft during the Vietnam war. But like them, he had managed to avoid it, getting through that difficult period without having served in the military. Nelson knew in his head that Walker, having been elected president, was his commander in chief and that he would obey his orders. But in his heart he found it difficult to have full confidence in the judgment of a man who had never served in the military.

"Sir, we're ready to go ahead with the mission in Iraq. Commander Nelson will be the on-scene commander, and I have brought him along to brief you."

As McKay spoke, Nelson took out his briefing charts and placed them on an easel.

"Before Chuck starts, let me emphasize a couple of points, Mr. President. This is an extremely risky operation and it violates almost all the rules of warfare that I've learned in my thirty-three years in the military. To take an air base, you would normally send at least a five-hundred-man Ranger brigade. We are sending forty-two men—counting the two helicopter crews. Only half the men are committed to the actual operation; the others are the backup. Ideally, we would have much more redundancy. Normally, we would have extensive support—scores of ships, and even hundreds of planes. For this operation, we have only the very minimum backup. All of these are compromises to preserve secrecy.

"As you know, we will also have a large-scale diversionary operation, but that will be quite separate from what Chuck and his boys will be doing."

Walker sat back on the couch with his feet on a coffee table, nodding as McKay spoke. As he listened, he couldn't help weighing this mission in the political scales. It was tilted far on the negative side.

The president had been elected three and a half years before over a strong candidate from the other party and a third-party candidate who had split the vote. The result was that he'd won with the votes of fewer than half of those who went to the polls—well short of a mandate. Now, with the next election approaching and with the long campaign season already beginning to heat up, Walker knew he had to do everything possible to shore up and add to his base of support. He could not afford a disaster like President Jimmy Carter had suffered in 1980 when the attempt to rescue hostages from Teheran came to grief in the Iranian desert.

He nodded toward Nelson, standing near the easel where he had displayed a map of the eastern Mediterranean showing southern Turkey and northern Iraq. "Go ahead, Chuck."

"Sir, we will be using two Pave Low helicopters provided by the Air Force Special Operations Command, flown by crews we train with frequently. We and the planes will be flown by C-5 to the Italian air base at Sigonella. Our arrival there should not attract any attention since we often operate in and out of Sigonella. On Night One, we will fly from Sigonella to the U.S.S. *Stennis*, which will be cruising to the east of the boot of Italy.

"Our landing on the *Stennis* should not create any problems for us. In recent years, the Air Force special ops folks have often trained with the Navy. The carrier will sail eastward, carrying out routine operations, launching and recovering its aircraft.

"We will remain on the *Stennis* two days. On the afternoon of the second day, the *Stennis* will go into a total electronic blackout. For all practical purposes, that ship, with nearly a hundred airplanes and a crew of six thousand, will simply disappear. In that condition, she will sail at flank speed northeast toward the Turkish coast, taking up a position north of Cyprus and about fifty miles off the Turkish coast just after dusk. She will continue to conduct flight operations.

"During a launch operation in which there will be a good deal of activity around the carrier, we will take off and fly northeast, remaining about two hundred feet above the water. About a dozen miles off the coast, we will be met by an Air

Force HC-130 tanker—a Combat Shadow—operating on a routine flight plan.

"We will tuck our Pave Lows up behind the bigger plane. Radar operators in Turkey, Syria, and Iraq will see a single image—the HC-130. The Air Force bird will provide us with a security cover and also top off our tanks. As the Shadow flies parallel to the Turkey-Iraq border, we will peel off and head south toward our target in Iraq. We will penetrate the mountains of northern Iraq at two hundred feet altitude. We have all the Iraqi radar sites plotted and we are confident we can avoid detection."

Walker raised his hand. "You're going to fly through the mountains at two hundred feet? Isn't that a little dicey?"

"Not really, sir. The Air Force special ops pilots do it all the time. We'll all be wearing night vision goggles. Our latest versions do a remarkably good job of enabling us to see in the dark, especially with the quarter moon on the night of our operation. And the Pave Low is probably the most sophisticated plane in the Air Force inventory. It has terrain-avoidance and terrain-following radar as well as forward-looking infrared. We will be able to find our way through the mountain passes in the dark. We've used this system many times in training, and I feel very comfortable with it."

Nelson paused to see if there were any more questions, then continued.

"I won't bother you with our exact timeline, but we expect to reach the Iraqi installation about midnight. According to our intelligence, the Iraqis normally conduct tests of their ramjet engines in a test facility for several hours every night. We expect the noise of those tests to mask the sound of our arrival. One Pave Low crew will deposit us inside the airfield complex and then take up a position with the other bird on the back side of a nearby hill to wait until it is time to come pick us up."

Nelson flipped over a new chart showing a satellite photo of the Iraqi air base.

"This is a picture of the base, taken a few days ago. It may be easier to follow our plan if I display a line drawing based on that photo.'' He flipped over another page, displaying a large drawing of the complex.

''We will land here.'' He indicated a point on the runway more than a mile from the hangar and other buildings. ''We will have two Air Force Special Tactics Team members with us, both equipped with small motorbikes. They will leave immediately to set out five infrared lights in what they call a 'box-and-one.' There will be four lights set in a square and a single light at the end of the runway to help Colonel Kaparov get himself oriented for his takeoff. When we arrive, we will immediately knock out the airfield power supply. They may get some power from generators, but not enough to power the runway lights. So the colonel will have to take off in total darkness.

''Two of my SEALs will also have motorbikes. The rest of us will ride in a Humvee, one of those big all-terrain vehicles, that we will bring along with us. It will be armed with a .50-caliber machine gun. Each of us, of course, will carry our own weapons and ammunition. Although there will be only sixteen of us, we will have as much firepower as an infantry company—while our ammunition lasts.

''Our intelligence . . . I guess I can tell you, sir. We have a human source in the Iraqi installation. . . . Our intelligence indicates that the plane will be fueled and ready for a test flight at the time of our mission. We will place Colonel Kaparov in the cockpit of the plane and help him to get settled. Then one of the Special Tactics men will take up a position in front of the plane on his motorbike. It will be his job to lead Kaparov to the end of the runway and get him oriented downwind for takeoff.

''As soon as the pilot starts those engines, of course, the shit is going to . . . excuse me, sir. We are going to be in the middle of a hornet's nest, and the hornets are going to be very angry.''

The president grinned. ''Yes, I can see. The shit really will hit the fan.''

Nelson continued. ''Our great advantage will be surprise. The Iraqis will not know what is happening. We will take up a position near the hangar. If the Iraqis do the logical thing, they will attempt to follow the plane and try to prevent its takeoff. If they do that, we will be on their flank and can chew them up with our weapons.

"While we are getting Kaparov into the plane, two of our men will move out on their motorbikes to place explosives at key points in the installation. We will trigger them by radio before we take off.

"We plan to break away in the confusion, rendezvous with our helicopter, and take off. We will place thermite grenades to destroy the vehicles we are leaving behind. Saddam will know we were there, but he won't be able to prove it."

The president took his feet down from the coffee table and leaned forward. "And that's it? You make it sound easy."

"No, sir, not easy," McKay broke in. "As we all know, 'the best-laid plans of mice and men. . . .' "

Walker turned to Nelson, still standing at parade rest beside the easel. "Relax, Chuck. Sit down. I want you to tell me what you think the odds are. Admiral McKay says this is a risky operation. How risky? What are the chances it will blow up in my face? I don't want another Desert One."

Walker liked the way Nelson looked him directly in the eye.

"Sir, in an operation like this, there are no guarantees. But this is a very well planned op. My SEALs and the Air Force men we will be working with are the very best. The American taxpayers have been very generous with us, giving us first-rate equipment and providing the funds for us to train to a very high level of efficiency. If it is important to get possession of that plane—not just to disable or destroy it—and to do that secretly, we are your best bet. We are the very best at what we do."

"I'm sure of that," Walker replied. "What do you think, Mac?"

"I agree with Chuck. This is going to be very difficult. But I think the chances of success are very good," McKay replied.

"Why are you using this little unit? How about the Delta Force or SEAL Team SIX, or whatever they call it now?" Walker asked.

"Sir, this was my choice to use the Eagle Force. Delta and SIX were set up by the Army and the Navy some years ago as hostage rescue teams. They are very good, but they have gotten quite large, a little bureaucratic. They are perfectly designed for carrying off a hostage rescue operation where we are operating in a friendly country. But they are not at their best operating secretly in hostile territory. That's why I encouraged the formation of this very small, very specialized unit to be available for covert operations.''

Walker rose and stood in front of the easel, studying the diagram of the Iraqi installation and then flipping the sheet to examine the map. Finally, he turned toward McKay and Nelson.

''Okay, gentlemen, let's do it.''

''Yes sir!'' the two naval officers replied in unison.

''One thing, Commander. I want to be kept informed every step of the way. As you can understand, this is not only a high-risk operation for you, but it also involves considerable political risk for me. I do not want any surprises.''

Nelson glanced toward McKay and saw him standing silent, waiting for the junior officer to respond.

''Sir . . . I'm sorry, sir, but we can't do that. Once we leave the *Stennis*, we will be operating in strict radio silence. Our whole mission, both getting in there and getting back out again, depends on secrecy and surprise. I will not take a chance on any radio transmissions that might endanger our mission—or my men.''

McKay looked particularly uncomfortable. For all his surface friendliness, Maynard Walker was not a man who was used to being told no. His temper, always under control in public, was well known to those who worked with him often. McKay had experienced it on more than one occasion and did not welcome a repeat.

Walker glared at Nelson. The Navy officer held his gaze.

After a long pause, the president spoke. ''Okay, Commander, I understand. You give me the good news as soon as you can.''

The president walked the two men to the door, a hand on the shoulder of each.

CHAPTER 8

FOR MARK RATTNER, THE LANDING NEAR THE STERN OF THE HUGE aircraft carrier was totally routine. The once-high barrier between the Air Force and the Navy had been lowered in recent years so Air Force Special Operations crews could become comfortable with landing and taking off from the Navy's carriers.

Following a young man with a lighted baton in each hand, Rattner taxied to a position in the shadow of the tower from which carrier operations were directed. One crew member, seated on the helicopter's rear ramp to serve as Rattner's eyes, confirmed that the second helo had landed safely.

If they had been flying the Navy version of the helicopter—the thirty-year-old design from which the Pave Low was derived—they would have quickly folded their large rotors and been towed onto one of the huge elevators used to move aircraft down for storage on the hangar deck. But the Pave Low's rotors did not fold, so it would have to remain on deck. Four Marines armed with M-16 rifles were posted to guard each helicopter.

There were a few curious stares from members of the ship's crew as the passengers and crew alighted from the Pave Lows and were directed to a secure area of the ship that had been set aside for them. It was not unusual to see Air Force crews on a carrier, but it was unusual to see such a hard-looking team of heavily armed men emerge from visiting Air Force planes. It was against the rules, but Nelson had insisted that his men be permitted to carry their personal weapons with them to their quarters on the carrier.

For the time they remained on the *Stennis*, the team members remained almost totally isolated from the ship's crew. For most of them, their only contact was with the orderlies who brought steaming helpings of food from the galley—food heavy on meat and potatoes, swimming in thick gravy and cholesterol, accompanied by pots of black coffee and finished off with mountains of soft ice cream.

Nelson and Rattner were the only two to leave their secure area to meet with the skipper of the ship to go over plans for their operation. Actually, the mission was not at all challenging for the crew of the carrier. They would be in the proper position for launch at dusk one evening and return at dawn the following morning to meet the returning helicopters. All of this would be carried out under a strict electronic blackout—which was also routine.

During the day of the mission, the helicopter crews took off from the carrier, flew out about fifty miles, and returned, checking all the planes' systems to make sure everything was working properly. The gunners fired a few rounds from each of the .50-caliber machine guns, one in each waist window and one mounted on the rear ramp. Rattner had learned through long experience that the best way to keep a flying machine in good condition was to fly it often.

As the SEALs and the Special Tactics men lined up to board the helicopters in the late afternoon, they were a fierce-looking crew. Their faces were darkened with camouflage paint. Even Bonior, the sole black member of the team, had coated his face to prevent it from reflecting light. All of the men carried .45-caliber pistols strapped to their waists, and most of them carried M-16 rifles slung on one shoulder. The exceptions were Chief Jack Berryman, who carried one of the big, powerful .50-caliber sniper rifles that had been especially developed for the SEALs, and HM3 Bill Wagner, the SEAL corpsman, who toted an M-60 machine gun capable of firing at the rate of as much as 550 rounds a minute. In an infantry company, the twenty-three-pound M-60 is operated by a crew of soldiers. The SEALs had made it a one-man weapon and

Wagner prided himself on the accuracy with which he could fire the weapon from the waist.

The oddest-looking member of the team was Kaparov, who was wearing a cumbersome suit designed to protect him and keep his blood from boiling at the extremely high altitudes he would be flying the Blackjack. He needed the help of two of the Air Force gunners to clamber up onto the rear ramp and make his way to his bucket seat on the side of the helicopter.

For all of the men, it was a tight fit. The center of the helicopter cabin was filled by the Humvee, with four motor-bikes strapped along each side.

The backup team had an equally tight fit. Except for Ka-parov, they had the same number of men and the same equipment as the lead team.

As the men lined up to board the helicopters, they welcomed the breeze across the carrier's deck. Inside, the cabins seemed to be filled with an oppressive, stomach-turning mixture of warm, moist Mediterranean air and diesel fumes. But they knew they would soon have an entirely different complaint. The Pave Low routinely flew with its waist windows and the rear ramp open. This gave a clear field of vision for the crew members who acted as the pilot's eyes and room to mount the plane's three machine guns. Going through the mountains of Iraq in the nighttime, it would be bitterly cold in the helicopter's cabin.

The helicopters rose, shuddering, pivoted to the northeast and then moved out on course, holding two hundred feet above the ocean surface. Almost immediately after they left the carrier deck, there was some relief from the oppressive heat as air rushed through the cabin.

Twenty-five miles ahead, a four-engined HC-130 circled lazily at ten thousand feet. The Combat Shadow was a C-130 specially modified to refuel special operations helicopters. Instead of a boom projecting from the rear like that on other Air Force tankers, it carried a hose curled inside each wing. Copying a system used by the Navy, the HC-130 unreeled a hose from one or both wings and it was up to the helicopter pilot to plug into the hose.

"Navigator to pilot: I have them on the screen. They're at

one-one-zero degrees, twenty-two nautical miles.'' The helicopters were two tiny dots on the screen of the HC-130 navigator's radar.

"Pilot to navigator: Okay, we'll start our descent now.'' The crew members heard the sound of the engines drop slightly and felt the down-elevator sensation as the plane began its descent toward the ocean.

The pilot made a wide circle to the right, swinging around to match the helicopters' course as he leveled off at an altitude of 1,000 feet, about three miles behind the Pave Lows. He held his speed at 200 knots. A few minutes later, he picked up the helicopters, clearly visible through his night vision goggles. Gently he eased back on the throttles until he passed over them and then settled at 140 knots.

Aboard the first Pave Low, S.Sgt. Ray Donovan, sitting cross-legged on the rear ramp, kept Rattner informed as he watched the tanker moving up behind them. As the Shadow passed overhead, Rattner pushed forward on his throttles to bring his craft up into the L-shaped space between the bigger plane's right wing and tail. From his right-seat position, he watched both the wing and the plane's looming tail, making sure his whirling rotors did not come too close to either one. The second helo moved into position on the left side.

Even for a pilot as experienced as Rattner, flying this close to another plane in the dark never became routine. But with the three craft this close together, they would appear as a single blob to any radar operator who picked them up.

With their pace set by the 110-knot speed of the helicopters, the three planes crossed the coastline just north of the Turkish city of Iskenderun and immediately began a climb to four thousand feet to skim over the mountains that rise quickly from the sea.

For nearly two hours, the three planes flew in tandem, paralleling the border with Syria and climbing steadily to remain above the mountain tops. As they approached the point where the borders of Syria, Turkey, and Iraq meet, the fuel hoses began to emerge slowly from both sides of the tanker. Through his night vision goggles, the "basket" attached to the end of the hose looked to Rattner like a huge white blob, a cobra's head at the end of a long snake's body waving sinuously in the darkness.

Easing back slightly on the throttle, he dropped back behind and then pulled up slightly higher than the tanker. Taking aim on the "basket," he dived forward, shifting his attention to the plane rather than the basket itself. The probe extending from the right side of the helicopter drove into the middle of the basket and connected to the coupler at the end of the fuel hose with a satisfying thump.

As soon as the connection was made, Rattner moved back and up to put as much distance between himself and the tanker as possible without breaking the link between the two planes.

He took every drop of the JP-8 fuel that his tanks would hold—a full 12,696 pounds, or 1,895 gallons. As soon as his tanks were filled, he simply moved back away from the tanker, breaking the connection, and turned to a new heading that would take him south and east across the Iraqi border toward his target, just at the northern edge of the great Mesopotamian plain. If Rattner had had time to let his thoughts wander, he might have pondered how this night's mission would add one more bit to the history of an area where history had begun. Their target for the night, in fact, was only a short distance from the ancient city of Nineveh, the capital of Assyria in biblical times.

There was no time for such thoughts, of course, as Rattner dropped down and began working his way through the mountains—some as high as nine thousand feet—trying to avoid the rocks while at the same time using the mountains and the rocky outcroppings to shield himself from the Iraqi radar sites indicated on his chart.

In the left seat, Maj. Jack Laffer, the copilot, flew without night vision goggles. It was his job to follow the progress of the flight using the helicopter's instruments, which were just a fuzzy blur as seen through Rattner's goggles. If the goggles ceased to work, Latter would take over immediately, using the plane's terrain-avoidance radar to work their way through the mountains.

As often as he had flown such missions, Laffer was never entirely comfortable flying so low in the dark. When he glanced outside the cockpit, there was only the faintest light from the quarter moon. And then suddenly a shape would flash by—a rocky outcropping, a snowbank, perhaps even a startled mountain goat. As quickly as one of these apparitions came, it was gone again. Who knew what other hazards lay ahead in the dark?

On the dashboard, one key instrument told Laffer the time and distance to each checkpoint set into their inertial navigation system and the expected time of arrival. By adjusting the speed slightly, he kept them right on schedule.

"Fifteen minutes," he told Rattner.

"Chuck, get your guys ready. We're fifteen minutes out," Rattner told Nelson.

To Nelson, it was a strangely disembodied voice. Because of the sound of the engines and the roar of the wind through the open windows, he wore earplugs inside the helmet that held his earphones tightly over his ears.

Actually, Nelson's team had been ready to go since they'd climbed into the cabin of the helicopter nearly four hours before. They had laid their weapons down, but it was too much trouble to take off most of the web gear that held all their equipment in place and put it back on again in the cramped confines of the cabin.

During the flight, several of the men fidgeted in their seats, already feeling the adrenaline coursing through their veins. Occasionally, one of them would grope his way forward through the darkness to use the relief tube near the left waist window. Others quietly chewed tobacco, spitting the black juice into plastic coffee cups. On takeoff and landing, all the men were strapped in, but during the flight a couple of them, feeling that strange calm that is one of the mysterious symptoms of fear, stretched out in the Humvee and went to sleep.

Donovan unbolted the machine gun from the rear ramp, clearing it for the team to move out quickly as soon as the helicopter touched down.

As Rattner approached the compound, he was flying so low that he had to pull up to hop over the twelve-foot-high fence. The Iraqis apparently did not expect this kind of visit. There were no watch towers and the outer perimeter was not lighted.

There were, however, bright lights surrounding the hangar area across the field.

As soon as the helicopter touched down, the ramp dropped to the ground. Jack Berryman was first to emerge, carrying his heavy .50-caliber sniper rifle. He set the gun on a tripod and took aim at the transformer linking a high-tension power line and the wires that fed electricity into the complex.

As Nelson stepped out of the Pave Low, he could hear the roar of an engine in the test cell overwhelming the sound of their craft's engines.

Chief Bonior drove the Humvee carefully out the rear cargo door as other members of the team unstrapped the four motorbikes and wheeled them out. As soon as they were clear of the plane, Rattner lifted off and skimmed over the fence to his hiding place a few miles away, where the backup bird was waiting.

Sgt. Tim Hutchins checked the wind. It was blowing at a steady 15 knots from the east, directly down the runway. Motioning to T.Sgt. Tom Shoup, they set off on their bikes to lay out the infrared lights that would guide Kaparov's takeoff.

Chief Ray Pratt, the team's explosives expert, and Chief Jeremy Merrifield mounted the two other motorbikes and raced across the field toward the hangar. Their job was to place explosives at key points in the complex.

The other members of the team took their places in the Humvee. Two of the men virtually hoisted Kaparov into the rear of the vehicle. Nelson sat in the right front seat next to Bonior, his "buddy." Each man worked with and looked out for his buddy and received support and protection in return. Chief Mark Raymond stood behind them in position to operate the .50-caliber machine gun mounted immediately behind and above the front seats.

As the others took their positions, Berryman peered through his telescopic sight, centered the cross hairs on the transformer, shimmering in the green light of his night vision scope, and held them there, steady, as he slowly squeezed the trigger. The team saw a sudden shower of sparks and the whole complex disappeared into the darkness. If they were lucky, the Iraqis would think the transformer had exploded on its own and not realize they were under attack.

Bonior shifted into gear and drove directly toward the shape of the plane parked in front of the hangar. The shroud had been removed from the aircraft and he could see figures working on it, apparently preparing it for takeoff. He was surprised how large the plane was—more than half a block long. Bonior held his speed at about thirty miles an hour, searching the area ahead through his night vision goggles for rocks or hidden holes. The Humvee is as rugged as they come, but he was taking no chances on spoiling the entire mission with a broken axle.

Bonior slowed before he reached the plane and stopped beside the hangar at a point where a corner of the building shielded the Humvee from the view of anyone near the plane. Motioning to Kaparov to remain where he was, Nelson and the other SEALs crept slowly around the edge of the building and then formed a semicircle, lying on the tarmac with the building at their back and their weapons all pointing outward. They remained in total silence for three minutes while Nelson observed the scene.

The men around the plane seemed to have taken the sudden blackout calmly. Several of them could be seen holding flashlights, talking among themselves. Guards remained at their positions, slowly pacing back and forth. To Nelson, it looked as though the Iraqis were used to frequent power failures.

Taking Bonior by the arm, he pointed to two armed men near the front of the plane. Turning to Mark Raymond, he pointed to two other guards near the rear of the plane. Then, holding each man by an arm, he urged them forward. Bonior ran toward the plane, dropped, rolled, waited a few moments, and then dashed forward again. Raymond followed the same pattern, heading toward the two men at the rear of the plane.

When the two SEALs reached within fifty feet of the plane, they paused, crouching low to the pavement. Bonior removed his HK MK23 pistol and affixed the silencer, watching to see that Raymond followed his lead. Then he raised his pistol over his head and slowly lowered it down, in one fluid motion drawing a bead with his laser aimer, firing at one man and then the other. Raymond matched his movements. The four

Iraqis dropped. But as their weapons hit the pavement, there was a brief clatter of sound.

Several of the workers near the plane ran back and forth shouting and swinging their flashlights into the darkness. And then, as the team members watched through their night vision goggles, the workers ran off toward the other end of the hangar.

Bonior lay flat on the pavement, watching the scene. After a full minute, he raised his right arm and motioned the other SEALs to join him. Berryman moved back around the edge of the hangar and urged Kaparov forward. The SEAL with his big sniper rifle and the pilot in his clumsy flying suit made an awkward pair as they scampered toward the plane.

Nelson signaled the remainder of his team around to form a new perimeter, this time facing toward the other end of the hangar while the other three SEALs helped Kaparov up through the nosewheel hatch into the cockpit. As they worked, Tim Hutchins and Tom Shoup emerged from the darkness after setting the lights to guide the takeoff. Shoup joined the SEAL perimeter, while Hutchins climbed up behind Kaparov to help him strap himself into the cockpit and connect his pressure suit and oxygen system to the plane's fittings.

Hutchins patted Kaparov on the shoulder, gave him the thumbs-up sign, and scrambled quickly back down to the ground. As Kaparov pressed the button to bring the giant engines to life, Hutchins scooted out in front of the plane. On the rear of his bike was a small red light to guide Kaparov through the darkness.

Two men pulled the chocks and the plane rolled smoothly forward, picking up speed. It was obvious Kaparov was in a hurry to get out of here.

As the plane began to roll, the hangar lights flickered, dimmed, and then came on in full brightness.

Blinded by the sudden burst of light, Nelson pushed his goggles onto his forehead and rubbed his eyes, trying to make his pupils contract.

"Shit," he muttered. "I knew this was going too good."

The seven commandos were in the worst possible position. Berryman and Raymond were still at the point on the parking apron where the plane had been. Nelson, Bonior, Marker, and Wagner, along with Shoup, were twenty-five yards back, closer to the hangar but still exposed under the glare of the blinding lights. They all hugged the pavement. But there was no place to hide.

CHAPTER 9

IN THE READY ROOM OF THE USS *GEORGE WASHINGTON*, CUTTING slowly through the steamy waters of the Persian Gulf, there were sighs of disbelief and groans of unhappiness as the night's mission was briefed.

For the F-14 pilots and radar navigators, the mission was routine, the same as they flew every day and night, only this time they would go further north, to Baghdad itself. Their job was MiG-cap—to shoot down any enemy aircraft that threatened the F/A-18s on their attack mission.

The grumbling came from the fighter-attack pilots. Their assignment was to penetrate Iraqi airspace, flying well north of the line that designated the southern limit of the no-fly zone imposed on the Iraqi air force. But instead of dropping bombs or firing rockets, they would simply simulate attacks and then return to the carrier. If they were attacked by Iraqi fighters or received indications they were about to be fired on by the Iraqi anti-aircraft units, they could of course shoot back.

"Who's bullshit idea is this?" one pilot demanded. "We're supposed to go to downtown Baghdad and get killed or captured for nothing?"

The officer conducting the briefing acted as though he hadn't heard the interruption. He felt exactly the same way but he wasn't going to say so. Orders are orders. And in this case the orders had been very explicit and they had come directly from the office of the chairman of the Joint Chiefs.

The first two-plane flights were catapulted off the bow of

the *George Washington* just as, unbeknownst to the pilots, the two Pave Low helicopters were breaking away from the Combat Shadow and heading south into northern Iraq. A few minutes later, Iraqi radar scopes began to dance with the images of scores of planes inbound from the darkness of the Persian Gulf. In Baghdad, air raid sirens shattered the night for the first time in months. A CNN correspondent called Atlanta with an alert. Within minutes he was broadcasting live through his satellite link as the first waves of planes swept across the capital, kicked in their afterburners, and hammered the city with sonic booms.

So far, it was all going just as Adm. McKay had explained the operation to the president:

"We're going to put enough planes over Baghdad and make enough noise to make them think World War III has just begun. We'll probably have to take out a few radar sites if they light up our guys, but otherwise we're not going to break anything or hurt anybody.

"Remember the Son Tay raid, back in 1970, when we sent a team of commandos to rescue a group of our men from a prisoner-of-war camp near Hanoi? That was a small operation. But they put on a massive diversion with more than a hundred aircraft swarming over the eastern part of North Vietnam. It kept the North Vietnamese looking the wrong direction long enough for us to get in and out. Unfortunately, the prisoners had been moved before our team arrived."

The president nodded. "Yeah, I remember reading about that. How come you don't have the Air Force involved in this thing?"

"That's the advantage of using an aircraft carrier," McKay responded. "The Air Force has planes in Saudi Arabia and Kuwait. But we'd have to get permission to use them on this kind of operation. That can be sticky, considering that the target is another Islamic country. This way, we just do it."

"Yeah, right. Just do it! All I have to do is explain what we're doing to the House and the Senate and our 'friends' around the world without being able to say what we're really doing or why we're doing it." The president sighed deeply, stared at the ceiling, and drummed his fingers on the arm of his chair. McKay simply kept quiet.

CNN, which was the only network that had kept a correspondent in Baghdad, had a clear beat on the story. With the flip of a switch, their man on the scene broke into the mid-evening news broadcast with his live report from his hotel room. With the time difference between the Persian Gulf and the East Coast of the United States, the broadcast came at prime time with millions of Americans in front of their screens.

ABC, CBS, NBC, and Fox were caught flat-footed. While their anchors raced to their studios in New York, their news departments went on the air with wire service reports based on the CNN broadcast—an embarrassing admission that they didn't really know what was going on.

At the White House, there had been only a few correspondents still in their cubicles taking advantage of the quiet to finish up stories for the following day. And then the press area in the West Wing began to fill with reporters. Sound and video technicians stood by their equipment in the press room and outside on the lawn, waiting for something to broadcast. While some of the reporters worked the phones in vain, others simply stood around the press room exchanging rumors, assuming White House officials would soon have something to say.

When the first broadcast came in from Baghdad, President Walker was in the East Room, circulating among the guests at a reception for African-American leaders. Even here, two Secret Service agents hovered nearby, trying to be as inconspicuous as possible but still alert for any threat to the president.

The president had just hugged a tall, handsome woman with a tinge of gray in her black hair.

"Amelia! Thanks for coming. You keeping things under control up there in Philadelphia?"

"Oh, yes sir, Mr. President. Getting out the vote. Getting out the vote." She was a veteran politician, but it still made her a little nervous talking directly to the president himself. They had often worked together when he was a candidate, but now that he was president, it was just a little different.

An aide worked his way through the crowd, touched the president's elbow, and whispered in his ear. Walker nodded.

"Keep up the good work, Amelia. We need you." He gave her a pat on the shoulder and then moved quickly toward the door that led down the hall to the other end of the White House and his office. The aide matched him step-by-step, talking in a low voice.

"The press is all over us. And the State Department is hearing from every country in the world."

Walker wrapped a big arm around the aide's shoulder.

"Okay, I knew this was coming. Here's what we're going to do. Have State get back to everyone who's called and tell them this is a very limited, one-time operation, a warning to Saddam to behave himself. I want Henry Trover over at State to make the calls personally to London, Bonn, and Paris. Then I want him to talk to Tel Aviv, Kuwait City, and the Saudis."

"I think Secretary Trover has already started fielding some of those calls." The aide struggled to take notes while keeping pace with the president. "That leaves us the press to deal with."

"The press and Congress. I talked to a few of the leaders a short time before the operation began, but most of the people on the Hill are going to be awfully surprised about this. And some of them are going to be awfully angry that they weren't considered important enough to be briefed in advance. We'll get a statement out to the press and then I'll start working the phones to the Hill."

Tucked as discretely as possible into one wall of the Oval Office were five television monitors, one tuned to each major U.S. network. In the past, most presidents had relied on aides to let them know if there was anything worth watching on TV. But Walker didn't mind the distraction of the images dancing silently as he worked. If he saw anything that caught his interest, he could immediately pick up the sound with his remote control.

As the two men entered the Oval Office, all five monitors

were filled with a single image: the face of Senator Richard Wilson.

"Well, shit. Looky who's here," the president exclaimed.

To the inside-the-beltway experts, Wilson's challenge to the president from within his own party didn't seem to have much of a chance. But with a seemingly endless supply of money, Wilson had put together one of the best media teams anyone could remember. Whenever anything important happened in the world, Wilson was first on the air. The networks knew they could rely on him for seemingly informed comments and for the pithy sound bites that could be repeated over and over through an entire news cycle.

Maynard Walker picked up the remote control from his desk and clicked on the sound.

". . . Irresponsible conduct of foreign affairs cannot be allowed to continue. I can only conclude that the White House is operating on auto-pilot, oblivious to the dangers that lie ahead. The man in the White House is a danger to this country—a danger to world peace.

"I have also been informed that our pilots were sent into harm's way with orders not to drop bombs or fire their weapons—orders not to shoot! What kind of idiocy is that? Our brave American boys deserve better leadership than this . . . better leadership."

The president clicked off the sound and slammed the remote control down on his desk. "He knows things he shouldn't know. Pretty good intelligence, that stuff about not dropping bombs. Our guys aren't even back on the carrier yet and he's on the air with their rules of engagement. Talk about endangering brave boys!"

Walker spent the next half hour working with his press secretary on a statement to be read to the hungry mob waiting in the press room. When they were finished, they both knew it was weak. Looking it over after a clean version had been run through the word processor, the press secretary shook his head: "They're going to kill me when they hear this stuff."

"Reminds me of a story," Walker said. "I remember, years ago, talking to Jim Hagerty. He had your job when Eisenhower was president. He told me he once said the same thing to

Eisenhower that you just said to me. You know what Eisenhower said?''

The press secretary had heard this story before, but he just grinned.

''Ike said: 'Better you than me, boy. Better you than me.' Okay, go on out there and do the best you can.''

As the press secretary left, Walker leaned back in his chair, feet on the desk and hands behind his head. Well, he thought to himself, everything's going just the way we planned. With the help of CNN and our friend Dick Wilson, we've got not only the Iraqis but the whole damn world looking in the wrong direction.

With the constant demands on his time, he welcomed even a few moments of solitude, time to think. But a few moments were all he ever got. The small red light on his office intercom blinked. ''Yeah?''

''Sir, the first lady has just returned.''

''Oh, good. Is she here now?''

''Yes sir, she'll be here in a moment.''

Walker strode to the door and opened it. Marcia Walker was dressed in a light brown tweed suit. A tan silk scarf was knotted around her neck and tucked into her jacket. Even after traveling halfway around the world and back, she was impeccably turned out, with every hair in place.

''Marcie. It's so good to see you. Sounds like a great trip.'' He grasped both of her arms and pulled her toward him.

She reached out with one hand to close the door behind her and then stepped back from him.

''Chip, we've got to talk.''

''Okay, Marcie, sure. What about?''

''I think you know. Do I have to spell it out for you?''

''No, I guess not.'' He turned and walked toward the window, staring outside for a moment, then swung back to look her in the eyes. ''Damn it, Marcie, I love you. I really do.''

CHAPTER 10

As the SEALs lay on the pavement, waiting for their vision to clear, five Iraqi soldiers armed with AK-47 assault rifles dashed around the corner of the hangar toward the position where the plane had been parked, trying to comprehend what was happening.

Wagner rose and opened fire with his .30-caliber machine gun, sweeping across the running figures. The sudden burst of fire from near the hangar caught the Iraqis by surprise. All five dropped without firing a shot. As Wagner fired, Bonior rolled over on his back and began shooting out the lights with his M-16 rifle.

Berryman and Raymond sprinted back to where the other SEALs had set up their thin perimeter. As they dropped to the pavement, a pickup truck carrying a squad of soldiers and mounting a .30-caliber machine gun raced around the corner of the building, a powerful spotlight sweeping the area. Nelson signaled to his men to hold their fire, buying at least a few seconds before they were spotted. The spotlight swept over the point where the plane had been parked and lingered on the bodies of the four men the SEALs had taken out.

At Nelson's signal, the SEALs scampered back, one by one, toward the corner of the hangar, establishing a new perimeter fifteen yards back. They still had not fired a shot at this new adversary. Then the spotlight swung around and caught them in its beam. Nelson fired first, taking out the spotlight. Berryman brought his powerful .50-caliber sniper rifle into play, sending a bullet through the pickup's engine block. The truck stopped, crippled. But seven soldiers jumped from the rear of the truck.

One soldier, remaining in the truck, swung its machine gun toward them but he didn't have time to fire. A bullet tore through his face, exploding his brain out the rear of his skull.

Three of the Iraqi soldiers spread out away from the truck but the other four remained hidden, firing toward the SEALs from its protection. Their fire in the darkness was not accurate, but it was enough to keep the SEALs pinned down until reinforcements arrived. Nelson realized that would occur in minutes, if not seconds, but his only option was to try to pick off the Iraqis clustered near the truck.

With the advantage of their night vision goggles, the SEALs quickly knocked out the three soldiers who had left the protection of the truck. But the muzzle flash from their shots gave the Iraqis hiding behind the truck a target to shoot at in the darkness.

Nelson was about to give the signal for the SEALs to pull back around the corner of the hangar. It was a tactic they had practiced often in which one man dashed back, hit the ground, rolled, and opened fire over the heads of his comrades, keeping up a steady suppressing fire until a new line had been stabilized.

But that option was suddenly cut off when two more pickup trucks carrying Iraqi soldiers emerged onto the parking area and quickly zeroed in on the SEALs with their searchlights. From the SEALs' viewpoint, the scene had suddenly become, in the old euphemism, very "target rich."

Jeff Bonior lay as flat as he could on the tarmac, carefully squeezing his trigger, picking off one Iraqi soldier after the other. Despite the danger and all the gunfire, he felt strangely calm, almost disengaged. As his body automatically did what it had been trained to do, his mind wandered back to that hospital room in Norfolk where little Denise lay so quiet. He didn't notice that Nelson, his buddy, lying a few yards away, was not firing his weapon.

Chief Ray Pratt and Merrifield had been quietly moving from one point to the next setting their explosives at key points throughout the complex. With the last package of C-4 plastic explosive in place, they mounted their cycles, and headed toward the hangar. The plan was to meet the other SEALs at the Humvee, abandon their cycles, and head for the helicopter.

As they raced toward the rendezvous point, they heard the initial exchange of gunfire, a moment of silence, and then more firing.

"Let's go," Pratt shouted, leading the way back toward the Humvee. When he reached it, Pratt jumped from his cycle, which careened on riderless and smashed into the hangar, then threw himself into the driver's seat. Merrifield vaulted into the back and grabbed the handles of the machine gun. With a roar, the powerful engine came to life and Pratt swung around the corner of the hangar with a screech of tires, taking up a position between the SEALs and the Iraqis while Merrifield raked the enemy positions. It wasn't the U.S. cavalry, but it was close enough.

Rex Marker broke radio silence for the first time: "Spark One! Code Red! I repeat, Code Red! Evacuate now!"

A short distance beyond the security fence, Rattner's helicopter crew—call sign, Spark One—had waited anxiously for the signal to pick up the raiding team. "Code Green" would mean they had been able to carry out the operation without being detected. "Code Red" meant they were under attack.

With the Humvee providing shelter, the men clambered aboard. As Bonior rose, he glanced over and saw that Nelson was lying strangely still. Reaching down, he touched his shoulder. His hand came away sticky with blood. Grabbing Nelson's web gear, he half-carried, half-dragged him to the Humvee. One of the other men reached down and helped pull him onto the floor of the vehicle as Pratt gunned the engine, swung around, and aimed toward the point on the runway where they were scheduled to meet the helicopter. He pressed the throttle to the floorboards, abandoning all the caution with which Bonior had driven the opposite route half an hour before.

As the team headed away from the hangar, they became aware of a roar that rose to ear-shattering intensity and then they saw the glow of the exhaust gases as Kaparov flashed past in a maximum performance takeoff, tucking up his wheels and heading steeply upward. The purpose of their mission had been accomplished. Now all they had to do was get themselves out of this mess.

Wagner, one of the team's two medics, as well as its sharp-shooter, knelt on the floorboards beside Nelson.

Pushing up his night vision goggles and holding a flashlight in his teeth, he examined the wound. The bullet had entered just at the edge of Nelson's body armor. His shoulder was torn open and blood was streaming down his side. It was a wound that should have put Nelson out of action. But strange things happen to men in combat. He had sensed only what felt like a gentle push on his shoulder and had continued to control his little team until nearly the end of the firefight. But then, still not realizing he had been hit, he lost consciousness.

Wagner pulled the cumbersome body armor aside and, us-ing his K-bar knife, cut Nelson's uniform away from his shoul-der and covered the gaping wound with a handful of thick compresses to stop the bleeding. He quickly wrapped a sling around the shoulder to hold the compresses tightly in place.

At 46 the oldest and most experienced SEAL on the team, Wagner had seen and treated a lot of wounded men—in South-east Asia, Grenada, Panama, and the Gulf War. He had more experience with combat wounds than most doctors. But there was only so much anyone could do until they got Nelson to the medical facilities on the carrier.

Tom Shoup, the Air Force paramedic, or ''PJ,'' as they are known, moved over to help, holding Nelson's wrist to take his pulse.

After a moment, he glanced at Wagner and almost imper-ceptibly shook his head.

Bonior leaned over, tapped Shoup on the shoulder, and shouted: ''How's he doing?''

''He's hit bad, Chief.''

''Damn! I didn't even know he'd been hit. I wasn't paying attention, doing my job.''

The Humvee was lurching wildly as it zigzagged across the open field toward the runway. Merrifield stood at the machine gun, firing at the Iraqi trucks pursuing them, but all his bullets seemed to go wide of the mark. Fortunately, the Iraqi gunners' aim was no better. But they all knew that as soon as the helicopter landed and they stopped to climb aboard, they would make a perfect target.

"Ah, Spark One, we could use a little help here." Marker, the communications expert, had never been in combat before, but he reacted as coolly as a veteran.

In response, Rattner, who had just crossed the perimeter fence, rose sharply and spun around to move in beside the leading Iraqi truck. From the left waist window, the gunner poured a rain of shells into the truck. It seemed to continue as though it were untouched and then exploded in flames.

Spark Two, the backup helicopter, pulled alongside the second truck and swept it with a long blast of .50-caliber fire. The truck swerved, rolled over, and burst into flames.

As the pilot pivoted close to the ground, it suddenly felt as though some giant hand had grabbed the controls.

"Sir, you've lost your tail rotor." The voice of the tail gunner was remarkably calm, almost matter-of-fact.

As they felt the machine jerk out of control, the men in the cabin reacted as they had been trained, lying one on top of the other, to form a kind of human body cushion. And then the damaged bird slammed into the runway, pivoting sideways and sending up a shower of sparks.

As soon as motion stopped, the men dashed for the open rear door. Perhaps because they had been only a few feet off the ground, none of them was seriously hurt. The smell of spilled fuel was strong in the air.

Ray Pratt slowed the Humvee long enough to permit the other men to clamber aboard and then hit the throttle again, putting as much distance as possible between himself and the wreckage. Moments later, the crashed helicopter burst into flames with a roar, punctuated by the sound of ammunition and grenades cooking off. If Pratt had lingered even a second or two longer, the Humvee and its passengers would have been shredded by the projectiles spewing from the wreckage.

Rattner landed about a quarter mile down the runway and Pratt pulled in close beside the rear ramp. Nelson, drifting back into consciousness, tried to stand up, but his legs gave way and he collapsed to the floor of the Humvee.

Nelson looked up, startled by his sudden weakness. He plucked at Bonior's sleeve and said, "Take over, Chief."

Shoup leaned down and, as gently as possible, picked Nelson up, slung him over his shoulder, and ran for the helicopter.

Bonior paused on the ramp and took a moment to count the occupants of the helicopter cabin to make sure that in the excitement no one had been left behind. Then he turned, tossed two thermite grenades into the cab of the Humvee, and gave a thumbs-up sign to the aircraft crewman standing on the open ramp. The helicopter had been on the ground only a minute and twenty seconds when it lifted off and headed out over the fence toward the north.

Rattner was pleased how well the helicopter handled. By leaving behind the Humvee and the cycles—to say nothing of the ammunition that had been expended and the fuel that had been burned off—he had more than made up for the weight of the men from the crashed chopper.

Pratt pressed the button on his remote detonator. Suddenly a series of explosions went off almost simultaneously, enveloping the entire Iraqi complex in flames.

Wagner quickly plugged into the plane's intercom. "Colonel, we've got a problem here. Mr. Nelson was hit. The wound is pretty bad. We've got the bleeding stopped, but he's lost a lot of blood and I'm afraid he's going to go into shock. This cold back here is not going to do him any good."

As he spoke, Shoup pulled a pack of serum albumin from his pack, inserted a needle into Nelson's good arm, and began an intravenous flow to replace the fluids he had lost. It was not the same as a transfusion of whole blood, but it could help to keep him alive.

"Okay, Sergeant, do the best you can. It's going to be a while before we can get out of here and get to someplace where he can be treated." Rattner knew there was a so-called golden hour during which a seriously wounded man's life could be saved if he received proper treatment. And he also knew they had a lot of hard flying ahead of them. They were going to need four golden hours.

Donovan crouched on the rear ramp, attached to the plane

by a long, thick nylon cord. He steadied himself with one hand on his machine gun, scanning the sky behind them through his night vision goggles.

"Tail to pilot: Sir, we have company."

As he spoke, Rattner looked out his right window and saw a stream of tracer bullets flash past.

"Well, shit, that's all we need," he muttered to himself, as he threw the plane into a hard, diving turn to the left.

"Tail to pilot: Looks like a Hind." Donovan crouched behind his weapon, trying to get a shot at the Iraqi helicopter which was flying behind and slightly above them—obviously afraid to get too low as the two craft headed up into the mountains.

The Hind is a Soviet-built gunship with a twin-barrel 30mm gun mounted in its nose. It is more agile and more heavily armed than the large American Pave Low. The contest between the two planes was something like a battle between a fighter plane and a transport. Sooner or later—and probably sooner—the transport would lose. To make matters worse, the Hind has heavy armor protecting the pilot and gunner in the nose while the Pave Low has no such protection in the rear.

The Americans did, however, have two things going for them: their ability to see in the dark, and their superior skill as pilots. The men in the back of the helicopter knew that if anyone could prevent them from ending up as a blackened scar on the side of some unnamed Iraqi peak, it was Rattner and Jack Laffer.

In the front of the cabin, just behind the pilots, Rex Marker crouched over the radio. He was pleased to be in the warmest part of the cabin—but it was still not all that warm.

He was under orders to avoid all radio transmissions that were not absolutely essential until they had left Iraqi territory. The best he could do was to listen to the radio and monitor what was going on around them.

"Eagle One . . . Jupiter." The faint sound broke through the static. Marker recognized the transmission as an AWACS calling an F-15 fighter plane. Around the clock, giant flying radar stations—Airborne Warning and Control System planes—circled over the area in northern Iraq where the Iraqis had been forbidden to fly their own aircraft. They were in constant contact with two-plane flights of Air Force F-15 fighters—ready to enforce the prohibition if any Iraqi planes were detected in the forbidden area.

"Eagle One," the lead F-15 pilot replied.

"Eagle One . . . Jupiter. I have two slow-movers on a heading of three-two-one degrees, twenty miles north of Checkpoint Y. They are not responding to IFF. We also have a fast-mover on a heading of zero-eight-seven climbing through Angels four-zero."

"Ah, roger, Jupiter. We'll take a look at the slow movers. Eagle One out."

Marker keyed his microphone. "Colonel, your Air Force buddies are coming after us. I just heard the AWACS vector in a couple of Eagles."

Rattner had known all along that this was one of the hazards of their mission. To preserve secrecy, neither the AWACS nor the fighter squadrons that patrol this area had been told about this operation. And to avoid calling attention to themselves, they had turned off their IFF—Identification, Friend or Foe—system that automatically transmitted a code signal to identify the plane as friendly. The AWACS and the fighter pilots, seeing two helicopters heading north through the no-fly zone, would understandably assume they were Hinds. The trouble in this case was that one—but only one—of them was.

Wagner and Shoup had laid Nelson, who had again lapsed into unconsciousness, on the floor of the helicopter and wrapped him in two blankets they had found on the plane. But still, he was awfully cold and might already be in shock. Wagner gently pulled back the blankets to check the dressing on the SEAL's shoulder. The gauze pads were wet with blood, but the heavy bleeding seemed to have stopped.

On the rear ramp, Donovan fired sporadically. On several occasions, he was sure he had hit the Hind, but the heavy armor protecting the pilot and gunner had deflected his bullets. The Iraqi gunner was obviously conserving ammunition. But when he did fire the guns mounted on the right side of his nose, the stream of tracers often came alarmingly close to the Pave Low.

The radio came to life again. "Jupiter . . . Eagle One. We have ID on trailing Hind and are preparing to attack."

"Ah, roger, Eagle One. Do you have visual ID? I repeat, do you have visual ID? Jupiter."

Marker listened intently. He knew the F-15 pilots could find them easily with their radar. But after a tragic accident in which two American helicopters were mistaken for Hinds and shot down, tight new security rules had been put in place. The pilots were required to actually see and recognize the target.

"Affirmative, Jupiter. Request clearance to fire."

"Eagle One . . . Jupiter. You have permission to fire."

"Sir," Marker called, "those Eagles are coming for us."

"What did you hear, son?"

"They said they had positive ID on the trailing Hind and have permission to fire."

"Roger." Rattner turned to his copilot. "Let's let them solve our problem for us." He stopped the violent evasive maneuvers he had been using to dodge the Hind. The Iraqi pilot puzzled for a moment and then leveled off to move in for the kill.

Donovan, crouching on the rear ramp, saw the stream of tracer bullets. They came straight at him, like floating balls of fire, and then seemed to veer off at the last moment.

Unfortunately, one of the bullets did find the fuel tank on the right side of the plane. Drop by drop, fuel began leaking from the tiny hole, the crew unaware of the new hazard.

Suddenly the Hind erupted in a blinding flash. Blazing chunks of debris rained down from the fireball. The occupants of the Pave Low stared out the rear doorway in awe.

"They'll be coming around for us in a moment," Rattner told his copilot. "Let's see if we can give them the slip."

Rattner turned abruptly up a small canyon and gently touched down as close as he could to the canyon wall. With luck, the fast-moving F-15s wouldn't be able to see the stationary Pave Low. And, if they did, they would have a hard time getting into position to hit it. Rattner, who had been an Eagle driver himself before becoming a helicopter pilot, knew, too, that the Eagles would have to break off soon and go in search of fuel.

"Holy shit!" It suddenly dawned on Rex Marker that, in his concern over the fact that the F-15s were coming looking for them, he had totally ignored the other half of the message he had heard in the first broadcast from the AWACS: "We also have a fast-mover on a heading of zero-eight-seven climbing through Angels four-zero."

Marker called the pilot: "Colonel, I think our Russkie is going home!"

CHAPTER 11

IT WAS THE FIFTH DAY AFTER SURGERY. DOROTHY BONIOR, WHO had slept in a small bed near her daughter, had risen early and showered. As she stepped out of the bathroom, Denise was still asleep.

One of the tubes had been removed from her mouth the night before and the wires had been detached from her head. She was beginning to look more like a little girl than some weird medical experiment.

Her mother bent over the bed and kissed her daughter on the cheek. "How's my baby this morning?"

She frowned. With the back of her hand she felt her daughter's forehead. It felt hot. She ran her hand down between the sheets. They were damp.

The nurse who had attended Denise each day entered the room and put an arm around Dorothy's waist. "How's our little patient doing?"

"Feel her forehead. I think she's got a fever."

The nurse leaned over the bed. "Denise. Can you wake up a little bit?"

The little girl opened her eyes groggily and stared at the nurse as she slipped a thermometer into her mouth and lifted her wrist to take her pulse. She retrieved the thermometer and went to the window to read it. "You're right. She has a fever. What is this, the fifth day after the operation? I'm going to call Dr. Robins."

The doctor, who had monitored the child's condition several

times each day, pulled back the covers and examined the wounds in her leg, abdomen, and head. He also checked the drain emerging from her left lung. The right side of her abdomen felt warm and the drain from her abdomen contained what appeared to be pus.

He stood for a few moments holding the little girl's wrist and staring out the window. He took the nurse aside and gave her instructions.

"Mrs. Bonior, I'm afraid Denise has an internal infection—probably in the area of her duodenum. Children this age are usually pretty good at avoiding infections. But there are a lot of bugs wandering around in the human body, especially in the digestive system. We'll run some tests and I'm going to place her on a course of antibiotics for the next twenty-four hours and see if we can knock this out."

"I thought she was already getting antibiotics."

"That's right. We gave her antibiotics both before and after the operation. But that apparently didn't do the trick. We'll try a different medicine and see if that will work."

"She's going to be all right, isn't she?"

He put his hand on her shoulder and they stood looking out the window.

"I don't want to raise any false hopes. You have a very, very sick daughter. She's lucky she survived at all. An inch one way or the other and that bullet in her abdomen could have killed her. I'm very pleased with the way we were able to repair the damage. But her recovery is going to be difficult. She hasn't had anything to eat for nearly a week and she won't be able to eat for another week until her stomach and other organs have had a chance to heal. That means she is weak and will continue to be weak. That will make it harder for her to fight off this infection."

Dorothy Bonior began to cry softly. Suddenly, the whole awful experience, which she had had to bear almost alone, bore down on her. She reached for a tissue from the bedside table, blew her nose, and dried her eyes. "I'm sorry, Dr. Robins. It all just caught up with me there for a moment. I'll be all right."

"Your husband is a SEAL, isn't he? Is he going to be able to be here with you?"

"No. He's off on a mission. I don't know where he is or what he's doing. But everything he does is dangerous. That makes it worse."

After the doctor had left, she sat by her daughter's bed and thought. Should she try to get a message to Jeff? Or would that just make him worry when he probably should be devoting all of his attention to his mission—whatever that was? Finally she reached for the phone.

When it was answered in the chairman's office, she identified herself and the aide who answered immediately responded: "Oh, yes, Mrs. Bonior, I was told we might expect a call from you. How is your little daughter doing today?"

"She has a fever and I'm worried. I don't know whether I should bother Jeff or not. I don't want him to worry any more than he is."

"Why don't you give me the information? I'll try to pass it on to him at the appropriate time. But I can tell you that we will not be able to be in touch with him for some hours, or even perhaps a day or two."

"I understand. In that case, I'll call you with reports whenever there's any change in her condition. I don't want you to pass along outdated information and worry him needlessly. Perhaps I can call you back in a little while with good news."

"That's fine, Mrs. Bonior. Please feel free to call at any time—night or day—and we'll pass the information along as soon as possible. And I want you to know that all of us here are praying for your daughter and you."

CHAPTER 12

THE CUMBERSOME SPACE SUIT THAT SERGEI KAPAROV HAD donned before they left the carrier was supposed to be air conditioned as soon as it was plugged into the bomber's air circulation system. But Kaparov was still sweating profusely as he followed the dim infrared light on the back of the motorbike as Tim Hutchins led him out to the end of the runway.

The moment he had stepped into the cockpit, he was delighted to see how remarkably it resembled the mockup in which he had trained back in Arizona. But still he was nervous: flying a plane bigger than anything he had ever flown before—a plane that had been drastically modified by the Iraqis—would be more challenging than any of the hundreds of flights he had made as a test pilot.

His eyes darted over the control panel, not only checking every gauge to make sure everything was working perfectly, but also checking to make sure that each gauge and switch was where he thought it was. One misread instrument, one control moved improperly, could end this whole adventure in a pyre of smoke and flame. The Air Force men had gone through a quick checklist with him before he'd begun to taxi, but now he was on his own, relying on his memory and luck to get everything just right for takeoff.

As he turned onto the runway, Kaparov could see the infrared lights of the box-and-one providing a bare outline of the runway's dimensions—two lights on each side of the strip and one at the end.

He stood on the brakes as he pushed the throttles full forward, going over the instruments one last time. The huge plane shuddered like a giant bird fighting against a tether.

Then he slipped his feet off the brakes and concentrated on the rudders, keeping the plane headed for that one small light at the end of the runway as the craft slowly began to move. Kaparov knew the takeoff roll would be a long one. He was using only the two conventional jet engines rather than cutting in the unfamiliar ramjet engines while still on the ground.

Even inside the cockpit, looming well forward of the engines, and with his head encased in the helmet of his space suit, Kaparov still heard the throaty roar of the engines. As suspected, the Iraqi engineers had replaced the original Soviet engines with General Electric F-404 engines which had been developed for the Navy's F/A-18 strike fighter. Noise suppression had been far from the thoughts of the GE designers. As the plane gained speed, Kaparov was grateful for every ounce of the thirty-two thousand pounds of thrust the engineers had been able to wring from the twin engines.

There were still several thousand feet of runway remaining when Kaparov cranked back on the stick, racked the plane into a steep climbing turn, and retracted the landing gear. Flying with a stick rather than a wheel, the huge craft handled almost like a fighter plane, even on two engines.

Kaparov could feel some of the tenseness drain from his body.

On his lap was the aeronautical chart he had prepared before he'd left Arizona. His route was a straight line, almost due south, from the airfield he had just left in northern Iraq to the Al Jouf airbase in northern Saudi Arabia used by American forces during the Gulf War. In his careful printing, he had noted his compass course and the radio frequencies he could use as a navigational aid. With a boost from his ramjet engines, he would cruise through Iraqi airspace well above the range of anti-aircraft guns and fighter-interceptors. Saudi air defense units along the border had supposedly been warned not to shoot at him—without being told who he was or what his mission was.

As soon as Kaparov heard the thump as the wheels locked in place, he tucked the chart down beside his seat. Gently moving a lever with his left hand, he swung the variable geometry wings back about halfway. With the wings tucked back against the fuselage and with all four of the original jet engines, the plane was capable of flying at twice the speed of sound at sixty thousand feet. But Kaparov was not out to set any speed records on this flight.

Still climbing sharply, he turned onto a new heading he had carefully committed to memory. In his mind's eye, he could picture the route. Instead of taking him south toward Saudi Arabia, his new route took him to the northeast. In a few minutes he would cross the Iraqi border into Iran, passing north of the capital of Teheran and out over the Caspian Sea. Back over land, he would cross over the newly independent state of Turkmenistan before finding his way to a former Soviet military base in the Uzbekistan desert.

As he rolled onto his new course, Kaparov was passing through thirty-eight thousand feet. He could feel his speed draining off as the two jet engines struggled to continue the climb. It was time to see whether the ramjet engines installed by the Iraqi engineers would do their job. Despite his experience test-flying all kinds of new and experimental planes, this was something new for Kaparov. He didn't know what to expect. When he pressed the switch to crank up the new engines, they could do one of three things: ignite smoothly and send him soaring up into the outer fringes of the atmosphere; do nothing; or explode, turning the plane and him into a shooting star that would flare for a few moments and then disappear.

He got the reaction he had hoped for—and more. The ramjets thrust him back into his seat so hard that he had to push forward on the stick to keep the plane from rocketing straight upward.

Kaparov watched, pleased, as the needles on the old analog altimeter spun off tens of thousands of feet. In the U.S. Air Force planes he had often flown, he had become used to the more modern digital readout gauges in the so-called glass cockpit. But he still felt a little more comfortable with the old circular dials that he had grown up with, and that made it a little easier to picture your position in space and time.

Every thousand feet was just a little more insurance as he crossed the border into Iran. If the technicians in the Iranian air defense sites were on their toes, they would quickly identify him as a potentially hostile intruder heading in the general direction of Teheran. Every anti-aircraft gun and rocket in northern Iran would swing in his direction. Interceptors on ground alert would take only a few minutes to become airborne. Kaparov worried most about the F-14 fighters the United States had sold to Iran when the Shah was still in power and Iran was one of America's staunchest allies. Time and a shortage of spare parts had undoubtedly taken a toll on the F-14s, but if the Iranians could manage to get any of the fighters into the air, they had the radar to find the intruder and the weapons to shoot it down.

With the subconscious reflexes of a veteran pilot, Kaparov's head pivoted constantly, searching the skies for any sign of danger—the contrails of a fighter or the plume of a surface-to-air missile. He felt naked and alone. On a combat mission into hostile airspace, a pilot would normally carry radar to warn him of a threat from fighters or anti-aircraft rockets, countermeasures to spoil the aim of the rockets' radar guidance, and guns and missiles to beat off an attack by a fighter plane.

Kaparov had none of these. The Iraqi engineers had stripped the plane of most of the heavy defensive equipment a bomber would normally carry, assuming that its ramjet engines would permit it to fly above the threat. That was now Kaparov's best hope: if he could get high enough soon enough, the Iranians couldn't touch him.

As he soared above eighty thousand feet, he began to relax. It would take a very lucky shot indeed to catch him at this altitude. As he continued to search the skies for signs of danger, he could not help but marvel at the view from here—so high that he could clearly make out the curvature of the earth.

Off to his right front, the lights of Teheran spread out in a great golden circle. Beyond, by the light of the quarter moon, he could make out the ghostly shape of the Elburz Mountains. And directly in front lay the Caspian Sea, its waters silvery in the moonlight.

Sergei Kaparov felt very pleased with himself. He had picked an opportune moment to betray his old colleagues in the Soviet Union when he'd hijacked the Backfire bomber and delivered it to the U.S. Air Force—an act that had made him a wealthy man. Now he had done it again, betraying his new friends in a deal that would make him even wealthier. In the months before his flight, he had quietly mortgaged his Arizona ranch and transferred much of his wealth into a bank account in the Cayman Islands, identified by a number rather than his name.

As he crossed the coastline, he switched off the ramjets and pulled back on the throttles of his jet engines. The plane dropped steeply toward the surface of the sea. Kaparov didn't expect much of a threat from the air defenses of the old Soviet Union. The Russian military had fallen on hard times and the defenses of the new republics that had been created with the collapse of the Soviet empire were even more threadbare.

But Kaparov did not intend to take any chances. He plummeted down until his radar altimeter showed that he was flying only two hundred feet off the surface of the sea. The flight plan he had memorized was designed to avoid the coastal radar. And by flying as low as possible, he should be below the fan of any radar station he should happen to pass.

At that altitude, he couldn't see ahead, as he had been able to at high altitude. He had only his compass to guide him. He tuned in the commercial radio station at Krasnovodsk, the nearest city in Turkmenistan. But he had not dared to try to bring along an aeronautical chart of the area, and he could not take his hands off the controls long enough to try to get a bearing on the station.

The coastline slipped beneath his wings and he climbed slightly to avoid the low-lying coastal mountains and then dropped down once more over the featureless Kara-Kum Desert that stretched for hundreds of miles. This was going to take some fancy dead-reckoning navigation.

As the plane crossed the coastline, Kaparov clicked the watch on his wrist to start the stopwatch. At the same time he nudged the nose of the plane three degrees to the south. At his speed of 425 knots, it should take him just about an hour and six minutes to reach the Amudar River, the only geographical feature breaking the monotonous landscape. He only hoped the river would be visible in the moonlight. Farmers upstream drained the river of its water to irrigate their cotton crops. At the point where Kaparov planned to cross the river, it might well be just a dry, sandy riverbed, hardly distinguishable in the dark from the surrounding desert.

As his watch ticked toward the time when he should see the river, Kaparov leaned as far forward as he could, peering into the darkness. And then, suddenly, there it was. The river was dry, as he had feared, but the moon cast a shadow on the low banks, drawing a dark line across the landscape. Kaparov turned ninety degrees to the left and followed the path of the riverbed to the north. It was a trick as old as the art of navigation, practiced by sailors for centuries: fly—or sail—to a line that passes through your destination; then turn and proceed along the line until you arrive. It is an almost foolproof trick, as long as you hit the line on the correct side of your destination. If you hit the line on the wrong side and turn the wrong direction, you are very lost.

That is why Kaparov had turned slightly to the right as he'd cross the coastline, to make sure he would hit the river to the right of his destination.

Once he had found the river, it was easy to follow it another twenty-seven minutes to the north until he came within sight of the lights of the small city of Urganch, on the Turkmenistan-Uzbekistan border. Swinging onto a new heading toward the east, over the Kyzul-Kum Desert, Kaparov set his stopwatch once again and began peering into the distance for the old Soviet airfield that was his destination. Suddenly he spotted it up ahead, a shadowy cluster of buildings alongside a long paved runway gleaming silver in the moonlight. He didn't see a single light.

As he came over the base at two hundred feet, the roar of his engines was loud enough to bring everyone below to a startled alert. As he passed over the end of the runway and began a climbing turn, the runway lights flashed on. He extended his wings fully and completed his turn, lined up with the runway, let down his landing gear, and greased the plane in to a smooth landing.

Braking to a slow roll, he spotted a jeep-like vehicle with a flashing red light off to his right. He turned and followed the light as it led him back down a taxiway. Up ahead he saw the cavernous interior of a huge hangar. Sand had been piled along its sides so that from even a short distance away it seemed to be part of the desert. The red light proceeded right into the hangar and Kaparov followed. As his huge vertical tail cleared the doorway, monstrous metal doors sliding on tracks closed smoothly behind him and the interior lights brightened.

As soon as he had closed down the engines, Kaparov unsnapped the cumbersome helmet that enclosed his head and pried it loose from the space suit covering his body. The air inside the hangar still smelled of the fumes from the plane's exhaust, but it was a relief to be free of the hardware that had made him feel more like R2-D2, the robot, than a human being.

As soon as the plane came to a stop, Kaparov heard someone open a hatch in the wheel well and clamber up into the plane.

"Welcome to Uzbekistan, Colonel," Ben Bernard said.

The second voice Kaparov heard was a surprise. The man just behind Bernard shouted up, in Uzbek: "Abdul. Welcome home."

Kaparov laughed. During his service in the Soviet military, he had passed himself off as Russian. To be a good Communist—and a Russian—those were the two secrets to a promising military career. But the man known as Kaparov had actually been born Abdulkhashim Karimov in the ancient Uzbek city of Samarkand. All during his military career he had carried a deep love for his native land—a love he had carefully kept hidden. But now that the Soviet Union had broken up,

Uzbekistan was free to pursue its own destiny. Perhaps even now he was playing some small part in shaping the nation's future.

Bernard helped the pilot from the plane and guided him across the hangar to a small office.

"Vodka?" Bernard filled a glass with the clear liquid. He filled his own glass from a bottle of Sapphire gin.

The two men touched the edges of their glasses and then drank in unison, emptying the glasses.

"Okay, now, here's the setup," Bernard began. Then he hesitated. "Hey, I don't know what to call you."

"Why don't we just stick with Sergei?" Kaparov replied. "My friends here can use my Uzbek name."

"Fine, Sergei. Now, the deal is this: I'm in charge here, under orders. . . ." Bernard was careful not to use Nash's name. "You understand?"

Kaparov nodded.

"I have a good security force here. Some are my own people. We've also hired a corps of former Soviet *Spetznaz* troops. They're good—not as good as my guys, but they're good. We've also put together a top-notch technical team. It's not hard to hire first-rate people who were cast adrift when the Soviet Union collapsed. They'll go over the plane to see what the Iraqis have done and to make sure everything is in good condition. They're also going to be doing some modifications. They'll be putting in a look-down, shoot-down radar and some weapons."

"Sounds good." Kaparov picked up the bottle and refilled his glass with vodka. "How long is this going to take?"

"We're not sure. Probably several weeks. We'll be informed when it's time for the next stage of this operation."

"Next stage?"

"Yeah. Our . . . uh . . . employer has some plans for this plane. I don't know what they are, and frankly, I don't want to know. That's none of my business at this point."

"Well, if we don't know, we don't know. At least it gives me some time. Can you fix me up with a car? I'm going to go into Samarkand. Been a long time since I've been there."

Bernard stared into Kaparov's eyes for a moment.

"Sergei, I want you to understand something. This place is locked down while this operation is under way. Nobody comes in. Nobody goes out. No Samarkand. No nothing. And no apologies. We'll try to make you as comfortable as possible, but you're not going anywhere."

CHAPTER 13

As soon as he had shut down the engines, Rattner unbuckled the harness that held him in the helicopter's right seat and climbed back into the cabin to kneel beside Nelson.

Picking up the SEAL's left wrist, he held it for a few moments, watching his wristwatch. Then, laying the arm gently down, he looked questioningly toward the two medics.

"Pretty weak. What do you think, Doc?"

Bill Wagner, the SEAL corpsman, spoke: "Colonel, he must have lost a lot of blood just lying there on the tarmac before we even knew he had been hit. I've given him a couple of packs of serum albumin and we've got his fluid volume restored, but that's not the same as blood."

"Have you been able to examine the wound?"

"Not really. There's not much point to fooling around with it. The thing now is to get as much fluids into him as we can, keep him warm, and get him to a real doctor."

The pilot shook his head. "That's going to be a while. We'll just have to do the best we can."

Rattner was not only a veteran special operator; he studied and taught the subject at the Air Force special operations school at Hurlburt Field, Florida. As he knelt, peering down at Nelson in the cabin's dim light, Rattner could not help thinking of the Israeli raid on the airport at Entebbe, Uganda, in 1976. Commandos of the Sayeret Matkal Counterterrorist Unit landed four C-130s in the dark, stormed the airport terminal building, and rescued a planeload of airline passengers held hostage by terrorists. It was one of history's classic commando raids. But Lt. Col. Jonathan Netanyahu, the Israeli commander, was hit in the chest, just under the collarbone, by a round from an AK-47. The commandos had both a doctor and a supply of blood with them, but Netanyahu, who had lain untreated as his men stormed the terminal building, had been wounded too severely to survive.

Rattner bent over Nelson's silent form for another few moments and shook his head. "God, I hope that doesn't happen to us."

Then, standing, he motioned to his copilot, Jack Laffer. The two men stepped out the side doorway and began a careful walk around the helicopter, looking for any sign of damage.

Rex Marker was already busy beside the helicopter setting up his satellite communications antenna. With it, he would beam a report straight up to a satellite hovering at 22,000 miles above the earth and bounce it back down to Washington without giving away their position to any Iraqi in the area or to the American AWACS. For the moment, the F-15s had gone to get fuel, but they would probably be back again soon enough.

The two pilots were surprised to see that their plane had almost miraculously escaped damage from the bullets fired by the Hind. Then Laffer shined his flashlight on the fuel tank bulging at the right side of the plane.

"Oh, shit!" he exclaimed, kneeling to peer more closely at the skin of the tank. A thin but steady stream of fuel flowed from a hole in the side of the tank and splashed on the ground.

"Chief!" Rattner shouted. "Have we got anything to patch this damn thing with?"

The Air Force crew chief was at his shoulder in a moment, a roll of tape in his hand.

"This'll stop it, at least for a while," he said. He plugged the hole with his finger, wiped off the surrounding area, and slapped a strip of tape over the hole. "You know, that fuel is a real solvent, but this stuff is supposed to stick. Let's see what happens."

He shined his light on the strip of tape and stood, watching. After a minute, he wiped his hand on the leg of his flight suit, ran his fingers over the tape, and then lifted them to his nose to sniff.

"So far, so good. I don't know how long this will last, but it's holding now."

Rattner patted him on the shoulder. "Okay, good. Now check and see if you can figure how much fuel we've got left. That sucker must have been leaking for at least a good fifteen or twenty minutes now."

The pilots continued their way on around the machine. No more damage was apparent. But that one little hole, where a bullet had apparently just struck a glancing blow to the thin metal of the fuel tank, was bad enough.

"How are you doing, son?" Rattner asked, kneeling down beside Marker where he crouched beside his satcomm device.

"We've got comm, sir," Marker replied. The team had been provided with special codes that gave them a secure link directly to the office of the Joint Chiefs at the Pentagon. Operators there could patch them through to any military installation in the world.

"That's great. I'll have a message for you to send in a few minutes."

Rattner climbed back up inside the helicopter and retrieved his aeronautical chart from the case beside his seat. Spreading it out on the floor of the cabin, he marked the point where they had landed and then measured the distance to the Iraqi border and from there back to the carrier that was supposed to be waiting for them offshore. Carefully, he wrote a series of coordinates and times on a small piece of paper.

The crew chief tapped him on the shoulder. Rattner looked up. "What's it look like?"

"We've lost a lot of fuel, sir. We should have enough for a couple of hours, but I figure we've only got about 1,650 pounds left. That will give us just about a half an hour of flying time—assuming we've got that leak plugged."

Rattner turned again to the chart, marking a point just north of the Turkish border. He underlined one of the coordinates written on the paper.

"It's going to be close, damn close."

Working his way back through the cabin, Rattner stepped

outside again and joined Marker. "Okay, Rex. I want you to whistle up a Shadow from Incirlik. Tell them to meet us here." He handed the radioman the slip of paper, pointing to the coordinate he had underlined. "We should be there at oh-one-two-five, give or take a few minutes. Tell them we're going to be damn near bingo fuel as we come across the border so we don't have any time to be mucking around. Oh . . . and tell them there's only one of us coming out."

Rattner knew the Combat Shadow tanker that had escorted them on their way in was waiting on the ground at the big North Atlantic Treaty Organization airbase at Incirlik, Turkey. All he had to do now was to find his way back through the mountains and link up with the Shadow before he ran out of fuel.

In his concern about the fuel, Rattner had forgotten entirely about the two F-15s.

"Sir," Marker said, "I've been listening to the AWACS. The Eagles made one more pass over here after they took on fuel and then I heard the AWACS tell them to RTB."

"Return to base? Good. Let's hope they stay there," Rattner replied. Then he turned to the crew and shouted, "Okay, men, let's get this show on the road."

He and his copilot moved up quickly through the cabin and strapped themselves in. As soon as they received the signal that all the men were onboard, they fired up the engines and the huge rotor began to circle slowly above their heads.

As they rose from the ground and pivoted carefully to head back out of the little box canyon in which they had hidden, a flurry of white flakes swept across the windscreen.

"Snow! That's all we need!" Rattner knew that the snow was a mixed blessing. The cold weather meant their fuel would last a little bit longer. If the F-15 pilots returned, the snow would certainly prevent them from getting visual ID. But the snow also meant their night vision goggles would be worthless. They would have to rely entirely on their radar to work their way back through the mountains.

In an airplane, a pilot could simply climb above the surrounding peaks and set his course in safety. But climbing vertically in a helicopter was both time- and fuel-consuming.

Their only way to safety was through the passes in the mountains, not over them.

Emerging into the floor of the valley, Rattner tilted the nose downward and began moving forward, his eyes riveted on the round radar monitor that gave him a picture of the terrain in front of him. As long as the horizontal line across the monitor was above the line indicating the terrain, he was okay. If it dropped below that line, he was headed for disaster in the next minute or so.

When the pilots and engineers developing the Pave Low back in the 1970s told the engineers at Texas Instruments that they wanted to be able to fly blind at a hundred feet, the engineers had a brief answer: "You're crazy." Even fighter pilots, with much more power and maneuverability, wouldn't dare stake their lives on terrain avoidance radar that low.

But the Pave Low team had insisted. If they couldn't fly that low safely, then they couldn't go into hostile territory and get back out again without being spotted and destroyed. With the engineers shaking their heads, the Pave Low test pilots took the plane out night after night, flying lower and lower until they proved they could do it safely.

It was that pioneering work Rattner was betting on now. Flying a few feet off the ground with just that little glowing dial to show the way was the ultimate in sweaty-palm flying. Rattner had to fight every normal human instinct: the instinct to pull up; the instinct to look outside and try to see where he was going; the instinct to flinch at imagined hazards. Most of all, he had to fight the temptation to succumb to vertigo and believe the messages his body was sending him rather than the truth reported by the little dial. This was the worst place in the world for seat-of-the-pants flying.

Laffer, sitting in the copilot's seat, followed Rattner's every movement, ready to take over instantly if his pilot succumbed to vertigo.

"Chief! Keep an eye on the fuel gauges," Rattner called. "Give me time, position, and fuel checks every five minutes."

Before they had even left the carrier, Rattner had carefully set the checkpoints for the entire flight into his inertial navigation computer. He had reset the computer with the known coordinates of the Iraqi airfield as he'd waited for the commandos to carry out their mission. They had done a little wandering through the mountains, but the computer should lead them from one checkpoint to the next with reasonable accuracy.

With the chief calling off vital information, he would not have to take his eyes from the radar monitor for even a moment. Laffer, monitoring the compass and the inertial guidance system, would advise him if he got off course.

The few flakes that had begun to fall as they took off soon turned into a blizzard. Rattner could feel the plane buffeted by the winds whipping through the mountain passes. He could only hold the craft as steady as possible and hope some errant gust didn't smash them into a rocky outcropping.

In the rear cabin, the crew members had closed up the side windows and the rear ramp. In this storm, there was no sense trying to look outside and there was no need to have the machine guns at the ready. With the hatches closed, the temperature in the cabin slowly rose.

Two of the SEALs stripped off their outer clothes and lay down, one on each side of Nelson. By surrounding him with their body heat, they were doing the best thing that could be done to help him survive the long flight to the carrier. In shock, the body protects itself by drawing blood to its most vital organs and gradually sacrificing the fingers and toes, the ears, the legs, the arms in a desperate effort to preserve life itself. But that effort places an added burden on the heart and other vital organs. A person in severe shock teeters on the borderline between life and death. By sharing their warmth, the SEALs could help tilt the balance in Nelson's favor.

Every five minutes, the crew chief reported the remaining fuel. Laffer added the other part of the equation by reading off the distance remaining to the point just over the Turkish border where they expected to meet the tanker.

"Damn!" Rattner muttered to himself. "It's going to be awful close." If worse came to worst, he knew, he would have to try to land the craft while he still had a few drops of fuel remaining. The chances of surviving such a landing in this rocky country ranged from zero to none.

As the plane neared the Turkish border, the terrain reflected on the radar monitor became smoother, less jagged. Rattner had been flying at about a hundred feet off the ground. He now began a gradual climb, working his way up to a safer altitude for the refueling operation. The snow tapered off and then stopped. It was still pitch black under the overcast, but Laffer slipped his night vision goggles into position. With them, he would be able to see the C-130 as it pulled in ahead of them while Rattner continued to use the terrain avoidance radar.

Now, it was all up to the Shadow crew to find the helicopter with their radar and move into position just in front of the chopper.

Back in the cabin, the crew members opened the rear ramp and the side windows, peering into the darkness for the first glimpse of the tanker.

"Tail to pilot: I have him at our five o'clock, overtaking on your right."

"Ah, roger that," Rattner replied. "Jack, you handle the linkup with the NVG."

"Roger. I've got it."

As Laffer looked back up to his right, he saw the four-engined tanker just above them and moving on out ahead. He climbed gently until he was slightly above the tanker and just to the left of its giant tail. The big basket, glowing white in his goggles, danced toward him on the end of the hose snaking out from the plane's wing.

Laffer eased forward, taking aim on the basket.

Just as he prepared to dive down to slide the probe sticking out from the nose of the helicopter into the basket, the engine coughed, sending a shudder through the craft. The sound of the engine smoothed out and then coughed again.

Rattner pressed the button on his radio control, breaking radio silence. "Shadow one. We are bingo fuel. Lead us down and we'll try to plug in."

The engine sputtered, dragging the last drops of fuel from the tank.

As Laffer dove forward to connect with the basket, the engine stopped and he had a sickening sensation in the pit of his stomach as the plane began to drop toward the earth. But the tanker was diving now, leading them down. The probe stayed in the basket and fuel began to flow.

In the cockpit of the tanker, the pilots fought the controls. They had deployed their flaps to slow the plane's forward motion and keep pace with the falling helicopter. The stall alarm screamed in their ears.

The command pilot, in the left seat, watched the altimeter as they plummeted downward. They had another two thousand feet—how much time? What? Another thirty seconds before they had to break the link and level off.

Rattner felt helpless, like a passenger on the *Titanic*, as his helicopter dropped toward the earth, following the tanker down. Without night vision goggles, he could not even see the tanker to which they were linked. But if they could get some fuel and get their engines going, he might have to take over within a few feet of the ground, again relying on the instruments alone.

"Fifteen hundred. Fourteen hundred. Thirteen hundred . . ." The copilot of the tanker read the figures off the altimeter as fast as he could speak. At five hundred feet, they would have to break off. That would give them barely enough room to get up to flying speed and pull up before they hit the ground.

"Ten hundred. Nine hundred . . ."

The engine of the Pave Low coughed, sputtered, and then caught. Laffer could feel the controls begin to respond solidly as the rotor bit into the air.

The tanker surged ahead abruptly as the pilot pushed his throttles forward and pulled back on the wheel. Laffer saw the basket jerk free of his probe and recede into the distance.

"Okay, Chief, what have we got?" Rattner demanded.

"Five hundred pounds, sir. About ten minutes' worth."

Laffer leveled off and then began another gradual climb as the tanker circled and again approached from the rear. The tanker crew knew as well as Rattner and Laffer that the chopper needed another long drink.

The Shadow moved into position in front of the helicopter once more and then turned onto a new heading toward the carrier waiting offshore. Laffer followed the big plane around and then dived toward the basket once more.

For the next two hours, the two craft flew in tandem. To radar operators down below, it looked like one C-130 on a routine training mission. Twice more on the way to the carrier, the helicopter moved in for another drink, replacing the fuel that had again begun to drip from the hole in the tank.

Dawn was just beginning to break over Asia, to their rear, as the two planes crossed the coastline. Minutes later, Rattner made out the dark shape of the USS *Stennis* cruising slowly toward them. Breaking off from the Shadow, he circled, settled gently on the carrier's flight deck, and followed a crewman who signaled him toward a group standing near the base of the towering superstructure that towered over the deck.

As soon as he came to a stop, four corpsmen darted up the rear ramp and gently lifted Nelson onto a stretcher. They carried him out carefully and then strapped him to a wheeled gurney. One of the corpsmen quickly inserted a needle in his arm and started the flow from a bag of Type O-positive blood.

Nelson stirred and looked around him as he was wheeled into the brightly lighted operating room. An aircraft carrier is the home to some six thousand of the healthiest young Americans gathered anywhere. But the ship's medical team must be prepared to deal at any time with the horrendous injuries that can be caused by bullets or shell fragments, the crushing trauma of a plane crash, or the burns from flaming aviation fuel.

"How are you doing, Commander? You okay?" The young woman flight surgeon leaned over Nelson, carefully observing his skin color. With her thumb, she peeled back the eyelid of one eye and then the other, checking his pupils with a small flashlight.

"What happened? Where am I?"

The fact that he could respond to her question was a good sign.

"You're on the *Stennis*. How are you feeling?"

"Confused."

"You've got some injury to your shoulder and you've lost a good deal of blood," the surgeon told him. "But you're in good hands now. We'll get you fixed up. I'm going to take a look at your shoulder now. It may hurt a little, but I'll give you something to deaden the pain as soon as I see what we're dealing with.''

With a large pair of scissors she cut away the jacket, shirt, and thermal underwear covering his torso and gently lifted the gauze padding covering his wound.

''Wow! That hurts!'' Nelson exclaimed.

''This will sting,'' she said, as she cleansed a patch of skin and plunged a hypodermic needle into his chest. He flinched but didn't cry out.

''Okay, now, can we roll you over a little on your left side?'' A corpsman stepped forward and helped as they rolled him over. The surgeon cut away at the fabric and pulled the rest of the uniform away. Then she ran her hand carefully over his back, searching for any sign of an exit wound. Often, a bullet makes a relatively small hole where it enters the body but then tears a large wound as it comes out the other side. In Nelson's case, the entry wound was large, but she found no exit wound.

''It looks like you were lucky, Commander. I think this bullet must have hit something that slowed it down before it struck you. But it was also tumbling when it hit so it's still done a good deal of damage. I'm going to get some X rays and see what we've got here.''

When Nelson entered the operating room, his color was ashen and his skin was clammy. But now the doctor could see the transfusion beginning to take effect. His color returned and his skin again felt normal.

But the doctor knew he was not out of the woods by a long shot. She had spent far too many nights in an urban emergency room treating gunshot and knife wounds and the devastating injuries of automobile and motorcycle accidents to relax just yet. She had seen healthy young people seem to emerge from shock and then go into cardiac arrest. She had seen arteries burst, pouring out blood faster than it could be replaced. Perhaps saddest of all, she had seen patients seemingly on their way to recovery suddenly felled by deadly infections.

All the risk factors were here. That long helicopter ride certainly didn't help. And who knew what kind of viruses and bacteria were already beginning to work their way through his system?

The surgeon slid one X ray after another up until they clipped onto a translucent glass wall frame that was lighted from behind.

At least some of the damage was obvious. The bullet had broken his right collarbone near the shoulder and shattered three ribs. She could make out three parts of the bullet and a number of bone fragments.

"Okay, Commander, we're going to put you to sleep while I try to clean up this mess."

The operation went smoothly. She got out as many pieces of bone as she could see, but she decided to leave one bullet fragment. If it caused any problems, it could be removed later.

When Nelson awoke after the surgery, Jeff Bonior was standing beside his bed in the ship's sick bay. He grinned, trying to put a reassuring look on his face. But his brow was still furrowed with worry.

"How you doing, Skipper?"

"Well, okay, I guess. How'd the op go?"

"I'll fill you in as soon as you're a little more awake. Look, Skipper . . . I'm really sorry about this. You're my buddy and I didn't even know you'd been shot. I let you down."

"Oh, bullshit, Jeff. You're not supposed to stop when you're in a firefight and start playing medic. I'm here on the ship and everything is okay."

"Well, if you say so, sir. But I still feel like shit."

CHAPTER 14

WHEN NELSON AWOKE THE NEXT MORNING, JEFF BONIOR WAS again sitting quietly beside his bed. Nelson tried to sit up and then dropped back onto the pillow. The cast encasing his right shoulder and upper arm loomed over his body. Fluid from a bag hanging above the bed dripped into a vein on his left arm.

"Feeling better today?" Bonior slipped an arm around behind Nelson's left shoulder and put another pillow behind his head.

"Not bad, I guess, Jeff. They tell me you almost lost me back there."

"Yeah, I guess that's true. Bill Wagner and Tom Shoup did a tremendous job in keeping you alive. But there was only so much they could do. We really have to thank the good Lord and his son, Jesus. I know I let you down back there, but I've been making up for it by praying."

"I really appreciate that, Chief. You think Baptist prayers work on an Easter-and-Christmas Catholic?"

"Well, you're alive, aren't you? From what the doctor tells me, that's pretty close to a miracle."

Nelson stroked the stubble on his chin. A shave would make him feel a lot better.

"Okay now, Jeff. Fill me in on the op. We got the plane off okay, didn't we?"

"It got off okay. But that Russkie didn't go to Al Jouf, like he was supposed to."

"He what?" Nelson started forward, but a wave of pain

swept through his shoulder and he fell back on the pillow. "You're shitting me . . . where is he?"

"We don't really know. Our best information now is that he headed kind of northeast, in the general direction of the old Soviet Union."

A corpsman entered and placed a cup of ice on the tray beside the bed.

"What time is breakfast around this place?" Nelson asked him.

"I'm sorry, sir. You had a general anesthetic. You won't get anything solid to eat until your bowels begin to function again. You can suck on some ice if you'd like." The corpsman handed him the cup of ice. Nelson grimaced and put a cube into his mouth.

"All right, now, Jeff. What are we doing?"

"Well, sir, if you remember, before you conked out back on the airfield, you passed the command on to me. I've been working with Colonel Rattner, but I've been acting as commander of our SEAL–Air Force team. I've set up a secure comm link to the chairman's office and to Mrs. Collins, back at Site Y in Arizona. She's running our intel operation from there."

"Good. I want you to remain in command. I'm probably still a little woozy from the drugs and the operation. But keep me informed. Now, what has Pat found out?"

"Well, she's getting some bits and pieces. One of our AWACS picked Sergei up shortly after takeoff on a heading of zero-eight-seven at forty thousand feet. At least, we think it was Sergei. The chairman gave Mrs. Collins a lot of clout. She's tasked the National Security Agency to search through their radio and radar intercepts for that whole area during the entire night. Those folks at Fort Meade suck up all kinds of electronic transmissions. The trick is to find what you're looking for in all that stuff. That's what Mrs. Collins has them doing right now, on the highest priority."

Nelson nodded, popping another ice cube into his mouth.

"So far, we know that the Iranian air defense went on a high alert just about the time Sergei would have crossed their border. They flushed two Tomcats, but they didn't get close to him before he was out over the Caspian Sea. Apparently NSA picked up some pretty frantic transmissions. He scared the heck out of them.

"Once he was out over the water, he apparently got down on the deck. He disappeared from Iranian radar. There was another partial radar contact as he crossed the coastline into Turkmenistan. He must have been flying really low. They didn't get any kind of a decent fix on him."

"And then . . . ?" Nelson waited.

"And then . . . nothing. He just disappeared. Mrs. Collins is in touch with the National Reconnaissance Office—you know, the guys who run the satellites. They have a camera bird that makes a pass over that area about every twelve hours. She's tasked them to look for anything that might give us a hint where he's gone. There are several old, deactivated Soviet military bases in that area. We've got them looking for any indication of recent activity—roads, traffic, new construction, anything like that. I don't think we're going to see that plane sitting out in the open."

Nelson shook his head. "That's for damn sure. I'll bet they had him under cover before his wheels stopped rolling."

When Bonior left the sick bay, he glanced frequently at a little map he had drawn before setting out, working his way back through the labyrinthine passageways, ladders, and decks of the huge ship to the small message-and-command center he had set up. As he entered, Rex Marker was busy typing a coded message to be transmitted by the ship's radio room. By doing their own coding and decoding, they could use the ship's crew for the actual transmission and receipt of messages without breach of security.

"Anything come in, Rex?"

"Might be something here, Chief. Mrs. Collins says there're signs of recent activity at an old, supposedly inactive airbase in the Kyzul-Kum Desert west of Urganch in Uzbekistan. Here, we've got the coordinates." He looked up at Bonior and grinned. "I wonder what Kyzul-Kum is like."

Bonior did not appreciate the double entendre. He glared at Marker: "Let's see where that is."

Marker called up the mapping software on his computer and

typed in the coordinates. Almost immediately, a map of Uz-bekistan began to unfurl itself down the screen.

"See that mark, looks like a little house? That's where the base is—at least, that's where these coordinates are. This software doesn't show details like military bases, but that gives us some idea of its location."

Bonior leaned down, peering over Marker's shoulder.

"Can you get any more detail?"

Marker clicked the down arrow with his mouse. "That takes us in closer, but there's really no detail there. That's right out in the middle of a desert. There are some low mountains off to the south, a dry riverbed to the west, and of course the Aral Sea, up here. But where we're looking, there's nothing to look at—just desert."

Bonior straightened up. "What about NSA? Are they getting any unusual communications traffic out of that place?"

"Mrs. Collins has them looking for it. But my guess is that they are running a pretty tight ship. They're probably using satcomm in short bursts, and that's almost impossible to pick up."

The tall chief stood with his arms folded across his chest, deep in thought.

"Can you get me through to Mrs. Collins?"

"Sure. We've got a secure phone right here. It goes through the ship's system, but it's encrypted on both ends." He picked up the phone and punched in the number of the Arizona base. "Mrs. Collins? Chief Bonior is here. He'd like to talk to you."

Bonior took the phone. "Pat, it looks like we've got ourselves a problem here."

Her voice came over with remarkable clarity, although with the slight delay caused by the time it took the message to travel to the satellite and back and halfway around the world. "I'm getting all the cooperation I could ask for. The chairman really put out the word."

"What do you think? Is the plane at that place in . . . what's it called? Uz . . . something?"

"We don't know, Jeff. But it's our best bet so far. I've just come across one interesting thing. I ran a computer check on some old Soviet records we've gotten access to since the Cold

War ended. You may be interested to know that our friend Sergei Kaparov is really Abdulkhashim Karimov. It may not mean anything, but it's interesting that he turns out to be an Uzbek, and we think the plane is now in Uzbekistan.''

"What other leads are you working?"

"Well, on the next pass, the satellite is going to focus in on this old airbase with photo, radar, and infrared coverage. That should help us see if there has been any recent activity there."

"Okay, good. Keep it up." Bonior was about to hand the handset back to Marker when he heard Collins's voice.

"Uh, Jeff . . . how is Chuck? Can you tell me what happened?"

With his concern for finding the missing plane, it had not occurred to Bonior to fill her in on Nelson's condition. But, now that he thought of it, they seemed to be pretty good friends.

"Oh, I'm sorry. I should have told you. He took a round in the shoulder—just at the edge of his body armor. He lost a lot of blood and we were pretty worried about him on the way back. But we got him to the carrier and he was operated on yesterday. The doc says he's doing fine. I saw him just a little while ago and he was complaining they wouldn't give him anything to eat but little pieces of ice. He should be back on the job in a few days."

"Thanks, Jeff. Tell him I . . . tell him I'm thinking of him."

"I'll do that, Pat. I'm going down to see him now, if I can find my way."

Bonior worked his way back through the carrier once more. He found Nelson sitting up in a chair, his cast supported by a pile of pillows. Nelson listened intently as the chief filled him in on what they knew and then sat staring at the wall for several minutes before he spoke.

"Jeff, I think we're going to have to go in there and see what's going on. Get together with Colonel Rattner and get the guys working on a plan. I don't want to jump in there . . . too much of a hassle getting back out again. See if you can find out what that desert is like. Can we land a Combat Talon and then work some of our people in close enough to get a look? Talk to Pat Collins and have her start putting together the intel we need: desert conditions, weather, approach and departure routes, the whole schmeer.''

Bonior took notes as Nelson talked. Then he snapped his notebook shut and rose to leave.

''And, Jeff . . . when you talk to Pat, tell her I . . . tell her I've been thinking about her.''

CHAPTER 15

"SENATOR WILSON. SIR, LET ME ASK YOU THIS: MANY PEOPLE are wondering how you can afford the expenses of a presidential campaign. You have even dispensed with Secret Service protection and have your own security people. Where is the money coming from?"

Wilson looked directly into the camera lens and smiled.

"I'm glad you asked that, Katie. You're right. I am not using the Secret Service, paid by the American taxpayers. I am not asking the taxpayers to pay to finance my campaign. I am not taking one dollar from the taxpayers. I am not accepting one cent from the interests—from tobacco, the banks, the insurance companies, from the telecommunications monopolies, from the so-called entertainment industry, from the big labor unions. No. Ask the other candidates where their dirty money comes from."

"But Senator, what I asked was . . ." Katie Couric normally had no problem forcing or cajoling guests on the *Today* show into answering her questions. But Wilson, with careful guidance from his media team, was an expert at sucking up every moment of air time and using it for his own purposes. He knew it would soon be time for the next commercial and the audience would be left thinking about what he had said and not about the unanswered question.

"The big problem in this country, as I see it, is the growth of these great, powerful conglomerates with their overpaid executives. Do you realize that the twenty highest-paid chief executive officers of American corporations are paid a total of more than a billion dollars a year? A billion dollars! At the same time they are slashing payrolls, laying off people, shipping jobs overseas. But are they cutting executive salaries? No! Their own salaries soar to obscene levels—money stolen from their workers. That is what the American people should be asking about.''

Katie Couric gave Wilson a wry smile. ''Thank you, Senator. I'm afraid our time is up.''

It was almost a year now since Wilson had first surfaced as a potential challenger to the president within his own party. His first tentative moves reminded veterans of the political wars of what had happened back in 1975, when Washington reporters began finding messages in their mailboxes from an obscure southern governor named Jimmy Carter. ''Jimmy who?'' they had asked themselves before dropping the letters into the trash.

Gradually, they'd heard more and more from Jimmy. And the next thing they knew, he had garnered enough primary victories to win the Democratic nomination, scoring a surprising victory over other, better-known members of his party.

Until Wilson began his campaign, he had been an obscure member of the Senate—a first-termer from a small western state with no important committee assignments—the kind of assignments most senators treasured because they were a great source of campaign contributions and because they were the key to, as they put it, ''getting things done'' for the folks back home.

Wilson's secret was to understand that the rules had changed. It was no longer important to be a loyal party member, gradually working your way up to a position of prominence. Even being perceived as a successful senator could be a disadvantage: you were seen as part of the Washington ''system.'' In the course of a year, with the astute use of paid commercials and as much free air time as he could garner, Wilson had made himself a major player on the national scene with a stridently populist message that was both simplistic and remarkably effective.

Now, with the party conventions coming up, it was hard to

turn on the television without seeing a smiling Dick Wilson, with his glib one-liners, attacking Washington, the "interests," Big Industry, Big Unions, Big Government—and President Maynard Walker. The insiders still didn't give Wilson much of a chance to topple the president in the party convention, but they weren't counting him out, either.

At the White House, Walker clicked off the sound on the TV and walked next door to the cabinet room. It was 8 A.M., time for the weekly meeting of his political advisers, the so-called Tuesday Breakfast Group.

Seating himself at the center of the oblong table, Walker said, to no one in particular: "Couric asked the right question. But he never answers. Where does he get the money?"

The president focused on an aide sitting back against the wall on the other side of the table. "Any dope yet, Tony?"

"No sir. But we've got some rough figures on what he's spending, and it is impressive. He's spending a lot of money in every state where there are still delegates up for grabs. He's got a slick operation. Before we can catch up with one lie or misrepresentation, he's got a new spot running."

The president shook his head. This was not the way things were supposed to be going. He had started early on this campaign—very early. His goal was to lock up all the important money as quickly as possible to head off a challenge from within his own party and spare himself the need to fight, state by state, to win in the primaries. And he had begun spending money early to position himself for the general election. But his effort to freeze out challengers had not worked with Wilson. He had some mysterious source of funds and he just kept spending.

With rare exceptions, presidential candidates work hard to qualify for federal funds—the money taxpayers provide by checking the box on their income tax returns that asks if they want to contribute three dollars to support presidential candidates. When they accept federal funds, candidates are required to make periodic reports on the money they have raised and how they have spent it. The law is full of loopholes, but the reports filed with the Federal Elections Commission give at least some information about where a candidate gets his money—and whom he is beholden to.

As Richard Wilson boasted at every opportunity, he had not taken any federal funds and did not accept any contributions to his campaign. He claimed to be financing everything out of his own pocket, and no law required him to say anything more.

The closest Wilson had come to dealing with the subject was when he appeared as a guest on one of the more contentious Washington talk shows.

"Senator," he was asked, "you claim to be financing this campaign from your own funds. Senator, where did you get all that money?"

"Let me say, in answer to that question . . ."

Another panel member broke in. Every residue of courtesy had been left at the studio door. "Senator, why don't you let us look at your income tax returns? President and Mrs. Walker have routinely made theirs available."

"Did you ever hear of the right of privacy . . ."

"Privacy!" Another panel member almost shouted. "Didn't you know that presidential candidates have no privacy? C'mon. Tell us where your money is coming from. Let us see your tax returns."

"I am under no obligation to make my private finances public. It is enough to say that I have been extremely fortunate in the investments I have made."

"So you refuse to, one, tell us where your money is coming from, and two let us see your income tax returns. Is that the bottom line?" The first panelist leaned forward, almost seeming to snarl his questions.

Wilson, as he often did, simply looked past the panelists directly into the camera and spoke to the audience.

"I think the American people are quite satisfied to have a candidate who is not beholden to any special interest and who is not taking one cent of public funds to finance his campaign. Why don't you ask the other candidates why they have taken millions in taxpayer dollars and, on top of that, have sold themselves to the very interests who threaten the future of our country? Ask them that!''

''Well spoken, Senator, well spoken.'' Luke Nash emitted a low, mirthless chuckle and clicked off the small television set on a corner of his large desk. Nash had a clear memory of the one and only time he and Senator Wilson had met face-to-face.

It was just a little over a year ago, now. Wilson had caught Nash's eye some months before. When he received a report on the senator from his staff, he was impressed with what he saw: a man with a pleasing personality who exuded a certain star quality on television; a man with unlimited ambition—an ambition that probably outstripped his talents; and, perhaps most important, a man with a very flexible moral compass, willing to do almost anything to further his ambitions.

When they met in the Colorado Springs compound, Nash came quickly to the point: ''Senator, I have been watching you, and I am impressed. I see you as a man destined for high office—much higher than the office you now hold. Will I surprise you if I say I see you as a future president of the United States?''

Wilson swelled almost visibly. ''Oh, that's far beyond my . . . do you really think so?''

Nash leaned forward. Wilson could not see the eyes behind the dark glasses but he could sense them burning into him like twin lasers. ''Yes, I do. President Wilson! President Richard Wilson! How does that sound?''

Wilson beamed. ''It sounds . . . well, it sounds good . . . good.''

''You have the talent, the experience, the television presence—all the makings of a successful candidate.''

Wilson nodded.

''What you lack is money. A lot of money.''

Wilson nodded more energetically.

''Now,'' Nash continued, ''what I would like to propose is that I make it possible for you to obtain the money you need.

I'm not going to give you money. What I *am* going to do is make you an extremely successful investor. With my guidance, you are going to become, very rapidly, a very wealthy man. If anyone asks where your money came from—and they *will ask*—you can simply say that you have been very, very fortunate in your choice of investments.''

Wilson smiled but he also shifted uneasily in his chair.

"And . . . ?" he asked. "And the strings?"

Nash's thin lips spread in a tight little smile. "No strings, Senator. Let's just call this my contribution to good government in gratitude for all this great country has done for me."

"When something seems too good to be true, I've found that it usually is," Wilson replied. "Really? No strings? No special legislation? No ambassadorship? Not even a night in the Lincoln bedroom?"

"My own bedroom is quite adequate, thank you. No, Senator, there are no strings. Let's just say that your candidacy and your election will also serve my purposes. All I ask you to do is run hard and win. Run hard and win! Is this acceptable to you? Do we have a deal?"

Wilson nodded. "Deal."

"Fine. Now, Senator, I am an arbitrageur. You're familiar with the term, I assume. What I do, to put it simply, is to buy low and sell high on the world market. Many of my transactions are in currencies, but I also deal in many other commodities. This is a very demanding and very risky business— and also very rewarding if it is done right. I won't expect you to master the art of arbitrage. What I will do is to have my people set up some accounts for you. You will contribute a small amount to begin the operation. Then we will trade for you. You will be pleased at the results."

Wilson shrugged. "Sounds okay to me. As you know, I am not a wealthy man."

"Yes, I know. But that doesn't matter. You will soon be a wealthy man—an extremely wealthy man."

Nash glanced at the watch on his wrist and pressed a button on the edge of his desk.

An aide appeared at the door almost immediately.

"My people will get things set up for you. Thanks for your

time, Senator.'' Nash turned his attention to the papers on his desk as though Wilson had suddenly vanished.

The senator sat for a moment, puzzled. He wasn't used to being dismissed so abruptly. He looked around and then rose and joined the aide at the door.

CHAPTER 16

NELSON WAS GETTING SICK OF HIS CAST, WHICH HELD HIS ARM UP away from his body and immobilized his shoulder. Every time he moved, it seemed, he banged into something. He shifted uneasily in his chair, trying to get comfortable while still remaining close enough to the table to make laborious notes with his left hand.

The flight surgeon had complained that Nelson was not ready to move. But as soon as the *Stennis* reached the Central Mediterranean, the SEAL commander insisted on being flown to Sigonella and then quickly on to Arizona. He still felt weak and found he had to make time for a nap every afternoon, but it was good to be back on his own home ground.

Tacked up on a wall opposite from where Nelson sat was a large map of Uzbekistan and the surrounding countries. To the south were Turkmenistan and Afghanistan. To the north and west was Kazakhstan. To the west were Kyrgyzstan and Tadzhikistan. Uzbekistan and all the other ''-stans'' except Afghanistan were newly independent parts of the old Soviet Union. A large part of the northwestern portion of Uzbekistan was taken up by the bed of the Aral Sea, which had been rapidly shrinking as farmers had drained off water from the Amudar River to water their crops.

Nelson glanced around the table. Rattner and Laffer, the two Air Force pilots, were there, along with two of their Special Tactics men. Bonior and Marker, the team's communications expert, sat to Nelson's right.

"This is the area we're looking at right now." Pat Collins stood near the map, indicating a spot in the Uzebekistan desert. "We're not sure that's where the plane is, but it seems the likeliest place."

Nelson turned to Rattner. "What do you think, Mark? Can we get in there with a Combat Talon or a Pave Low for a little look-see?"

"I dunno, Chuck. It's going to be tough. As you can see, we don't have a lot of real good friends in that area: Iran? Afghanistan? Russia? Forget about it. We might be able to stage out of Turkey, but Turkey is going through some difficult times politically right now. We've always pretty much gotten along with their military people, but I'm not sure they would welcome any more problems at the moment. And staging an operation out of one of their airbases would be a problem.

"I guess our other alternative is to see if we can work something out with one of the small Persian Gulf states. Some of them—Oman, for example—have been very helpful in the past, so long as we didn't advertise what was going on. But as you can see from the map, to get from down there along the Gulf up to Uzbekistan involves flying over Iran or Iraq or even Afghanistan. I don't think we want to do that."

Nelson shook his head and stared at the map.

"Well, say we could find a staging area. Do you think we could land a bird in that desert and get back out again?"

"We could certainly get a Pave Low in and out. But you're talking about a big logistics operation with at least a couple of refuelings both going and coming. A C-130? I'm not sure. We'd almost have to get someone in there on the ground to take a look at the desert, test the soil, and see if it will support a plane that big. What do we know about the desert, Pat?"

"As far as we know, it's just sand. If there's a wind, it's blowing sand. And there are dunes."

Rattner shook his head. "Not good, Chuck. We could get bogged down in that stuff and then we'd have a real problem on our hands."

"Sir." Rex Marker, the youngest and most junior man at the table, broke the silence. "Sir, I have an idea."

Nelson, his concentration disturbed, turned awkwardly to stare at Marker. His question was abrupt: "Yes?"

"Sir, why don't we go as tourists? Fly in to one of those cities there, like Samarkand or Tashkent, rent a van, and go check the place out?"

Nelson looked at Marker and then at Rattner and finally broke into a grin: "Out of the mouths of babes . . ."

"Okay, Rex, keep talking."

"It would be easy, sir. We can say we've come to photograph the dunes or look for traces of the old caravan route through that area. We bring along our cameras and our binoculars. Then we just drive up there, sneak out in the night, and look this place over. We give you a report and fly home."

"How big an operation are you talking about?" Bonior broke in.

"Not big. Maybe four guys. We can even put on a little cover operation. I speak German and so does one of the Air Force guys. We fly in from Germany and say we're German. Nobody's going to guess who we are or why we're there."

Nelson stared at him for a moment. "Not bad. Not bad at all. Okay, let's do it."

That night after dinner, Nelson drew Pat Collins aside. "Pat, would you like to go for a drive in the desert?"

She smiled. "Good idea. Let me get a sweater and I'll be right with you."

Nelson found the keys to one of the base pickup trucks and handed them to Collins. "I guess I could try to drive with this thing on, but I'd better not." She took the keys, opened the door on the passenger side, and helped him fit himself into the seat.

Even in the darkness, the heat of the summer sun radiated up from the earth, but there was the first hint of the evening's coolness in the air as they drove to the top of a nearby hill. Far off in the distance, they could see the glow of the lights of Tucson and the looming presence of the Santa Catalina Mountains. "Why don't we stop here for a few minutes?" Nelson asked.

Collins laughed. "How romantic. Parking in a Navy pickup."

"I guess we sailors take our romance where we can find it," Nelson laughed. "Want to take a little walk?"

Except for the sound of an airliner far overhead, it was absolutely still. The delicate aroma of the desert, a mixture of sage and dry sand, reached their nostrils as they walked hand-in-hand along the side of the road.

"This *is* kind of romantic. You know, I've always been a sea person. But in the short time we've been out here, I've grown to love the desert. I like the way it changes its appearance in the different light, from dawn to dusk, from day to day." She took a deep breath. "I even like the way it smells."

"Yeah, me too . . . you know, there's something else I like."

She turned to look at his face, only faintly visible in the darkness. "What's that?"

He hesitated a moment. "I like . . . I like you."

Her grip on his fingers tightened. "Oh, Chuck, that's sweet."

"Ever since we first came out here, I've been thinking about you . . . thinking about us . . ."

"I think I know how you feel, Chuck. I guess I've been thinking, too. I've been thinking about us."

"Thinking what?"

"Well, Jim and I didn't have too much time together. I loved him, but I now realize that I also loved being married. I liked the feeling of having someone who was mine. The feeling of belonging to someone. I miss Jim . . . miss him a lot. But I also miss that feeling."

Nelson was quiet as they walked hand-in-hand. Then he said, "I think I can understand what you're talking about. I've always been a bachelor. I've seen too many guys who tried to divide their love between a wife and the teams—and the teams won. The shores at Coronado and Little Creek are littered with wrecked marriages. I guess I just felt it wasn't fair to a woman to do that to her."

"And yet there are also many happy marriages. My marriage to Jim was a happy one, even though I worried every time he went on an op. And we have two wonderful children to remind me of him.''

"I really like your kids, Pat."

Still holding his hand, she turned and started back toward the pickup. She gave him a sideways look. "Chuck, I'm confused. I really don't know what I want. I like you, but I guess I'm kind of scared, too. I still haven't gotten over the loss of Jim—maybe I never will. Why don't we just kind of play this by ear and see how it works out?"

"That's another thing I like about you," he said. "You're a sensible woman. The way I'm beginning to feel about you, I'm not sure a sensible woman is what I want. But I think you're right. Let's play it by ear."

She helped him back into the pickup and drove slowly back down to the base.

CHAPTER 17

AS THE ILYUSHIN AIRLINER CIRCLED FOR A LANDING AT TASH-kent, the four young men peered out the window at the dramatically contrasting landscape. To the east was the Chatkal range of mountains. To the west was the featureless expanse of the Kyzul-Kum Desert. Rex Marker strained as the plane turned to keep the mountains in his view: if he had his choice and it were a little later in the year, he would be heading in that direction on a skiing expedition rather than driving out into the heat of the desert.

During their stopover in Frankfurt, the four men had been provided with a full set of documents: German passports and drivers' licenses, receipts from German stores, and German credit cards. Most important, each carried a properly endorsed invitation to visit the country from the Uzbek government. Although the new country had begun to adopt some western ways since the breakup of the Soviet Union, it still kept a careful eye on who visited the country and why. Without an invitation in hand, a would-be visitor would find himself on the next plane back to where he'd come from.

As they had expected, the line through the customs and immigration checkpoints was both long and slow-moving. But they had carefully scheduled their trip to allow plenty of time for such delays. The last thing they needed was a hassle with officials at the border. The officials spoke a little English, but no German. That relieved the two men who did not speak fluent German from the need to attempt to fake their way through the immigration process.

Once outside, the four obvious westerners were quickly surrounded by cab drivers shouting for their attention. One man in the rear of the crowd muscled his way toward the front and shouted in English: "Visit the sights of Samarkand! Visit the sights of Samarkand!"

The cab driver had olive skin, dark eyes, and a massive black mustache. Perched on his head at a jaunty angle was a Chicago Bulls cap.

Marker grabbed him by the shoulder: "Are you the expert on Samarkand?"

The man grinned. "I am the expert on Samarkand."

The phrase "expert on Samarkand" was the password the team had been told would help them identify their contact.

"This is our man," Marker said, handing him his bag. The other three fell in line behind him and headed toward a decrepit old Soviet-built cab.

The cab driver jammed as much of their luggage as he could into the trunk and then stuffed the rest inside on their laps.

Pulling out of the airport traffic toward downtown Tashkent, he introduced himself: "I'm Johnnie, the Chicago kid."

Marker introduced himself: "I'm Rex. Behind you are Tom Shoup, Tim Hutchins, and Ray Pratt. You've been to Chicago?"

"Yeah. Five years. That's where I learned English and how to drive a cab." He swerved sharply, cutting in front of a car whose decrepit condition was signaled by a cloud of oily smoke pouring from its exhaust.

"What's the plan, Johnnie?"

"I'll take you down to the Uzbekistan Hotel. It's the best in town and badly overpriced. The rooms are small but clean. Shower, no bath. Maybe air conditioning, maybe not. Today's Saturday. I'll pick you up in the morning and we'll go shopping."

The next morning, Johnnie was waiting as promised when the foursome emerged from the hotel. Marker carried his laptop computer and a small global positioning system receiver. With them he could pinpoint their location and navigate accurately from one point to the next. He wasn't taking any chances leaving such valuable equipment in the hotel room.

"You've got dollars?" Johnnie asked.

"Yeah, lots of dollars. Why, what are we going to buy?"

"You'll see pretty quick." Johnnie navigated them out of the downtown area and onto the road toward Samarkand. As they approached the outskirts of Tashkent, they saw a large hippodrome.

Johnnie found a place beside the curb and parked near a large open lot covered with scores of vehicles in various stages of repair—or, in many cases, disrepair. There was at least one representative of every vehicle that had rolled off a Soviet production line in the last quarter century, from little Fiat-like cars and motorcycles to large trucks, plus a smattering of vehicles that had somehow made their way here from the West.

"Welcome to the Tashkent Sunday morning *avtobazar*," Johnnie exclaimed, waving his arm to take in the scene.

"Is this where people go instead of church?" asked Shoup.

"Well, not really. Since this is an Islamic country, our holy day is Saturday instead of Sunday. But yes, a lot of people worship here—in a way."

Scores of men wandered through the narrow spaces between the vehicles. Here and there, men bargained intently.

"Okay, let's see if we can find some good transportation for you. You need something that will be reliable and big enough to carry you and your equipment." Johnnie led the way.

"Yeah, what we really need is something like a Land Rover. But a van of some sort will probably be okay. We also want to find some dirt bikes. Do you think we can find something like that?" Marker asked.

"If we don't find it, we'll get somebody to go get what we want," Johnnie replied. "You'd be surprised what you can buy if you start waving a few dollars around. Cash speaks here, and dollars speak loudest of all."

Their search was simplified by the fact that what they were

looking for was a fairly bulky vehicle, one that stood out above the roofs of the smaller cars.

"How about this one?" Johnnie asked, stopping beside a faded green Volkswagen bus of indeterminate age.

The four men walked around it. Tim Hutchins bent down to look at the tires. Pratt inspected the tiny engine.

"I dunno, Johnnie . . ." Pratt was not impressed.

They moved on.

"Here's something," Shoup said, leading the way to a big tan Chevrolet Suburban with a sunroof.

"That's better," Marker said, opening the door and sliding into the driver's seat. Depressing the clutch, he moved the shift through the gears, pumping the brake pedal with his right foot. "What do you think?"

"Oh, yeah, this is great!" Pratt exclaimed. "My dad had one of these—before I was born. The tires are pretty shitty, but it's the best thing we've seen."

"Don't worry about the tires," Johnnie broke in. "I'll take care of that. I've got a friend and I'll have him look it over for you. He's not going to make it like new, but he'll replace the radiator hoses and the fanbelt, put in some spark plugs, stuff like that."

The owner hovered nearby, keeping up a constant sales talk in Uzbek.

"You want it?" Johnnie looked around. The four men nodded. "Okay, let me handle this."

He spoke rapidly to the man in Uzbek, both of them gesticulating with their hands. Finally, he turned to the Americans. "Have you got eleven hundreds? Give them to him."

Marker handed over the money and then the two Uzbeks leaned on the hood of the truck making out the paperwork for the sale.

"You guys can't drive until we get the van licensed. Once we get that done, your international drivers' licenses will be all you need. He'll take the van over to my friend's place and let him get to work on it. Come on, let's see if we can find some bikes."

They worked their way across the lot and finally found four bikes in reasonable condition. Marker paid the owners and

Johnnie arranged for them to be picked up later.

As they drove back toward the hotel, Johnnie filled them in. "It's going to take about three days to get the paperwork done to transfer the titles. You can poke around town. You'll see that much of the town is new. It was pretty much leveled in an earthquake thirty years ago. You can see the big TV tower from your hotel. You might want to walk down there and get a good view of the city. It doesn't look like much now, but there's a lot of history here and several fairly good museums, if you like that kind of thing."

"Yeah, we're real museum-type people." Marker laughed. "Johnnie, you know there are some other things we're going to need?"

"Yeah, I know. But we don't have a Sunday morning market for machine guns. I'll do a little shopping for you. But that's no problem. With soldiers selling off their weapons and the Afghanistan war just across the border, there are so many guns floating around this place it's a wonder you don't stumble over them in the street. Four AK-47s, four pistols, and ammo? That be okay?"

"How about a box of grenades and at least a couple grenade launchers?" Marker asked.

"No problem. You guys enjoy yourselves." Johnnie pulled up in front of the hotel. "I'll be in touch."

They spent Monday and Tuesday working their way through the paperwork, getting clear title to the van and the bikes. It was worth the delay to make sure there'd be no hitches with curious officials down the road. By Tuesday evening, they were ready to depart early the next morning.

When Johnnie arrived at the hotel driving the Suburban, they could see he had been busy. Two of their motorbikes were lashed to the top of the van, one had been jammed inside, and one was tied to the rear. Johnnie's friend had added a frame on the rear which held half a dozen twenty-liter jerry cans of gas.

Johnnie handed the keys to Rex. "You'll need those," he

said, gesturing toward the cans. "You're not going to find any gas stations where you're going . . . wherever that is."

The Uzbek had been given detailed instructions by his intelligence contacts. He had been told everything he needed to know—but nothing more. He did not need to know exactly where the Americans were going or why they were going there.

Johnnie drew Rex aside. "There's some space under the floorboards in the rear. The stuff you wanted is hidden there. You've got AKs, ammo, grenades. The pistols are old Soviet Army issue, not the best, but not bad. I even picked up some silencers for you."

"Good man, Johnnie. Al Capone would be proud of the Chicago Kid." Rex clapped him on the back.

"Al Cap . . . oh, yeah, the famous gangster. Right!"

During their stay in Tashkent, the team members had carefully studied a detailed map of the area and made careful mental notes of their route. They did not mark the map, just in case it might fall into someone else's hands.

The first stage of their trip took them west toward Samarkand on the four-lane M39 highway. But they decided not to take the direct route, which cut across a tiny corner of Turkmenistan. Instead, they detoured off to the left on the M34 through Gulistan and then took the M376 back onto the M39. That kept them safely within Uzbekistan the whole way. No sense taking chances on a possible search and discovery of their small arsenal by border agents.

The road to Samarkand was not bad, but with the detour it was a long, 350-kilometer ride. It was late in the evening when they rolled into the city, once a fabulous trading post on the legendary caravan route between China and the West. They had to use a map to find their way to the center of town and the Hotel Zerafshan, where they had made a reservation. Unlike western cities, with their bright streetlights and neon signs, there was no glow in the sky to point the way to downtown. Rex, who was at the wheel, had the feeling that the end of the world might be just beyond the dim rays from their parking lights. Johnnie had warned them not to take a chance on getting picked up by the police by keeping their brights on once they entered the city.

None of the four looked forward to the drive scheduled for Thursday. It would be a long, dull, hot day. Their route took them west to the little town of Navoi about ninety miles, and then out through the desert another 165 miles to the even smaller town of Uckuduk. Looking over the map the evening before, they decided to allow about six hours of driving time, plus another hour for good measure. If they wanted to reach Uckuduk about dusk, that meant leaving their hotel in the early afternoon.

Taking turns driving, they tried to hold the speedometer at a steady fifty miles an hour—not so much because of fear of speed cops, of which there probably weren't any, as for concern for the fragile nature of their aging van.

With the windows and the sunroof open, bathed in the blistering desert air, they could almost feel their skin and bodies drying. In addition to the extra fuel cans, they had also added a five-gallon container of water. On the front of the van they hung two large canvas bags of water. Evaporation from the canvas kept the water inside remarkably cool.

At several points along the way, they pulled over to the side of the road to drink from one of the canvas bags and stretch their legs. After the roar of the vehicle engine, the silence of the desert was almost overwhelming. The only sound was the faint whisper, almost a song, as the breeze gently caressed the sand.

At the last rest stop, Marker checked his watch.

"We're doing great. Right on time. We'll slip through that little town up there and it will be good and dark when we get to the base."

"How much farther from the town to the base?" Hutchins asked.

"Our satellite images show seventy-six klicks to the eastern perimeter of the base. It stretches along the road for about ten miles to the western fence line. I'm allowing about an hour from the town. . . . Okay, ready to go?"

The four men climbed back into the van and tried to get as comfortable as possible for the last stretch of their trip.

Uckuduk seemed almost deserted as they rolled slowly through town. Lights glimmered from a few windows but there wasn't a soul to be seen on the streets.

"Just as well," Marker thought. He hoped that no one had made note of the heavily laden van with its four passengers as it turned and headed west into the darkness of the desert.

Marker was at the wheel on this last stretch, watching the odometer as it reeled off the kilometers. As the distance from the town approached fifty kilometers, he switched off the lights and stopped beside the road until his eyes had become accustomed to the dark. Then he moved forward again, peering ahead for the first indication they were near the base.

Off to the right, in the distance, he spotted an upright post. As he got closer, he could see the sign atop the post carried the picture of a camera with a slash across it.

"No photographs," Marker thought. "Well, we'll see about that."

Up ahead, he saw a dip in the road where the view in both directions was obstructed by hulking dunes. Pulling off to the side of the road, he stopped while Shoup got out and walked up the little valley created by the dunes. He returned after a moment: "Okay, Rex. It's plenty solid."

Marker drove slowly up the shallow gully, far enough so the van would not be spotted by anyone passing on the road.

The four men dismounted from the van and quickly unloaded the dirt bike crammed into the rear of the van and the one attached to the back, working by the dim light of flashlights shielded with red lenses. They then pulled up the floorboards to uncover the little arsenal Johnnie had prepared for them. Each took an AK-47 and a pistol, checked them over carefully, and loaded them. Johnnie said he had cleaned and oiled the weapons, and they were happy to see he had done a good job. Two of the men took a grenade launcher each and a supply of grenades. Working silently, they smeared their faces and the backs of their hands with dull green camouflage paint.

Each man was equipped with a small radio with an earphone

and microphone to permit hands-free operation. They would use the radios only in emergency, and then only in coded messages that would be on the air for just a fraction of a second.

"Okay, we're all set. Tom, you and Ray take the van down to the other end of the base. You know what you're supposed to do: move in there, and if we need it, create a diversion. Then you come back by here with the van and we'll be waiting for you."

"Hooyah!" Pratt exclaimed.

"Hooyah? What are you talking about?" asked Shoup, the lead Special Tactics man.

Marker laughed. "Oh, that's just SEAL talk, Tom. Don't worry about it. He'll get over it."

Shoup backed the van carefully out onto the road—not that there was any traffic to be worried about—and headed slowly west, driving without lights.

Marker and Hutchins mounted their bikes, crossed the road, and drove slowly up the gully between the dunes. What their bikes lacked in power, their little engines made up in silence. They emitted only a little more sound than a bicycle.

The two men had studied satellite photos of the base for hours, measuring distances, looking for obstacles, trying to gauge the time from one point to the next.

Marker raised his right arm directly above his head and then swept it down in an arc to point to his right. Hutchins followed as they turned toward the perimeter fence. Looming in the darkness beyond the fence, they could just make out the shape of the large, sand-covered hangar that was their target.

Guard towers stood at two corners on the east side of the compound. A searchlight on each tower rotated so that their beams intersected at a point on the fence halfway between the two towers. The two men hid their bikes behind a mound of sand and then worked their way to the top of the dune where they lay prone, timing the two circles of light. As the lights swung toward them, they shut their eyes to preserve their night vision.

Hutchins broke the silence. "There's a zone of darkness between those two cones. We can get almost to the fence before we can be seen. And then . . . what do you figure? About thirty seconds of darkness after one beam passes until the next one hits that point? Not much time.''

''No, we've got time. We'll crawl up there and cut the fence while it's dark. We should be able to cut it in two periods of darkness, say forty seconds. Then we go through in the next period of darkness. Simple. You know, the fact they're using searchlights is probably a break for us. It means they're not using night vision goggles.''

Marker checked his watch. ''Let's stay here another twenty minutes. That'll give Tom and Ray time to get into position. Let's see what kind of security op they have here.''

He put a small pair of binoculars to his eyes and began sweeping them across the compound. He finally handed them to Hutchins.

''Holy shit! Look at what they've got there. Looks like they're expecting World War III.''

Hutchins studied the compound for several minutes. While he did, Marker spoke softly into his microphone, recording what he had seen into a small tape recorder. He had counted half a dozen anti-aircraft guns along this side of the compound alone. A circular array indicated the site of a surface-to-air missile battery. Beyond the hangar was a barracks area large enough to accommodate at least a battalion of infantry. Beside the hangar was a parking area filled with armored vehicles. On the runway, he could see several helicopters, although he could not tell how many there were.

The two men glanced frequently from side to side, as they had been trained. This focused the little available light on the cones to the sides of their eyes rather than on the rods in the center of their eyes, enabling them to see better in the dark. They had reluctantly left their night vision goggles at home to avoid having to explain them as they passed through customs.

''Okay, let's get started,'' Marker said, after glancing at his watch. He moved quickly down the dune and ran toward the fence while the lights were sweeping away from them. Hutchins followed closely behind. As the lights swung toward them, they dropped and hugged the sand.

It took five dashes to reach the fence. When they were about fifty feet away, they stopped and lay on the sand as the lights flashed past. Marker pulled a small pair of bolt cutters from his pocket. He dashed forward another thirty feet and then dropped. In the next period of darkness, he reached the fence and quickly began cutting two sides of a rectangular hole, leaving the wire at the top untouched.

As the lights swung toward him once more, he retreated back from the fence and lay flat in the sand. In the next period of darkness, he finished the hole and pushed the wire through so it hinged at the top, creating a small opening. He retreated once more and then he and Hutchins darted through the hole in the next period of darkness. Marker turned and pushed the wire back in place. He pressed a scrap of paper over one protruding wire end to mark the hole for their retreat. Anyone seeing the paper would think it had been lodged there by the wind.

Most of the area from the fence to the hangar was left in the dark as the searchlights atop the guard towers circled. Marker and Hutchins ran forward, stopped, moved to one side, ran, stopped, moved, quickly covering the distance toward the hangar in the brief periods of darkness between sweeps of the searchlights. Both knew that if they jumped the gun even by a second, if they were at all impatient, they could be discovered and so doom the mission.

They aimed toward the rear corner of the huge building. Since sand had been banked up against the sides to camouflage the structure, they would have to go to one end or the other to try to peer inside.

Both men advanced with their pistols in hand, silencers attached. At the corner, Hutchins guarded the rear while Marker peered around the corner. The area was dimly lighted. Marker could see no one along the entire rear of the building. They waited five minutes. Still no one. Marker slipped around the corner and motioned Hutchins to follow.

They crept along the wall of the building. Marker paused and pointed upward. There was a row of windows. But the sills were seven feet off the ground. Marker pulled out his digital camera and slung it around his neck. Then he motioned to Hutchins to boost him toward the window. Hutchins braced his back against the wall, held his hands cupped in front of him. Marker put one foot in his cupped hands and vaulted to his shoulders. The Air Force man remained crouched, his pistol grasped in both hands, watching for any sign of movement along the wall.

The windows were shaded, but Marker was able to see through a crack. Inside he saw the immense bulk of the bomber, its tail rising so tall it almost touched the roof. A number of men were at work on the plane, some climbing in and out through the wheel well, others on tall scaffoldings, apparently checking the engines and the aircraft surfaces.

With his digital camera set on infinity, Marker carefully braced it against the window ledge and snapped a series of pictures. He didn't know enough about the plane to tell what was happening, but perhaps the experts could tell when they saw the pictures.

Then he noticed a familiar face among those in the hangar. Before he could get a better look, Marker was jolted and almost lost his balance as Hutchins shifted suddenly to the right and fired a single shot from his silenced pistol. A soldier, apparently a guard on patrol, had appeared around the corner and shouted in Russian. Hutchins's shot caught him square in the forehead, but the man's AK-47, set on automatic, released a burst of shots as he fell.

The sound of the rifle seemed to Marker to be the loudest noise he had ever heard.

He jumped to the ground, and motioning Hutchins to follow, ran around the end of the building and dashed toward the hole in the fence.

As they ran, a loud siren began to wail and they could hear the throaty roar as armored personnel carriers came to life. Bright lights suddenly illuminated both ends of the hangar.

The two Americans thought as they ran that the lights might be to their advantage. The guard force would not know which way they had gone and would have difficulty seeing beyond the glare of the lights.

Maybe we can make it, Marker thought to himself. As he ran, panting, toward the fence, he clicked on his radio and barked one word: "Firestorm!"

Lying in the sand on the other side of the compound, Shoup and Pratt heard the message.

"Oh, shit. We've got problems," Shoup exclaimed.

Attaching the grenade launcher to the muzzle of his rifle, he aimed at the guard tower on one corner and fired. As he did so, Pratt fired at the other guard tower. Quickly the two men fired again, aiming at the fence between the two towers. They didn't really hope to cause much damage, but they were sure they were causing a lot of confusion among those guarding the base.

As the flash of the grenades lit up the fence, the two men dashed back toward their bikes, hidden behind a nearby dune. They raced back to the van, ditched the bikes, and roared down the road toward the pickup point for Marker and Hutchins.

They drove with lights out, hoping that the guards were so busy looking in other directions that they would not notice a vehicle passing on the otherwise deserted road.

As they approached the pickup point, they saw Marker and Hutchins crouched beside the road. Shoup slowed, but kept rolling as the two men climbed in.

As Shoup shifted into second gear and jammed his foot down on the throttle, the sound of their engine was drowned out by the distinctive clop-clop-clop of a helicopter's rotor.

"We've got company," Marker muttered, as he rose and pulled open the sunroof. He and Hutchins stood in the opening, their AK-47s at the ready. The helicopter came slowly along the roadway, its searchlight swinging back and forth. Suddenly they were caught in the light. The muzzle flash of the nose-mounted machine gun lit up the night. And then there was the light of the tracers chewing their way up the roadway toward the van.

Hutchins and Marker fired. Hutchins aimed for the cockpit, Marker for the rotor. Bullets hammered the top of the van inches from the two men. And then the chopper veered away, swerving out of control. In the dim light, the men in the van could sense the pilot fighting to bring the craft down as gently as possible in a semi-controlled crash landing. The crew of the chopper had suddenly lost all interest in pursuit of the van.

"Man! That was close!" Pratt exclaimed.

"Okay," Marker said, "let's get this thing up there." He handed a small satellite antenna to Hutchins to attach to the edge of the roof.

Marker began dictating a report into his computer. He was thankful for this new software that would convert his spoken words into written words.

"The aircraft is in the hangar. Photos follow. The base is heavily guarded, with anti-aircraft guns and missiles. There may be as many as a battalion of guards. They have APCs and helicopters.

"Note: I saw Dick Hoffman in the hangar. He's in that outfit Big Dog Bernard organized. They are probably in charge of the guard force.

"Desert surface appears too soft for C-one-three-oh. Bringing samples of sand."

Marker then took his digital camera and downloaded the images into the computer. When both his written report and the pictures were ready, he transmitted the entire package in a brief electronic burst that traveled to a satellite and quickly back down to the team headquarters in Arizona.

Marker sat back in the seat and covered his eyes with his hand. It had been a tense few minutes. But his thoughts were far away, at another time and another place.

It was in the summer, three years ago. Marker and Hoffman had gone through BUD/S together and been assigned to the same team. They were not only swim buddies, but also had become best friends. It was only natural that they had both been selected at the same time to attend the SEALs' high-altitude jump school at El Centro, California.

They had been through the Army's jump school at Fort Benning, Georgia, and considered themselves experienced parachutists. But this was something different. Ground school was intermixed with jumps that gradually increased in difficulty.

On the first couple of free-fall jumps, an instructor goes with the student, holding onto his webbing. Then the student learns to free-fall by himself and gradually adds more equipment.

The class was getting close to graduation that day in July and all of the students were feeling pretty cocky. Suddenly, as they were still climbing toward altitude, the alarm bells in the plane rang and the lights flashed. The instructors anxiously signaled to the students to jump as quickly as possible. Within seconds, they were out the door and into the bright California sunshine.

In his hurry to get out, Marker jumped too close behind the man in front. As he jumped, the other man's foot came up and around and slammed into his shoulder, hard.

The force of the blow caused Marker to begin to rotate, almost like an airplane out of control in a tailspin. One arm hung useless, apparently paralyzed by the blow. The other arm seemed to be immobilized by centrifugal force.

Marker began to spin faster and faster. Hoffman, who had followed Marker out the door, was about to pull his ripcord when he realized his buddy was in serious trouble. Pulling his arms in tight against his body, he streamlined himself and dived toward Marker. Marker's spinning motion caused him to fall slightly slower than Hoffman, so Hoffman was able to get below him. Then he spread his arms, slowed to Marker's speed, and "flew" in carefully toward his spinning body. There was no sense getting himself hurt or knocked out in the process.

He reached out, snagged Marker's parachute harness to stop his spinning, and then drew him toward him.

"How you doing, buddy?"

Marker did not respond. He was unconscious.

Hoffman checked his altimeter: three thousand feet. Only a few seconds to act.

Hoffman pulled Marker's ripcord and held on until he saw the chute begin to deploy. Then he pushed Marker away and pulled his own ripcord. His chute had barely blossomed above him when he hit the sand of the desert floor. Marker drifted down a short distance away. Hoffman quickly loosened his chute and ran to knock the air out of Marker's chute before he was dragged away.

Ever since that day, Marker had felt even closer to Hoffman

than before. They were not only buddies and best friends, but he truly owed his life to his friend.

When their term of service neared an end, the two men spent long hours discussing what they should do next. Both wanted action—to prove themselves in combat. Marker finally decided to sign on for another tour of duty in the SEALs. But Hoffman heard that Ben Bernard, under whom he had once served, was setting up a new team in civilian life and promising plenty of action.

In the months after Hoffman left the service, he and Marker stayed in frequent contact through the Internet, exchanging gossip about mutual friends and girls they both knew. But with both assigned to clandestine units, neither felt free to tell the other what he was doing.

Marker knew Hoffman might be off on a secret mission, but it was a shock to see him in that hangar.

Now, what had they gotten themselves into? Were they going to end up fighting against each other? Marker had heard about that happening during the Civil War, with best friends and brothers finding themselves on opposite sides of the battle line. No. That couldn't happen to him and Dick Hoffman.

CHAPTER 18

PAT COLLINS TAPPED ONCE ON THE DOOR AND THEN STEPPED INTO Chuck Nelson's office.

"Chuck, we've got a satcomm report from Marker."

Nelson looked up from the papers on his desk. Doing paperwork with his left hand while his right arm remained encased in its cast had proved to be one of the most difficult things about his injury.

"What's he say?"

She handed him a sheet of paper. "Here. The plane's there. They got a look at it and some photos. Dr. Malcolm's studying the photos now to see if we can tell what condition the plane is in. Marker also saw a friend of his in the hangar. He thinks it means Ben Bernard's people are in charge of security there."

"Good old Big Dog!" Nelson shook his head. "You can expect him to turn up whenever something bad is happening. Let me look this over. And Pat, please call Rattner and a couple of his Air Force types and Jeff and Dr. Malcolm. We're going to have to figure out what this means and get a report off to Admiral McKay as soon as possible."

Half an hour later, they were all assembled around the conference table in Nelson's office.

"Why don't you fill us in first, Doctor?" Nelson said, turning to Dr. Malcolm.

"These photos help, but our information is still pretty sketchy," Malcolm said. "You can see, here, some of the equipment associated with the weapon—the *Cockatrice*. It looks as though they are ready to install this stuff. My guess is that they are fairly well along in overhauling the engines. They're doing a little sheet metal work on the wings, tail, and fuselage but that looks like minor stuff. I think they're also going to hang a couple of air-to-air missiles on her.''

"How long until it's ready to fly?" Rattner asked.

"Well, as I say, it's pretty sketchy and there's a lot of guess-work. But I'd say maybe a week until she's operational. I really don't think it will be much less than that, and it could be more. According to Marker's report, they know we have penetrated their operation so they will be pressing to get every-thing operational as soon as possible.''

"Jeff, have you looked over the stuff on the security setup?"

Bonior shook his head. "Looks pretty rough, Skipper. Marker says they have triple-A, both guns and missiles, as much as a battalion of infantry, personnel carriers, helicopters. They've got a real little army there. And my guess is that these are not just some crumb bums. Probably *Spetznaz* veterans— you know, the Soviet version of our Special Forces, willing to do anything for a buck. I'd say that's a real hard target.''

"Well, what do you think?" Nelson pressed him. "Can we get in there and at least disable the plane?"

"No way, boss. I wouldn't go in there with less than a battalion of Rangers—preferably a couple of battalions. And I wouldn't do that until the place had been pretty well softened up.''

"We could sneak a one-nineteen in there, put a bomb right inside that hangar," Rattner offered, referring to the F-119 Stealth bomber.

Nelson shook his head. "No, I don't think so. We're talking about a bombing attack on a friendly country. Even with a Stealth, we'd need a lot of backup, including tankers. I think the chances of getting in and out without a lot of people know-ing about it are somewhere near zero.''

"Well, if we don't do something soon, they're either going to use the plane or move it, in which case we're back to square one," Rattner responded.

His remark was followed by a long period of silence with everyone lost in thought.

Nelson finally broke the silence. "Well, this whole thing is, as they say, above our pay grade. I'll put together a report for Admiral McKay, outline all the lousy options, and let him decide what to do. That's what he gets paid for."

————— ★ —————

Admiral McKay stood leaning against the tall navigator's desk in his office on the second floor of the Pentagon's E-ring as he studied the decoded message from Nelson. He went over each of the options Nelson had suggested, shaking his head as he read each one. This, he finally decided, was above his pay grade, too.

He pressed a button on the side of the desk: "Joannie, please call the White House and tell them I need to meet with POTUS as soon as possible." Normally, McKay made it a point to avoid, as much as possible, the acronyms that have become so common in military terminology. But he loved "POTUS," reducing the august office of the president of the United States to a five-letter term that sounded almost like an obscenity.

————— ★ —————

It was almost dark when a few minutes were shoehorned into the president's schedule for his meeting with McKay.

Walker motioned him toward a seat on the couch. "The sun's well past the yardarm. Want a drink, Mac?"

As the president knew he would, McKay refused. He liked a drink when the day was done. But he made it a habit to wait until he had left the office for the evening before relaxing with it. Even then, he set his limit at two. Too many times, he had thought everything was wrapped up for the day only to be called abruptly back to duty. And those late-night calls were always the worst, dealing with some tough and unexpected problem, and demanding a clear head.

"Mr. President, we got a team into Uzbekistan. I don't know how those boys do it, but they're good. They got inside the compound, even got pictures of the plane. Unfortunately, they were spotted and had to shoot their way out. So whoever has that plane knows we know where it is and have some idea of about how soon it will be operational.''

''How long do we have, Mac?''

''Probably about seven days. Could be more, but we can't count on it.''

''Seven days. Shit, Mac, that's getting close to the convention. Do you think there's any connection?''

McKay shrugged at Walker's single-minded focus on politics. ''Could be just a coincidence. The fact is, we simply don't know. We've got all the questions, and whoever it is has all the answers.''

''What are our options?''

''That's the reason I'm here, sir. If there were any good options, I would have made the decision about what to do. Commander Nelson and his guys have gone over it pretty well. They've ruled out a raid by their outfit. The target is too hard —and our surveillance operation has certainly placed them on the highest alert.

''The other options are, one, bomb the plane before it can be moved or used; or two, send in at least a battalion of Rangers, preferably more, to seize control of the airbase.''

''Sounds like a war to me. No, Mac, we just can't do that. I'm not worried about the Uzbeks. If we offend them—well, that's just too bad. But I've got to worry about the Russian reaction. We've been through this whole difficult business with them over the expansion of NATO. They're still not happy with that, to say the least. The whole situation has changed a lot since the collapse of the Soviet Union, but Russia is still a nuclear power and I can never forget that for a minute. I let you carry out this little surveillance operation because it was small enough to avoid detection. But we simply can't go heavy-footed into a country that is independent but that the Russians still consider part of their sphere of influence.''

McKay sat silently, waiting, the unanswered question of what to do next hanging between them. Walker rose and began to pace, stopping, as he so often did, to stare out at the Rose

Garden. How many other presidents, similarly perplexed, had sought inspiration by gazing through these windows? And how many had found it? All Walker saw were roses. But when he turned around, he had reached a decision.

"I've decided to punt, Mac. Let's not do anything right now. But I want everything we've got focused on that place. I want as much warning as we can get of when the plane moves and where it goes. If you see anything at all, you let me know immediately. I want the guys at Fort Meade to make it an absolutely top priority to find out who the people at that base communicate with and who tries to communicate with them. I want to know who's behind this whole business."

"Yes, sir. I've already alerted the National Security Agency. They're running a full-court press on this one."

"There's one more thing I've been worrying about, Mac. How did whoever took that plane right out of our hands know enough about our operation to pull it off?" He pivoted and glared at McKay. "I think you've got a security leak. Someone leaked information about that first operation in Iraq. That would have gone perfectly if someone hadn't let the word get out."

"Yes, sir. I'm concerned about that, too. I am frankly perplexed. Our guys were all locked down out in Arizona. They couldn't even make phone calls to their wives. In my own office, this was kept very tightly. It was on a strict need-to-know basis, and the number with an overall view of the operation was only a handful of people who report directly to me."

"What about the people in Arizona? None of them was off the base?"

"No, sir . . . well, I take that back. Master Chief Bonior's little daughter was wounded in a drive-by shooting. I personally arranged for him to fly back to Norfolk to visit with her and be with his wife at the Children's Hospital down there. But Commander Nelson assured me that Chief Bonior is totally reliable."

Walker spun around and pointed a finger at McKay. "That's your leak, Mac! Your boy must have done some talking. You get on it. If he was the leaker, I want him out of there. This whole thing is so secret we probably can't send him to Leavenworth. But we can sure as hell put an end to his Navy career.''

McKay looked pained. ''We have to deal with this very delicately, sir. I can't bring in the Naval Investigative Service without blowing a real hole in our security. I may have to handle this myself.''

''Maybe you ought to start by getting this chief out of the operation, Mac.''

''Give me a little slack on this, sir. The team is locked down again, and since we don't know what we're going to do next, they don't either. Rather than disturb the team, let me see what I can do very discreetly. There's still time to move him out, if we need to. But at this point, he's still a vital part of the team.''

Walker stared hard at McKay and finally agreed. ''Okay, Mac. Do it your way. But you make damn sure there are no more leaks. And keep me informed. Okay?''

''Yes, sir. I'll report every development.''

CHAPTER 19

SPECIAL AGENT CINDY CARSON HAD WORRIED FOR DAYS AND many sleepless nights before she'd finally called for an appointment with Derek Shepherd, the head of the Secret Service White House detail. When she walked into his office, she was more nervous than she had ever been but determined to go through with it.

Shepherd, who had been guarding presidents for forty years, was half cop and half politician. To become head of the White House detail, you not only had to be good at your job. You also had to be good at dealing with people. The White House seemed to be a magnet for prickly personalities and you had to get along with all of them.

"Sit down, Cindy. What's on your mind?"

"Sir, I don't know how to say this . . . well, I guess I'll just say it. This is not what I thought I was getting into when I was assigned to the White House. Perhaps I was naive. But I thought this would be not only a very demanding job, but also a kind of glamorous one. It may sound overly dramatic, but I really was prepared to lay down my life to protect the president. I still am. But now, I'm a . . . a *pimp* for the president. There. I've said it."

Shepherd sighed. "I'm glad you came to me, Cindy. Let's talk about it. I've been protecting presidents since Dwight Eisenhower. There were things we've always had to do to protect the privacy of the president, whether it was covering up for the number of times Eisenhower was out playing golf or covering up for the women visiting with John Kennedy. We covered up for Woodrow Wilson's illness, Franklin Roosevelt's crippled condition, and other health problems such as Kennedy's Addison's disease.

"We are not instigating or encouraging any activity we might personally find offensive. One of our jobs, in addition to protecting the president—the person and his family—is to provide him with as much privacy as we can so he can live his own life as he feels he should live it while exposed to this unmerciful glare of publicity that comes with the presidency. If the president wants to do something, that's his decision."

Shepherd leaned forward, speaking slowly and choosing his words carefully, trying at the same time to ease his agent's concerns and remind her of what her priorities should be.

"It's not our role to say, 'Mr. President, you can't do that,' or 'Mr. President, that's immoral.' It's our job to provide him with the coverage, you might say, to carry on his life as he feels he should live it. It is not up to us to act as guardians of his morality. We sometimes find our two jobs somewhat in conflict. I'm sure you've heard about John Kennedy and his relationship with Judith Exner, who was also sleeping with Sam Giancana. We have to ask: Is this really a question of the security of the president? In the case of Judith Exner, J. Edgar Hoover finally confronted the president."

Carson smiled. "Yes, I've heard about that. That must have been an interesting session."

"To say the least. . . ." Shepherd paused, reminded of other "interesting sessions" in his own career, then continued. "We often have to tread a fine line. We sometimes have to decide whether to object if the president does things that could be harmful to him, either physically or politically. What if he wants to have relations with a woman who may have been exposed to the HIV virus? Is it our role to say, 'Hey, wait a minute, Mr. President, that's not a good idea'?

"If we find his relationship with a woman, for example, could be not only harmful politically, but also a danger to him and to national security—he could, for example, be blackmailed—then it's our job to try to do something about that by talking to him, by conferring among ourselves, perhaps by talking to other members of the White House staff or other members of the government, although we have to be awfully discreet about that.

"In this case, I haven't asked you to do anything I haven't done myself with some considerable personal misgivings. I think you can in good conscience do this, recognizing that you are carrying out your job of helping our country to function by permitting the president to live his personal life, even though he is our most public official."

Carson sat silently for nearly a minute and then said, "I hadn't thought about it that way, sir."

"Why don't you think about it some more? I'm certainly not going to have anyone doing anything that goes against her conscience. So think about it, and if you're still personally troubled by it, we'll make some other arrangements."

Shepherd leaned back in his chair and swiveled to look out the window behind him. "You know, Cindy, this has probably been a problem for the people assigned to guard powerful men since the beginning of history. My favorite is the biblical story of David, who was chosen by God to lead His people. And what does he do? He falls for the woman next door, sends her husband off into a battle where he is sure to be killed, and then sets the widow up in his palace. And yet David is still revered as a great leader.

"Maybe some degree of sexual promiscuity comes with the job. You've heard the stories about President Harding and his illegitimate child, and Roosevelt, and Kennedy. When François Mitterand, the president of France, was buried, his wife, his mistress, and his illegitimate child all showed up at the funeral.

"No, Cindy. I'm afraid this is something that comes with the territory, and we have to deal with it as best we can."

Marcia Walker stood firmly in the center of the sitting room on the family floor of the White House, her arms folded across her breasts in what an expert in body language would have called a defensive posture. But her attitude was anything but defensive.

"We just can't go on this way, Chip. We've been through this before. You've sworn off, and then it happens again. I can't understand what's the matter with you. Are you sick?"

Walker, clearly agitated, walked back and forth. "No, I try . . . I'm not sick! I'm just a normal man. You're gone all the time. We don't have any privacy." He shrugged.

"Well, what are we going to do about it? This . . . this is going to leak out. It's going to end up in the newspapers. You know how things are these days. The *National Enquirer* pays somebody, and the next thing you know, it's being taken seriously by the *Washington Post*, the *New York Times*, and the networks. We don't need that! I don't need that! I'm not going to put up with it."

"Aw, Marcie. All right. I'll stop." He turned to her. "I love you. I've always loved you. We make a great team. We work together well in this business. You have your own career. This is the only time a first lady has been able to do that. We're not . . . we're not doing badly."

"Not doing badly? What kind of a dream world are you living in? I think we're right on the edge of a real problem here. If you can't control your . . . your *zipper* . . . then something's going to have to be done about it."

"I don't know what you mean by 'be done about it.' "

"As you say, I have my own career. I can afford to live on my own. David and I can just move out."

"C'mon, Marcie. You're the first lady of the United States. You are not going to move out of the White House!"

"You think about it. I'm just not going to put up with this anymore."

"Okay, okay, I'll knock it off."

After the confrontation with his wife, Maynard Walker knew he was skating on thin ice, but he decided to have one last meeting with Michelle, to tell her this was the end, that he wouldn't be seeing her anymore. It was the decent thing to do.

Late that afternoon, they met once more in the upstairs sitting room. Walker stood a few feet away from her, his hands thrust deep in his trouser pockets, as she sat on the sofa looking up at him. He cleared his throat and then came right to the point.

"I'm sorry, Michelle, but this is the last time I'll be seeing you."

She looked up startled, and started to rise. He motioned to her to remain seated.

"I've really looked forward to our meetings. Not just the sex. I enjoyed that, but I also enjoyed your company. Often, it seemed, you were the only one I could relax with, get things off my mind."

She bowed her head and bit her lower lip, trying not to cry. Finally, she looked up at him, tears in her eyes.

"I understand, Mr. Pr . . . Chip. But I will miss you." She stood and stepped toward him and he felt her body against his, her head buried on his shoulder. Slowly she raised her hands up under his jacket and began gently caressing his chest. She was experienced enough to know what many men will not admit: that a man's breasts can be a source of intense sexual stimulation. He felt himself rising against her loins.

"Michelle, we shouldn't . . ."

She raised a finger and pressed it against his lips and murmured, "For the memories . . ."

Walker tilted her chin toward him and kissed her deeply. Their hands were busy loosening belts, zippers, and buttons. Walker felt like an adolescent boy, unable to control his lust, as he knelt over Michelle and felt himself penetrate deep inside her.

Afterward, they lay still for long moments, gently caressing each other.

"We . . . I shouldn't have done that. But it's so good to relax with you. I'm going to miss it. It seems like I can never catch my breath long enough to think. It's always one thing on top of another.

"Here I've got the convention coming up and this asshole Wilson is screwing everything up. I'll take care of him, but it's a pain in the ass. And on top of that, I've got this other thing . . . this thing I can't tell you about."

She lay still against him, listening quietly, until he began speaking again.

"I've got this thing going in Uzbekistan, of all places. I can't tell you about it, but it's a situation where I'm going to have to move, and move fast."

It was several moments until she responded, and then her tone was one of almost bored indifference. "You mean you're going to attack this place, this Uz . . . ?"

"No, no. Well, I sure hope not. But we've got to do something about this situation."

Finally, he rose and helped her to her feet. He held her close for a moment and gave her a brief kiss on the cheek.

"I'm sorry, Michelle. Good-bye."

———— ★ ————

Ben Bernard was trained to deal with bad news. At its most basic, that was what SEAL training was all about—to teach a man that he had the inner strength to keep going when everything had turned to shit. Those who couldn't summon that inner strength were the ones who didn't make it through Hell Week and never pinned on the Budweiser. But being trained to deal with bad news and liking it were not the same thing. Bernard hated it especially when he had to be the bearer of bad news, and that was what he had to do in this case.

As soon as he received word of the helicopter crash, he called off the chase. Whatever damage they had suffered had already been done. No sense taking any more risks or losses. He didn't have to know any more to be certain in his mind what had happened: Chuck Nelson's guys had penetrated his perimeter and gotten a look inside the hangar. They had also gotten a good look at his security operation. Their report was already on the way. Catching or killing them was not going to change anything—no matter how much better it might have made him feel.

Bernard straightened his shoulders, took a deep breath, and reached for the secure phone. His call was answered instantly.

"Bernard here. Put him on the line."

"Yes." Nash's tone was flat, toneless. Not a question or a statement. Just an acknowledgment that he was listening.

"Sir, our perimeter has been violated. A small group of men—at least two, perhaps a few more—cut through the fence and approached the hangar. They killed a guard, but he fired his gun and that alerted us. We pursued them but they shot down our helicopter. I called off the pursuit at that point."

"What did they learn?"

"They were in a position to scope out our security. They also got a look at the plane, so they know it's here. We don't know whether they learned anything about the status of the plane or the weapon. I recommend we move the plane as quickly as possible."

"When I want your recommendations, I will ask for them, Mr. Bernard." His use of the word "mister" rather than "captain" was not lost on the mercenary. "I am very displeased about this breach in security. However, I will deal with that later. You are to continue to carry out my orders. Carry them out precisely. Is that understood?"

"Yes, sir." Bernard thought he had been chewed out by experts, but the brutal chill in Nash's voice was more unnerving than anything he had ever heard.

"Please instruct the engineers that I want the plane and the weapon put in condition to carry out a mission within the next seven days." Nash was confident that his intelligence network was good enough to tell him if any attempt would be mounted within that time to attack or seize the plane. After its mission, it could be landed at a new base.

"And now, Mr. Bernard, you will turn over responsibility at your present location to your second in command. He will take charge of the security force you have assembled there. And then I want you and the rest of your people to come here to Colorado Springs to help enhance our security."

"Yes, sir. I'll make arrangements immediately and report

when we will arrive.'' Bernard put down the phone with a grunt of relief. There might still be a reckoning with Nash for the security breach, but that was in the future. For now, everything seemed to be back on track.

CHAPTER 20

CHUCK NELSON AND JEFF BONIOR WAITED NERVOUSLY IN THE small office they had borrowed at the Tucson International Airport.

"Any idea what this is about, boss?" Bonior asked.

Nelson shook his head. "All I know is that Admiral McKay asked me to get a room and meet him here, with you. He should be here any minute."

Bonior sat staring at the wall. He felt nervous, not knowing why he had been called to meet with the chairman of the Joint Chiefs. But his nervousness did not overshadow the joy he felt in his heart—the joy he had felt ever since he had talked to Dottie on the phone on their return to Site Y.

"Oh, Jeff." He could hear the relief in her voice at being able to talk to him. "I've been so scared."

"It's about Denise?"

"Yes, she was so sick, darling! I thought we were going to lose her after she got through the operation and all."

"What happened?"

"A few days after the surgery—while you were away—she came down with a high fever. She had a terrible infection in her little tummy. She just got weaker and weaker. She just lay there unconscious. She looked so tiny and helpless with all those tubes."

"How is she now?" Being so far away made his heart ache.

"I think it's a miracle. She was so sick. She wasn't even moving. And then her fever just went away. She opened her eyes and she smiled at me. It happened so fast. She was barely alive, and then all of a sudden she was getting better.''

"What does the doctor say?''

"They're going to take the tube out of her stomach tomorrow, and then she can start eating a little bit. The doctor says she'll gain strength very quickly then. He thinks she's out of the woods.''

"How's her leg?''

"It didn't even need a cast. She'll have to use a little walker for a while, but the doctor says it's healing nicely. She'll have some scars on her leg and her tummy, but they should disappear as she grows older.''

"How much longer does she have to stay in the hospital?''

"I don't think she's going to have to stay more than a couple more days. She's already out of intensive care and the stepdown unit, and she's got her own little room up on the eighth floor. As soon as they release her, I think I'll take the kids out and stay with Momma for a week or two. You have the number there, don't you?''

"At your folks' place in Saint Louis? Sure, I've got it. I'll call you when I can. I wish I could be there with you. You give her a hug for me. And thank the Lord. Our prayers have been answered.''

"I do, Jeff. I've been praying day and night for her to get better. Now it will be prayers of thanksgiving.''

Bonior was brought abruptly back to the present as the door opened. Normally, the chairman of the Joint Chiefs couldn't go to the head to take a leak without a retinue of aides and horse-holders trailing along behind. But when McKay entered the small office, he was alone. Only his pilot knew where he was and only the admiral knew why.

Nelson and Bonior jumped to attention.

"At ease, men, at ease. Take a seat,'' McKay said as he pulled out a chair. He turned to Bonior. "Master Chief Bonior?''

"Yes sir.''

"I understand your daughter is coming along fine. She had us worried for a while.''

"Yes, sir, she sure did. But I think she's pretty well out of the woods now."

McKay reached across the table and gave him a firm handshake. Then he turned to shake with Nelson. Nelson's arm was out of the cast, but he turned awkwardly to shake with his left hand.

"How's the shoulder, Chuck?"

"Still sore, sir, but I'm getting some motion back in it."

The two junior men sat rigidly in their chairs, waiting expectantly.

"This is very sensitive," McKay said. "That's why I've come myself. Gentlemen, we have a leak in our operation. Someone knew you were going after that plane and knew enough to snatch it right out of your fingers."

Nelson and Bonior nodded.

"The question now is where the leak came from. We simply can't afford that sort of thing."

"Yes sir," Nelson replied.

"This is the kind of thing where we would normally call in the Naval Investigative Service for a thorough investigation. But we can't do that without telling them a lot of things I don't want anyone to know. So let's see how far I can get doing my own investigation. I'm not a cop, but I've got a law degree and I was commander of the NIS for a while."

The two men nodded.

"So . . . to put it bluntly," he said, turning to Bonior, "the question is, were you the source of the leak? You were the only one who left your compound out here and had any contact with the outside world. So I've got to ask both of you some questions."

Nelson and Bonior looked at each other, concern showing in their faces.

"Now, Chief, when you left here and went to visit your daughter, did you discuss this operation with your wife . . . or with anyone else?"

"No, sir. Not a word."

"Did your wife ask you where you had been or where you were going? Did she ask you what was so important that you couldn't remain with her and your daughter?"

A small smile crept across Bonior's lips. "No, sir! Dottie has been a SEAL's wife for fifteen years. I never tell her when I'm on secret ops, and she never asks. It's one of those things that she just knows."

"Even in this case, when neither of you knew whether your daughter would live or die?"

"Even then, sir. She knows I have to do what I have to do."

Nelson leaned forward as though he had something to say, but he was hesitant to interrupt the admiral.

McKay turned toward him. "Okay, Chuck, what's on your mind?"

"Sir, Jeff couldn't have been the source of the leak. I ran a very strict need-to-know operation. Jeff knew enough to carry out his job, but nothing more. Jeff did not have to know exactly where we were going or exactly when, and so he didn't know. At the time he went to visit Denise, he didn't know enough to be a source of this leak."

"How about afterward, after he returned here?" McKay turned to Bonior. "Did you have any telephone conversations with your wife that might have been overheard?"

Nelson responded, "No sir, he couldn't. As you know, we arranged for reports on the condition of his daughter to be relayed through your office. He had no opportunity to talk with anyone."

Bonior nodded emphatically. "That's right, sir. All I knew about the op was enough to do my job. I really didn't know enough to leak useful information to anyone."

McKay studied the faces of both men for several moments. Then he turned to Nelson.

"You're absolutely certain then, Chuck . . ."

"A *physical* impossibility, sir. When Jeff was in a position where he might have divulged some information, he simply didn't have any information."

McKay looked from one man to the other and then shook his head. "I suppose even the incomplete information Chief Bonior had might have enabled someone to piece together details of the mission. Which leaves us with a mystery." McKay paused for a moment, a deep frown on his brow. "If it didn't come from your team, then it had to have come from my office . . . or from the White House.''

The three men sat silently. McKay suddenly found himself thinking about the beautiful woman he had seen waiting in an antechamber when he'd left the president's office a few weeks earlier. The two SEALs barely heard him murmur, ''I wonder. . . .''

Then McKay rose suddenly. ''Well, thank you, gentlemen. Get back to work,'' he said, then shook their hands distractedly, and strode out the door.

Before the collapse of the Soviet Union, the senior scientist had enjoyed a privileged life in a secret city that was off-limits not only to foreigners but to most Soviet citizens as well. It did not even show up on maps—except those prepared by the American Defense Mapping Service. He lived in a comfortable apartment furnished by the government and sent his children to a first-rate school. He and his family enjoyed the finest medical care. Best of all, he had his choice of equipment in a superbly equipped laboratory where he pursued his research in particle physics.

Life at a remote airbase in the endless desert of Uzbekistan did not compare with his former existence. But it was better by far than the fate of many of his colleagues who not only had lost their laboratories but were reduced to close to starvation. Life here was not too bad and the scientific problems he faced were among the most challenging of his career. He did not really know who had recruited him. All he knew was that he had been hired to perfect an amazing device that Iraqi scientists had been working on. After studying what they had done, he was impressed. This was a revolutionary new weapon and it was almost operational.

''Now, Andrei, are you satisfied with the controls of the plane? We do not have the luxury of any test flights.''

Sergei Kaparov had not been happy since he'd arrived in Uzbekistan. He was only a few miles from his old home, but he had been locked in the airbase for days with very little to do.

One thought had kept him from open rebellion—not that that would have done much good. Before his flight to Iraq with the American commandos, a secret numbered bank account had been opened for him in the Cayman Islands. He had a receipt showing that half a million dollars had been deposited in his account, with another half million to be deposited when he had finished the remainder of his mission. It was the same account into which he had transferred much of his wealth, including the proceeds from the heavy mortgage on his ranch.

"Sure, I can fly it. I got it here, didn't I?" Kaparov replied.

"This afternoon, we will go over your mission profile," the scientist told him. "Your responsibility will be to fly the mission exactly as planned. You must hit all of your checkpoints precisely. You will have limited communications capability. If there are any deviations from the plan, even the slightest, they must be reported to us. We want you to be precise. Not as precise as possible, but absolutely precise. Is that understood."

"Yeah, right. What about that thing back there?"

"You don't worry about 'that thing back there.' Forget it's there. It will be operated by remote control. All you have to do is fly the plane.

"Now, let me fill you in on a few more things. We have added a modest self-defense capability to the plane. Are you familiar with look-down, shoot-down radar?"

"I know about it but I've never really used it."

"You probably won't need it, but I'll brief you on it later today. In addition to the radar, we've installed two Acrid AA-6 rockets in pods on the wings. You can use them if you are attacked. You've fired those missiles before, haven't you?"

"Yes, many times."

"Meet me here this afternoon and we'll go over the radar system, and then I'll fill you in on the flight profile."

In the broadcast box hanging near the ceiling of the cavernous Trans World Dome at the America's Center convention hall in Saint Louis, Brent Benedict, network television's most popular anchor, checked to make sure the red light on the camera was off, then stretched his arms over his head, yawned a giant yawn, and checked his watch.

What a bore! National political conventions had changed dramatically from the days when the whole nation tuned in to watch the old guys like Walter Cronkite. Now, Benedict wondered, was there anybody out there at all? The convention had become just a programmed ritual for the anointing of the candidate everyone knew would be nominated. The governor of Florida, new to national politics, had surged into a surprisingly strong lead in the primaries. By the time the delegates gathered in Saint Louis, he had the nomination neatly sewn up.

The other party's convention, later in the month, would at least have a smidgen of suspense, with the challenge against Maynard Walker from within his own party by Richard Wilson. Still, everyone knew how it was going to turn out. If Walker didn't score a clean win on the first ballot, that would be news. But he would certainly win on the second ballot, and then it would be back to the same old boring speeches, the same old party-organized choreography. This convention was all choreography with no drama at all to keep viewers in front of their screens. Benedict could almost hear the sound of millions of remote control switches changing stations.

Sergei Kaparov was already airborne. He had taken off from his base in the Kyzyl-Kum Desert and quickly climbed to altitude. When he cut in the ramjet engines, he felt a great surge of power as the plane rocketed above 100,000 feet and rapidly accelerated. As he leveled off at 120,000 feet, he cut back on the throttles and seemed almost to coast along at nearly eight times the speed of sound. Although still in the outer reaches of the atmosphere, he was almost in orbit.

He was surprised how easy the plane was to fly at that great altitude and high speed. A slight touch on the controls would send him into a lazy, sweeping turn. His route had been planned, however, to require as few turns as possible. When he did have to make corrections in his course to compensate for the fact that the earth was turning under him, he began the turn early and then gradually leveled out on the new course.

Flying almost directly north, he passed high over Russia. He gave only a passing thought to the possible danger from the notoriously ineffective Russian air defense system. Far below he saw the great expanse of the polar ice cap as his course took him almost exactly over the North Pole. Years ago, he might have worried as he passed over the string of radar stations designed to protect North America from attack by Russian bombers. But with the end of the Cold War, the warning line had been largely mothballed. If he did show up as a blip on a radar screen, odds were that no one would pay much attention.

Northern Canada was covered with clouds and Kaparov had an eerie sensation, as though he had somehow departed from the familiar earth and existed alone in his own little free-flying world. Flying so fast that he left the noise of his engines far behind, he heard only the faint murmurs of the plane's instruments and the occasional slight movement of a control surface.

His course took him down the spine of the northern Rocky Mountains, and then over central Nevada. As his plane approached the tiny California desert town of Mojave, a red light on his instrument panel flashed and Kaparov felt a subtle vibration and a faint hum in the body of the plane behind him. The vibration and the sound lasted for less than a minute and the light on the panel went out.

———————— ★ ————————

It was just a little before 5 P.M. in Saint Louis. In Mojave, fifteen hundred miles to the west, the clock was approaching 3 P.M. and students in the one-story Mojave Elementary School were fidgeting restlessly, waiting for the bell to ring.

In Miss Canepa's third-grade classroom, one little clock-watcher saw the timepiece on the wall begin to rattle.

"Earthquake!" He dived under his desk, as he had so often been trained to do.

Miss Canepa felt the shaking. "Everybody, under your desks!" she commanded. "Cover your heads with your hands.'' She looked over the room to make sure that all the children had obeyed her command and then she crawled under her desk at the front of the room.

The first faint sounds that the teacher and her students heard grew to a mighty roar, like that from a giant blast furnace. Embedded in the roar was a cacophony of snapping, crackling sounds, like a huge steamroller smashing a pile of wooden boxes.

''It's all right, children. It will be over in a minute,'' Miss Canepa called. In this earthquake-prone area, she had experienced more quakes than she cared to recall. She knew there were a few moments of terror, then you checked yourself over, found you had survived, and set about cleaning up the mess.

But this, whatever it was, was different. The sound grew to a deafening bellow. Miss Canepa saw the walls of the classroom suddenly disappear. Before she could scream, she and her third graders also ceased to exist.

A few blocks west, Dorothy Manor was cleaning off the tables and filling the sugar bowls and the salt and pepper shakers in the little town's most popular restaurant, one of the businesses strung out in a long row on the east side of California Route 14, trolling for the trade of the trucks and autos steadily streaming by.

Manor looked up and cocked her head as she heard the first sounds. Across the road, she saw a long freight train headed south on the Burlington Northern Santa Fe Railway line that snaked through town, seeking its way around the Tehachapi Mountains down into the Los Angeles basin. But the noise she heard wasn't coming from the train. It sounded almost like a hard rainstorm. But there wasn't a cloud in the sky. And it was getting louder.

As Manor looked toward the windows, they didn't shatter. They melted. The curtains were gone in a flash. Manor gasped. Then she was consumed.

The wave of destruction had swept through the little desert town from northeast to southwest. The wave hit the airport, to the east of town, first, vaporizing the hangars of the Tracor Company, the firm that built the *Voyager*, the tiny plane that flew around the world nonstop.

A giant Boeing 747, parked at General Electric Flight Test Operations, had exploded like a huge firecracker. A score of older commercial airliners, mothballed in the dry desert air, were picked up by the great wind created by the conflagration and flew about like children's toys, smashing into each other and the hangars until they, too, were all vaporized. The school went next, and then the few rows of small houses between the schoolyard and Highway 14 evaporated. The one-street business district and the railroad yard were the last to go. From beginning to end, the obliteration of Mojave took only fifty-five seconds.

As suddenly as it had come, the wave of destruction ceased. A few fires crackled at the edges of town, but most of the community and its airport had been reduced to a powdery residue. There was nothing left to burn.

Brent Benedict, relaxing off-camera, was just finishing a ham and cheese on rye and a Coke when he heard an urgent voice in the earphone hidden in his left ear.

"Something has happened in Mojave, California. The town has been destroyed. You will be live in thirty seconds."

Benedict washed down the bite he had just taken and pushed the paper plate and the remnants of his sandwich to the side, out of sight. He ran his tongue along his front teeth to make sure no scrap of food was lodged where the camera would see it. An aide handed him a sheaf of wire service reports. Key items had been marked in bright yellow. Benedict glanced at the clock on the opposite wall, counting off the seconds to air time, and then leafed hurriedly through the one-sentence bulletins.

The monitor to his left suddenly went blank. Then a brief message appeared: "News Bulletin." A disembodied voice said: "Ladies and gentlemen, we interrupt this program to bring you a special report from our convention newsroom. Brent Benedict."

Benedict loved the surge of adrenaline he felt whenever he had to go on air live, with no time to prepare and little information to go on. Everything now depended on him and his skill, his ability to perform under the most intense pressure.

"We have this bulletin just in," he began, reading from one of the wire service reports. " 'The small California desert town of Mojave was destroyed this afternoon by a mysterious blast. There is no immediate report on casualties.' "

Benedict improvised smoothly while he waited for more information.

"Mojave is a small city in the desert northeast of Los Angeles. It is the nearest town to the huge Edwards Air Force Base. The town lies near the Tehachapi Mountains, which have often been the site of severe earthquakes. We do not yet know whether it was an earthquake or some other force that has struck Mojave.

"According to the most recent census, Mojave had a population of 3,763. But many residents were probably at work at Edwards Air Force Base or in the nearby towns of Lancaster and Palmdale, so the actual number of casualties is not known."

Moving around off camera, an aide slipped another wire service bulletin onto the desk in front of him.

Benedict took a moment to read the bulletin, shook his head slightly in disbelief, and then looked into the camera.

"We have this word just in: The first rescue personnel to reach the scene report that there are no known survivors. The entire town seems to have been obliterated. Ladies and gentlemen, this is an awful, awful disaster, one of the worst catastrophes in our nation's history.

"So far as we know, the damage seems to have been limited to the town of Mojave itself. There are no reports of damage from any nearby cities or from Edwards Air Force Base. The California Highway Patrol has blocked traffic on Highways 58 and 14 through Mojave. Service on the Burlington Northern Santa Fe railway and the Union Pacific line through Mojave has also been severed."

Benedict looked around. There were no more bulletins immediately available.

He had been through enough emergency broadcasts to be intensely aware of the pressures bearing on him and in fact the entire network. Everyone knew the rewards of being first with the news. For Benedict and others, there were bonuses in the making. For corporate executives in New York, there was the knowledge that they would be able to trumpet a lead of seconds over the other networks into full-page ads that would translate into millions of dollars in advertising revenue. But Benedict, who had learned his trade first as a newspaperman, always remembered the adage: "Get it first, but first get it right."

In this electronic business, with the constant pressure to fill air time, there was always the temptation to go on the air with a guess or a rumor that later turned out to be erroneous—to the great embarrassment of the anchor and the network. With the absence of new bulletins, he played it safe with a comment on the convention.

"It is not immediately clear what, if any, impact this disaster will have on the political situation. It will not affect tonight's nominating vote here in Saint Louis. But it could have an impact at the next convention. Richard Wilson, the challenger from within the president's own party, may already have enough votes to deny President Walker the nomination on the first ballot. His challenge to the president has, all along, been based on questions about President Walker's firmness and his ability in dealing with a number of problems, both domestic and foreign. This event in Mojave might just be enough to tilt some votes into the challenger's column."

At 6 P.M., when the delegates began streaming back into the convention hall and assembling in their state delegations for the evening's nominating speeches and vote, it was still not clear what had happened in Mojave. The California Highway Patrol had blocked all access to the town to leave the way clear for emergency vehicles. But the rescue workers who were first to arrive on the scene quickly radioed back their grim report: the entire town had been reduced to a kind of white, powdery dust. There wasn't a structure standing high enough off the desert floor to shelter a possible survivor. They

radioed that there was no use sending more rescue equipment.
The first units to approach the outskirts of the former community also reported a suspicious level of radioactivity and
recommended that no one enter the area without protective
gear.

Overhead, helicopters circled with television cameras. Photos of the grim scene soon appeared on television screens
throughout the world. But there was very little to see—just a
large white rectangle on the face of the earth.

Moments after the red light went out, Kaparov passed over
the coastline just north of San Diego and saw the deep blue
of the Pacific far below. He eased back on the throttles of the
ramjets. It felt almost as though the plane had dropped away
from under him as it descended rapidly toward the ocean. As
he began his descent, Kaparov made a long, slow turn to the
left, a turn that brought him back over land south of Mexico
City and then carried him northeast toward the Yucatán Peninsula.

Kaparov was delighted with his navigation instruments.
They had guided him easily over the Pole, and now, as the
checkpoints slid by, he looked ahead and saw the long green
runway, bordered on each side by seemingly endless jungle,
stretching ahead of him right where it was supposed to be,
deep in the heart of the state of Quintana Roo.

Back in the Kyzyl-Kum Desert, Kaparov had been unhappy.
But accommodations at this landing spot in the middle of the
Yucatán jungle were enough to make him homesick for Uzbekistan. A small team of technicians had been flown in ahead
of time and set up shop in a series of small buildings along
the edge of the jungle. A large camouflaged tent was quickly
erected to shelter the plane. They had brought with them a
collection of spare parts and a full load of fuel for the plane.
But there were few creature comforts.

The runway was one of perhaps hundreds of similar landing
strips scattered through Mexico, Central America, and the islands of the Caribbean, carved out of jungle or desert and used

from time to time by planes carrying loads of high value cargo north to the great heroin, cocaine, and marijuana markets of the United States. It had been a simple matter for Nash's agents to locate the airfield and to pay generously for its use—no questions asked, no questions answered on either side.

Maynard Walker was at the White House. When he saw the first reports on the Mojave disaster on one of his TV monitors, he immediately called Admiral McKay over the secure phone on his desk, part of the intricate system of communications that permit the president, the secretary of defense, and the chairman of the Joint Chiefs—the national command authorities with responsibility for the nation's nuclear arsenal—to be in instant contact with each other.

"Mac? What do you know about this Mojave business? Is that the whatchamacallit, the *Cockatrice*?"

"We're not sure yet, sir. But it sounds very much like it. The reports of the total destruction are compatible with what we know about the weapon. Some of my people are preparing to analyze the residue, but we've been delayed by the radioactivity in the area. We should have a report soon and I'll keep you informed."

Chuck Nelson, Mark Rattner, and Jim Malcolm left Site Y in Arizona and headed for Edwards Air Force Base as soon as they heard of the disaster. Pat Collins began combing all her sources of information.

She put in a call to her contact at the North American Air Defense Command headquarters, carved into a mountain in the Rockies near Colorado Springs. She knew that the plane, if it was the source of the disaster at Mojave, would have been flying too high to show up on air traffic control radar. But perhaps the people at NORAD, who monitor every satellite and try to keep track of every piece of debris in space, had picked up something.

"I'd like you to go over your records for the period from

twenty-one hundred to twenty-four hundred GMT today,'' she said. "See if you find any unexplained object, probably crossing the United States from north to south at an altitude above a hundred thousand feet. If you find anything, let me know immediately."

Her contact at NORAD knew enough not to ask questions. She recorded the details and said, "Okay, Pat, got it. I'll get back to you."

———— ★ ————

Half an hour later, her contact called back. "Bingo, Pat. I don't know what you're looking for, but there was something up there. It was at about a hundred twenty thousand feet. That's well below the zones we normally monitor, but our equipment did pick it up. We have a timeline with altitude and speed. Generally, it shows that this object entered North American airspace over the Pole about twenty-two twenty GMT and exited off the West Coast at about twenty-three ten. It descended over the Pacific and we lost contact. I'll fax you the report."

Pat Collins felt a tingle of excitement run down her spine. This was it! Her thrill of discovery was immediately followed by new concerns: Where had the plane gone? And where would it show up next? She hadn't a clue.

As soon as she completed her conversation with NORAD, she went to Nelson's office and picked up the direct line to Admiral McKay's office. She was immediately put through to him.

"Admiral, Commander Nelson is on his way to Mojave, but I thought this was too important to wait. I have just confirmed with NORAD that an unidentified object passed over Mojave at a very high altitude at the time of the disaster. This is almost certainly the Blackjack with the *Cockatrice*."

"Okay, Mrs. Collins. Good work. Let me know immediately as soon as you know more. I guess we're going to have to wait for an analysis of the material at the scene to be sure what we're dealing with."

"Yes, sir, that's right. Dr. Malcolm is with Commander

Nelson. They should already be on the ground at Edwards. We have made arrangements for a chemical and physical examination of the residue to be done as soon as Dr. Malcolm has collected a sample.''

The networks, desperate to fill air time, were delighted when Richard Wilson's press secretary called to say he was available. Wilson took the elevator near his office in the Philip A. Hart Building—the newest of the three Senate office buildings—to the basement and rode the subway to the basement of the Capitol. Another elevator took him to the third floor. A network television crew was waiting for him there in Room S-308, the large studio adjoining the Radio and Television Correspondents' Gallery.

Wilson, who spent more time in the studio than any two other senators, strode briskly across the room and took up his familiar position near the podium. An aide had already pulled back the blue drapes behind him to reveal a painting of the Capitol that would look, to viewers, like the real thing.

He stood patiently as one of the TV crew members slipped a small earpiece into his ear and ran the cord to a little box attached to his belt under his jacket in the rear. A microphone was clipped to the lapel of his jacket. Wilson felt to make sure his necktie was in place and then turned toward the camera.

''Senator,'' a voice in his ear said, ''we will be live in thirty seconds.'' Wilson nodded.

Through his earpiece, he heard the voice of Brent Benedict. The red light on the camera across the room came on. He could hear Benedict, but he could not see him.

''Senator Wilson, as a candidate, you have been given regular intelligence briefings by the administration. Can you give us any insight into what has caused this disaster at Mojave?''

''First, Brent, I want to offer my most heartfelt sympathy to the people of Mojave. I am sure that every family in that city has suffered losses, and my heart goes out to the survivors who must now attempt to put their lives back together again. If this was some kind of terrorist attack, it overshadows any other such incident in our history—even the loss of a hundred sixty eight lives in the Oklahoma City bombing.''

''Yes, Senator, the reports we have received indicate this is a terrible tragedy. You mention a possible terrorist attack. Can you tell us anything more about that possibility, Senator?''

Wilson knew no more than anyone else, no more than had come out in the news service bulletins. True, as a presidential candidate, he did receive a daily intelligence briefing, but to-day's briefing had been in the morning, before the Mojave disaster. He did not let a lack of knowledge stop him.

''Brent, I know very little more about this incident than you do. However, I can say that this has all the earmarks of an attack on American soil by someone—or some thing—that intends to do us harm. Why Mojave? Why now? Is it possible Edwards Air Force Base was the target and Mojave was struck by mistake? I don't know.''

''Sir, you referred to 'some *thing*.' Are you suggesting that this was an attack by aliens from outer space?''

''Oh, no, no!'' Wilson was too astute a politician to permit himself to be associated with the fringe element that believes in the reality of unidentified flying objects. But he also knew that this casual reference to ''some *thing*'' would attract attention.

''Brent, our information at this point is very scanty. All I can tell you is that, once again, our president has been found wanting. The American people should ask, 'Has he fulfilled his most elemental duty to protect our nation?' I think this horrible disaster at Mojave is just one more example of the failure of President Walker to carry out his most basic duties.''

''Senator, do you think this incident will have an impact on this year's presidential contest?''

''Our party will not meet for its convention for several weeks, and when the time comes, the delegates must, of course, vote their conscience. But I must say that if this dis-aster causes some of the uncommitted delegates to give re-newed thought to their choice, then yes, this incident could have an impact on the convention and the election. As I have constantly told you and the American people, the outcome of this nominating procedure is not a foregone conclusion.''

It was late in the evening when an aide thought to whisk away the plate containing the half-eaten sandwich Benedict had set aside when the news of the destruction of Mojave had come in. Buzzing with news of the attack, the delegates hurried through the formality of selecting the governor of Florida as their presidential candidate. The traditional demonstration following the vote was noticeably shorter and less enthusiastic than such rituals normally were.

"And there you have it, ladies and gentlemen. The governor of Florida has, as expected, been nominated to represent his party in the presidential election in November. The party went through the motions, but it was clear the minds of the delegates were really not focused on the business here in Saint Louis on this very sad day for all Americans.

"We're leaving you from the America's Center now. But stay tuned for up-to-the-minute reports as we continue our coverage of the disaster at Mojave. This is Brent Benedict at America's Center in Saint Louis saying, good night to all."

CHAPTER 21

BAD NEWS TRAVELS AROUND THE WORLD FROM WEST TO EAST, registering its impact on one stock exchange after another: Tokyo, Hong Kong, London, and finally, New York's Wall Street.

One thing stock traders hate even worse than bad news is uncertainty. The mysterious destruction of Mojave combined the two and the stock markets reacted predictably by dropping abruptly, one after the other.

At his dimly lighted retreat above Colorado Springs, Luke Nash watched the monitor on his desk with satisfaction as it recorded the market collapse. As soon as the Tokyo exchange opened, he began buying from a list of stocks he had carefully selected in anticipation of just such a drop in prices. For him, this was not the disaster it seemed to many, but a golden buying opportunity—one he had personally created.

By the time the shock wave had traveled around the world and reached New York, Nash had invested nearly a billion dollars in stocks that had dropped far enough to make them attractive to him. A number of other stocks had not yet fallen far enough to meet his standards. He knew he could wait and that another buying opportunity would soon arrive.

When he was through, he would have a controlling interest in a number of the world's most critical industries: communications, energy, and transportation. These were the industries that dominated the economic and political life of the modern industrialized world and Nash intended to make his influence felt—as always, from behind the scenes.

"Let's get a little altitude, Mark. We don't need to get tangled up with those fellows down below." Malcolm sat in the left seat in the Huey helicopter as they approached Mojave. Below them, helicopters from every television station in southern California swirled above the area where the town had been. "Let's fly over the town from east to west. I want to get a good look at the pattern of destruction."

After taking off from Edwards Air Force Base, Rattner had swung out toward the east and then headed back in toward the town. Flying at five thousand feet, they could see a stark white rectangle where Mojave had once stood. The rectangle was bordered by a line of black where fire had burned.

"That's exactly what I would expect," Malcolm said, "an area of utter destruction where the ray cut through the town with fires along the edges in the area that was not destroyed."

Malcolm balanced an aeronautical chart on his lap and marked the boundaries of the destroyed area. It measured out to about two thousand yards wide and just a little over thirty-five hundred yards long.

With a small scientific calculator, Malcolm made a rough estimate of the energy required to cause such complete destruction. He did not know exactly how long it had taken, but from the eyewitness reports coming in from those who were nearby, it was all over in less than a minute.

Malcolm whistled softly.

"That is one powerful beam!" Then he turned to Rattner. "Okay, Mark, I've seen enough. Let's get back on the ground."

Nelson was waiting for them when they landed. "Is it what we think it is?"

"Yeah, I'm almost positive. I want to see the analysis of the residue, but that will just be icing on the cake." He paused and shook his head. "Not a very apt figure of speech. . . . Have you got a secure phone set up?"

"Right over here," Nelson replied, motioning to a small office at one end of a large hangar.

As soon as Malcolm entered the office, he placed a call to Adm. McKay. Because of the need for security, the chairman of the Joint Chiefs had been reduced, in a sense, to acting as a messenger between members of the team and those at the Pentagon with a need to know and the president.

"It's our boy, all right," he told McKay. "The pattern is amazing, a sharp, distinct rectangle of utter destruction. I can't imagine any other force that could cause this kind of pattern. We're still waiting for the chemical analysis, but I think we can proceed on the assumption that whoever has that weapon has used it and may be prepared to again."

"What makes you think he'll use it again?" McKay had been thinking the same thing, but he wanted to hear Malcolm's opinion.

"Sir, this is just guesswork and certainly not very scientific. But Mojave is just a little desert town—an isolated target. It seems logical to me that we should view this as both a test and as a warning of worse to come."

"Mm-hmm. That's exactly what I've been thinking. The stock markets are all going to hell. You can imagine what would happen if it hit a big city."

"I've done some calculations on that," Malcolm replied. "I think the width of the beam is fixed at about the width of the destruction in Mojave: about two thousand yards, or somewhat more than a mile. But if we're right in our guesses about the technology involved, there's no limit to the length of the area of destruction. This device, so far as we know, does not require any fuel source. It is simply a focusing mechanism. Once it is activated, it just turns everything in its path into dust until it is turned off again."

"Bad news!" McKay was stunned by the potential damage that could be caused.

"Yes sir," Malcolm replied. "Lay this beam over Manhattan, from the Hudson to the East River, and it's gone, just evaporated. For all we know, it could tear the heart out of any city—or even a number of cities in rapid succession."

Nelson reached for the phone. "Sir, this is Commander Nelson. It occurred to me that this attack on Mojave was intended as a kind of warning of worse to come. Have we gotten any communication at all from any terrorist group, perhaps demanding a ransom or some kind of action on the part of the U.S. government?''

''We've thought of that, Chuck. We've got the FBI, the CIA, and the National Security Agency checking both for messages and any intelligence we can gather on any terrorist group that might be involved. So far, the answer is zilch. No messages. And most of the terrorist organizations don't have the sophisticated skills to pull off something like this. Right now, we're up a tree. And if there's going to be another attack, the clock is ticking.''

''Okay, sir. We're going to hang around here for a little longer and then go on back to Site Y.''

Nelson, Malcolm, and Rattner had left their base in Arizona so rapidly that they had not had time to pack a bag or even bring along a toothbrush. In the hot desert climate, they were all beginning to feel a little gamey.

''I'm going to take a run into Lancaster and pick up a few things,'' Nelson said. ''Why don't you guys each make a list: toothpaste, toothbrushes, razors, shorts, shirts, socks?''

''We can probably get everything we need at the base exchange,'' Rattner said.

''Yeah, we could. But I just want a little time to get off by myself and think. Anyway, we have to wait for the chemical analysis.''

Nelson was pleasantly surprised to find the highway almost bare of traffic. Immediately after the disaster, Route 14 had been jammed with cars and trucks, many of them stalled for hours. But the word had gotten out and through traffic was finding other ways around Mojave. He pulled off the highway in Lancaster and turned into the parking lot of the first shopping mall he spotted.

His first stop was a large drugstore. With his list in one hand and pushing a shopping basket with the other, he worked his way along the men's toiletries section, dropping deodorant, razors, shaving cream, and other items into the basket. As he neared the end of the row, Nelson looked up to find the aisle that contained men's underclothes.

He found himself standing only a few feet from Ben Bernard, who looked as startled as he.

Nelson was the first to recover from his surprise.

"What the hell are *you* doing here?"

Bernard glared for a moment and snarled, "None of your business, asshole." He turned on his heel and strode away.

Well, Nelson thought to himself, one more piece of the puzzle. But it's still a puzzle.

He looked around the store and spotted a bank of pay phones against the wall. He quickly keyed in his credit card number and then dialed the office of Adm. McKay.

"This is Commander Nelson. I am calling from a nonsecure phone. Please tell Admiral McKay this is urgent."

There was no sound on the phone for nearly half a minute, then McKay came on the line: "What's doing, Chuck?"

"Sir, I'm on a non-secure phone in a drugstore in Lancaster. I just ran into Ben Bernard. He's here—or at least, he *was* here until he saw me. His people were at that place overseas. Can we get a tail and a tap on him?"

"Chuck, you get out there and see if you can tell what kind of car he's driving, get a license number if you can. I'll see what I can do."

As soon as he had hung up, McKay turned to an aide. "Set up a secure conference call with the attorney general and the director of the Bureau ASAP."

Moments later, the connection was complete. McKay filled the two officials in on the situation, telling them only what they needed to know, but emphasizing its importance.

The director of the FBI moved fast. "I'll have our guys out there get on this immediately. But if and when we find him, we re going to need special authorization to tap his phone."

"I'll get the paperwork moving on that," the attorney general broke in. "We have a special panel of judges that have to rule on wiretaps in national security cases. It's a little more complicated than getting a wiretap subpoena in a domestic case, but it can also move a lot faster if it has to.''

"Well, in this case, you move it just as fast as you can," McKay responded. "I'll get background information and a picture of Bernard to you in the next few minutes. Keep me informed."

Nelson ran to the nearest exit from the drugstore and scanned the parking lot, looking for Bernard. As he had expected, there was no sign of him among the hundreds of cars in the lot. Nelson shook his head and resumed his shopping trip.

Acting as a security force at Luke Nash's compound was not at all what the former commandos had expected when they'd signed on with Ben Bernard: they wanted action. But all they were getting was boredom—not much more exciting than being a rent-a-cop in a WalMart. But one thing they could not complain about: the food was not only plentiful, but very good.

Dick Hoffman lingered over his large slab of apple pie à la mode and a cup of coffee, reading a paperback novel. Gradually, other members of the team drifted off to their rooms or the rec room where they gathered when they were off duty.

Hoffman stood and stretched, looking around the room. He was alone except for a single kitchen worker gathering up the last of the dinner dishes. He tucked his paperback under his arm and strolled out the door. Once outside the dining room, he looked up and down the corridor, then turned and walked quickly in the opposite direction from the way the other men had gone. He slipped hurriedly through a fire door that led into a long corridor.

At the third door on the right, Hoffman stopped, took another quick look up and down the hallway, then slid a credit card between the door and the jamb, flicking the lock open. Inside, three quick steps brought him to a row of computers. Pulling up a chair, he sat in front of one of the machines, turned it on, and waited for the familiar desktop of Windows '95 to appear. As soon as the icons appeared, he clicked on the symbol for E-mail, typed out a brief message, clicked on "send," and then, as soon as the message had been transmitted, deleted it from the computer's memory.

Shutting down the computer, he slipped back into the corridor, passed through the fire door, and then sauntered casually into the team's rec room.

One of the men looked up from a card game as Hoffman entered the room. "Hey, Dick, you're just in time. You want to take my hand? I've got to go on duty."

Hoffman sank into a chair across the room. "Naw, no cards tonight. I want to see how this book comes out. At least it's more exciting than this 'action' Big Dog has got us into."

The other man dropped his cards on the table as he rose. "You can sure say that again. This place is boredom center U.S.A."

CHAPTER 22

"SIR, I STRONGLY—STRONGLY—SUGGEST YOU DELAY THIS TRIP until we know more about the situation out there. I am very uncomfortable with the degree of risk involved."

Derek Shepherd, the chief of the Secret Service White House detail, stood almost at attention as he addressed the president.

Maynard Walker waved a hand as though to brush him away.

"I know, I know, and I appreciate your concern. But if I always listened to you guys, I'd never get out of this house. The people out there are hurting, hurting bad, and I'm going to go talk to them. You do whatever you have to do, but I'm going."

He turned quickly to an aide standing at the side of the room.

"Have you got it laid on?"

"Yes, sir. We're getting things set up in a hangar at Edwards where you can meet with the family members of the victims." He turned toward the Secret Service agent. "The president will land at the airbase, meet with the people, and then fly back out from there. That should provide as much security as you could ask for."

Shepherd shrugged, nodded, and then turned to speak to the president. "If you'll excuse me, sir, I'll make the security arrangements."

As Air Force One began its descent, Maynard Walker looked up from the desk where he had been busy with paperwork and gazed north along the spine of the Sierra Nevada Mountains, rising in a steep escarpment on the eastern side and then sloping down to the west into California's central valley. Looking from the south, he could see only a few patches of snow lingering in shady folds in the rock at the higher elevations. He thought wistfully of the days when, shortly after their marriage, he and Marcie had hiked those mountains. He had traded that kind of freedom for the trappings of the nation's highest office. At times like this, he wondered if he hadn't made a bad bargain.

He sighed as he pulled the shade over the window, then lifted a phone that connected him with the cockpit.

"Jim, before we land, please make a couple of turns over Mojave. I want to see what it looks like."

"Ah, roger, Mr. President. We've already had traffic cleared out of that airspace. I'll let you get a good look and then we can go on in and land. Sir, you might be able to see better if you come up here in the cockpit."

Walker walked up the aisle. As he entered the cockpit, the copilot slipped out of his seat, motioned to the president to sit down, and handed him his earphones.

"Sir, if you look right out there at twelve o'clock, you can see what's left of Mojave." The pilot pointed straight ahead at a white blotch on the ground far in the distance.

As they circled the area, Walker could not see the remnants of even a single building rising above the surface of the flat white rectangle. "That's awesome," he murmured.

"Yes, sir," the pilot replied. "I can't imagine anything that would cause that kind of destruction. It sure wasn't just an earthquake."

"No, you're right. We've got our best people trying to figure out what happened." The president was one of the handful who knew the cause of the destruction—and the danger of another attack on a large city.

——— ★ ———

When Walker entered the hangar, more than a hundred men, women, and children were seated on folding chairs. A kind of a stage had been erected by laying planks across the teeth of two forklifts. They turned to look at him, uncertain how to react, and then a ripple of applause came from the group.

A young woman and her two small children stood by their seats in the front row. Tears ran down her face.

Walker broke away from the Secret Service agents, presidential aides, and Air Force officers who surrounded him, strode directly to the woman, and took her in his arms.

He patted her on the shoulder and murmured, "There, there."

She choked back her tears. "Oh, Mr. President. They're all gone. Everybody's gone."

He let go his embrace and held her hands. "What's your name, dear?"

"Angie . . . Angie Peterson, Mr. President."

"I'm so sorry, Angie. I'm so sorry." He put a finger under her chin and lifted her face. "You've got to keep your chin up. Can you do that for me?"

She sniffed, dabbed at her eyes with a damp tissue, and tried to smile. "I'll try, sir. I'll try. And thanks for coming to see us."

Walker turned and walked to the improvised platform, his head bowed in thought. An aide held his arm as he stepped up onto the planks.

"Ladies and gentlemen, I flew over Mojave a few minutes ago and I was appalled at the destruction. I cannot do anything to restore your loved ones to you. But I wanted to be here with you, to offer whatever comfort I can. I have already ordered the director of our Office of Emergency Management to make available whatever help you need to begin to get on with your lives.

"And now, please, each of you take the hand of your neighbor and join with me in a prayer."

Walker spread his arms in front of him, the palms of his

hands facing upward. "Lord, we cannot know the mysterious ways in which your power works among us. We only ask, Lord, that you bring comfort and solace to those gathered here who have lost so much, not just in physical objects but in the lives of loved ones who are no longer with us. Have mercy on the souls of those whose lives were taken and bring comfort to those they have left behind. Amen."

As the prayer ended, Walker climbed down from the platform and walked along the front row of the group, shaking hands and offering words of solace. Soon, many of those from the rear pressed forward until he was surrounded by people reaching out for his touch.

Friends often thought that it was at times like this that Maynard Walker was at his best. Somehow, people knew that he was not just a politician going through the motions and saying the right words. The deep personal feeling he experienced when he was with people who were suffering seemed to flow out through the look on his face, the movements of his body, even the tips of his fingers as he reached out to touch those who surrounded him.

The president stayed with the people for more than half an hour, shaking hands and talking briefly with each of them. Then, once again surrounded by aides, he walked toward the door, looking back over his shoulder to wave as the group applauded. Several raised their voices to shout, "Thank you, Mr. President."

CHAPTER 23

CHUCK NELSON'S REPORT THAT HE HAD RUN INTO BEN BERNARD went through the Lancaster office of the FBI like an electric shock. Because of the unusual circumstances of the Mojave disaster, the bureau had moved a contingent of agents from its large Los Angeles office to Lancaster. So far, they had had little to do.

Now, with a name to go on, they went eagerly to work by telephone, checking motel registrations and rental car agencies. It was not a big surprise that Bernard had not registered or rented a vehicle using his own name. The next step was to canvass the same places on foot, showing Bernard's picture to as many people as possible. The agents carried two pictures, one showing a clean-shaven Bernard from the Pentagon files, and another enhanced with the beard Nelson had seen Bernard wearing.

It was two full days before the surveillance began to pay off. First, a clerk at a rental car agency in Los Angeles recognized the bearded Bernard as the man who, using a different name, had rented a car earlier in the week—the day before the destruction of Mojave. He had returned the car at LA International about four hours after Nelson had spotted him in Lancaster.

The agents went from one ticket counter to the next at the same time of day Bernard had presumably left Los Angeles, showing the pictures to scores of airline clerks. Finally, one recalled selling a ticket to Albuquerque to a man who looked like Bernard. The FBI bureau in Albuquerque was alerted and asked to check rental car agencies there. None of them had rented a car to anyone looking like Bernard.

At FBI headquarters in Washington, an agent contacted AT&T, MCI, and Sprint to see if Bernard had used a telephone credit card in the last few days. Sometimes a person who wants to avoid surveillance will go to elaborate extremes to equip himself with false identification and then carelessly use a memorized telephone credit card number. Sure enough, Bernard's calling card record showed a series of calls to three different unlisted numbers in the 719 area code that covers southwestern Colorado, including Pueblo and Colorado Springs.

The director of the FBI placed a call to McKay. "Admiral, we've turned up calls charged to Bernard's calling cards to three numbers in the Colorado Springs area. Each appears to be a residential phone. We're checking the names of the phone customers against our files, but so far we haven't found anyone with a criminal or terrorist record.

"Can you tap those phones?"

"Yes, we're running it through the special national security court and we should have bugs in place this afternoon."

A small office was set aside in the FBI headquarters in Colorado Springs and three agents were assigned to monitor the three phones in relays around the clock. The agents were ordered to avoid listening to what sounded like personal conversations. If they did record such conversations, they were ordered to erase the tapes of those portions.

For several boring days, the agents heard nothing but brief, apparently innocuous conversations. Then, on the third day, an agent monitoring the unlisted phone registered to Laszlo Nash sat up when he heard a click indicating a call had been connected. And then he heard a pulsating screech similar to the sound made by a fax machine. He pushed the "record" button and taped the sound until the connection was broken three minutes later. To his trained ear, it sounded not like a fax machine, but a sophisticated scrambling device.

As soon as the sound stopped, he placed a direct call to the

FBI laboratories in Washington and arranged to have the experts there listen to the sounds and see if they could break the code that had turned the conversation into gibberish. He knew it would take hours, perhaps even days, and might require help from the National Security Agency—the government's codebreakers—to get a clear text of the conversation. Even with the government's top experts, there was no assurance they would be able to break the code.

The special agent in charge of the Colorado Springs office called the director in Washington: "Sir, we have an intercept from one of those three phones with a scrambled conversation. We may be onto something here."

"Good work," the director replied. "Let's get some very quiet surveillance on that place. I don't want anything obvious. But I want to know who's going in and out, and anything we can find out about how many people are there."

"Did you come up with anything on this Nash fellow?"

"Not much. We seem to be stuck with a dry hole on Laszlo Nash. We've found a record in New York that a Laszlo Nagy changed his name to Laszlo Nash in 1961. Immigration tells us they have a Laszlo Nagy who entered the country from Germany in 1960. He was apparently one of the young men who got out of Hungary when the Russians took over in 1956.

"I wouldn't be surprised if he worked for the Agency in Germany in the late fifties. A lot of those Hungarians did. But Langley is being a little slow checking their records for us—as usual.

"A Laszlo Nash, of the Colorado Springs address, is listed with the Securities and Exchange Commission, but he does not seem to be connected with any of the large brokerages."

The special agent in Colorado Springs took swift notes as his boss gave him the rundown. "Not much to go on there, is there, sir? No criminal record? No ties to bad guys?"

"None. He seems to be a man who likes his privacy. But that's not a crime."

"No, it's not. Well, we'll keep an eye on his place and keep monitoring those phone lines. I'm also setting up surveillance on any cellular phone traffic around Nash's place. I guess there's not much more we can do."

CHAPTER 24

As soon as Chuck Nelson, Mark Rattner, and Jim Malcolm arrived back at Site Y, they gathered in Nelson's office with Pat Collins.

"Okay, Pat, what do we know?" Nelson asked.

Collins had posted a large map of the world on the wall, but she had also brought along a globe, which stood in the center of the conference table.

"I've been talking with a friend at NORAD," she explained. "This is what we think happened: if the plane was in Uzbekistan, as we believe it was, a great circle route would take it directly north, over the North Pole, and then south over North America. It would cross Mojave on a course from the northeast to the southwest."

She traced the route on the globe.

"That's just the pattern we saw on the ground out there— northeast to southwest," Malcolm said.

Collins continued: "Before it was modified with the addition of the ramjet engines, the Blackjack bomber had an unrefueled combat radius of 4,535 statute miles. We don't know what the substitution of the ramjet engines did to its range, but let's assume that number is still in the ballpark. That's not enough to get it from Uzbekistan to Mojave and back again. So our question is: 'Where is it now?'"

Mark Rattner broke in. "You know, this is beginning to sound familiar—déjà vu all over again. Back in the Cold War, we used to play some elaborate war games, figuring all the ways the Soviets might attack us. Of course the big worry was missiles. But we also worried about their bombers—perhaps more than we needed to.

"We figured they could make a pretty good-sized bomber attack on this country—but they couldn't get their planes home again, either because some of the bombers weren't equipped for refueling, or because we didn't think they could refuel the planes that were equipped.

"Would they make a massive, one-way suicide attack? Well, maybe, if we're talking about an all-out Armageddon. But probably not. Air crews want at least some chance of survival. What we came up with as our solution to their problem was to come over the Pole, bomb the targets in the U.S., and then recover at airfields in Cuba. The Soviets gave some credibility to our theory when their bombers began flying training missions to Cuba. It was a scenario with some obvious holes in it, but it was the best we could do."

Pat Collins nodded. "That's almost exactly what we've been thinking, Mark. NORAD lost the plane after it crossed out over the Pacific. Our assumption is that it then descended and came back in for a landing somewhere here." She went to the wall and laid a hand across the map, covering most of Mexico and Central America and part of the Caribbean.

"We monitor air traffic in and out of Cuba and in much of the Caribbean pretty well. We're still checking, but I don't have any reports yet of anything that sounds like what we're looking for. Our own coverage of Mexico and the Central American countries is much thinner. So our best guess is that he landed somewhere here."

She drew a circle with her finger to indicate southern Mexico, the Yucatán Peninsula, and Guatemala.

"This is an area of nearly eight hundred thousand square miles. A lot of it is water, but it is still a big, big area."

Nelson laughed. "Well, Pat, now that we've got it narrowed down. . . ."

"Right, Chuck. We are talking about a very big haystack."

The room was silent for nearly a minute as they all stared at the map. Finally, Nelson looked around the table. "Any ideas?"

"Not beyond the obvious ones, Chuck," Rattner volunteered. "I assume we're doing everything we can to check radio transmissions and radar intercepts. Can we get a U-2 over that area?"

"We're checking radio and radar as well as we can, Mark," Collins responded. "But we're limited, especially when it comes to asking other countries for help. We don't want to reveal exactly what we're looking for, but if we don't tell them, there's a limit to how helpful they can be. As far as a U-2 is concerned, we've already begun recon flights out of Florida, recovering in Panama. We'll leave it to the State Department to smooth things out when some of those countries start complaining about violation of their airspace. By then, we should be finished."

"I sure wish we had a Blackbird," Rattner broke in. The SR-71 Blackbird was the world's super spy plane, flying much higher and faster than the U-2, which was more like a motorized glider. But the Blackbird, with its highly sophisticated sensors, had been taken out of service in an ill-advised fit of penny pinching. With it, the search for possible landing sites for the Blackjack would have been faster and more likely to produce results.

Jim Malcolm had been silent, studying the map and the globe, throughout the discussion.

"I've been thinking . . ." he began. The others grew silent and turned toward him. "Even if we don't know where the plane is, exactly, even if all we know is that it's probably somewhere in that eight hundred thousand–mile circle, we can still make some realistic guesses about what might come next."

He rose and moved over so he could reach the globe. "Look at this. If the plane is here, where is it likely to go next?" He looked around the room and then continued. "My guess is that he'll go home, back up over the Pole."

Malcolm leaned over and traced a line on the globe with his finger, up to the North Pole and then back down to Uzbekistan.

"See where that takes him? Right up the Mississippi River valley. If my assumption is correct that the attack on Mojave was just the rehearsal for something truly dreadful, then perhaps we can make an educated guess at what the next target—or targets—might be.''

The others gathered around the globe.

"Look at the cities, here,'' Malcolm continued. "We've got New Orleans, Memphis, Saint Louis, perhaps Chicago, and Minneapolis–Saint Paul. We're talking about cities with a combined population of . . . what? Four or five million?''

The four of them stood staring at the globe.

"Could he hit them all?'' Collins asked.

"Technically, I think it's possible,'' Malcolm replied. "As near as I can figure, that device doesn't require any fuel. As I've explained before, it simply focuses the energy with which the earth is constantly bombarded. He could probably fly up the valley, turning the device on and off, zapping one city after another.''

Collins shook her head. "That's awful.''

"No question. The destruction of Mojave was already something awful. But let's pursue this a little further.'' Malcolm had begun to sound almost like he had back when he was lecturing college students. But in this case, he was laying out his thoughts as they came to him rather than working from a carefully prepared lesson plan.

"Let's say whoever is controlling this weapon wanted to make a demonstration at Mojave—to get our attention. I don't think it was an accident that the attack occurred during a national convention. Now, let's say he wants to do something very destructive, perhaps aimed at creating turmoil in this country and probably in much of the world. Does he need to destroy four or five cities and kill four or five million people?''

Still playing the professor, he looked around the room to make sure everyone was following his argument. "No. I don't think he needs to do anything that destructive. Wiping out a single one of these cities would be sufficient to create as much turmoil as anyone could wish for. Anything more than that would be overkill.''

"But Jim, this is all crazy.'' Nelson was clearly disturbed. "We're dealing with a guy who should be in the loony bin.

If some crazy person has control of this weapon, why wouldn't he zap all the cities and the people he can?''

"I'm a physicist, not a psychiatrist, Chuck. But I don't think that whoever has control of this weapon is crazy in the sense that he is out of control. Everything we have seen so far indicates that he. . . ." Malcolm paused and nodded toward Collins. "Perhaps I should say 'he or she'—equal opportunity terrorism—everything indicates that he or she is acting according to a rational plan. Snatching the plane and the weapon out from under our noses indicated a superb intelligence capability, careful planning, and almost certainly, virtually unlimited purse strings.

"I think we can call this person 'diabolical' or 'amoral' or 'depraved,' but I don't think we can write him—or her—off as crazy. Whoever is doing this has a very clear purpose in mind—no matter how distorted that purpose might seem to us.''

"So. . . .'' Nelson summed up. "We have a perfectly rational person doing perfectly irrational things. Is that it?''

Malcolm grinned. "Something like that, Chuck.''

"Let's take a break,'' Nelson concluded. "Pat, I'd like you and Dr. Malcolm to put together a report summarizing what we've been talking about here and get it off to Admiral McKay as soon as possible. Make a clear distinction between what we know—which is damned little—and what we have been speculating about. Let's get back together here in about forty-five minutes or an hour and talk about what we can do about this thing—if anything.''

An hour later, the same group assembled around the conference table in Nelson's office. He began the session with a question addressed to Mark Rattner.

"Mark, what kind of radar coverage does the Air Force have facing in that direction? If this guy takes off and heads north, can we spot him?''

"Yeah, we really do have pretty good coverage. We've got a lot of radar looking for drug courier planes trying to slip into the U.S. Our guy would probably be above that coverage by the time he reaches the CONUS.'' Rattner did not even realize he had slipped in an acronym for Continental United States. ''We also have some powerful radar focused in that direction to give warning of attack by submarine-launched or orbital missiles. This plane wouldn't really be on the kind of trajectory those radars are designed to detect, but they should be able to pick him up if they're alerted to look for him.''

''NORAD is already watching that corridor,'' Collins interjected.

''So, there is a chance that we can detect the plane if and when it takes off from somewhere down there and heads in our direction. Is that right?'' Nelson asked.

Rattner nodded. ''I think the emphasis is on the word 'chance.' If we're lucky, we'll spot him. But there are no guarantees.''

''Say we spot him. What do we do next?''

Rattner shrugged. ''*Nada.* There's nothing we can do.''

''What do you mean, nothing? Why can't we shoot him down?''

''Yeah, right. Shoot him down with what? We don't have any anti-aircraft guns or missiles that can hit anything flying that high and that fast. We don't have any planes that can get up there and tangle with him. Remember back in the fifties, when we flew the U-2 over Russia and they couldn't hit it? Not until they had a lucky shot and brought down Gary Powers. Same thing. We don't have anything that can get up there.''

Collins shook her head. ''You mean the U.S. doesn't have any defense against a bomber flying over this country?''

''Nope. Not at that altitude. Same goes for missiles. We've been talking about a missile defense for forty or fifty years now, and we still don't have one.''

A glum silence settled over the room. Finally, Malcolm spoke. ''Mark, refresh my memory. You're an F-15 pilot, aren't you?''

''Yeah, I was an Eagle driver before I switched over into special operations as a Pave Low pilot. Great airplane. But if you're thinking of trying to get up that high with an F-15, forget it. When the Eagle runs out of air and stalls out, this guy is another eight miles straight up.''

Malcolm, under pressure of the anti-smoking campaign and the frowns of friends, had given up smoking his pipe indoors, but he took it out now and placed the stem between his lips as he thought.

''I'm trying to remember, Mark. Didn't the Air Force at one time do some tests using an F-15 as a satellite-killer?''

Rattner sat with his chin resting in the palm of his right hand, deep in thought, for several minutes. Then he sat abruptly upright.

''Jim, you may be onto something. That was before my time, but you're right. I remember hearing about it from an instructor in flight school. He had been one of the test pilots. As I recall, the idea was to fly an F-15 just as high as it would go—maybe something like eighty thousand feet—and then pop off a missile with its own guidance system that would go on up and knock out a satellite.''

''That's right,'' Malcolm said. ''What did they call that thing, Mark?''

''I'm not even sure it ever got a name.''

''Maybe that's our answer,'' Nelson broke in. ''Are there any of those systems still around?''

''I don't know, Chuck. You know, all of us in the military are relatively young. We have the institutional memory of a five-year-old.''

''Can you find out?''

''I can try. But it will mean making a lot of phone calls. What about our opsec?''

''That's a problem, all right. With caller-ID, almost anyone you call can know the number you're calling from. I don't like that.''

Collins broke in. ''Chuck, why don't you have Mark and perhaps someone else go into town, check into a motel, and call from there? Even if someone picks up the phone number, it won't make any difference.''

''Okay, I guess that's the best we can do. Mark, why don't you take Marker with you and do as Pat suggests?''

''Sounds good, Chuck. Rex is a sharp kid.''

When Rattner met with the group the next morning, he had a handful of pages torn from a pad of yellow foolscap paper.

"What did you find out, Mark?" Nelson asked.

"We're still trying to put things together, Chuck. But from what we found out, this thing just might work. We're going to have to work fast to make all the pieces fit together, but this is what we learned.

"Dr. Malcolm was right. The Air Force did do a lot of work on this system between about 1979 and 1985. It was essentially a two-part system, a specially equipped A model of the F-15 carrying a two-stage missile. The plane would fly as high as it could and then fire off the missile. The business end of the missile was a little warhead designed to home in on the satellite target. 'Warhead' is probably not the right word. It didn't carry any explosive. It was more like a big rock. It slammed into the target at something like eleven thousand miles an hour and just blew it away."

"Did the system work?" Malcolm asked.

"Technically, yes. Politically, no. They ran some tests out of Edwards in 1984 in which the warhead was aimed at the infrared signature of a star. In other words, it just flew off into space. But on September 13, 1985, they fired it at an actual satellite—the six-year-old *Solwind* satellite, which had been put in orbit to gather information on the radiation coming from the sun.

"The system worked perfectly. The F-15 climbed at an angle of more than sixty degrees and fired off the missile while flying at just under the speed of sound at about eighty thousand feet. The satellite was in a polar orbit at an altitude of about three hundred twenty miles. The warhead found the satellite, homed in, and destroyed it on impact.

"That, unfortunately, was the first and last live test for the system. The scientists involved with *Solwind* were pissed. Even though the satellite had lasted longer than expected, it was still transmitting data—and of course that stopped abruptly. And the system was also criticized by arms control advocates, who were generally opposed to the deployment of anti-satellite systems.''

"So it never became operational?" Nelson asked.

"Not really. The program was officially dropped in 1986. But I found out that three or four F-15s were modified to carry the system and were actually delivered to interceptor squadrons at McChord Air Force Base in Washington and Langley in Virginia.''

"Where are those planes now?" Collins asked.

"They're probably up on concrete piers, serving as lawn decorations at some Air Force base," Rattner replied. "But I've got some lines out now to see if any of them is still around.''

"Mark, even if you can find one of those planes, we'd still need a missile. Are there any available?" Malcolm asked.

"Finding one of them may be harder than finding a properly equipped plane, Jim. The Vought Corporation developed the weapon. But with the shrinkage of the defense industry in the last few years, Vought was gobbled up, then gobbled up again. We'll be lucky to find anyone who even remembers this system. I think our best hope is that one or more of the missiles might be in storage out at Edwards, where the tests were conducted. We're checking that.''

"It seems to me the key is finding the missile," Malcolm suggested. "If we can do that, perhaps we can configure another F-15 to carry it.''

"I'm not sure it would work, especially considering that we probably have little or no time to put this all together. The modified F-15s had a backup battery, a microprocessor, and a data-link for mid-course guidance of the missile. I really doubt we can cobble together such a system in the time we have with any assurance it would work. For example, the computer in the plane is going to have to talk to a missile that is more than a decade old. In computer terms, that's a lot of lifetimes. We'll almost certainly need a mid-eighties computer in the plane to make it work. We're going to have to find one of those three or four planes.''

"Looks like we've got our work cut out for us," Nelson broke in. "More like *you've* got *your* work cut out for you,

Mark. If any of the rest of us can help, let us know. Otherwise, you and Rex keep after the plane and missile.''

———— ★ ————

As the others drifted off, Nelson looked at his watch. This was the hard part—just waiting. Until the U-2 surveillance flights turned up something and Rattner tracked down an old F-15 and found a missile in storage, there wasn't much more they could do.

"Want to take a ride in the desert?"

Pat Collins smiled. "Why not? We're not doing much good here biting our nails."

Nelson, with his shoulder feeling better every day, took the wheel and drove once more to the top of a nearby hill with a sweeping view over the desert in all directions. A large golden moon was just peeking over the horizon.

Collins leaned back and stretched. "It's good to get out of that place for a little bit. I'm beginning to feel what it's like to be in prison."

"Yeah, I know what you mean. I really worry about our guys. Those young animals are not used to being cooped up. I try to keep them busy training, but they know we don't have a mission and they're starting to get frustrated. I wish I could send them into town for a night to let off some steam. But I know a couple of commanders who've done that. They're not commanders any more."

"Well, it won't be too long now. I don't see how this can go on very much longer. It'll all be over, one way or the other."

Nelson had his hands on the steering wheel in front of him. As they talked, he thought about putting his arm around the woman next to him and pulling her close to him. But reaching out with his right arm didn't seem like the smart thing to do. Any unusual motion was sure to send a stab of pain through his whole upper body.

"Pat," he said, turning toward her. "Would you like to come over here?"

"I thought you'd never ask." She turned and lay across his lap, facing him. "Is this better?"

Nelson drew her toward him with his left arm and leaned down until their lips met. When they came up for air, he murmured, "Yes, much better."

"You know, I've really gotten to rely on you since we've been out here, Pat. I guess I shouldn't feel this way, but I'm almost happy this whole thing has happened because it has thrown us together." As he spoke, he gently undid the buttons of her white blouse. His hand slid under the strap of her bra and pushed it down off her shoulder. "Do you mind?"

"No. I like." She smiled up at him and drew his head down for another long kiss as she felt his fingers caressing her breast. She ran her own hand up under his T-shirt, being careful not to touch his still-tender shoulder wound.

"Here," she said, pulling up on his T-shirt. "Let's get rid of this." She pushed it up over his head as he reached his arms upward. Then she kissed him on the neck and gently, very gently, drew her tongue across the red gash where the bullet had torn into his shoulder.

With his left hand, he reached back, awkwardly unfastened her bra, and helped her slip off her shirt and bra. She leaned against his chest and moved slightly from side to side, sliding her breasts across his bare skin.

He grinned down at her. "Do you think we can get a little more comfortable?"

She giggled and rubbed against him again. "You're not comfortable?"

He put a hand on her breast and kissed her again. "I said *more* comfortable. Why don't you lean back and let me scrunch around and get on my left side." He pushed the gearshift up into "low," out of the way. After an awkward moment, they lay side by side on the long flat bench seat of the pickup truck.

Nelson loosened the belt of her shorts and slid his fingers down her hip and onto her thigh. She moved herself slowly back and forth, pressing back gently against the pressure she felt between her legs.

"I love you, Commander Nelson. I love you very much."

"I love you, too, Mrs. Collins. Can you feel how much I love you?"

"Yes, I feel you." She pushed his shorts down and took him in her hand. "Yes, I like the way you feel."

He pulled her shorts further down and gently caressed her, feeling her moistness as she responded to his touch.

"I feel you, too."

They pulled aside for a moment as both kicked off their clothes and then they rolled together. Nelson balanced above her, holding himself with his left arm, and then, as she guided him, entered deep within her body.

Perhaps because they had both been holding their emotions in check while privately anticipating this moment, they could feel each other coming to a pulsing climax with one shuddering wave of sensation building upon another.

Pat pulled his lips down to her, murmuring, "Don't move. Just hold me close."

Finally, they rolled over onto their sides and lay together, feeling each other's closeness.

She rose on an elbow and looked down at Nelson. "Chuck, I needed that." She sighed. "We're getting deeper into this business than I thought we would. What are we going to do?"

He lay back and stared at the ceiling of the pickup. "Yeah, I know what you mean. I haven't thought things through. But all I know now is that I'm very much in love with you. Why don't we just relax and see how things work out?"

"Right now, I don't care. All I know is that I love you—and that you're a wonderful lover." She reached down and gently caressed him. "A wonderful lover."

When they pulled up in front of Nelson's office, Jeff Bonior was standing on the steps.

"Evening sir . . . Mrs. Collins."

Collins took one look at his face and thought to herself, "Oh, God. He knows!" She quickly excused herself and went to her room.

"What's doing, Jeff?"

"Colonel Rattner and Rex Marker are back, sir. The colonel says he has some good news to report."

"Okay, Jeff. Would you please tell him I'm in my office?"

"He's waiting for you inside, sir. Marker said he had something he wanted to discuss with me. I'm going to go check him out."

Nelson bounded up the steps and into his office.

"What's the word, Mark?"

"We're in luck, sir. The Air Force turned one of the planes we're looking for over to NASA as a test bird. They have it out at Edwards. And they also found one of the missiles in storage out there."

"That's great, Mark. Can you fly it?"

"Sure. Once you learn to fly, it's like riding a bicycle. You never forget."

"How long will it take to get it ready to go?"

"The NASA folks are working on it right now. The bird itself is operational. But they'll have to check out the special equipment associated with the missile. That hasn't been used for a long time."

"Well, that leaves us with the problem of where to position the plane and the missile. We're only going to get one shot and we don't know where he's coming from or when. Big problem."

"I've been thinking about that, Chuck. Remember this afternoon how Jim Malcolm ran up the Mississippi River valley? My guess is that the target will be Saint Louis, since the recent convention focused a lot of attention there and the other party will soon be convening in the same place."

"I'd forgotten about the next convention. That makes sense. So you think you ought to position the plane in Saint Louis?"

"No, I don't think so. We could be wrong. If he decides to take out New Orleans or Memphis while we're sitting and waiting for him in Saint Louis, he wins. I'd feel safer waiting further south. Then, if we get any kind of advance radar warning, I can go for him while he's still out over the Gulf. That way, even if we're right that the target is Saint Louis, we will have taken care of the problem."

"That makes sense. How long does it take you to get up there to release the missile?"

"I'll be carrying a full load of fuel and a twenty-seven

hundred–pound missile. If I were in just the right place, I figure it would take me about ten minutes from takeoff to weapon release. Add thirty seconds or a minute from that point until impact. But I'll probably have to do some maneuvering to get in position, so it'll take longer than that.''

''Okay, Mark, you get on out to Edwards tonight and get that plane into position as soon as possible. When does the next convention begin?''

''I think it's a week from tomorrow. But I'm not going to assume we've got that much time. We just don't know.''

CHAPTER 25

As Nelson and Rattner conferred, Bonior strode quickly down the street and rapped on the door of the small room Marker shared with another enlisted man.

"What's up, Rex?"

"Let's take a little walk, Chief." Marker closed the door behind him and led the way out into the desert night.

They walked silently for almost a minute until they were away from the buildings.

"Chief, can I tell you something and it'll stay just between us, it won't go any further?"

Bonior paused before answering. "I guess the answer is yes, Rex. But I may tell you very quickly that I don't want to hear any more. What's on your mind?"

"I know I'm not supposed to, but I . . . well, I got bored and started playing around with the Internet."

"That's not what you were supposed to be doing."

"Yes, I know. But the bad part is that I checked to see if I had any E-mail. I guess that's a pretty big security violation, isn't it?"

"Did you send any messages?"

"No, I just downloaded what was on the server."

"I guess technically somebody could trace that connection and find out where you were."

"The problem is that I got a message that may have to do with what we're doing here. I think it's important, but how am I going to tell Commander Nelson about it without admitting I broke opsec?''

"What's the message?"

"It's from Dick Hoffman. You remember him. He's my best friend . . . the guy who saved my life. Anyway, here's the message." Marker pulled a piece of paper out of his pocket and handed it to Bonior. The big chief stopped and moved over under a streetlight and held the printout so he could read it. He skipped over the heading to the message:

"Rex: In a hurry. Don't want to get caught. We're at a place in the Rockies above Colorado Springs. Guarding the place. They call it the Rock House. I don't know what's going on, but I think this has something to do with what happened to Mojave. Scares me. Dick sends."

Bonior turned to look at Marker. "How long have you had this, Rex?"

"I retrieved it just before the colonel and I left town—not more than an hour and a half."

"Come on, let's go see the commander. I'll try to protect you if there's a problem over opsec. But this is too important to sit on. It may just be the clue that'll blow this whole thing wide open."

He turned and jogged toward Nelson's office, Marker trailing just behind.

Bonior knocked quickly on Nelson's door and then entered breathlessly, without waiting for a response.

"Look at this, skipper," he said, holding out the message. "Marker picked this up off the Internet. Here, read it!"

Nelson held the paper under his desk lamp and quickly scanned it.

"Holy shit! How long ago did this come in?"

"Like I told the chief, not more than an hour and a half ago, sir," Marker replied.

"Rex was worried about violating opsec, sir. He waited to tell me about it."

"Oh, the hell with opsec. Good work, Marker. Rig up your computer and check your E-mail every half hour to see if there are any more messages."

Nelson picked up his phone and dialed Pat Collins's number. "Pat, please come on over to my office. I think we've got a big break here." He turned to Bonior and Marker. "You two hang loose. I may be needing you."

Bonior and Marker left as Collins entered the room.

Nelson glanced at his watch. It was just after 11 o'clock, well past midnight back in Washington. He picked up his secure line to the chairman's office.

"Yes, I know it's late. I don't care if he's asleep. Patch me through!"

There was a pause, and then Nelson heard a rattling sound as though someone had groped for the phone in the dark and didn't yet have a firm grasp on it.

"Sir, I think we've got a break here. One of my young SEALs picked up a message from the Internet. Here, let me read it to you."

Nelson paused a moment until he was sure Adm. McKay was fully awake and then read the brief message.

"Just what we need, Chuck. Please fax the message to my office and I'll send it on to the FBI. This is beginning to firm up. Chuck, you get your guys up to Peterson Field in Colorado Springs right away. We may need you there."

"Roger, sir. We'll be on the ground there by noon tomorrow, our time."

McKay slipped carefully out of bed and groped for his robe in the dark. His wife stirred fitfully but didn't awaken. She had long ago grown used to phone calls in the middle of the night. The only time she became upset was when someone called with trivia that should have been handled at a lower level. One of the McKays' long-standing family jokes concerned an early morning call that did wake her up. When the admiral had finally hung up the phone, his wife had asked irritably, "What was that all about?"

"We may be at war before dawn," he whispered.

"Oh, that's all right," she'd murmured sleepily, before turning over and dropping off to sleep again.

McKay quietly closed the door, stepped across the carpeted

hall into his den, and slipped into the executive chair in front of his large, heavy oak desk. One wall of the room was covered with pictures recording the admiral's Navy career, from the fading picture of the fresh-faced young ensign on his graduation from the Academy to the mature naval officer shaking hands with the president.

He picked up the green phone that linked him directly through a secure line to his office in the Pentagon.

"Get me the director of the FBI," he instructed.

Moments later the director came on the line, sounding not at all sleepy.

"Did I wake you?" McKay asked.

"No, I couldn't sleep. I'm down at our command center watching this thing. It's getting pretty damned frustrating, Mac. We've got surveillance on that place in Colorado Springs and we're monitoring all their telephone and radio transmissions but we're not getting anything worthwhile. We suspect they're using encrypted satcomm. We intercepted one brief message, but we've only gotten a few words out of it."

"Well, I think we really have something here. One of our young SEALs got a message from a friend on the E-mail that we think came from that place in Colorado Springs. It says he thinks there's some link to the Mojave incident. That's the firmest thing we've had so far."

"Can you get the text of that message to me?"

"You should have it any minute. I told my people to fax it to my office at the Pentagon, and they'll zap it right on over to you," McKay replied.

"You know, this really could be our big break. I've been wanting to get a look inside that place, and this may be just what we need to get a search warrant. Where are you now?"

"I'm at home in my den. They woke me up when this message came in."

"Well, there's not much for you to do now. I'll let you know as soon as there are any developments."

CHAPTER 26

BEN BERNARD ALWAYS THOUGHT OF HIMSELF AS THE KIND OF man who occasioned fear in the hearts of others rather than one who suffered such fear. But he could not hide from himself that this strange man for whom he worked was able, without even raising his voice, to cause his stomach muscles to tighten and to send a chill down his spine.

It was early on the morning after the vote on the presidential nomination and the sun was just working its way across the vast expanse of land from the Mississippi to the Rockies.

Bernard hesitated in the doorway as his eyes grew accustomed to the dim light and then walked toward Nash's desk.

"Yes?"

"Sir, we've got a problem."

"What kind of a problem, *Commander*?" Bernard wished the son of a bitch would not use his old rank that way.

"We're under surveillance."

"How do you know?"

"My men have been monitoring the road out there. They've seen the same vehicles pass a number of times."

"How do they know they're the same?"

"License numbers."

"What else?"

"One car parked near the entrance to your compound. One of the old tricks. Guy got out and put up the hood as though he had engine trouble."

Nash shrugged. "Maybe he did."

"Yeah, maybe. But when you see a car parked in your driveway with 'police special' tires, it makes you wonder."

"Yes, it does, doesn't it? What happened?"

"One of our guys walked across the street and offered to help. Gave him a chance to size up this fellow. He was about thirty-five, neatly dressed. Had a bulge under his left armpit. The car had a whip antenna."

"So, what do you think?"

"We're in the county here. Wouldn't be a city cop. And it didn't look like a sheriff's deputy to me. My guess: FBI."

"Is he still there?"

"No, he told my guy he had called for a tow. He had a cellular phone in his hand. And sure enough, a little later a commercial tow truck came by and hauled him away."

Nash stood and strode across the room and back. Bernard had never seen him leave his chair before. He was impressed by the way the older man carried himself, like an athlete in superb condition.

"So they're watching us. What does that mean?"

"Sir, we've had our scanners monitoring the channels used by the police and the FBI. There's been an unusual amount of traffic, but nothing that tells us very much. The only interesting thing has been several references to 'Mojave.' We can't tell from what we've heard whether it has something to do with us or whether it's just the fact that Mojave is in the news."

"I don't like this, Mr. Bernard."

"I don't either, sir. Our security here is ironclad. But this makes me nervous just the same."

"Let me think about this. And keep me informed of any developments."

"Yes, sir." Bernard started to leave.

"Oh, Mr. Bernard. One other thing."

Bernard turned, halfway to the door.

"There is that matter of the security lapse in Uzbekistan."

Bernard stood silently. He thought that had been forgotten.

"I have kept you in my employ because you have otherwise performed well and this is not the time to bring in a new security team. But as I told you when we first met in this office, I demand absolute precision in carrying out my orders."

"Yes, sir."

"In view of your lapse, I am reducing your personal payment for that segment of your assignment by fifty percent. Do you understand me? I am reducing your *personal* payment. I do not want to penalize the men working for you, but I want you to be personally aware of the penalties for even the slightest failure."

Bernard, whose financial condition always teetered on the brink, felt as though he'd been kicked in the gut. But he was in no mood to argue. All he wanted to do was to get out of this dim room, away from this sinister creature with those eyes that he could feel but never see.

"Yes, sir. Will that be all, sir?"

"Yes, you may go."

As Bernard left the room, Nash picked up the phone and spoke a few words.

A moment later, a tall, thin man entered the room. His face was so pale that someone who did not know him might have thought he was ill. He was one of the stable of top-notch lawyers that Nash relied on to keep his operations just inside the law—or to be able to defend him whenever he crossed that line. Even though it was early, the lawyer had already been at his desk for nearly an hour. He had learned that it did not pay be to caught sleeping when Nash called.

"Sit down." Nash gestured toward a chair. "Bernard thinks we're under surveillance by the FBI."

The man nodded.

"Our physical security is as good as we can make it. I'm not worried about that. But let's just play a game here. Suppose the FBI comes up, knocks on the front gate and says they've got a search warrant. What do we do?"

The lawyer made a steeple of his fingers and let the hint of a smile creep across his lips.

"We invite them in and offer them a cup of coffee."

"And. . . ."

"Well, first, I'll try to get advance warning if such a thing is going to happen. We have friends in both the local and federal courts. I suspect this will be handled by a federal court. If a warrant is issued, I'd like to see the supporting affidavits. They will try to do this in secrecy, but we may still get a look at the documents. If they do come here, have your people stall them as long as possible. The search warrant will have to specify what they are looking for. I will want to examine it very carefully and make sure that their search doesn't go beyond the bounds of the warrant. If the wording of the warrant is limited, we may be able to tell them to go ahead and search.''

''I don't want the FBI mucking around here.''

''Neither do I, sir. But we may not have much choice. And I will of course attempt to have the warrant quashed or withdrawn. This, I'm afraid, is one of those things we're just going to have to play by ear. Meantime, if there are things you don't want the bureau to see, you might make them hard to find. But I don't want anything overt—no moving vans carrying stuff out of here, if you know what I mean.''

As the lawyer left the room, Nash paced back and forth across his office, thinking of what should be hidden—and how. He concluded there really wasn't too much to be worried about. In preparation for just such an emergency, his technical people had prepared an extra hard drive for each computer in the compound. In effect, Nash kept two sets of electronic books. One accurately reflected all his transactions. The other was a dummy set that left out all of the more interesting items but still contained enough transactions to appear credible.

Nash picked up the phone. ''I think it's time to switch the hard drives.''

Within the next half hour, all hard drives in the compound's computers had been changed and the originals carefully hidden away. Although Nash and his technicians did not realize it, they had, in the process, hidden away the electronic record of the message Dick Hoffman had sent surreptitiously from one of the compound's computers.

Nash's remaining worry was the security of the command center from which he controlled the weapon. But then he shrugged. To any outsider, the room simply looked like a communications center, not unusual for a business with worldwide interests. He decided the FBI could look around the room if they wanted to.

———— ★ ————

At Edwards Air Force Base, the sun had not yet emerged over the eastern horizon when Mark Rattner arrived at the hangar where the old F-15 was stored. As he entered the building, he saw a group of men clustered around the plane. One of them broke away from the group to greet him.

"Colonel Rattner? 'Morning. We're the Tiger Team from Boeing." The F-15 had been developed and built for the Air Force by the McDonnell Aircraft division of the McDonnell Douglas Corporation, which had recently been taken over by Boeing. "Let's take a walk around the plane. The bird looks to me as though it's in first-rate condition. But it hasn't been flown for a while, and I don't like that. As you know, airplanes are meant to be flown. When they just sit around, all sorts of bad things happen."

The plane was painted white with a bold "NASA" in red on the fuselage and the vertical stabilizer.

"Let me take a look in the cockpit," Rattner said. He climbed the ladder leaning against the left side of the plane. He had sometimes wondered why fighter planes were mounted from the left side. Was it some sort of holdover from the old cavalry days, when horses were mounted from the left?

Rattner checked to make sure that the ejection handle was locked in the safe position and then climbed into the cockpit and settled himself into the seat. The instrument panel looked very much like the one in the first F-15 he had flown, years earlier. Later models of the plane had a so-called glass cockpit in which the pilot received almost all his information from a screen like that in a small television set. This cockpit still had a collection of the older round dials in addition to several small cathode ray tubes.

The McDonnell man leaned over his shoulder. "Look familiar, Colonel?"

"Just like home. I won't have any problem with this. How

long is it going to take you guys to get this system operational?''

''Normally this would take a couple of weeks. But we'll do it a lot quicker. That's why they call us the Tiger Team. Give us a couple of days. We'll run up the engines and check them out and go over the avionics. If things go smoothly, we should have you ready for a test hop about three days from now.''

Rattner climbed back out of the cockpit and joined the Boeing man at the foot of the ladder.

''Colonel, we flew one of our A models out from Saint Louis. It's not equipped to handle the missile, but you can fly it for the next couple of days to familiarize yourself with the plane. That way, as soon as we've brought this bird up to speed, you'll be ready to go.''

''Sounds good. I not only want to get the feel of the plane again, but I want to practice the profile of the mission I'll be flying.''

''We don't know anything about that, Colonel. All we were told was to get this plane and the missile ready to go. From then on it's up to you.''

''Roger that. I'll take it from there.''

The special agent in charge of the FBI's Colorado Springs office sat at his desk making a careful list on a pad of yellow foolscap of the items he would need to present to a judge to obtain a warrant to search Nash's Rocky Mountain hideaway.

At the top of the list was the E-mail message from Dick Hoffman to Rex Marker. He also would tell the judge, in a series of affidavits, about telephone calls to and from Nash's place and list several vaguely suspicious intercepted conversations. Agents watching the compound had turned up nothing out of the ordinary, just the normal traffic of people going and coming to and from work and a few delivery trucks.

When he had completed the list, he leaned back and tapped his front teeth with the eraser on his pencil. Except for Hoffman's message, it was a short and not very impressive list. Despite the early hour, several agents were busy preparing affidavits, trying to make them as persuasive as possible. They would be ready when the judge arrived in his chambers as he did every day promptly at 9:30 A.M.

Just before 9 o'clock, the FBI man gathered up his notes and the affidavits that had already been prepared and went to meet with the U.S. Attorney.

"Pretty thin stuff," he told him. "The best thing we have is this E-mail message one of the SEALs received, but it's awfully vague."

The U.S. Attorney glanced over the list. "I don't think the old man's going to buy it. He really has a hangup about the Fourth Amendment. I can just hear him rattling it off by memory." His voice took on a deeper tone: " 'The right of the people to be secure in their persons, houses, papers, and effects, against unreasonable searches and seizures, shall not be violated, and no warrants shall issue, but upon probable cause, supported by oath or affirmation, and particularly describing the place to be searched, and the persons or things to be seized.' "

"Yeah, I've heard it, too." The FBI man shook his head. "But I think we've got to try. We're talking about perhaps thousands of American lives."

"You know that and I know that. But you try telling it to the judge. Do you think you come close to 'particularly describing the place to be searched, and the persons or things to be seized'? I think he's going to see this as a fishing expedition and he's not going to go for it."

The FBI man glanced at his watch. "I told his clerk we'd be down there at nine forty-five. Why don't we go on down and see what happens?"

"Do you have your guys ready to swear to the affidavits?"

"Yeah, they'll meet us there."

The FBI man, the U.S. Attorney, and three more FBI special agents crowded into the judge's chambers. To one side sat the court clerk and a court reporter with a small tape recorder and a stenotype machine on which she kept a record of everything said.

The U.S. Attorney quickly ran through the arguments for a search warrant and then introduced the FBI agents. Each of them swore to the accuracy of the affidavit he or she had prepared.

The judge, dressed in a white shirt with bright red suspenders arcing down over his ample belly, sat impassively as the agents and the U.S. Attorney presented their case.

"All right, gentlemen . . . and ladies," he added, nodding toward a female FBI agent. "I will take this matter under advisement."

"Your Honor, we believe the request for this search warrant bears directly on the security of many citizens of the United States. May I ask when you will reach a decision?" The U.S. Attorney studied the judge's face for a clue to his feelings.

"Yes, yes, I understand. The government is always in a hurry. The government is always concerned about national security. But I must remind you that the controlling issue here is not either of those things that seem so important to the government. The controlling issue here is the Fourth Amendment to the Constitution of the United States. It is my duty to stand firmly against 'unreasonable searches and seizures.' " He glanced at his watch. "I have an important matter before me this morning, but I'll try to have a decision for you by one o'clock."

The court clerk gathered up the affidavits, carried them into her small office next door, and set them on the edge of her desk. Stepping into the corridor, she signaled to a court bailiff and said, "Keep an eye on my office, will you? I've got to run down the hall to the bathroom. Too much coffee this morning."

The bailiff stepped to the door and watched as she walked down the hall. As the clerk entered the ladies' room, the bailiff stepped into her office and quickly glanced through the affidavits lying on her desk. The one containing the brief E-mail message caught his eye. He ran off a copy on the copy machine and then placed the affidavit back where he'd found it.

When the court clerk returned, the bailiff smiled and opened the door for her.

Not long afterward, during his morning break, he slipped into a phone booth and quickly dialed a familiar number.

The pale-faced lawyer at Nash's estate took notes as he listened.

"What'd you say the name was?"

"Dick Hoffman."

"Okay, I've got the message. Good work. We'll take care of you, as usual." The line went dead.

If the lawyer had looked out his window with a pair of powerful binoculars, he might have seen a four-engined olive drab C-130 drift in for a landing at Peterson Field, down in the valley.

Chuck Nelson and his team had spent most of the night checking their weapons, packing their gear, and preparing for the three-hour flight to Colorado Springs. Each of the canvas bucket seats in which they sat along the sides of the plane seemed to have been carefully designed with a metal bar that struck each man just below the shoulder blades. Despite the discomfort, most of them slept soundly from wheels-up until the gentle bump and the sound of the tires rumbling along the runway at Peterson.

Two military buses were waiting when they arrived and parked at an out-of-the-way corner of the field. Nelson detailed four men to remain to guard the plane and their equipment until he could arrange for a guard force provided by the base commander. The buses took them to an old, empty bachelor officers' quarters. An Air Force major was waiting when they arrived. He didn't know who these folks were or why they were here, but he had been impressed by the explicit directions from Washington to provide Nelson and his men with quarters and anything else they needed.

"Major, I'd like some kind of an office or conference room, and we'll need secure communications," Nelson told him.

"Yes, sir. There's a room here that you can use as an office and conference room. We have already received orders to install communications for you, and as you can see, our people are already at work." He motioned to two men on ladders working on a telephone line.

"Okay," Nelson said, "let's get to work. I want to see Mrs. Collins, Dr. Malcolm, Chief Bonior, Marker, and Major Laffer in the office. Rex, do you have any civilian clothes with you?"

"Well, sort of, sir. I've got a pair of slacks, a sports jacket, a sport shirt, and a pair of loafers. No suit or even a necktie, if that's what you mean."

"No, that'll do fine. As soon as our bags are brought over from the plane, you get changed."

As the small group gathered in their makeshift office, Nelson filled them in on their potential mission.

"We have reason to believe that the person or persons responsible for the destruction of Mojave is in a guarded compound up in the foothills west of here. It's possible that they may already be planning an attack on another, larger American city. We have orders to be prepared to assault the compound and prevent them from carrying out their attack."

Laffer, Rattner's copilot, was now the senior Air Force officer in the commando team. "What kind of defenses are we going to come up against?" he asked.

"We're still checking that out, Jack. The FBI has had the place under surveillance since sometime yesterday, and we've run one high-altitude photo flight so far. We don't want to go in too close yet. From what we know now, the compound seems to be pretty heavily defended. It has a secure high wall. The FBI people think they have seen what could be .50-caliber machine gun emplacements, but that's not firm. Those guns could give us a lot of trouble—if that's what they are. We'll know more about that later. We don't know how big the guard force is, but we think at least some of Ben Bernard's people have recently arrived to supplement whatever normal security force they have. With Ben's people there, we certainly don't want to underestimate what we might run into.

"Rex, I want you to go in town to the courthouse and see what you can find out about this place. Check the assessment records. That should tell you how big the place is. They might even have a diagram of the land and grounds. Then check the building permit department. If we're in luck, you should be able to see the plans that were submitted when the place was built. Check the dates on the assessment record. That should show if there were any building permits issued later for modifications. And then make sure you get those plans, too. Think you can handle that?''

"I'm sure I can, sir. I worked several summers in our courthouse back home, so I have a pretty good idea of what to look for and where." He paused for a moment and then added, "If I'm going to get copies of these records, I'll need some money. I've got a credit card, but I've only got thirteen dollars in cash."

Nelson looked around the room. "I don't have any idea how much it might cost. Some of these local bureaucrats charge an arm and a leg to let the public look at 'their' records. Guess we'll have to take up a collection."

Slowly, those around the table began emptying their pockets. Pat Collins counted the stack of bills and change.

"We've got a little over seventy-five dollars," she announced. "What a bunch of high-rollers."

Laffer shifted uneasily in his chair, then pulled out a fat wallet and counted out five one-hundred-dollar bills. "Not much to do back there at Site Y except sit around and play a little cards," he said sheepishly.

Marker gathered up the money and bowed. "Thank you, brethren and sister. The Lord will bless you."

At the courthouse, Marker found his task remarkably simple. The clerks in the assessor's and building permit offices not only were helpful, but seemed eager to help him find what he wanted. Before noon he left the building with a thick sheaf of copies of the public documents—and minus a hefty portion of the $575 with which he had entered the building a few hours before.

The tall, slim attorney glided noiselessly across the floor to a chair facing Nash.

"We have a mole in our midst, sir."

"Go on." Nash's face showed no evidence of surprise or alarm. It was not that he expected a security leak; he had long trained himself to be prepared mentally to deal with the unexpected.

"The U.S. Attorney has requested a search warrant and the judge has taken it under advisement. I was able to obtain information from one of the affidavits submitted to the judge—apparently the most persuasive of the documents. It indicates that someone—a person identified as Dick Hoffman—sent an E-mail message to a friend connecting our establishment here with the destruction of Mojave."

"Do we have a Hoffman on the staff?"

"Yes, sir. He is a young former Navy SEAL who is employed by Mr. Bernard. Our assumption is that he somehow got access to one of our computers and sent this message to his friend. And the friend apparently turned it over to the government."

The lawyer could feel the eyes burning into him.

"I think we had better rid ourselves of this Hoffman."

"I beg your pardon, sir, but I think that might be premature. We don't know at this point whether this Hoffman might have been able to transmit other, more revealing messages. Unfortunately, since we have already switched out the hard drives, it will take a while to go back over the last few days to find out if he was able to send any more. We should begin that task immediately."

"Why don't we just ask him? Gently, of course."

"Whenever I carry out an interrogation, I like to know not only the questions, but the answers as well. That tends to keep the subject honest. If you'll bear with me, sir, I suggest we assign Hoffman to some task where he cannot cause further harm while we search the hard drives—without, of course, alerting him that he is under suspicion. Then we will be in a better position to ask him intelligent questions and to get honest answers."

"You're right—as usual. That, of course, is why I pay you so well." Nash swung around toward the shaded windows and added, after a moment, "I wonder . . . do you think he might be induced, at the appropriate time, to send another message or two—messages that we would write for him?''

"That's a brilliant thought, sir. While we're searching the hard drives, I'll spend a little time composing a couple of misleading messages that he might, as it turns out, be quite eager to send. We could just send them ourselves, now that we know the E-mail address of his friend. But it would be best if he inserted a personal touch to make the messages more believable.''

"Yes," Nash said, turning to the papers on his desk. "Get on with it.''

CHAPTER 27

NELSON SPREAD OUT THE DOCUMENTS MARKER HAD BROUGHT from the courthouse. Tapping the pages from the building permits department with his finger, he exclaimed, "These are just what we need. They really lay out what that place looks like."

Marker stood beside the table with a pleased grin on his face. "I have an idea, sir. Let me see if I can scan these images and get them into my computer. Then we'll be able to manipulate them. It'll be almost like walking through the corridors."

"Do you think you can do it, Rex?"

"How do we get in touch with that major who's supposed to be taking care of us? The Air Force must have a scanner at a base like this."

Nelson picked up the phone on his desk and pressed a button. "Major? Chuck Nelson here. Could you drop by my office, please? Okay, see you in a few minutes.

"Rex, you get those scanned in and get back to me as soon as you do. Incidentally, have you had a chance to check your E-mail today?"

"I checked before I went into town. That was pretty early in the day and there were no messages. I'll keep after it."

Two hours later, Marker was back at Nelson's office with a small portable computer and a projector he had borrowed from the Air Force.

"Look at this, sir!" he exclaimed, as he connected the computer to the projector and flashed a picture onto the wall.

As he manipulated the mouse on his computer, the image on the wall twisted and turned, displaying a corridor, then a corner, and then another corridor.

Marker clicked the mouse and another level of the building was revealed. He picked up a ruler from the desk and pointed to the wall. "It looks to me as though this space here is the main office suite. That's where Mr. Big probably hangs his hat. You can see the entranceway here, the outer offices, the entrance to the big office here, the windows facing out onto the swimming pool here."

Nelson stood beside Marker, studying the image.

"Rex, if they're controlling that plane from here, there should be some sort of a communications room or control center. Do you see anything like that?"

Marker clicked the mouse one more time and moved down to a basement level of the building built back under the cliff behind the structure.

"An awful lot of wiring goes into this room back here, sir. I'd guess that's the comm center."

"Okay, Rex, keep that on the screen. Let me get some other folks in here."

Within a few minutes, Laffer, another helicopter pilot, Bonior, Collins, and one of the Air Force Special Tactics men had crowded into Nelson's office.

Nelson quickly explained the layout of the compound. "Having these images really gives us a leg up. We can see exactly where we want to go and how to get there."

Bonior stopped him. "Skipper, let's back up a little bit. If we go in there, what, exactly, are we supposed to be doing? Where do we want to go and what do we want to do?"

"Good question, Jeff. I guess I was getting ahead of myself. Okay, if we go in, what we want to do is to disable their communications so they can't control that plane. We assume that if the device is under positive control from the Rock House, the controls would be in this area." He pointed to the underground room Marker had designated as the probable communications center.

The room was silent for a minute as they all studied the images on the screen.

"Rex, what are we talking about here, three stories?" the special tactics man asked.

"Yeah, an upper story, apparently with offices and maybe some bedrooms. A second floor, probably offices. Then a main floor. It opens out at ground level in the front, but faces up against the cliff in back. Then another floor that is largely underground. It has an opening at ground level here, where the land slopes downward, but most of it is underground, and part of it is actually dug back under the cliff."

"So what we have to do is get in there and get to that comm room down under the cliff? Tough!"

Bonior, the most experienced person in the room, walked to the wall and studied the image.

"Rex, can you let me see what the rooftop looks like? Okay, now the upper floor. Good. Here's what I suggest: you see these two stairways at each end of the building? I think those are our fastest route to the basement room.

"We'll want to hear what Major Laffer thinks about this, but I'd like to see us come in real low and fast with two Pave Lows. Half of us fast-rope onto this end of the building, half on the other end. The helos drop the ropes, as usual. We blow holes in the roof at each end. Then we rig our ropes and fast-rope down those two stairwells. I figure we can be in the basement within one minute from touchdown."

Fast-roping was a relatively new technique. Instead of using a clamp on the rope to slow his descent, a man simply grasped the rope with heavy gloves and plummeted to the earth. A squad of men could fast-rope from a helicopter in a few seconds.

"I like it, Jeff," Nelson said. "How's it look to you, Jack?"

The helicopter pilot nodded. "No problem. But how much fire are we going to take? No sense getting ourselves shot up before we get to the building."

"The FBI has had the place under surveillance," Nelson replied. "They have spotted what they think could be .50-caliber machine gun emplacements. We can hammer them as we come in. Or if we're lucky, we can get in and out of there before they know what's hit them. Once we're over the roof, they may have trouble firing at us without hitting the building. Actually, I'd like to take them by surprise so we don't alert the folks inside the building until we blow the roof."

"Let me make one suggestion," Pat Collins broke in. "At some point we should take out as much of their antenna system as possible. They may well have backup systems, but we might as well disrupt everything we can."

"Good point, Pat. We can shoot up the antennas just as the charges on the roof go off. And maybe the helos can do some damage on their way out. Now . . . does anyone have any other suggestions or questions?"

The Special Tactics man raised his hand. "Sir, the only other way I can see that we can take this place—unless we want to drive an M-1 tank up the driveway—is to land over here . . ." He went to the image on the wall map and pointed to the area where the underground floor seemed to have a ground-level entrance. "If we landed here, we would be on the right level and we could bang right on in."

Laffer shook his head. "No. I don't want to take our birds in that area on the way in. There are trees, other obstructions. We'd probably have to unload one helo and then another. There's not enough room for both of them to get in there at the same time. Coming in on the roof makes a lot more sense to me. It may make it more difficult for you guys, but I think the chances of success are a lot better that way. If you want, we can use the lower level area for extraction."

"You're the expert," Nelson responded. "Let's go with the vertical envelopment. Jeff, you and Major Laffer get together and work out a training program. I think we can practice landing on one of these buildings here. The tricky thing will be practicing fast-roping down a stairwell. Some of us are going to get banged up doing that. Okay, let's get busy."

As they streamed out of the room, Collins remained behind.

"Chuck, I don't think any of your guys are going to ask you this, so I will. Is your shoulder well enough for you to take part in this operation? You're going to be firing your weapons, fast-roping. That's tough on a sore shoulder."

"I've been thinking about that, Pat. I've been working out

hard every day. I've been doing a lot of push-ups and pull-ups, and I've even done some rope climbing. I'm sure as hell not going to put a shotgun up against this shoulder and fire it. But there's nothing we're going to get involved in that I can't fire from the hip. I can handle it."

"Okay, Chuck. It's your decision. But you know it's not fair to your men to get yourself into a situation where they're going to have to risk their lives to get you out just because you were trying to be too macho."

He drew her to him and kissed her on the lips.

"You're right to ask, Pat. Thanks for keeping me honest."

The search of the old hard drives was still going on, but the lawyer decided it was time for action. He pressed a buzzer on his desk and one of the security men who seemed to move silently, almost invisibly, through the corridors of the compound entered his office.

"Tri, there is a young man, a man named Hoffman, on Mr. Bernard's security force. Please bring him to my office."

Tri returned the lawyer's gaze impassively. "Yes sir, I know which one he is."

Moments later, he returned, guiding Hoffman ahead of him into the office. He grasped him above the elbow of his right arm and pushed him toward a chair. "Sit there."

The muscle in Hoffman's arm was so large that Tri's hand went only partway around it. Hoffman flexed his arm, shook off the man's grasp, and glared at him before sitting down. Tri took a position directly behind the chair, flexing his fingers. He was so close that Hoffman could sense his presence.

The lawyer made his instinctive steeple with his fingers and stared at the young SEAL.

"Mr. Hoffman, I have received some very disturbing information about you."

Hoffman glanced over his shoulder at the man standing behind him and then turned to the lawyer. "What the hell is this all about? Does Captain Bernard know about this?"

Tri moved a hand forward. Hoffman could feel the fingers dig into his shoulder with a grip of steel.

"Please, Mr. Hoffman. I will ask the questions here and you will provide the answers. Is that understood?"

"Screw you!"

The fingers dug deeper into his shoulder.

The lawyer picked up a piece of paper from his desk. "Did you send a message to someone whose E-mail address is 'rex-mark'?"

Hoffman glanced nervously over his shoulder.

"I want to see Captain Bernard!"

"No, I don't think so. As you can see, you are not in a position to demand anything. You are in our power. You will answer my questions truthfully, and you will do exactly as I tell you to do."

Hoffman set his jaw, clamping his lips tightly together. He folded his arms across his chest.

"Let me ask you again. . . . No, I'll make it a statement. You did send an E-mail message to this person, who is apparently a friend of yours. Here, let me read the text of the message." He reached up, adjusted the desk lamp and held his handwritten notes up under the light.

"Rex: In a hurry. Don't want to get caught. We're at a place in the Rockies above Colorado Springs. Guarding the place. I don't know what's going on, but I think this has something to do with what happened to Mojave. Scares me. Dick sends."

"Scares you? *What* scares you, Mr. Hoffman?"

Hoffman remained impassive, feeling the grip on his shoulder dig deeper.

"What scares you, Mr. Hoffman? We don't want anyone here to be frightened, do we, Tri?"

Hoffman glared at the lawyer. As he did, he leaned forward slightly, brought his hands down by his sides, and grasped the edges of the chair seat. With a sudden lunge, he stood, driving the back of the chair sharply up under Tri's chin. His jaw broke with an audible crack. Whirling, Hoffman grasped the startled man by an arm and the back of his neck and drove his head into the edge of the desk. The lawyer jumped up and backed toward the window.

"You want to play games? Okay, we'll play games." Hoffman started around the desk toward the frightened lawyer.

"Mmmmffff." Hoffman heard a strange sound and glanced to his left. Tri had struggled up off the floor and was cupping his broken jaw with one hand. In the other hand, he held a .38-caliber automatic. He gestured upward with the gun.

"Don't shoot, Tri!" the lawyer commanded. Turning to Hoffman, he said, "He wants you to raise your hands. I think he also wants to kill you."

Hoffman glared at the lawyer and then slowly, reluctantly, raised his hands over his head.

"Tri, why don't you leave the pistol with me and go seek treatment for your injuries?" Tri nodded, handed over the pistol, and walked toward the door, holding his jaw in his hand. The lawyer motioned Hoffman to pick up the chair and sit down. "I think you may be seeing Tri again, Mr. Hoffman. I don't think you will enjoy your encounter.

"Now . . . where were we? Oh, yes. We were discussing your message to your friend, 'rexmark.' Why don't you tell me a little bit about your friend? Who is he? Where is he? Why did you send this message to him? What did you think he could do after he received this message?"

Hoffman glared at the pale lawyer. Behind Hoffman's impassive face, his mind was racing, dredging up every memory of the painful course he had undergone at the Air Force survival school at Stead Air Force Base in Nevada. He remembered the fear he had felt under interrogation by his "enemy" captors, even though he knew it was only training and that he would not be seriously injured by their simulated torture. Now, strangely, he didn't feel fear. Instead he felt a cold, calculating anger, a determination to beat these people at their own game, whatever it was.

One word coursed through his mind, as steady and strong as his pulse: "*Resist! Resist! Resist!*"

The lawyer laid the gun down on the desk but kept his fingers within a few inches of the weapon. "I'm not going to shoot you, Mr. Hoffman. At this point, at least, you can be of more use to us alive than dead. Now . . . this message was apparently sent two days ago. Have you sent any other messages to this Rex—is that what you call him, Rex? Or to anyone else?"

Hoffman stared at him defiantly.

The lawyer shrugged. "We'll know the answers soon enough. We're reviewing our computer files right now to see if any other messages were sent. I'm sure you erased the text of your transmission, but of course an electronic record remained in the computer's memory."

Even though he was the one under interrogation, Hoffman processed the information the lawyer had inadvertently given him: the lawyer had somehow gotten a copy of his message to Rex before he had found anything on his own computer files. Hoffman's heart sank. If this meant there was a mole within the Eagle Force, he was in even more trouble than he had thought a few moments before—and the nation was in more danger, too.

"Where'd you get that message?" he demanded.

"Let me remind you, Mr. Hoffman, that I'm the one asking the questions. Let's just say we have our sources. Now, did you send other messages?"

"Yeah. I sent copies to everybody I know . . . at least everybody whose E-mail address I could remember."

"Interesting. Our search of the files will soon tell us if you are telling the truth. Meanwhile. . . ." He pressed a button. Moments later a man dressed, like the injured Tri, in a black single-breasted suit and white shirt entered the room.

"Branco, please tie up Mr. Hoffman and take him . . . take him down to the ground floor. There's a storage room with a secure lock. Leave him there—with the lights out. By the way, Branco, do we still have a problem with the rats down there?"

Branco grinned, exposing a shiny gray steel incisor tooth. "Oh, yes, sir. Big rats. Very big rats. Very hungry." Producing a nylon cord from his pocket, he lashed Hoffman's hands behind him and then tied his ankles so that he could walk, but only with short steps. Hoffman tensed the muscles in his wrists, trying to create a little wriggle room that might permit him to get loose.

"I'm going to let you sit there in the dark and see if that makes you want to be a little more cooperative," the lawyer said. "We may want your help a little later in sending another message to your friend Rex."

Grasping him by the elbow, Branco guided Hoffman down the hall to an elevator and took him one floor down. Opening a thick metal door to what appeared to be a storage room, the man pushed Hoffman inside. The room was empty, without even a chair or table. As the door closed, Hoffman was left standing in darkness as deep as that inside a tomb. There wasn't even a faint line of light to remind him where the door was and to keep him oriented.

CHAPTER 28

AFTER MEETING WITH THE FAMILIES AT EDWARDS, MAYNARD Walker had made three more stops in California and then touched down in four other states as he worked his way back toward Washington. As he went through the political motions with all the charm for which he was famous, the president's mind kept bringing up pictures of the destruction he had seen at Mojave and the grief exhibited by the people he had met in the Air Force hangar. He called ahead and asked Adm. McKay to meet with him as soon as he arrived back in the White House.

When McKay received word that Air Force One had touched down at Andrews Air Force Base, he pushed aside the pile of work on his desk and strode briskly down the hall from his second-floor office to the Pentagon's river entrance. His driver was waiting at the bottom of the steps with the motor running and the air conditioning blowing cold air. Mc-Kay glanced at his watch. He knew from long experience that barring unforeseen delays in traffic, he'd arrive at the White House a few minutes before the president's helicopter touched down on the south lawn.

His driver circled down around the edges of the huge Pentagon parking lot and eased into the stream of Washington-bound traffic. McKay pulled the reading lamp, attached to the shelf behind the back seat, down into position so he could leaf through the handful of documents he had brought along. But as they crossed Memorial Bridge, he indulged in a few seconds of daydreaming. He could see the rowing crews gracefully slicing through the smooth surface of the Potomac and recalled how simple life had seemed when the biggest thing on his mind was Saturday's regatta.

The road curved around behind the Lincoln Memorial onto Constitution Avenue. On the right were the long expanse of the Mall, the Washington Monument, and far ahead, the white dome of the Capitol. Ever since the bombing at the federal building in Oklahoma City had caused panicky security officials to close off Pennsylvania Avenue in front of the White House, traffic in that whole area of the city had become a nightmare. But McKay's driver had found a way to beat the system. From Constitution Avenue, he turned up Seventeenth Street and then, as he approached F Street, swung right into a narrow gateway leading under the Old Executive Office Building, just to the west of the White House. From his parking spot there, it took McKay only three minutes to stride across to a side entrance of the White House.

Maynard Walker was first out of the helicopter, bounding down the stairs. He spotted McKay and swung an arm over his shoulder, pulling him rapidly along toward the Oval Office.

"I need a fill-in on this whole situation, Mac. We're going to have to make some decisions."

As the two men entered the Oval Office, Walker grasped an aide by an elbow. "We'll need some coffee . . . and see if they've got some of those little biscuits, the ones with the jam on top. Know what I mean?"

Walker motioned McKay to a seat in front of the fireplace and took a seat opposite him. "Okay, let's have it! With all this politics, I've been kind of out of touch."

"The situation hasn't changed dramatically, sir. But this is the way it stands: the U.S. Attorney in Colorado Springs asked for a warrant to search the Nash compound. The judge turned him down flat. So our knowledge about what's in that place and what's going on there is limited.

"We're making several assumptions. One, we think the plane is at some isolated airfield, probably in Mexico. We've got very limited satellite coverage of that area and we've flown several U-2 missions, but we haven't been able to locate it.

Two, we think he may be planning an attack on Saint Louis at the time of your party convention, starting next week. Three, we suspect the plane will be flown by Sergei Kaparov—the same fellow who stole it from us. But we don't know whether he controls the ray device. There is evidence of considerable communications capability at the Nash compound, and it may very well be controlled from Colorado Springs.''

The president rose and strode toward the windows, then stood with his hands clasped behind his back, staring outside.

McKay paused and then added, ''I should emphasize, sir, that at least half of that is guesswork.''

''So. . . . What are we going to do about it?''

''We have two plans, sir. Actually, one plan and a backup plan. First, we are resurrecting an old weapons system from the mid-eighties. It was designed originally to shoot down satellites, but it can probably take out a high-flying plane as well. One of the pilots on our commando team used to fly the F-15—that's the plane that carries this anti-satellite weapon— and he's preparing to take up his position somewhere on the Gulf Coast. If and when we detect the plane heading toward the U.S., he'll take off and try to shoot it down.''

''And if he misses?''

''That's when things get a little dicey. I've had Commander Nelson move his team to Peterson Field in Colorado Springs. If Colonel Rattner—he's the F-15 pilot—misses, Nelson and his people will make an assault on Nash's compound and try to disable their communications before the ray device can be triggered.''

Walker whirled around. ''What are you thinking about? You can't even get a search warrant, and here you're talking about attacking this place with a commando team? Didn't you ever hear of Waco? You're going to go blasting into this guy's home? What if you kill his wife and children and his pet dog and it turns out he's just some law-abiding citizen sitting on his mountainside, minding his own business? The press and the opposition would eat me alive! Did it occur to you that this is an election year?''

McKay uncrossed his legs and sat up straight with his hands flat on his thighs. Then he stood and faced the president. He drew himself up until he almost seemed to be standing at attention.

"Yes, sir, I've thought about all those things. But I don't have to remind you that this device has already wiped out one American city with the loss of several thousand lives. If this ray is used against a major city such as Saint Louis, it would be the worst single disaster in American history. The casualties, in a few moments, could exceed the number killed in all the wars this nation has fought in more than two hundred years."

The president stared at him for a few moments and then nodded. "You're right, Mac. I'm sorry I lost my temper. I guess we really don't have much in the way of options. I'll tell you what: you have my authorization to attempt to shoot down the plane with the F-15. It's likely no one will even know about that, whichever way it goes. Meanwhile, go ahead with the planning for the assault by your team. But they don't move until I personally give the okay. Is that understood?"

"Yes sir." McKay stood staring at the president, his lips tightly compressed and his jaw rigid, as he debated whether to say anything more. Then he spoke. "Sir, I understand your reluctance to assault the Colorado compound. But if Colonel Rattner fails, we are going to have precious little time to carry out our operation before that plane will be over Saint Louis. If this were a straight tactical decision, I would urge that we move on the compound just as soon as we can—as early as tonight, if possible."

Walker returned McKay's stare.

"No, Mac, I'm not going to do it now. The evidence is too flimsy. We are not going to carry out that assault until and unless we have exhausted every other alternative. I will promise you one thing: you and I will remain in constant communication. If Colonel Rattner fails, I will give you an immediate decision on the assault."

At Peterson Field, as soon as it was dark, Jeff Bonior ran the team through the first dress rehearsal for their assault. Us-

ing two Pave Low helicopters that had been flown in from the
Air Force Special Operations training base at Kirtland Air
Force Base in Albuquerque, New Mexico, the team flew a
simulated approach that took them skimming through canyons
and over wooded hillsides in the foothills of the Rockies. Then
they returned to the airfield and hovered over a vacant three-
story building.

Tumbling out of the helicopters in rapid succession, the men
fast-roped to the rooftop, took up defensive positions with
their weapons, and simulated blowing holes at each end of the
roof. Inside the building was a stairwell similar to those they
expected to encounter. Attaching their ropes to the top railing,
the men practiced plummeting down the stairwell, bouncing
off the railings as they dropped.

Later that night, Bonior met with Nelson.

"It's all going to work okay, boss. But getting down that
stairwell is going to take some practice. The guys kept getting
their weapons and their equipment caught on the railings.
Slowed us down."

"Yeah, I expected that, Jeff. We're just going to have to
work on it."

"How long do we have?"

"Wish I knew. Our guess is that the target may be the
opening of the next party convention in Saint Louis next week.
That gives us over the weekend. But who knows? It could
come sooner."

"We'll keep working on it, sir. Except for the stairwell, it's
almost a routine thing. Give us a couple more nights and we'll
be in good shape."

Bonior turned to go and then paused. "Excuse me sir. Are
you . . . are you going to lead us?" He glanced meaningfully
at Nelson's shoulder.

Nelson looked up and grinned. "You, too? Pat Collins
asked me about that the other night—the shoulder and everything. Yes, Jeff, I'm going to go. I don't want to take part in
your training yet. There's no sense banging my arm around if
I don't have to. But don't worry, I'll be with you."

Bonior saluted. "We need you along, sir . . . but only if you
feel up to it."

CHAPTER 29

MARK RATTNER LEVELED OFF AT EIGHTEEN THOUSAND FEET OVER the Nevada desert. Off to the west rose the majestic mass of the Sierra Nevada Mountains. Down below, the hot, dun-colored desert spread in all directions.

After a quick call to the air traffic controller for clearance, Rattner began a series of maneuvers to regain his familiarity with the flight characteristics of the F-15. He found flying the swift, responsive fighter a pleasant change from the demanding task of flying the big Pave Low helicopter. A grin spread over his face under his oxygen mask as he thought to himself, This is fun!

Slowly he rolled over and flew inverted, enjoying the strange sensation of viewing the world upside down while hanging suspended from his shoulder straps. Then, with a quick snap of the stick, he rolled right side up again and pulled the plane up into the beginnings of a tight loop. At the top of the loop, he rolled out in a maneuver known as an Immelmann and threw the plane into a series of contortions known as the squirrel cage.

Rattner could feel his stomach muscles knotting as he fought the force of gravity, sensing the pull of up to seven times his normal weight. He grunted and strained to keep the blood flowing to his brain and to keep from blacking out.

Leveling out again, Rattner found himself breathless. It had been a long time since he'd had such a workout. He flew in a lazy circle, catching his breath, then rolled over into a steep dive to build up speed, pulled back sharply on the stick, and rocketed almost straight up, feeling the surge of power pressing against his back.

As the plane broke through fifty thousand feet, he pulled back on the throttle and began a long, shallow descent back toward the long runway at Edwards.

"How did it go, Colonel?" The leader of the Tiger Team met him as he locked the ejection seat and climbed down out of the cockpit.

"Great. You know, that helicopter is a challenge. You feel like you are flying it with your own two hands and feet. But this bird is more fun. I really had a good time up there today."

"Well, we've got some good news for you. We've got your plane all checked out. We've even loaded the missile on the center fuselage station. You can take it up for a test anytime you want to."

"Let me get a sandwich and something to drink," Rattner said. "I want to check it out and get out of here as soon as possible."

Half an hour later, Rattner was back on the flight line. He was surprised to find that the Tiger Team had even found time to repaint the plane in the light sky blue that was supposed to make the Eagle invisible to enemy pilots and replaced the NASA logo with Air Force markings.

"We thought this would make you a little less conspicuous," the Tiger Team leader explained. "That white paint job with the red NASA seemed to us a little gaudy."

Rattner walked around the plane appreciatively. It was almost like having his own brand new sports car. Ducking in under the swept-back wing, he examined the eighteen-foot-long missile attached along the center line of the fuselage.

"The first stage—back here—is basically an AGM-69," the Boeing man explained. "That's the SRAM—the short-range attack missile—carried by the B-52s. The second stage is a modification of the Altair III rocket. And this small section up here, that's the business end."

"Okay," Rattner said, backing out from under the fuselage and standing up in the shade of the wing. "Let me get this straight. I zoom up, lock in the target with my radar. Then the computer passes the lock-on information to the missile. When I release it, its guidance takes over and zeros in on the target.''

''That's right. You have to remember that this system was designed to shoot down a satellite, in a known orbit around the earth. It will work against a plane, but only if the plane stays on a fairly steady course. The missile's guidance will follow mild maneuvers, but if he begins jinking around, you're going to miss.'' The Boeing man, a veteran pilot himself, held his right hand up to simulate the target and swung his left hand in an arc to mimic the track of the rocket. As his left hand neared his right, he moved his right hand abruptly to one side and his left hand passed on by.

Rattner patted the missile. ''Does this thing affect the flight characteristics very much?''

''No, we don't think so. It weighs less than a ton and a half, far from a full payload for the F-15. We've been able to dig out the records from 1984 and 1985. There were five launches, only one against an actual satellite. All the records indicate that the missile didn't degrade the performance of the plane. At least the test pilots didn't list that as a problem.''

''What about separation?'' Rattner asked. He knew the critical point with any weapon released from a plane came at the moment when the missile was cut loose and began flying on its own. Rattner had seen plenty of films of test flights in which a new bomb or missile was released and then flew through the wing or the tail of the test plane.

''No problems—at least, according to the records we've found. The missile drops away and then goes on its own course. If there was any problem in those five live launches, I'm sure we would have seen a lot of comments about it.''

That afternoon, Rattner took the sleek, newly painted plane for a test flight, zooming up over the desert to familiarize himself with the launch of the missile.

Early the next morning, he climbed into the plane, tucked a small bag with a change of clothes behind the seat, and set his course for Eglin Air Force Base on Florida's western panhandle.

——— ★ ———

"Are you sure we've got good C-cubed, Pat?" Nelson used the military acronym for command, control, and communications. "If this thing blows, we're going to have to know what's happening in real time and be ready to move fast."

"It took a little while to get things set up here, but I think we're in very good shape now." She gestured at the lineup of phones on the desk. "These Air Force types really did a job for us after they got a little jolt from the E-ring at the Pentagon. I've got a direct line to NORAD and another to Colonel Rattner at Eglin. I'm glad we decided to have him go to Eglin instead of New Orleans. This not only gives us better communications, but he'll have any support he needs right there.

"He found his old wing man behind a desk at Hurlburt Field—that's one of the satellite fields at Eglin. He called and arranged for him to meet him at Eglin. They're going to take turns in the cockpit of the plane—four hours on, four hours off. That way, they can launch within a couple of minutes of getting the go-ahead. There's some security risk in getting another person involved, but Colonel Rattner and I agreed it was the only way to maintain a constant alert.

"We've got round-the-clock AWACS coverage flying out of Tinker Air Force Base in Oklahoma. They'll be able to vector Colonel Rattner in and monitor his reports on the mission. I've got another direct line to AWACS ops at Tinker. Colonel Rattner should land at Eglin in less than an hour. Give him a little time to get refueled, and everything will be in position. I'd say we're in pretty good shape."

Nelson shook his head. "Yeah, good shape—except for holes in our intel so big that everything could fall through. We have only the foggiest idea of where that plane is. We really don't know whether he's going to target a city. If he is, we don't know what city. We don't know when. And we don't really know a damn thing about what's going on just a few miles from here up at the Rock House. Otherwise, we're in great shape."

———————— ★ ————————

As soon as Branco's footsteps faded away, Hoffman groped his way until he felt the wall and then sat down. He sat absolutely still, listening. If there was one thing he hated, it was rats. Even the thought of a rat, with its dirty-looking coat, its beady eyes, and its hairless tail, made his skin crawl. As he'd gone through BUD/S training, it wasn't the cold or the lack of sleep that had almost caused him to drop out. It was the creepy, crawly things, especially the things he couldn't see in the dark. And rats were the worst.

He sat for a minute, two, three. He wasn't sure how long, but it seemed like a long time. He heard nothing except the faraway sound of water gushing through the pipes after a toilet was flushed. He began to relax. That talk of rats was just to scare him.

Leaning one shoulder against the wall, he began working at the cord that bound his wrists behind his back. He had not been able to create much slack when he was tied up, but gradually he was able to work one loop of the cord down over his knuckles. The tension cut off the flow of blood to both hands and they began to tingle. Suddenly the loop slipped free, permitting him to reach the knot with the thumbs and index fingers of both hands. Moments later his hands were free.

He quickly untied his ankles. Carefully, he retrieved the cord, rolled it up, and placed it in his shirt pocket. Then he began to grope around his improvised cell. He worked his way around the walls and crisscrossed from one corner to the other. Then he went around the room again next to the wall, reaching as high as he could.

His exploration confirmed his impression that he was in a totally empty room with cinderblock walls. There was no furniture and no shelves that could be fashioned into a weapon or a tool. He dropped to his knees and ran his hands over the floor, hoping to find it was made of tiles that might be pried up to form a weapon. With the side of his hand, he swept away the grit and dust covering the floor and ran his fingers over the seamless surface. It was apparently part of the solid concrete foundation poured when the building was built.

He sat again against the wall and resumed his careful listening.

"I almost wish there were rats," he thought to himself. "I'm so hungry I could eat one."

After a while, Hoffman lost all sense of time. The only reminder that several hours must have passed was the growing urge to urinate. He finally gave in, walked to a far corner of the room, and relieved himself against the wall. Then he returned to his spot against the wall, looped the cord loosely around his ankles and wrists, and dozed off.

The rattle of a key in the lock awakened him with a start. He shut his eyes tight, knowing that the burst of brightness when the door was opened would temporarily blind him. He heard a click, the creak of a hinge, and a few steps on the floor, then felt a hand on his arm, pulling him up. Hoffman opened his eyes, squinting, to see Branco leaning over him. He struggled awkwardly, his back against the wall, his hands behind his back, and his ankles close together. He seemed to lose his balance, leaning heavily against the other man. Then, in one swift motion, he pulled Branco's arm behind his back, snapping the bone out of the shoulder socket, and extracted the pistol from the holster under his left armpit.

He jammed the muzzle of the pistol hard behind Branco's right ear. It was only then that he looked toward the door and saw Nash himself, the light behind him shining on his bald head. A sardonic grin showed beneath his dark glasses. In his hand was what looked like a long-barreled .45-caliber pistol.

The trace of a Hungarian accent was still audible in Nash's speech. "And so we have a standoff, just like in the movies. Mr. Hoffman, did you ever see that wonderful film *Speed*?"

Hoffman looked at him incredulously. Was this guy for real?

"Remember that marvelous scene, very similar to this, where the mad bomber holds one officer and his buddy is ordered to drop his gun? What should the buddy do?"

Hoffman squinted at him and shook his head, bewildered.

"*Shoot the hostage!*" Inside the concrete-walled room, the sound was deafening. Branco collapsed, falling heavily against Hoffman and throwing him off balance. Nash stepped forward quickly and kicked Hoffman's weapon to one side. He glanced down and murmured, "Sorry, Branco."

"My people tell me you have been somewhat less than cooperative. Perhaps we can change your attitude. Tri!"

Tri wore a high, stiff neck brace, and Hoffman could see that his mouth had been wired shut to immobilize his broken jaw. In his hands he carried two bags.

"Let's see what treats Tri has for you, Mr. Hoffman. Open that bag, Tri."

Tri reached into one of the bags and pulled out what looked like a small wooden cage. It appeared to be made of bamboo, with closely spaced bars running side to side and up and down.

Hoffman stared at the object. Oh shit, he thought.

One of the worst stories he'd heard about combat in Vietnam from some of the older veterans was a form of torture reportedly used by the Vietcong. A cage was placed over a man's head and then a rat was inserted into the cage. At first, the rat just scratched the man's head and face as it tried to get free. Then, as it became hungry, it began to eat the man's flesh: his nose, his cheeks, his ears, his eyes. The torture could go on for days.

"Show him what's in the other bag, Tri."

He reached inside and brought out a large rat confined in tightly wrapped netting. The animal writhed from side to side as Tri held it firmly behind the head, but its mouth and claws were constricted by the netting.

"Oh, God," Hoffman groaned, turning his head away.

CHAPTER 30

THE MEMBERS OF BERNARD'S SECURITY FORCE WERE BEGINNING to get bored by their duties at the Rock House, defending the compound against attack from the outside.

From the beginning, Bernard had thought the addition of his force to the twenty-five or so men Nash already had on his staff, primarily responsible for security inside the building, was overkill. But the pay was good—very good—so who was he to complain?

For Bernard's men, the duty involved patrolling the fence around the compound and checking traffic on the road that ran by the front entrance. They were the ones who had first noticed what appeared to be FBI surveillance. They also manned a series of machine gun and mortar emplacements, disguised as part of the landscaping, that covered the eastern approaches to the compound. Approach from other directions was blocked by the cliff against which the compound was built.

They were housed in a barracks-like building adjoining the main compound. It had a recreation room and well-equipped exercise room. But aside from watching television, reading, sleeping, and exercising, there was little to do in the long hours between duty assignments.

"Captain, how long are we going to sit around here?" one of the men asked, as Bernard walked into the recreation room. It was a familiar refrain from his action-oriented men.

"Yeah, when are we going to get some action?" another asked.

The off-duty men began to gather around Bernard. He paused and leaned against a table and gestured for quiet.

"You men are professionals, and I want you to act like professionals. I'm getting sick of this bitching. You're getting paid well to guard this place, and that's what you'll do." Scowling, he stared around the room.

One of the youngest members of the team was the first to break the silence.

"Skipper, what's happened to Dick Hoffman?"

"Yeah," another man broke in. "That creepy Tri guy came and dragged him away a couple of hours ago, and we haven't seen him since."

Bernard looked puzzled. Even when he was in the Navy, he had never been a stickler for record-keeping. Now, running his own outfit, he had dispensed with such routines as a daily accounting of the men available for duty. Until the question was asked, he had not been aware that Hoffman was missing.

"Oh, he's probably around. I'll check on him."

"Dick has this theory," one of the men cut in. "He thinks this place has something to do with that disaster at Mojave. What about it? We don't want to be involved in any of that kind of shit."

A murmur of agreement ran through the room and the men crowded in more closely around Bernard.

"Big Dog, you know we'll follow you anywhere and fight anybody you tell us to fight. But we don't want anything to do with wiping out cities. That's not our thing."

Bernard backed slowly toward the door. "All right. All right. Take it easy. Take it easy. You guys, just calm down. I'll check on Hoffman and let you know where he is."

Bernard paused outside the door, deeply worried. He was used to almost blind obedience from his men, who regarded him with something bordering on idolatry. He had seen them restless and eager for action before, but this was the first time he had ever had them question an assignment. How close, he wondered, were they to open mutiny?

He walked across the small courtyard from the barracks area to the main compound, inhaling deeply the tangy pine scent of the mountain air and feeling the warmth of the sun on his shoulders. He strode the few yards to Nash's office.

Nash looked up and waited as Bernard crossed the room and stood in front of his desk.

"Where's Hoffman?"

Nash regarded him for a few moments before answering. "I have detained Mr. Hoffman because he was involved in a very serious breach of our security."

"What are you talking about?" Nash had not offered him a seat and Bernard remained standing awkwardly in front of the desk.

"Mr. Hoffman sent an E-mail message to a friend, a Rex Marker, telling him he thought our operation here was involved in the attack on Mojave. We are questioning Mr. Hoffman about this incident."

"Where is he?"

"You don't need to know that, Mr. Bernard. A bigger question for you is what kind of security you have in your team. Are any other members of your team raising questions about Mojave?"

"No." Bernard lied.

"Do you have any doubt that your men will do what it takes to defend the Rock House against any threat?"

"No. No doubts." Bernard lied again.

"Just make sure that remains true, Mr. Bernard. Remember what I have told you on more than one occasion: I expect my orders to be carried out precisely . . . precisely."

Bernard nodded.

Nash waved a hand dismissively. "That will be all."

"I still want to see Hoffman. He's one of my men."

"You are all *my* men." Nash stared at Bernard through his dark glasses for a moment and then turned his attention to the papers on his desk. As Bernard left, Nash pressed a button, summoning the lawyer from his adjoining office.

The man took a seat without being invited, made a steeple with his fingers, and waited for Nash to speak.

"I think it's time we get this over with. What time does the convention convene tomorrow?"

"TV coverage begins at seven in the evening, our time, eight o'clock in Saint Louis. Most delegates are in the hall an hour or two before that. The president's acceptance speech is scheduled for nine o'clock, and knowing him, it'll probably last about an hour.''

Nash made a swift calculation with a small calculator and jotted some figures on a pad of foolscap paper.

''So . . . say between nine-fifteen and nine-thirty Saint Louis time for maximum impact?''

The lawyer nodded.

''Will you please transmit the necessary data to our base in Mexico? By my rough calculations, takeoff should be between eight-thirty and eight forty-five, again Saint Louis time. Have our people make the precise calculations. And I want to speak with Sergei before the mission.''

''I'll inform you when the data has been transmitted.'' He rose to leave.

''What's the status of that Hoffman fellow?''

''We've just about completed a check of our hard drives. We found his message to Marker, but nothing else. He was lying to us about sending copies to other people.''

''You've still got him downstairs?''

''Yes, sir. We're letting him think about Tri and his little friend. When we're finished here, I'm going to have a little discussion with him. I would like him to send another E-mail message—one we write for him. But I need something from him to make Marker believe it. I know this won't take attention away from us completely, but it may well buy us enough time to complete what we have in mind.''

When the lawyer and Tri entered Hoffman's makeshift cell a short time later, he was right where they'd left him, securely tied, hand and foot, to a chair in the middle of the room. The two men paused in the doorway as Hoffman sat blinking in the bright light, looking to make sure that he hadn't worked his way free again.

Tri strode quickly to where Hoffman sat and back-handed him across the face, drawing blood from his mouth and nose.

''That's enough of that, Tri!'' the lawyer commanded. ''We may let you have him later. But not now. Untie his feet so he can walk. Untie him from the chair but keep his hands tied behind him.''

Tri tilted the chair with its back against the floor as he worked to free Hoffman's ankles. That made it possible for him to loosen the cord while still standing at arm's length, where he couldn't be kicked.

"Bring him along," the lawyer said. "I want to talk to him up in my office."

Tri roughly pushed Hoffman into a chair in the office and again stood behind him—far enough back not to be hit again.

"Mr. Hoffman, I would like to have you send another E-mail message to your friend, Rex. We have prepared the text of the message. What I need is a little help from you. I want you to tell me something we can use to authenticate this message—something personal that will convince Marker it comes from you."

Hoffman sat impassive, staring at the lawyer.

"Tri. Would you give Mr. Hoffman a little reminder?"

The man walked to the side of the room and reached into the bag he had had with him earlier. He pulled out the big rat, still trussed up.

Walking toward Hoffman, he thrust the rat at his face. Then he held the animal across his mouth and nose so he couldn't breathe without inhaling the rodent's sour stench.

"That's enough, Tri. Now, Mr. Hoffman. . . ."

Hoffman shuddered and spit on the floor. "Shit!" he exclaimed. "Shii . . . iit!"

"Precisely. Now, Mr. Hoffman, would you like to help us?"

Hoffman shuddered again. "Just keep that damn thing away from me! What do you want?"

"Think back, Mr. Hoffman. Is there anything you and Marker share in common? Any mutual memory that will authenticate our message?"

Hoffman sat silently.

"Tri?" The lawyer said, motioning toward the bag.

"No, no. Don't do that. I'm thinking."

"Yes, fine. Think. Search your memory."

"Okay, I've got something. Back when Rex and I were in training at El Centro, we had a double blind date with a couple of honeys. And both of us scored that same night. Man, that was nice!''

A thin smile crept across the lawyer's face. ''And you think Marker remembers this incident?''

''Man, does he remember it!''

''So you think some reference to this incident will have meaning for him?''

''Yeah. Tell him something like, 'Remember El Centro. Let's do it again, man.' ''

''Tri, take Mr. Hoffman back to his room. And Tri, do not mistreat him. Do you understand me? We may need him again.''

Hoffman glanced apprehensively toward the bag containing the rat as he was led from the room.

Late that night, Marker rapped quickly and then entered Nelson's office. ''Skipper, I've got another E-mail from Dick.''

Nelson looked up. ''Let's see it.'' He took the paper, held it under the desk lamp, and read aloud: ''Rex. False alarm. Man, was I screwed up. These folks need security, but it's a strictly legit operation. Let's get together when we finish up here. Remember El Centro? Let's do it again, man. Dick sends.''

''What do you make of this, Rex?''

''They're twisting his thumbs, sir. Somehow they found out about that other message and they made him send this one to call us off.''

''How do you know?''

''That bullshit about El Centro, sir. I don't know what he told them, but the only big thing that happened in El Centro was that time when we were in advanced jump school. I was knocked out going out the door, and Dick dived down and pulled my ripcord. Saved my life.''

''Not something you want to do again?''

''Never.''

''Well, I guess this tells us two things: one, we should believe the first message, that this place is involved in the Mojave incident, and two, Dick is in big trouble.''

''What can we do about it, sir?''

''Not a damned thing, Rex. I'll pass this on to Admiral McKay and give him your analysis. It will help confirm what we already suspected. But we've done everything we can. We're just going to have to play it out.''

A small red light on Nash's telephone console blinked. Nash pushed a button to activate his speaker phone.

''Yes?''

''Sir, I have Mr. Kaparov on a satellite link.''

''Good, put him on . . . Sergei?''

Sergei was in a bad humor. He had just run his hand along the edge of the old desk at which he sat and punctured the skin of his index finger with a wooden splinter. The tropical sun beat down on the metal roof of the building nestled on the edge of the jungle next to the long grass runway. Sergei, who had allowed himself to become a little overweight, felt like a plump goose in a hot oven.

''It's hot down here. I want my money and I want to get out of here.''

''Yes, Sergei, I understand. We are in the process of depositing your funds in your account.''

''What do you mean, 'in the process'? That money was supposed to be there when I finished the job.''

''The funds will be there when you are in a position to draw them. There's nothing to worry about. Now Sergei, I have one more task for you.''

Nash held the phone away from his ear as Kaparov unleashed a torrent of curses in Russian, a language much better suited for a good cussing-out than English, or even German. Even if Nash had not understood Russian, he'd have had no doubt about the broad message Kaparov was trying to convey.

When the voice on the other end of the line finally subsided, Nash paused a moment and then snapped out a brief response in Russian—something about Kaparov's mother's relationship with barnyard animals—then quickly added: "Now that we have that out of our systems, let's get down to business. I have one more assignment for you. When we reach agreement, I will place another half million dollars in your numbered account. When you complete this final mission, another half million will be deposited and you will be free to do as you wish."

"I'm listening," Kaparov said.

"This assignment is almost a repeat of the flight you have just completed," Nash responded. "Was that so difficult . . . so dangerous?"

"No. The whole thing went very smoothly. What do you have in mind now?"

"I want you to repeat your flight in reverse. You will fly north, over the Pole, and back to your original point of departure."

"A million dollars? Say, what is this all about, anyway?"

Nash rolled his eyes and thought, I guess our security is pretty good after all. This joker doesn't know that he just wiped out a town of three thousand people.

"Don't worry about that, Sergei. This is all part of something bigger. You needn't bother your head about it."

"How much longer do I have to stay in this pest hole?" He added a few well-chosen words in Russian.

"Just a few more hours. The technicians have the flight data and are programming your systems, setting each of the checkpoints in your navigational computer. I want to emphasize again that it is of the utmost importance that you fly this mission precisely. If for any reason there are any deviations, you are to report them to us immediately. Is that understood?"

"Yeah, I know all that. All I want to do is get in that plane and get the hell out of here."

"That opportunity will come very shortly. Good luck, Sergei."

The line went dead and Kaparov slowly put the phone back in its cradle.

Moments later, Nash placed another call to the base in Quintana Roo. This time, the call went directly to the Russian scientist in charge of the plane.

Nash spoke in Russian. "Is everything in readiness?"

"Yes, sir. The plane and the device are both in excellent condition. They are ready to go when you give the word."

"Once this flight is finished, we will not be needing the system again. Have you carried out the arrangements I ordered in my message to you?"

"I received your message, sir. You really want me to. . . ."

"Yes, I can understand your feelings. But I am paying you to carry out my orders. Is that understood?"

The Russian sighed. "Yes, sir. I understand. I will make the arrangements."

CHAPTER 31

BRENT BENEDICT FELT A TINGLE OF EXCITEMENT AS HE LOOKED out over the delegates milling about on the convention floor down below. The mysterious destruction of Mojave two weeks before had triggered a sharp change in the political situation. President Walker's popularity had plummeted, and Senator Wilson had come on strong as a challenger. Some polls even gave him an edge over the incumbent if the election were held today. The animation in Benedict's voice was not feigned.

"In the last two weeks, ladies and gentlemen, we have seen a remarkable transition in this political convention. Before the destruction of Mojave, there was every reason to believe the delegates to this convention would quickly nominate President Walker for a second term. But the train carrying the president to victory is teetering, if it hasn't actually been derailed. The president's men have been working frantically to get the train back on the tracks again. With the vote this evening, we will soon see how well they have succeeded.

"I must say that the mood of this convention is dramatically different from what we felt when the other party was meeting in this same hall in Saint Louis. Those delegates seemed to be simply going through the motions, more intent on celebrating themselves or on positioning themselves for future political races. Now, as you can hear on every side as you walk across this convention floor, there is a palpable air of excitement.

"Earlier today, I spoke with Senator Carlyle Johnson, who

has probably attended more political conventions than anyone else here.'' Viewers saw Benedict look left at his own monitor, then their screens switched to a tape of the anchorman and the senator seated in the broadcast booth.

''Senator, have you ever seen anything like this?''

''No, Brent, nothing quite like this. To find another real cliff-hanger, you'd have to go back at least to nineteen sixty. That was the year that John Kennedy was nominated by the Democratic Party at its convention in Los Angeles. We now know, of course, that Kennedy was nominated and elected president. It is hard to remember now, but Kennedy's chances were in doubt up to the last minute, with some strong candidates fighting for the nomination. There were Lyndon Johnson and Adlai Stevenson and Estes Kefauver—any one of whom might have won.''

''That's right, that was a close one,'' Benedict interjected.

''You know, Brent, for much of our political history, the candidates were chosen at the party conventions, often only after a series of close ballots. Sometimes there were real surprises. My favorite is the Republican convention in 1940, when Wendell Willkie, an outsider, came in and 'stole' the nomination from Senator Bob Taft, who was the choice of the party's insiders.''

''Perhaps we're getting back to something like that here.''

''Oh, I would say this is probably an aberration, Brent. The party primaries have become too important and the amount of money needed to conduct a nationwide campaign has become so immense that the weaker candidates tend to be weeded out long before the convention. But this . . . this is like the good old days. It makes an old politician's heart beat faster just to be part of a convention that has some suspense in it.''

''Well, this one has certainly picked up a load of suspense. Thank you, Senator.''

In a small room just off the stage, three men met with the door closed. They were the party chairman, the chairman of the president's reelection campaign, and a special assistant to the president.

The president's special assistant looked worried.

"How much more time can you give me?"

The party chairman was clearly irritated.

"Not a hell of a lot. I've stalled a vote as long as I can. How much more do you need?"

"People scattered last night. I think some of them didn't want to be found. But now that they're coming back on the floor, we can get to them. Can you give me a few hours—say you start the balloting at seven P.M.?"

The chairman looked at his watch. "Okay, seven o'clock. But I'm liable to have a riot on my hands. These folks are all keyed up—more keyed up than I've ever seen at a convention. They all want to see how this is going to come out. Stalling this thing is going to cause me problems. Big time!"

"I understand, I understand. But I've been talking to the president and I can assure you he will be very grateful for your support. He remembers his friends."

The chairman gave him a wry look as he headed toward the microphones. He had to check himself to keep from retorting: "Yeah, I'll believe that when I see it."

Out on the floor, the delegates were assembling around the signs carrying the names of their states. From the podium, the roar of the hundreds of voices—each trying to be heard over the din—seemed like an overwhelming physical presence, a *thing* trying to reach out and snatch up whoever might be standing at the mike.

In the past, conventions always ran far behind schedule. In the last few years, that had changed as the convention managers had put together a carefully scripted show designed to capture as much free air time as possible and divert attention from any problems the party might be having. But this afternoon, the party chairman had thrown away the script. Instead of fighting to keep the convention on schedule, he had decided to dump the schedule, stall as long as possible, and only then try to fill the time with speeches and parliamentary maneuvers.

His tactic worked until nearly 6 P.M. Then a few voices began to chant: "*Vote! Vote! Vote!*" Gradually, the roar of the many voices coalesced into that single word, repeated over and over.

The chairman listened for five minutes, ten minutes, as the demand for a vote became louder and more insistent. Then he strode to the front of the stage and began slowly and methodically to hammer his gavel near the microphone, syncopating his sound with the chant: *"Vote!"* "Bang!" *"Vote!"* "Bang!" *"Vote!"* "Bang!"

"I can't hold this crowd too long," he shouted to one of the president's aides, who was standing at his shoulder. "We're going to have to vote before seven o'clock."

"Okay. Give us as much time as you can."

Suddenly there was a new sound from the rear of the auditorium. It was coming from a small brass band: drums, two trumpets, a trombone, and a big bass horn. Slowly they came down the aisle, leading a parade of demonstrators carrying posters:

WILSON FOR PRESIDENT.

DUMP WALKER.

TIME FOR A CHANGE.

There were even hastily lettered signs demanding: VOTE NOW!

The chairman shrugged, put down his gavel, and walked to the rear of the stage, his arm over the shoulder of the president's assistant.

"Hear that? That's music to my ears."

The aide leaned close to hear his words and then shouted to reply, "What do you mean? Wilson's getting free air time. And who knows how many delegates he'll sweep along from sheer emotion?"

"You wanted time? Wilson is buying you time," the chairman shouted back. "I'll let them demonstrate until those trumpet players' chops give out. If you guys can't get the votes in the time you've got, then ... well, you just can't get the votes."

Luke Nash watched the small television monitor on his desk with satisfaction. Like many—perhaps even most—television viewers, he saw the Wilson demonstration as an indication of strength that might even lead to victory. Astute as he was in financial matters, Nash did not have the political sophistication to look beyond the demonstration to see the behind-the-scenes fight for votes and realize that it was this struggle, not the visible show on the screen, that would determine the outcome.

How the vote at the convention, and, in fact, the November presidential election, came out were matters of intense interest to Nash. But they were not matters over which he lost sleep. If Richard Wilson won the nomination and the election, or if he challenged the president as a third-party candidate and won, Nash would have his own man in the White House. He had assured Wilson there were no strings attached to his offer of help, but of course Wilson would feel the tug of those strings every day he served as president. If Wilson lost and faded into obscurity as just another also-ran, Nash could accept that, too. His support for Wilson and his obliteration of Mojave had already made him significantly richer and more powerful.

By 6:30 P.M., the party chairman was dealing with a near riot from the impatient delegates.

"We're going to have to vote—now!" he told the president's men. "If this goes on much longer, you're going to have a hemorrhage of votes. You're just going to have to take your chances on a vote now. If you've got the votes, you'll win. If not . . . well. . . ."

The president's assistant for domestic affairs nodded glumly as he used a small pocket calculator to tote up the votes one last time.

It took the chairman nearly fifteen minutes of constant pounding with his gavel to bring the convention under a semblance of control and begin the voting process.

As the spokesman for each state came to the microphone and announced the vote, President Walker and Wilson, the challenger, were neck and neck, with a few votes going to a scattering of favorite sons from various states.

The professional politicians and the network vote-counters were not fooled by the closeness of the vote.

"In this rollcall vote, we are seeing only the first phase of this round of balloting," Brent Benedict explained. "As you will notice, some of the key states—California, Pennsylvania,

New York—have all passed up their turn. Only after the chairman has run through the entire roll call will they step up and announce which way they are going. Those three states together—and perhaps any one of them alone—have enough votes to swing this nomination one way or the other.

"Our correspondents on the floor tell us that a furious behind-the-scenes battle for the votes of those three big states is still going on."

In New York and Hollywood and Atlanta, network producers were frantically shuffling their schedules. Under the party's carefully scripted plan, the voting should already have been wrapped up. But if the voting went on much further into the evening, as now seemed likely, they would have to decide whether to continue with live broadcast of the convention and sacrifice the revenue from their most popular evening shows, or to stay with their scheduled programming and be accused by media critics of putting commercial interests above this dramatic story of the choice of a president.

The party chairman stood at the podium supervising the balloting, but he made no effort to hurry it up. Why bother at this point? And with all the air time he was getting now, he couldn't help think that this moment could be the beginning of his own candidacy four years from now.

At the White House, Maynard Walker stayed at his desk into the evening. On one wall, the images from the TV screens blinked and flashed silently. Occasionally he reached for the remote control and brought up the sound when something on the screen caught his attention.

All day, the president's secretaries and other aides had done whatever they could to avoid entering the Oval Office—or "the den," as they called it among themselves. Confronted with the challenge to his political future at the convention and with the threat of the destruction of another American city, the president was angry and frustrated by his inability to do anything about either problem—and he took it out on anyone who came close. Except for occasional bursts of anger, which could flare with sudden ferocity and then subside just as quickly, he was normally pleasant and considerate of those who worked for him. But today he was curt and testy with everyone. His longtime secretary hadn't seen him so irritable since he'd quit smoking, years ago.

Walker looked at his wristwatch and then sat drumming with his pencil on the edge of the desk, staring with unseeing eyes at the array of television screens.

A plan took shape in his mind: if he won on tonight's ballot, he would fly to Saint Louis first thing in the morning and go quickly to the convention hall to deliver his acceptance speech. Normally, the candidate chosen by the party would speak during the prime evening hours. But that would mean more time for Richard Wilson to work whatever mischief he had in mind. By making his speech about noon, Walker would give the impression of a man in charge—a president so busy with momentous events that his acceptance speech was just one more thing to be shoehorned into a busy schedule.

Maynard Walker had the unusual ability to compartmentalize his mind. Once he had made his decision about the acceptance speech, he shut that topic away and turned his full attention to the Blackjack and the *Cockatrice.*

He stood up and began to pace back and forth in his office, pausing occasionally to glance at the television screens.

He couldn't recall ever facing such a difficult situation. His decision to make his acceptance speech at noon could throw off the timing of whoever was controlling the weapon, but that was only a hope. He didn't know where the plane was. He didn't know who was controlling it. He didn't know when, or even if, it would strike again. All he knew was that the nation could be about to confront the most deadly disaster in its history. If that weapon could obliterate a little town like Mojave in less than a minute, what would happen if it were aimed at a major city? Casualties could be in the hundreds of thousands—even the millions.

Maynard Walker stood for a long time, staring outside as darkness settled over the Rose Garden.

CHAPTER 32

THE PARTY CHAIRMAN GLANCED DOWN AT THE SMALL COMPUTER screen built into the podium. Displayed in neat columns were the names of the states, the number of each state's voting delegates, and the status of the voting.

On a split screen down below, the votes for each candidate were listed. Up in the corner of the panel, backlighted, was the number of votes that would put the winning candidate over the top.

"It's going to be close . . . close," he thought to himself, as the numbers blinked and changed. If the president didn't make it on this ballot, he knew, the whole convention might blow up. Wilson, the challenger, could be nominated. Or the votes could suddenly and unpredictably swing to a favorite son. And, good Lord, what if they *tied*? This convention was in danger of going completely out of control.

Already, the chairman's sources in the state delegations told him, backers of a number of the lesser candidates were busy making promises and trading votes, preparing to show their muscle if the convention went into a second ballot. That was one reason, of course, several of the big states were holding back their votes. The other reason was that they were using whatever leverage they had to extract promises from the two leading candidates. No one knew how many dams, highways, post offices, appointments to high office, and pieces of questionable legislation might be spawned in the few hours the nomination hung in the balance.

The chairman began pounding his gavel in a slow rhythm as the roll call came to an end and it was time to go back and pick up the states that had passed the first time around. Gradually, the level of sound in the auditorium ebbed slightly.

"The State of California?"

"Mr. Chairman, under the unit rule, the great golden State of California casts its votes for our present and future president, Maynard 'Chip' Walker."

The numbers on the screen blinked, adding up the votes.

"Still awful close," the chairman thought.

"The State of New York?"

"Mr. Chairman, the great State of New York—the Empire State—casts half its votes for President Maynard Walker and half its votes for Senator Richard Wilson."

The numbers changed again. Wilson couldn't win on this ballot, but Walker was still short of a victory.

"The Commonwealth of Pennsylvania."

"Mr. Chairman, the Commonwealth of Pennsylvania—the Keystone State—casts its votes to assure the nomination of our President Maynard Walker as the candidate of our glorious party for a second term in the White House."

With the addition of the votes from Pennsylvania, the monitor indicated Walker's total had passed the magic number needed for nomination.

A demonstration quickly formed, with delegates parading up and down the aisles holding "WALKER FOR PRESIDENT" signs. A great din filled the hall and the chairman let it continue until the delegates were hoarse. Normally, in a well-ordered modern convention, such a demonstration would have been neatly choreographed and carefully limited to avoid eating up too much valuable air time. But after this cliff-hanger vote, there was no way, the chairman knew, that he could control the emotions of this multitude.

After the demonstration had gone on for nearly half an hour, he once again began the heavy banging of his gavel. Gradually the sound subsided and the delegates drifted back to their seats.

"Mr. Chairman! Mr. Chairman!" the leader of the Pennsylvania delegation shouted.

"The gentleman from the Commonwealth of Pennsylvania is recognized."

"Mr. Chairman, I move that the nomination be recorded as unanimous."

The chairman carefully failed to notice the delegate from Wilson's home state frantically appealing for his attention.

"It has been moved and seconded that the nomination be recorded as unanimous. All in favor, Aye ... all opposed, Nay ... the Ayes have it. The nomination of President Maynard Walker as the presidential candidate of our party will be recorded as unanimous.

"This convention will be in recess *sine die*." The chairman would have to talk to the president's men about when he intended to make his acceptance speech. He would then notify the delegates when to convene again.

Brent Benedict had remained silent through the latter part of the balloting, letting the drama on the floor unfold by itself. As the chairman banged his gavel, he resumed his commentary: "There you have it, ladies and gentlemen. As is customary, even though the president won a narrow victory, the vote has now been recorded as unanimous. This does not, of course, end the divisions within the party. We expect to hear shortly whether Senator Wilson will accept the decision of the convention or whether he will—as he has threatened—carry on a third-party campaign."

At the White House, the president had assembled a small group of his closest associates to be with him in the Oval Office as the voting reached its climax. Gathered in front of the bank of TV sets were Marcie Walker and their son, David; the chief of staff; and two cabinet officers who were also old friends. Many of the other high-ranking officials of the administration were already in Saint Louis for the convention.

When the balloting ceased, an aide entered the room carrying a tray with glasses of champagne. The president, standing in front of the TV screens, took a glass and raised it: "To politics. It never gets better than this."

The chief of staff raised his glass: "To four more years, sir. And congratulations."

"Okay, we've got work to do," Walker began, putting down his nearly full glass. "I'll fly to Saint Louis first thing in the morning. I'm going to make my acceptance speech at noon."

"At noon?" Marcie Walker was surprised.

"Yes. I don't want to keep those folks in Saint Louis any longer than we have to. This will keep up the momentum—give people the feeling we know what we're doing. . . . How's the speech coming along?" he added, turning to the chief of staff.

"I think it's in good shape, sir. As we discussed, it lays out your vision for the future without getting into a lot of specifics about legislation or new programs."

"That's exactly what I want—a broad vision. And you tell those guys with their word processors I want well-timed applause lines. And . . . listen to me . . . I want some memorable lines. I want words they'll use in the headlines—words someone, someday, will carve on my tombstone. 'Four score and seven . . . ,' 'Ask not what your country. . . . ' You know what I mean? Words for the ages."

The chief of staff made notes, keeping his head bent down toward the clipboard so Walker would not catch his eye. As long as he had been working for Maynard Walker, sometimes he could not be quite sure whether he was deadly serious or whether he was pulling his leg.

"Okay, you guys get to work." The president leaned down to talk to his son. "David, can you get yourself upstairs? I'm sure you have some homework to do."

The boy gave his father a grimace, quickly followed by a grin, and then followed the others out the door.

"Marcie, there's something you have to know." He turned from his wife and pressed a button on the intercom. "Please send Admiral McKay in."

"Evening sir . . . ma'am." McKay was resplendent in summer whites. Walker envied the military, who had the good sense to dispense with neckties in the Washington summer.

"Mac, please fill Marcie in on this *Cockatrice* business. She's going to have to make some decisions about herself and David." The president led the way to the couches at one side of the Oval Office.

McKay remained standing. "Briefly, Mrs. Walker, this is the situation we face. Someone—we're not sure who—has obtained control of a very deadly weapon carried by a modified Soviet bomber. It is this weapon that was responsible for the destruction of Mojave two weeks ago. We fear the weapon may be used again in the near future."

The president's wife leaned forward, staring intently at McKay. "How soon? Do you know where?"

"We really don't know, so we're assuming the worst-case scenario. We have some partially decoded intercepts that indicate the next attack could come as soon as tomorrow—directed at Saint Louis during the president's speech."

Marcie Walker put a hand to her mouth. "That's awful. Can you evacuate the city?"

Her husband answered the question. "We've thought about that. But we have no evacuation plan. Any attempt to move everyone out of a city the size of Saint Louis would create unimaginable traffic jams and confusion. And what if we were wrong and there was no attack? No telling how many people would be killed and injured in the panic involved in an attempted evacuation."

"We've also thought, Mrs. Walker, of adjourning the convention and getting the delegates out of town," McKay said. "Perhaps that would make the city less tempting as a target. But how would we explain such a drastic action without causing widespread panic?"

"So, what are we going to do?" she asked.

Walker signaled to McKay to continue his explanation. "We have two plans. One, we are prepared to try to shoot down this plane. Two, we have identified a compound in the Rockies above Colorado Springs. We suspect—but we really don't know—that the weapon is controlled from that compound. If the shoot-down effort fails, we will assault the compound and attempt to disable the control system before the weapon can be activated.''

''So you have two chances to stop this thing?''

McKay shook his head. ''No, I would say we have one chance, or perhaps a chance-and-a-half. Our best chance is to shoot down the plane. That solves the problem. If we fail in that effort, we can only hope that the weapon is controlled from the Colorado Springs compound and that we can get to the controls in time. If it is preprogrammed or if the pilot controls the system, then our assault will be futile.''

The president's wife sat silently, her face grim.

McKay cleared his throat. ''Mr. President, there is one other thing. I think it would be prudent to have those in the immediate line of succession to the presidency—the vice president, the speaker of the House, and the secretary of state—stay away from Saint Louis and remain in safe places.''

''Yes, I've already made arrangements,'' Walker replied. ''And, Mac, I want you to remain here in Washington. I will delegate my authority over our nuclear forces to you and you will be available to work closely with my successor, if it comes to that.''

''Yes sir. I think that's prudent. But let's hope and pray that it doesn't come to that.''

''Hope and prayer may be our best bets,'' the president replied. They were all silent, lost in thought. The president broke the silence. ''That'll be all, Mac. Would you excuse us, please?''

As McKay left the room, Walker turned to his wife and took her hands in his.

''Marcie, this whole thing has been very hush-hush. Only Mac and I and a few of his commandos know as much as he has just told you. Now, you have to make a decision. Knowing the danger, do you and David want to accompany me to Saint Louis for my acceptance speech tomorrow? I leave the decision entirely up to you.''

She gazed at him, looking directly into his eyes for a long moment, and then she stood, continuing to hold his eyes with hers.

''Chip, you know I have been very unhappy with you. I

thought I had your promise to change your behavior. But I'm not a fool. I know what goes on."

Her husband looked away and then strode across the room to lean with his back against the edge of his desk.

"Marcie, I'm sorry. I swear to you, it's all over now." He paused and then added: "I need your support. I really do."

She stared back at him, her lips set in a grim straight line. "As far as I'm concerned, promises don't go very far. You're still on probation. Now, as far as the convention is concerned, I think there is only one answer: of course we'll come with you."

Walker smiled and moved quickly across the room to kiss his wife. "Thank you, Marcie. Thank you very much."

CHAPTER 33

THE TELEPHONE BUILT INTO THE HEADBOARD OF NASH'S BED rang only once before he reached up, pressed the speaker button, and muttered, "Yes?"

The lawyer, all business, did not bother to apologize for waking his employer. "Sir, the Associated Press has just carried a news media advisory. It says the president's acceptance speech will be at noon today rather than tonight, as we had planned."

"What time is it?"

"Four thirty-four."

"Send a message to Quintana Roo moving up the schedule. Everything is ready. That should be no problem. Make takeoff at what . . . ? Eleven-fifteen or eleven-thirty?"

"By our earlier calculations, it should be about eleven-thirty, reaching Saint Louis at about a quarter past noon."

"Right, make it eleven-thirty." He snapped off the speaker phone, rolled over, and was quickly asleep again.

—————— ★ ——————

Senator Wilson had slept a total of only about half an hour during the night. He had spent almost all the hours since his narrow loss to President Walker on the phone, talking to advisers and backers, weighing the question of whether to split from the party and launch a third-party challenge to the president.

As the first rays of dawn groped upward from the eastern horizon and through the windows of his fourteenth-story suite, he had made up his mind. He strode back and forth across the room, a microphone in hand, as he dictated the statement that would be released later in the morning.

"I come before you at a critical point in American history. We stand on the threshold of a marvelous new age, with the prospect of peace and prosperity—prosperity unparalleled in human history—lying before us. But in order to enter this great new era, we need leadership.

"Unfortunately, we do not have that leadership. We are being led by men—by a man—who is blind to the opportunities that lie before us. Instead of stumbling blindly into the future, we must be guided by a vision of a new America.

"In my vision, I see a land where race will no longer be a barrier to opportunity—but where onerous laws will place no barriers to the achievements of every man and woman.

"In my vision, I see a land where the working men and women of this country will be protected from the rapacious greed of the few. It makes my stomach turn every time I stop to realize that while the average American working person takes home less than twenty-five thousand dollars a year, a few corporate executives pocket more than a hundred thousand dollars an hour . . . one hundred thousand dollars *an hour*. These are the same executives who are throwing thousands of workers out of their jobs. I call that obscene and it must be stopped.

"In my vision, I see a land in which the hardworking people of this country are protected from the threat of cheap foreign labor—whether it is foreigners working in sweat shops in their own lands or whether it is foreigners coming here to take jobs from Americans at substandard wages."

Wilson continued, ticking off every divisive hot-button issue in American politics.

"I consider it my duty to my God and to this country to offer the nation a vision of the future and to lead our beloved nation into that future. Therefore, I am announcing today that I will run in every state as the candidate of the New America Party for the presidency of the United States. I intend to run

... and to win ... to give this nation the leadership it deserves.''

Wilson pressed a buzzer on his desk. Moments later, his press secretary entered the room. His collar was unbuttoned, his necktie was loose, and he had a mug of coffee in his hand. His clothes looked as though they had been slept in, although he, too, had not been to bed that night.

The senator popped the cassette out of his dictation machine.

"Here, get this transcribed. And call a press conference here in the hotel at noon.''

The press aide took a sip of coffee and looked at him quizzically. "Noon? While the president's speaking?''

"Yes, noon. Set it up.''

The aide took another sip of coffee, shrugged and left the room.

News of Wilson's plan to hold a press conference—in effect, nominating himself and giving his own acceptance speech—at the same time the president was speaking had caused consternation in the upper reaches of the network.

Brent Benedict, his producer and network executives in New York were linked up in a conference call to decide how to handle this unprecedented situation.

"I know Wilson is a loose cannon, but this is news!'' Benedict almost shouted.

The network executive was one of that sizable group of fortunate individuals who had spent a night in the Lincoln bedroom as a guest of the president. A perk like that wouldn't influence his news judgment, but still. . . .

"Brent, we're dealing with the president of the United States here. We owe him the courtesy of full coverage of his acceptance speech. This is information vital to the American public.''

"Sir,'' the producer broke in, "we can handle it with a split screen. We can show both the president and Senator Wilson.''

"No,'' the voice from New York insisted, "that won't

work. We can't do sound from two places at once. We'll go with the president's speech and fill in what Wilson has to say later.''

''You're right about the sound,'' Benedict broke in. ''But here's what I'd like to do. I'll come on the air before the speech and explain that Wilson's scheduled a press conference. We'll go with the president but show Wilson on a small split screen. If he says anything really newsworthy . . . if he says he's going to run as a third-party candidate . . . we'll fade out the president's speech and I'll come in voice-over with a brief report. How does that sound?''

''Okay, I'll buy that,'' the executive said. ''I just don't want to seem to be disrespectful. After all, he *is* the president.''

Maynard Walker, accompanied by his wife and son, arrived in Saint Louis early in the morning and moved into a suite at the same hotel where Wilson was staying. A large sitting room had been arranged as an office for the president.

He quickly leafed through a sheaf of wire service reports lying in a neat pile on the desk.

''What is this son of a bitch Dick Wilson up to now?'' He turned to an aide, waving a handful of paper.

The aide shrugged. ''All we know, sir, is that he has called a press conference for the same time you'll be delivering your acceptance speech. We've got our guys trying to find out what's going on, but they're running a very tight operation. He could just be causing trouble. Our guess is that he's about to split from the party and run his own campaign.''

''Oh, great! That asshole screwed up the convention, and now he's going to screw up the campaign!'' The president shook his head. ''The worst of it is, he seems to have the money to do it. Where is all that money coming from? That's what the press should be digging into.''

''You'll beat him, sir,'' his chief of staff assured him. ''He's just a flash in the pan.''

Walker whirled and fixed his aide with a glare. ''Don't you understand? This is trouble! Big trouble!''

"But . . . third-party candidates never win. Even Teddy Roosevelt couldn't win, back in, what was it—1912?"

"Right. The Bull Moose Party." Walker had made such a close study of presidential politics that it was almost as though he had lived through every era throughout the more than two hundred years of the nation's history. "But remember what happened: Roosevelt split the Republican vote and Woodrow Wilson, the Democrat, became president. History could repeat itself this year. Don't you see what Wilson's done to us? He forced us to spend all through the primaries. Then he carries his fight into the convention and gives the people a picture of a divided party. Now we go into the general election nearly broke. We'll pick up our public financing. But Wilson's paying for his campaign himself. He can spend as much as he wants."

The chief of staff nodded in agreement. "You're right," he muttered.

"We can beat Wilson," the president continued. "We already beat him in the primaries and at the convention. And we can beat the other party, too. We've got the polls going in our direction. But can we beat them both at the same time? Wilson could siphon off just enough of our votes to cost us the election. We've got our work cut out for us."

The president glanced at his watch and then dismissed the chief of staff. "Give me a little while to go over this speech."

As soon as the door closed, Walker picked up the secure phone that had been installed during the night to connect him to Adm. McKay in the Pentagon.

"Any word, Mac?"

"No, sir. We're all set. All we can do now is wait and hope."

"Yes, hope. I've been thinking. I'm going to have to give you permission right now to carry out that assault if the shootdown fails. I'm going to have to leave it in your hands and rely on your judgment. Can I do that?"

"Yes, sir. If the shootdown fails, we really have no other alternative. To fail to act would be . . . well, it would be almost criminal."

The president sighed. "Yes, I suppose so." There was a

long pause as the president thought. "Okay, Mac, go ahead. But tell your team to get that guy Nash alive. We want to talk to him. And, Mac, try to minimize casualties."

"Yes, sir." McKay shook his head. Politicians were always worrying about minimizing casualties. Wouldn't they ever learn that the best way to minimize casualties was to attack violently with lightning speed and get the battle over with as fast as possible?

"I'll put this in an order and cable it to you: 'You are authorized to act in accordance with our conversation of such-and-such a time.' That'll cover your ass if this whole thing turns to shit."

McKay chuckled at the president's choice of words. "If that happens, sir, my derriere will be the least of our worries."

CHAPTER 34

MARK RATTNER GLANCED AT HIS WATCH ONCE MORE. ONLY TWO minutes had passed, but it seemed like hours. If something didn't happen soon, he feared, he would either drown in his own juices or short out all the electrical systems in the plane.

Rattner was strapped in the cockpit of his F-15, parked on a ramp at the end of the major active runway at Eglin. Next to the plane, a crew of Air Force technicians had rigged up a sheet of canvas to shade them from the humid heat of the Florida summer. Off to one side, an auxiliary power supply unit hummed, providing power for Rattner's radio and other electronic equipment. The ground crew had even stretched a canvas awning over the cockpit and hooked up an electrical fan directed at the pilot. Nothing short of firing up the turbine engines and turning on the plane's air conditioning, however, would make a dent in the almost nauseating heat in the cockpit.

Finally, Rattner saw a pickup truck slowly rolling toward them along the taxiway. Relief at last! He began unfastening the straps that tied him to the plane's ejection seat, getting ready to turn the hot seat over to his friend. He was out of the cockpit and standing under a wing when the pickup stopped.

"Sorry," Rattner greeted his friend. "It's going to get even hotter out here."

The other pilot patted Rattner on the shoulder. "Okay, go get a good cold shower. Hear anything?"

"Nothing. NORAD and the AWACS are both on the alert, but they haven't picked up a thing."

"Well, we'll get it when they do. See you back here in a couple of hours."

As soon as President Walker had given McKay the discretion to go ahead with an assault on the Rock House if the shootdown failed, the admiral had picked up another phone and called Nelson.

"Here's the situation, Chuck. If the shootdown fails, I want you to be in position to hit that compound within seconds. That means you'll already be airborne before we know whether the F-15 attack succeeds.

"We're going on the assumption that the attack will be directed at Saint Louis during the president's speech."

"Yes, that makes sense."

"Incidentally," the admiral said, "you know the president's moved his speech up from the evening and now plans to begin speaking at noon?"

"I know. That means we've got to do this whole thing in broad daylight?"

"Yes, I'm afraid so."

"That's going to make it tough, sir. We were counting on our ability to operate in the dark to give us an edge."

"Sorry, Chuck, but that's the way it is."

"I understand, sir. We'll do our best."

Jeff Bonior had been sitting quietly during the conversation. When he heard the words "Saint Louis," he rose to his feet in alarm.

As soon as Nelson hung up, he leaned over the desk.

"What's this about Saint Louis, boss?"

"We're going on the assumption that the next attack will be on Saint Louis during the president's acceptance speech."

"But that's where Dottie and the kids are, visiting her folks while Denise recovers. I've got to get them out of there."

Nelson shook his head as he held Bonior's gaze. "No, Jeff.

We're locked down here. No phone calls. No contact with anyone. I'm sorry."

Bonior stared back for a moment, biting his lower lip. Then he shrugged and left the room.

Just before 10 o'clock, Rattner's pickup pulled up beside the F-15. The sun was now high in the sky and the heat was visible, rising off the tarmac in shimmering waves.

"Still nothing," the other pilot reported, as he climbed down from the cockpit. "Hope you have a busier day."

"Yeah, me too," Rattner replied, as he grasped the edges of the ladder and started up the seven steps to the cockpit. "This can't go on too much longer . . . I hope."

The pilot settled himself in the cockpit and carefully went through the pre-flight check list. He had done the same thing four hours ago, and his friend had repeated it two hours after that. But, just to be on the safe side, he double-checked everything.

"Looks good," he said. A ground crewman, wearing a set of headphones connected to the plane's communications system by a long cord, gave Rattner a thumbs-up signal.

Rattner adjusted his helmet to make sure his built-in earphones were not pinching his ears and then settled down to listen to the chatter on the radio . . . and wait . . . and wait . . . and wait.

A few minutes after 10 A.M., Senator Wilson was alone in the hotel room that had been converted into his private office. He had left orders that he not be disturbed as he worked over the statement he planned to make at his press conference a short time later. He looked up in irritation as a knock at the door broke his concentration.

"Yes? What is it?"

The bulk of the chief of his security guard seemed to fill the doorway. The man wore a black business suit, carefully tailored over his bulging muscles.

"Will you please come with me, sir? I have orders that we are to leave Saint Louis immediately."

Wilson stood and glared at him. "What are you talking about? I'm not leaving Saint Louis."

Two more members of the security detail stepped into the room.

"Yes, sir. You are to come with us. Now!"

The two other men advanced and took up positions on each side of Wilson. One of them began to withdraw an automatic pistol from the holster under his left armpit. Wilson glanced at him in alarm.

"No, Markovitz. We don't need any weapons. I'm sure the senator understands the situation and will come with us peacefully—and quickly."

One of the men held Wilson's suit coat for him and then each man took an arm and urged him forward. Wilson began to protest and then shrugged, shaking off their hands, and walked toward the door. Ever since he had declined Secret Service protection, he had felt comfortable, surrounded by the members of a team of former commandos provided by Nash. Now he realized that they were there not only to protect him, but to control him. He had no choice but to go with them.

His limousine was waiting at the side entrance to the hotel. As soon as the door was closed, the vehicle sped away behind a police escort. At Lambert Field, a small executive jet was waiting. Later that morning, the plane landed at the small airport in the hills north of Atlanta and Wilson was whisked away to the compound Bernard had set up as his team's headquarters.

During the flight, and even after his arrival, Wilson got no answers to his questions about what was going on—just a curt, "Orders, sir." All he knew was that Nash must have some very urgent reason to want him out of Saint Louis.

The network began its convention coverage at 11:30 A.M. with Brent Benedict at his anchor position high above the floor.

"Good morning once again from America's Center in Saint Louis, where we will soon be bringing you live coverage of President Walker's speech accepting his party's nomination as candidate for election to his second term as president. This convention has been full of tension and surprises and we have yet one more puzzling development this morning.

"Senator Wilson, who was narrowly defeated last night, has called a press conference to coincide with the president's speech. But we have just been informed that the senator, accompanied by members of his private security team, was seen hurrying to his limousine a short time ago. The limousine, with a police escort, sped to Lambert Field and the senator entered an aircraft which immediately took off.

"Senator Wilson's staff had already issued the text of a statement he intended to read at his press conference announcing his intention to form a new party—what he calls 'the New America Party'—and challenge President Walker in the November election.

"We will continue to keep you informed of developments in this bizarre situation as it unfolds. Meanwhile, we have just been informed that the president's motorcade has entered the convention center. He will soon be taking his place on the stage in preparation for his speech."

In the cavernous, windowless cabin of the AWACS, circling at forty thousand feet, far out over the Gulf of Mexico, radar operators stared intently at their screens. Each set was tuned to provide a different resolution. One gave a broad view of much of the Gulf and the western portion of the Caribbean. Another focused in on Mexico's Yucatán Peninsula, jutting out far to the east of the rest of the country. A third scanned back and forth across the terrain. It was powerful enough to detect a plane on a runway several hundred miles away—but it helped to know where to look.

"Sir! I've got a fast-mover coming up out of that jungle." The operator with the narrow focus on the terrain leaned forward to follow the movement on the screen.

An officer peered over his shoulder, watching the trace on the screen. "That's it!"

He keyed his radio and used the AWACS call signal: "Jungle Jim to Tinker control."

"Jungle Jim, Tinker."

"We have a fast-mover on a course of three-five-eight degrees. Present location. . . ." He leaned down and studied the radar screen. "Present location 22.31N 89.22W. Estimated speed, Mach one-point-five."

"Ah, roger, Jungle Jim." The Tinker controller had already picked up the hotline to Nelson's office at Peterson Field.

"Mrs. Collins, I think we have your boy." He gave her the position and speed relayed from the radar plane.

Moments later, Mark Rattner heard the voice of the control tower operator at Eglin in his earphones. "Eagle five, Mrs. Collins is on the line. I'm patching her through."

Rattner raised his right hand, his index finger extended, and rotated it in a circle, alerting the ground crew he was about to start engines.

"As soon as you're airborne, contact Jungle Jim to vector you in." She gave him the radio frequency for the radar plane. "Good hunting, Mark. Collins out."

Rattner called the tower for permission to take off. A C-130 on its final approach was waved off as the Eagle pivoted into position, paused for a moment, and then rocketed down the runway on a maximum-performance takeoff. Rattner felt himself pressed back firmly against the seat as the plane accelerated almost straight up. Looking back over his shoulder, he could see the long white ribbon of the runway stretching through the green of the Florida swampland.

"Jungle Jim, Eagle five." Rattner checked in with the radar plane as he climbed out over the greenish-blue waters of the Gulf.

"Eagle five. This guy is really moving! He's gone through ninety thousand feet, still accelerating. We clock him now at Mach three."

"Ah, roger, Jungle Jim. Can you give me the vector for an intercept?"

"Eagle five. Remain on your present heading. We will vector you in as soon as he levels off and we have a firm reading on his speed, altitude and course."

Rattner leveled off at forty thousand feet and continued on to the southwest, toward a point over the Gulf south of New Orleans. He would not begin his zoom until he had better target information.

Inside the AWACS, the radar operators watched in amazement as the plane climbed steeply and then leveled off at 120,000 feet.

Maynard Walker approached the podium a few minutes before noon, waving and smiling broadly. A short time before, Adm. McKay had alerted him that the attempted intercept was under way.

The president's wife and son took seats a short distance behind him. She put an arm around the boy, drew him to her, and kissed him on top of the head. He squirmed uncomfortably and pulled away.

As the crowd quieted, Walker turned to look at his wife, give her the thumbs-up sign, and mouth the words "I love you."

"My fellow citizens. Before I begin this address, let me take a moment to express the gratitude of myself and our nation to the many members of our armed forces who, at this very moment, are standing guard in many parts of the world to protect our people and our freedoms. Let us pray for their success in missions of which many of us may never be aware."

He paused for a moment and then, looking through his Teleprompter screen, began his prepared address.

Brent Benedict spoke softly, his voice audible over the first words of the president's speech. "The president has begun his address with an unusual tribute to the armed forces. That paragraph was not in the original text of his speech. We have no explanation of why he chose to add that statement."

Far ahead, Sergei Kaparov could see the long curve of the Gulf Coast, stretching from Houston to the east of Pensacola. He checked his instruments. Everything was working perfectly. He found it a remarkably peaceful sensation to skim through the thin upper reaches of the atmosphere, running ahead of the sound of his engines. He relaxed and sat back, almost like a passenger, content to enjoy the view.

"Eagle five. We have an intercept vector." The radar controller read off the course and speed figures.

Rattner read the numbers back, then rolled over in a steep dive to pick up speed. As his speed approached nearly Mach 2, he pulled back sharply on the stick and zoomed almost straight up.

The radar antenna in the nose of the plane tracked rapidly back and forth, searching the sky for the other aircraft. Rattner watched intently as a tiny blip appeared at the top of the screen. He pressed a button to tune the radar into target acquisition mode. Moments later, the instrument indicated his radar had locked on the target.

As Nelson approached, the rotors on the two helicopters were already turning. He saw the members of his team standing silently a short distance away, gathered in a circle around Bonior. Their shoulders sagged under the weight of weapons, bandoliers of ammunition, radios, first aid kits, and other equipment. Their faces were streaked with dark green camouflage paint. From the center of the fierce-looking group, Bonior's deep voice emerged.

"Oh Lord, we ask you to bless these your servants on our mission today. Shield us from our enemies. Strengthen our bodies and our minds. Sharpen our vision and our hearing. Help us to prevail that evil may be defeated. Protect each of us from injury or death. And have mercy on those whom we may destroy this day."

Bonior paused for a moment and then added, in a strong

voice: "And, Lord, please, please care for our loved ones and keep them safe." He remained standing silently, head bowed, and then concluded, "Amen."

Nelson had reached the outer circle and joined with the others in echoing Bonior's "Amen."

Jack Laffer and the other helicopter pilots had carefully studied the approaches to the Rock House. With one of the combat controllers from the Special Tactics Team, they had even driven out into the hills and hiked through a neighboring valley and up to a ridge overlooking the compound. By the time they were through, they had spotted every power line and every other potential hazard in their approach route. They almost felt as though they knew every pine tree by name.

From Peterson Field, they swung north and east around the city before turning back south over the Air Force Academy, hugging the foothills. Their course took them up a V-shaped canyon neighboring the valley in which the compound was situated. They settled down in a small pasture and sat waiting, engines running and blades turning, ready to take off at a moment's notice.

An urgent buzz in his earphones and a flashing light on his instrument panel stirred Kaparov from his reverie. His instruments had an urgent message: he was about to be attacked. It was the last thing he expected, to find himself targeted by hostile radar.

Kaparov switched on his own search radar and began sweeping the space below and in front of his plane. Suddenly he was glad that the technicians back in Uzbekistan had fitted the plane with look-down, shoot-down radar.

A blip on the screen showed Rattner climbing rapidly toward him. Kaparov adjusted the fire control mechanism and watched in satisfaction as the radar screen indicated lock-on. He selected the Acrid missile under his right wing and then pressed the firing button on his control stick.

Off to the right, he saw the bright flame as the missile

streaked out in front of him and then arced downward.

He continued steadily on his course. No sense jinking until he knew whether the other plane had been able to launch a missile at him.

"Oh, shit!" The radar operator tracking Kaparov's plane detected the launch of the missile almost as soon as it had ignited. "Eagle five! Break! Break! Break!"

Mark Rattner felt his speed begin to drain off as he passed through seventy thousand feet, climbing at an angle of sixty-five degrees. As he prepared to fire his weapon, he heard an urgent buzz in his earphones, warning that he was under attack.

Almost at the same moment, he heard the warning from the AWACS operator. His instruments picked up the missile and began to track its course.

The commander of the AWACS radar team leaned over a screen that showed both planes, with a dot representing the Acrid missile streaking toward the F-15.

"Eagle five. You are under attack. Break now! I repeat, break now!"

Rattner held the plane steady as he strained upward to eighty thousand feet. Holding the lock on the plane far overhead, he pressed the button to fire his anti-satellite missile. As he felt the jolt of the missile falling away from the F-15, he threw his plane into an abrupt diving turn to the right.

Suddenly his plane was rocked, as though swatted by a giant hand, and engulfed by a dazzling burst of light as the Acrid missile exploded.

In the AWACS, all of the operators zeroed in on Kaparov's plane and the missile fired by Rattner, tracking the two objects on their collision course.

"Go! Go! Go!" one of the radarmen chanted, almost like a football fan cheering on a runner heading for the goalposts.

"We've got him!" another man almost shouted into his microphone.

The blip representing the plane continued steady on its course. The missile arced across the screen as it tracked the rapidly moving plane.

They didn't notice Rattner fighting his controls.

Kaparov watched the missile on his radar screen, almost hypnotized by the tiny dot and amazed at its rapid acceleration. His body was so tense it ached, every muscle straining. He felt as though his body was trying to shrink itself down and become invisible. But there was nowhere to hide.

At the last moment, mimicking the evasive maneuver Rattner had taken a few seconds before, Kaparov threw his control stick hard to the right and down. But the plane was agonizingly slow to respond. At its high speed, with little air to grab onto, it tended to obey one of the most basic laws of physics and continue on its course.

Kaparov watched helplessly as the missile curved toward his new course. If the two speeding objects collided, he knew, he and his plane would be vaporized.

Rattner fought the controls as the F-15 tumbled away from the explosion. As the plane leveled off and came back under control, Rattner craned his neck, turning to check his tall twin vertical tails. He gently worked the rudder and ailerons and moved the throttle back and forth to satisfy himself that the plane had not been damaged.

At the same moment, Kaparov saw the tiny homing device flash past his windscreen and hurtle on out into space.

Letting out a long breath, he checked his radar screen. Far below he saw the other plane on what appeared to be a course away from him. He turned his attention to his navigation system, adjusting his instruments to get back on track and on his tight timeline.

Once he had, he reported the attack to the control center in the Rock House at Colorado Springs.

He heard Nash's voice, faint and scratchy with static. "That's fine, Sergei. Continue your mission."

The radar operators greeted the near-miss with a gloomy silence. There was nothing they could do except pass the news to Tinker and on back to Mrs. Collins in Colorado Springs.

Rattner flew in a large circle, tracking the other plane on his radar and monitoring the time of flight of his missile. As the time of impact passed and the plane continued on its path, Rattner set his course back to Eglin, deeply disappointed.

Pat Collins picked up the direct line to the chairman's office. McKay was already holding on the line.

"Sir, we missed. The plane is approaching the Gulf Coast."

"Is the team in place?"

"Yes, sir. They are in a holding position forty-five seconds from the compound."

"Give them the go signal. Go get 'em, and God bless."

An aide carrying a glass of water walked to the front of the stage and handed the glass to the president. As he did so, he slipped a note onto the lectern.

The president took a quick drink of water and glanced down at the message: "Admiral McKay reports phase two has begun."

Except for his wife, he was the only one in the auditorium who knew that within the next fifteen minutes they and thousands of others in Saint Louis could be vaporized. Pushing the note aside, Walker continued smoothly with his address.

CHAPTER 35

FLYING IN TIGHT FORMATION, ONE BEHIND THE OTHER, THE TWO big helicopters slipped up over the crest and then down toward the compound. Laffer had timed it carefully: only fifteen seconds from the time they came over the ridge, into sight and sound of the compound, until they would be over the roof.

Machine gunners in the side windows and the open ramp of each helicopter searched the ground below for any sign of hostile action. They were under orders not to fire unless fired upon. By holding their fire, they might get to the roof without being detected.

In a machine gun emplacement guarding the approaches to the right of the building, one of Bernard's team was the first to detect the sound of the helicopters as they came over the ridge. He swung the muzzle of the weapon toward the sound.

Beside him, his teammate hit his arm and shouted, "Don't shoot. Those are Pave Lows. They're our guys."

The gunner looked at him, puzzled. "What do you mean, *our guys?*" He pulled the trigger.

But in his moment of hesitation, the two helicopters had passed overhead and reached the building, hovering so low over the roof that the structure was between them and the machine gun emplacement. The team members streamed down their fast-ropes. And then the choppers were pulling sharply upward and away. One machine gun fired a long burst, but its tracers arced behind the departing helos.

The members of the team had landed, as planned, at both ends of the main building of the compound. Nelson commanded the group on the left, Bonior the unit on the right. Both formed defensive perimeters as they landed while demolition men quickly placed explosives above the stairwells. Smaller charges were placed against the antenna masts.

Speaking into a microphone attached in front of his lips, the demo man in the left unit counted down: "Three, two, one." He concluded with a shouted, "Fire in the hole!" The other demo man echoed his shout. Members of both teams lay flat as the explosive charges tore jagged holes in the roof and toppled the antennas.

While pieces of wood and roofing material still clattered down around them, the door of a stairwell in the center of the building flew open and three members of Nash's security force emerged, holding machine guns. They dropped to the roof, blinking in the glare of the bright midday sun, trying to make out what was going on.

Bonior's men, firing so as not to hit their own teammates at the other end of the roof, quickly picked the three men off. Two SEALs dashed to the stairwell door. Each threw a grenade down the stairs and then stepped back as a muffled roar and smoke emerged from the doorway. Even before the smoke cleared, they stepped to the door and raked the area with automatic rifle fire.

Sergei Kaparov crossed the coastline to the west of New Orleans just before noon, local time. The sun was almost directly overhead, casting great gray shadows from the row of thunderheads along the coast. Down below, he could see the broad fingers of the delta where the Mississippi groped toward the sea. His course took him almost directly north along the great river valley toward Memphis and Saint Louis.

Members of the two units dropped down through the holes in the roof to the third floor.

Nelson looked down the stairwell. Members of Nash's internal security force were racing up the stairs, firing upward as they ran. He ducked his head back and dropped to the floor, signaling his men to do the same. Pulling two grenades from his web gear, he pulled the pin on one, counted "one thousand one, one thousand two," and dropped it down the stairwell. It went off in midair just after leaving his hand. He quickly followed it with another grenade.

As the second grenade burst, members of his team leaned over the railing, raking the stairs with short bursts of fire.

As they ceased firing, they heard one more rattle of an automatic weapon from the other end of the corridor, followed by silence.

"All clear, going down." Nelson heard Bonior's calm voice in his earphones.

Nelson's men were already rigging two fast-ropes. As soon as they were secure, the men vaulted over the railing and dropped downward, kicking as they went to keep from getting entangled in the stair railings. Two men remained on each floor to guard the stairwell and then followed their teammates down.

As they hit the deck in the basement, Bonior's men ran through the corridor to join Nelson's unit.

Nelson grabbed Bonior's arm and pointed at a closed door. Bonior shot the lock off the door and kicked it open. Nelson and Bonior led the way through the opening, weapons at the ready. Other members of the team set up a perimeter around the doorway while Sgt. Tim Hutchins led two other Special Tactics aircraft controllers outside to guide the helicopters back in to pick them up.

Nelson took in the scene in a glance.

Nash was seated at a communications console built into the opposite wall. Bernard stood at his shoulder. Both men looked up, startled.

To one side of the room, a man with a neck brace stood with his pistol pressed to the temple of Dick Hoffman, who was bound to a chair, his blood-streaked head hanging down on his chest.

Three of Nash's security team, armed with light machine guns, brought them to bear at the sound of the door crashing open.

Sergei Kaparov had begun to relax once more as he sped north over the Mississippi valley with no further sign of attack. Far ahead, he could make out the sprawling mass of Saint Louis, with the city spreading out to the west and East Saint Louis stretching off to the east, divided by the broad, muddy ribbon of the great river. He checked his instrument panel: right on course and on time.

Four shots rang out at almost the same instant. Nash's security men, including the one holding his pistol at Hoffman's head, fell dead, each with a bullet hole in the center of the forehead.

"Freeze!" Nelson shouted, and started across the room toward Bernard and Nash.

Bernard moved to meet him, swinging a chair. Nelson blocked the chair with the butt of his M-16 and ripped the muzzle of the rifle down across Bernard's face. Bernard dived toward Nelson, driving him backward.

Nelson stumbled, then regained his balance. Grabbing Bernard's head with both hands, Nelson used the other man's momentum to pull his face down while he brought his knee up. There was a sound of breaking bone as Bernard's nose shattered.

"Son of a bitch!" He roared with rage, spraying Nelson with flecks of the blood streaming from his broken nose.

He grabbed the webbing stretching across Nelson's chest with his left hand and drove his fist into Nelson's diaphragm. Nelson reeled backward, gasping for breath. The room turned a fuzzy gray and he blinked, trying to restore his vision.

Nash, seemingly oblivious to the violent confrontation, remained seated at the control console, staring intently at a large clock face on the instrument panel. The black hand indicated twenty-three seconds remaining before it would reach the twelve o'clock position. The index finger of Nash's right hand was poised over a switch on the desk. A few more seconds and he could push the switch—the switch that would obliterate the party convention and cut a wide swath through Saint Louis. But at the speed Kaparov was flying, he might miss the city entirely if the switch were pushed too early or too late.

The major features of downtown Saint Louis were now clearly visible to Kaparov, ahead and far below. He could easily make out the outlines of Busch Stadium, the Kiel Center, where the hockey and soccer teams played, and the immense Trans World Dome, spreading over fourteen acres at the heart of America's Center.

In the convention center, Maynard Walker held the attention of the normally restless delegates with a speech that ticked off the accomplishments of his first term in office and outlined the ambitious agenda for his second four years. Slowed by frequent prolonged applause, he was running just a little bit behind schedule. He thought with satisfaction that the speech writers had, if anything, overdone it on the applause lines he had demanded. Off to the side, Marcie Walker sat with a smile frozen on her face, clapping enthusiastically at each applause line. To the television audience, she seemed the very picture of a devoted presidential spouse. No one noticed that she could not keep from glancing nervously at her wristwatch, wondering if she was living the last few moments of her life.

As Nelson reeled backward, gasping, his foot came down in a pool of blood that had formed near the head of one of the dead security men. He lost his balance and fell heavily on his right shoulder.

Bernard was on top of him, screaming curses and slamming his face with a powerful right fist. As Bernard raised his fist for another blow, Bonior stepped forward and cracked him on the side of the head with the butt of his rifle, sending him sprawling back toward the console.

Bonior stepped over the body of Bernard and reached for Nash. But Nash turned and pushed violently, sending Bonior back, tripping over Bernard. He turned once more to the clock.

Bernard staggered to his feet and shouted, "Let's get out of here!" He grabbed Nash by the shoulder.

Nash leaned back toward the console, his gaze still on the clock. It showed seven seconds to go. "Wait! Wait!" He shouted.

"Bullshit!" Bernard exclaimed, and dragged him bodily through a door in the back of the room. The lock clicked shut.

Bonior leaned over the console, puzzling what to do. Was there some switch he should throw to prevent the device from going off? Should he shoot up the console? As he pondered, the hand on the clock reached the twelve o'clock position and stopped.

Bonior stared at the clock and then shrugged. If anything was going to happen, it had already been triggered automatically. Thinking of his family in Saint Louis, he prayed that nothing had happened.

He glanced over his shoulder. Nelson, smeared with blood from the dead man and clutching his right shoulder, was sitting up.

"Rex! Let's go!" Bonior shouted. He tried the door Bernard and Nash had gone through and then stepped back and put a shot through the lock.

As the door swung open, Bonior found himself looking down a long, brightly lighted corridor that curved to the right. As far as he could see, the corridor was empty, but he could hear the footsteps of two running men receding in the distance.

He and Marker ran down the hallway, holding their weapons ready at waist level.

As they rounded a curve, Marker suddenly stopped and grabbed Bonior's web gear.

"Hold it, Chief! This tunnel is mined!" Marker pointed to a tiny fixture on one wall. A small beam of light shone across the corridor to a sensor on the other wall. As the two men sized up the situation, they saw another similar light at knee level.

Marker pulled his canteen off his belt. "Let's see what these things do," he said, as he tossed the canteen through the lower beam.

As the canteen broke the beam, a ten-foot section of the ceiling crashed to the floor, blocking the hallway. The lights went off, plunging the corridor into total darkness.

Both men pulled out flashlights. As the dust cleared, they could see a narrow gap at the top of the pile of rubble.

"We can get through there, Chief," Marker said, pointing to the gap.

"No way, Rex. We don't know what other surprises are waiting for us down there. Do you know where this corridor goes?"

"Let me think. Yeah, I remember seeing something like this on those plans I got at the courthouse. I bet this goes down to the runway."

"That makes sense. Maybe we can head them off." Bonior adjusted the microphone in front of his mouth and keyed his transmitter to call Jack Laffer in his helicopter. "Bravo team to Flash One. Bravo to Flash One. . . ."

He hesitated, waiting for a reply. All he heard in his earphone was a crackle of static.

"Flash One, do you read me? Come in, Flash One."

There was no answer.

"Come on, Rex, let's get out of here," Bonior exclaimed. "The radio signal must be shielded down here."

Back in the communications room, Bonior quickly established contact with Laffer.

"Two fugitives are heading toward the runway, sir. If you get over there, you may be able to stop them before they can take off."

"Roger, Bravo One. Will do."

Turning, Bonior found Nelson still sitting on the floor, holding his shoulder.

Bonior leaned down. "Are you okay, boss?"

"My shoulder hurts like a son of a bitch, but otherwise I'm okay."

Over against the wall, Marker was untying his friend. With one hand, he held his head up and looked into his face. "Can you talk, Dick?"

The injured man gazed around the room and then murmured, through swollen lips, "Get outa here. Going to blow."

Marker leaned down, putting his ear close to his mouth. "What's going to blow?"

"Building rigged. I heard these guys talking. Going to blow. Get out!"

"Captain!" Marker shouted. "Hoffman says this place is rigged. It's going to blow."

"Okay, let's go." Nelson turned to Bonior. "How do we stand, Chief?"

"We've got problems, boss. One of the helicopters is heading for the runway. We can bring the other bird in but he may have a problem getting us all out in one load. After all, we're up about seven thousand feet here."

Nash and Bernard felt the shock wave as the collapse of the roof sent a blast of air through the tunnel.

"That ought to hold them." Nash led the way into the rear of a small hangar where an executive jet was sheltered. Bernard recognized it as the same plane that had brought him here for his first encounter with Nash.

Bernard looked down and saw that Nash was carrying a small and obviously heavy suitcase.

"What the hell are you carrying?"

"The keys to the kingdom." Nash grinned. "You get the doors."

Bernard pushed the doors open and then scrambled into the plane. Nash was already in the left seat, pressing the starter button. As the engines roared into life, he began to taxi.

Nash leaned back and touched the suitcase to make sure it was where he had put it. Inside were the hard drives containing the detailed secrets of his worldwide holdings.

As the jet emerged from the hangar and turned onto the runway, Laffer racked the Pave Low around in a steep bank, diving down toward the plane.

Bernard, sitting in the plane's right seat, looked out his window, and saw the helicopter diving toward them.

He grabbed Nash's arm and pointed out the window. "There's a Pave Low behind us."

Nash didn't even look over his shoulder. He pushed the throttles to the forward stop and the plane seemed to leap down the runway.

As Nelson stepped out into the sunlight, Hutchins grasped him by the left arm. "Sir, we've identified two machine gun positions there . . . and there." He pointed with his left hand. "They're going to have to be knocked out before we can bring the bird in."

"Are we in danger down here?"

"I don't think so. They can't see down into this area. But they sure as hell can hit a helo coming in."

Nelson looked up at the building rising four stories up behind him.

"Jeff, you take some of your men up there," he said, pointing to the second floor. "You can shoot down on those guns."

Bonior turned, called out the names of four of his men, and led them at a run up the stairway. Bill Wagner, struggling up the stairs with his heavy .30 caliber machine gun, brought up the rear.

Bonior, leading the group, looked back down and shouted: "Let's move it, Wagner. We need your firepower up here."

At the second floor landing, Bonior and his men paused, peering around the edges of a large window.

"There!" he exclaimed, pointing to one machine gun position camouflaged as part of a rock garden. "And there's the other," he said, pointing off to the right.

He spoke into his microphone. "Okay, we're in place. Bring in the bird. Tell him we'll mark the two positions with smoke. He'll take the green smoke. We'll hit the yellow."

"Roger, Chief. Will do," Hutchins replied. He switched channels and called in the helicopter.

Bonior listened intently to his earphones. Then he heard the warning signal: "The bird is fifteen seconds out."

He stood back and shattered the window with a short burst from his M-16. As the glass fell away, two of his men fired flares at the machine gun positions. Then all five men opened fire on the position marked with the yellow smoke.

The helicopter came into view, hammering the other machine gun with .50-caliber fire. Neither position got off a round.

Moments later, the helicopter settled near the basement door of the compound and the team clambered aboard. The craft was on the ground no more than twenty seconds when Nelson gave the signal for liftoff. The plane rose slowly, fighting to lift its heavy load in the thin mountain air. It rose gradually and then turned to race down the hillside away from the compound.

Laffer flew parallel to the runway, staying just far enough to the right to permit the gunner in the left window a clear shot at the fleeing jet. Fifty-caliber shells tore a line in the tarmac, chasing the plane down the runway. Then the plane was off the ground and climbing sharply. The gunner took one last shot and then ceased firing to avoid hitting the rotor circling above.

Laffer turned and joined the other helicopter headed back down the valley toward Peterson Field.

Nash eased back on the throttles and turned onto a course to the south along the eastern slope of the great mountain range. He reached over his head and carefully adjusted one of the radio dials. When he was satisfied that he had the right frequency, he clicked his microphone button once, sending a signal back to a receiver in the compound they had just left.

"Holy shit!" Marker exclaimed. "Look at that!" The whole mountainside containing Nash's compound blossomed like a giant, fiery flower as a series of explosive charges, planted at key points throughout the structure, erupted.

A moment later, the helicopters were violently jolted by the blast wave, the roar clearly audible over the sound of the aircraft engines.

Marker watched until the explosions ceased and then crawled up through the cabin to check on Hoffman. Shoup, the Air Force medic, had already given him some water and washed the blood from his face.

"How you doing, Dick?"

Hoffman smiled weakly. "Pretty good, I guess. That son of a bitch really worked me over. But I broke his jaw. Guess we're even."

"More than even, Dick. He's dead."

"Yeah, more than even."

"You really got in with some bad company there."

"Nah. They're a bunch of good guys. We just wanted some action and Big Dog said he could provide it. But that Nash . . . that bugger is *evil*!"

"I'm afraid we had to take out some of your buddies."

"I was worried that was going to happen. I've been having a bad feeling about this whole thing."

The delegates, unaware that they had come within seconds of being incinerated, greeted the conclusion of Walker's speech with prolonged applause, followed by a boisterous demonstration that serpentined up and down the aisles through the huge auditorium.

Kaparov, equally unaware that he had come within a few seconds of killing the president, the delegates to the party convention, and hundreds of thousands of people in Saint Louis, was enjoying his ride. Down below, he could see the sun glinting off the water of the Great Lakes, and far up ahead he thought he could make out the line marking the edge of Hudson Bay. It wouldn't be too much longer until he was back in Uzbekistan and then, he told himself, he would have time to spend with all his friends and his family in Samarkand. Time enough then to collect his millions from the bank in the Cayman Islands and plan the rest of his life. As he streaked northward, the outline of the great bay became clearer and, beyond it, the beginning of the great polar ice cap.

It was peaceful here, far above the earth. Kaparov thought it was strange to be astride such a powerful machine and yet hear nothing more than the faint murmur of the plane's instruments and the occasional sound of a control surface gently changing position. What he did not hear—or at least, did not distinguish from the other sounds—was a tiny timing device buried deep in the fuselage behind him. On orders from Nash, it had been placed there without Kaparov's knowledge shortly before he had blasted off from the strip in Quintana Roo.

Sergei Kaparov had not quite reached Hudson Bay when the timer completed its cycle and set off the explosive device to which it was attached. The boom of the explosion was quickly left far behind as the bits of the plane hurtled onward and then gradually slowed and fell in a long arc into the icy waters of the bay. A few villagers down below stirred in their sleep as the boom rolled across the landscape. One or two hunters saw the flash and told each other it was a particularly big shooting star.

Monitors at NORAD, who had been following the plane's path since shortly after it had taken off earlier in the day, noted that it had suddenly and without explanation disappeared from their radar screens.

When Adm. McKay was told of the radar report, he breathed a sigh of relief and picked up the hotline to inform the president.

CHAPTER 36

IT WAS THREE WEEKS AFTER THE ELECTION, BUT MAYNARD Walker was still savoring his narrow victory and the prospect of four more years in the White House. For all the money Richard Wilson had seemed to have at his command, he had rapidly faded in popular appeal, much as Ross Perot's strident message had lost its strength during the course of an earlier election season. Wilson was plagued during the campaign by questions about where he had disappeared to during the summer convention. He was never able to come up with a satisfactory explanation for his strange behavior.

When the votes were counted, Wilson had deprived Walker of the majority vote—the mandate—he'd badly wanted, but the new third party had not garnered enough votes to deny the president re-election.

Cindy Carson was puzzled. She had no idea why she had been ordered to report to Derek Shepherd, the head of the Secret Service White House detail.

Shepherd strode across the room to shake her hand and guide her to a chair. He pulled up another chair and sat down beside her.

"How are things going, Cindy?"

"Better, sir. That problem we talked about before seems to have solved itself. The president has been. . . ." She glanced at Shepherd with a quizzical look on her face. "How should I put this? Let's say . . . the president has been behaving himself."

Shepherd chuckled. "Sometimes things like this take care of themselves." He paused and looked at the young agent. "Cindy, you handled this whole thing very professionally. How would you like a new assignment with more responsibility?"

"I'd like that, sir. What do you have in mind?"

"We're making some staff changes. I'd like you to be the new head of the detail protecting the first lady."

She looked at him for a moment and broke into a broad grin. "Oh, I'd like that, sir. I'm a great admirer of Mrs. Walker. It would be a real privilege to protect her."

"It's a tough job, Cindy. As you know, Mrs. Walker has her own business and she travels a great deal. That means you'll have to deal with situations that are outside our normal routine. I've been impressed by your performance and I'm confident you can handle it."

She rose and shook his hand firmly. "You can count on me, sir. And thank you."

The military men, proudly wearing their uniforms, with wives in new dresses and children in tow, had begun lining up at the East Gate of the White House early in the morning, eager not to be late.

They were escorted into the building and to the East Room, the large ceremonial ballroom, and seated in rows facing the east side of the room.

The president and his wife entered the room from the door opposite the podium at exactly 10 A.M. and moved through the room, waving and shaking hands. The president stepped to the lectern and raised his hands. A hush quickly fell over the room.

"Meeting here with you this morning, I am reminded of Winston Churchill's words at the time of the Battle of Britain: 'Never in the course of human events have so many owed so much to so few.' It is no exaggeration to say that you, like those few Spitfire pilots, saved your nation from a terrible danger. But whereas those pilots won their victory in the skies over southern Britain in aerial battles visible to thousands of their countrymen, your victory was achieved in secret. Only a few of your fellow Americans will ever know of your contribution to their safety.

"You men—and Mrs. Collins—know what you did, and you are justified in feeling a great deal of pride in a job well done. But I must apologize to the wives and children with us here this morning. All you know is that your husbands and fathers disappeared one day without being able to tell you where they were going or what they were going to do and that they came back another day, forbidden to tell you where they had been or what they had done. Let me simply say that if your husbands and fathers had not gone where they went and had not done what they did, this nation would have suffered the worst calamity in its history.

"It gives me great pleasure to award the Silver Star to each of the officers and the Bronze Star to each of the enlisted men in this unique unit. This, unfortunately, must remain a secret between us. I ask you not to wear your new ribbons outside this room. But the award will be made a classified portion of your military record and the fact of the award will be available to promotion boards."

The president and Mrs. Walker stepped down from the speaker's platform. An aide held a tray containing the medals. As the men lined up, the president pinned a medal on each man's chest. A special civilian distinguished service award was presented to Pat Collins. Adm. McKay stood to the president's left and shook each person's hand.

"Mr. President." Nelson stood nervously. "On behalf of the Eagle Force, I would like to thank you for the recognition we have received here today. Let me say that we appreciate the opportunity to be of service to you and our country. Whenever there's an impossible job to be done, call on us."

His brief remarks were greeted with laughter and applause. The president smiled. "I may take you up on that, Commander. But let's hope it never gets as hairy as this last assignment.''

As the ceremony ended, the president and his wife circulated among the guests, smiling and shaking hands. Catching sight of Bonior, the president pumped the big man's hand.

Bonior introduced his wife and children. The president crouched down.

"So this is Denise. I heard you were a very sick little girl. Are you feeling all right now?"

The six-year-old stared at him with big eyes and pivoted back and forth on her heel, speechless.

"Oh, yes, Mr. President," her mother volunteered. "For a little while there, we were afraid we were going to lose her. But you know how children are. She bounced right back. She's as good as new now."

The president rose and patted her on the head.

"Mrs. Bonior, I can't say how much I admire your bravery and your competence in these very difficult circumstances. It pains me that we had to take Jeff away when Denise was in such critical condition. But let me just say that he has made an incomparable contribution to the safety of our nation. And you, in your way, were part of that.''

"Thank you, Mr. President. You know, sometimes SEAL wives have to be just as tough as SEALs.''

He shook her hand again. "Or even tougher. . . .''

As the president left the room and entered the long corridor running down toward his office, he put an arm over Adm. McKay's shoulder.

"Say, Mac," he asked, "did you ever find the source of that leak?"

"No, Mr. President. We couldn't carry out a full-scale investigation, but I personally felt satisfied the leak did not come from within the team itself."

"Which means . . . ?"

"Which means it must have come from my office or . . . well, it may have come from the White House. It worries me. It's the kind of thing that could cause us all kinds of problems in the future."

"I doubt it came from here. Who in the White House knew enough about the operation to leak it?" The president paused, thinking, then added: "Well, keep working on it. We can't afford that sort of thing."

If You Enjoyed *Desert Thunder,*
Then Read On For a Preview of

TERROR AT TARANAKI,

the Next Exciting Thriller
in the **SEALS EAGLE FORCE** Series
Coming Soon from Avon Books

A SLIVER OF THE MOON IN ITS LAST QUARTER CAST A SILVER glow across the four-foot swells coursing toward the shore, two miles away. An unusually soft wind from the east carried the fresh spring smells of the earth out across the waters.

Silently, the U.S.S. *Kamehameha* broke the surface of the water in the South Taranaki Bight, off the west coast of New Zealand's north island. As soon as the submarine came to a stop, gently rocking with the movement of the water, the door of the large dry deck shelter bulging from the aft deck swung open. Crew members quickly slid two SEAL delivery vehicles out onto the deck.

Cdr. Charles Nelson stepped out of the shelter and touched the arm of the submarine crewman in charge of preparing the SDVs.

"Chief, let's make sure we get the ballast right." Nelson recalled an incident during the Vietnam war when an improperly ballasted SDV sank to the bottom and was damaged when the submarine rolled against it.

The submariner turned and flashed him an "I know my business" look, but all he said was, "Aye, aye, sir."

Standing behind Nelson were eleven members of his combined SEAL–Air Commando force, each man clad in a wet suit and a Draeger underwater breathing apparatus. One man carried a heavy .50-caliber sniper rifle, and another shouldered an M-60 machine gun. The others carried their own favorite weapons. Several preferred the light H&K MP-5 submachine gun, so smooth-operating that a man could spray out its 30-round magazine while holding the weapon in one hand. Others favored the Navy-issue M-16 rifle, coated with teflon and fitted with drain holes to operate after long immersion in saltwater. Each of the men carried an automatic pistol strapped to his waist. Several of them carried the standard issue K-bar knife, but others had their own special knives. Two were encumbered with heavy coils of rope, carried over one shoulder and across the chest.

At a signal from the chief, the men quickly took their places in the SDVs and connected their masks to the crafts' air supply. Two men—a driver and a navigator—took the front seats of each SDV.

At a signal from Nelson, the two SDVs were slipped over the side, one after the other, and quickly submerged.

Moments later the submarine disappeared. It had been on the surface no more than fifteen minutes. No hint remained that just below the waves there lurked a powerful nuclear-powered ship and two tiny battery-powered submersibles carrying a dozen of the world's deadliest commandos.

Master Chief Jeff Bonior was at the controls of the lead SDV with Nelson beside him, acting as navigator. Bonior and Nelson concentrated on the instruments before them, glowing eerily in the darkness. Behind them the other members of the team sat with nothing to do, in total darkness, shivering in the fifty-eight-degree water that surrounded them. As they moved slowly toward shore, their fingers and lips turned blue with cold. Their bodies drew blood toward their hearts, and then, sensing the accumulation of fluids, signaled their kidneys to expel some of the liquid. A flow of urine down a leg provided a pleasant but fleeting sensation of warmth.

When the two craft reached a point a hundred yards from the rocky shore, Bonior gently parked on the bottom. The other boat pulled in behind him. Nelson set an electronic signal that would permit them to find their way back to the SDVs, if necessary. The men released their safety belts, formed up in two-man buddy teams, and swam toward shore.

They surfaced just to the seaward side of the breaker line and watched the waves crashing against the rocks. Then, swimming rapidly to follow a wave in, each of the men grabbed a rock and swung around to put the rock between himself and the following breaker. As the wave receded, they scrambled quickly to the top of the bank and dropped flat on the beach grass. Between the sounds of the ocean hammering the shore, they listened intently and scanned the area in front of them for any sign of light or movement.

After lying motionless for nearly five minutes, Nelson gave an arm signal and the men moved forward by twos to a stand of tall eucalyptus trees. In their shelter, they quickly stripped off their breathing rigs and wet suits, buried them in a hole they dug in the sand, checked their weapons and radio equipment, smeared camouflage paint on their faces and the backs of their hands, and then sat down to wait. Smoking was not permitted, lest the flare of a match or the smell of smoke give away their position. Several of the men quietly chewed tobacco, occasionally turning to spit into the sand.

As his men prepared for their mission, Nelson stood looking north at the almost perfectly symmetrical volcano rising more than eight thousand feet above him. In the faint light of the moon, he could see the mantle of deep snow that capped the mountain and reached far down its south side in sheltered crevasses.

Capt. James Cook, sailing past in 1770, named the mountain for John Perceval, Second Earl of Egmont and Britain's First Lord of the Admiralty in the years preceding Cook's voyage. But the Maori, who had colonized the islands of New Zealand hundreds of years before the coming of the white man, had long known it as a sacred mountain. With their name, they honored a god who took the form of a mountain.

"So this is Taranaki," Nelson murmured to himself.

But Nelson lost no time admiring the mountain's name or its spectacular beauty, which rivaled that of Japan's Mount Fuji. Instead, he concentrated on the job ahead—the most difficult and demanding he had ever faced in the more than a decade and a half that he had served as a Navy SEAL.

The words of Adm. Norris McKay, the chairman of the Joint Chiefs of Staff, remained vividly in his mind: "I don't have to tell you how important this mission is, Chuck. Your job is to rescue the hostages and bring them home safely. Failure, or even partial success, are not among your options. You must succeed!''

Nelson and McKay had had a long and friendly relationship. The older officer had served as a kind of "sea daddy" to the younger man, making sure at each step of the way that his career remained on the fast track. And it was McKay who had tapped Nelson to head the Eagle Force, made up of picked men from the SEALs and the Air Commandos, to be available for just such demanding missions as this.

In the years that he had been associated with the admiral, Nelson had never heard him speak in almost formal terms of the urgency of success on an assignment. Previously, the importance of the mission went without saying. They both understood that the Eagle Force was called on only when the stakes were high, as were the odds against success.

But this mission, of course, was different. No military unit had ever been called upon to carry out one quite like it, one which involved both national security and the strongest personal emotions.

Staring at the mountain, Nelson knew the hostages were up there somewhere. He could only hope that they were still alive and in good health and that by this time tomorrow, he and his men would be celebrating a successful operation.

Nelson turned back to his men, quietly moving among the trees, finishing their preparations.

Dick Hoffman, a SEAL chief petty officer, and Air Force Master Chief Tim Hutchins were standing off to one side, talking quietly, as Nelson approached.

"Okay, you guys know what you have to do. If you end up in jail, you're on your own.''

Hoffman, who had rejoined the SEALs after serving briefly in a mercenary commando outfit, laughed. "Being thrown in jail would probably be a lot better than being caught by some angry New Zealander.''

Hutchins and Hoffman quickly moved out, jogging along the side of the road that led to the little town of Opunake, a mile to the west. As they approached the town, they left the pavement and moved over into the shadows beside the road.

Hoffman took the lead, moving up the right side of the road from one parked car to another, quietly trying the doors.

He stopped beside a Land Rover, eased open the door, and checked the gauge. It showed a half tank of gas. Hoffman turned and gave Hutchins a thumbs-up signal.

As Hoffman slipped into the Land Rover, Hutchins continued down the street until he came to a van with the doors unlocked. The gas tank was nearly full.

Hutchins slid into the driver's seat on the right side of the van. Pulling a chisel and a hammer from a pocket on the leg of his coveralls, he knocked out the steering wheel lock with one sharp blow. Reaching under the dashboard, he quickly located the ignition wires. Then he looked back toward the Land Rover.

Once he saw Hoffman wave his arm out the window, Hutchins crossed the wires under the van's dash. The engine caught, Hutchins put the vehicle in gear, and after Hoffman passed him in the Land Rover, he rolled quietly down the road without lights, following Hoffman out of town. Behind them, a lone dog barked frantically, and then, as the two vehicles disappeared in the darkness, lapsed into silence.

Hoffman pressed the button on his radio and spoke a single word into the tiny microphone suspended in front of his lips: "Heist."

"Okay," Nelson said. "They're coming."

The ten men formed up beside the road in two five-man squads, ready to climb quickly into the stolen vehicles as they crept past.

Nelson got into the front seat of the Land Rover next to Hoffman.

"Any problems?"

"No problems at all, sir. Just like when I was a kid."

"One of my men, a car thief?"

"No, not really, sir. But we all knew how to do it."

"You're okay on the navigation?"

"Yeah, I've got it memorized. . . ." He paused as he swung to the left onto a road coming in from the north. "We take this road up past Taungatara, and then we turn off on a new road that goes up the mountain alongside the . . . the . . . I forget the name of the river.''

''Waiaua, or something like that.'' Nelson helped him out.

''Right, the Wye-oo-a. We go up that road and stop before we get to the guard post.''

''Good.'' Nelson scrunched down in his seat, crossed his arms over his chest, and shut his eyes. It was going to be a long night.

''Sir.'' Nelson felt the vehicle slowing and was instantly awake.

''Getting close?''

''Yes, sir, I think so. According to our intel, there should be a guard post and a barricade across the road about a mile from here.''

''Okay, Dick. Kill the lights and let's creep up here just a little further.''

Hutchins, in the following vehicle, switched off his lights and followed Hoffman until he pulled to the side of the road and stopped.

The four men designated during the pre-mission planning to take out the guard station stepped forward.

''This has to be done quietly,'' Nelson whispered. ''We don't want to give them time to set off an alarm and we don't want them firing their weapons.''

The team members nodded and started up the road, keeping in the shadows to the right of the pavement, spaced out in the traditional formation of an infantry patrol.

Jeff Bonior moved ahead as point man. A quarter mile later he raised his hand to stop the column. Ahead he could see a guard leaning against a bar like that at a railroad crossing, blocking the road. Another man was visible in a lighted guardhouse, apparently absorbed in a paperback book.

Bonior studied the scene. Both men were vulnerable. But the challenge was to take out both of them without giving either one time to alert the other or anyone else.

A plan formed in Bonior's mind. He signaled the SEAL

behind him to move forward and then whispered instructions in his ear. The man worked his way up the side of the road toward the guardhouse, keeping well over in the shadows, moving slowly, deliberately, gently.

When he came within twenty yards of the guard, he edged into the woods and hid behind a tree. Then he threw a handful of gravel into the trees in front of him.

The guard straightened up and turned toward the sound. Holding his automatic rifle at the ready, he walked across the road, peering into the darkness. As he stepped into the shadows, the SEAL stepped from his cover, grabbed the sentry from behind, and drew his knife across his throat. The man died without a sound.

Lowering the body to the ground, the SEAL wiped his knife on the dead man's uniform and then turned his attention to the guardhouse. The sentry inside was still busy with his paperback. Moving again with great care, the SEAL worked his way around behind the guardhouse. From the holster at his waist, he pulled out his Sig Sauer P-226 9-mm pistol and attached a silencer to the muzzle. He liked the Sig Sauer because its only safety device was a double-action trigger. When he pulled the trigger, he knew it was going to fire. Holding the pistol at the ready in his right hand, he quietly grasped the door handle with his left. Then, jerking the door open, he pressed the tip of his silencer against the base of the guard's neck and fired a single shot. The movement was so fast the guard didn't even have time to turn his head, let alone cry out, before he died.

The SEAL leaned over the body and pulled the lever to raise the barrier. He spoke a single word into his microphone: "Clear."

Moments later the two vehicles carrying the commandos rolled past the guardhouse, paused to pick up their man, and continued on up the mountain without lights.

"Let's take it real easy here, Dick," Nelson told his driver. The guardhouse seemed to have been located at the snowline. Almost as soon as they passed that point, they saw piles of snow on either side of the road, and Hoffman could feel the thin patches of ice where the snow had melted during the day and then frozen as the temperature had dropped after dark.

Nelson shined a light on the dashboard and watched the odometer as they crept up the road.

"I figure it's a mile from the guardhouse to the compound," he said. "Let's allow about a quarter of a mile and then go the rest of the way on foot . . . okay now, just a little bit further. . . . Here. Let's pull off here."

Hoffman eased the vehicle to the side of the road, careful not to slide on the ice. Hutchins stopped behind him. The men climbed out, stepping cautiously to avoid slipping, and formed up in two six-man squads, one on each side of the road. Nelson stepped out as point man of one squad; Bonior headed the other. Normally the unit commander would not take the point, but Nelson wanted to be where he could assess the situation and direct their action.

Silently, the two squads snaked up the road.

Nelson pressed the little button that illuminated his wristwatch. It was a quarter to one in the morning.

He inched forward around a bend and then signaled to his men to lie down. He pulled a pair of night vision binoculars from a case at his waist and scanned the scene in front of him.

From the satellite photos he had studied, he knew it would be tough getting into the compound where the hostages were held. But seeing the situation they faced in person was a shock.

Rising in front of him was an almost sheer wall of black lava thirty feet high. Where the road passed through a narrow cut in the rock wall, it was blocked by two tall steel doors. A small guardhouse nestled against the wall to the right of the doors. Nelson could see only two guards in the small building.

Raising his glasses, Nelson scanned the top of the lava wall. As he had feared, it was topped by rolls of razor-sharp concertina wire.

Nelson raised an arm and motioned to the left. Bonior and his men moved off in that direction. Nelson led his men to the right, toward the base of the rock wall.

One man in each squad carried a roll of rope over one shoulder and diagonally across his chest. Nelson signaled his rope-carrier forward. He laid the rope on the ground, pulled out an end to which a grappling hook with four barbs was attached, twirled it around, and threw it high up on the wall. He pulled on the rope to set the hooks and then he and another man put their full weight on the rope. The hooks held. A short distance away, on the other side of the road, Bonior's squad made the same preparations.

"Okay, get up there and make sure that thing is secure." Nelson tapped the rope-carrier on the shoulder.

The SEAL went up the rope hand over hand, bouncing his feet against the rock as he went. In a few seconds he had reached the top of the wall and checked the hooks. He pulled the rope up and down as a signal, and the other men quickly clambered up the cliff, spreading out along the ledge.

When they had all reached the top, the man who had been carrying the rope unwrapped a tightly woven mat that he had carried around his body. He spread the mat over the concertina wire and then lay down on it. He lay still as the other men, one after the other, used his body as a stepping stone to vault over the wire.

As the men crossed the wire barrier, they spaced themselves out in a single line. From their position, the lava sloped sharply downward. Ahead of them, about fifty yards away, they could see the outline of a three-story building. The roadway blocked by the large steel doors entered the building at ground level through another set of tall doors. It looked as though the entranceway had been designed so that trucks could move heavy equipment directly into the building.

Nelson studied the scene through his night vision binoculars. He found himself wishing he could turn the clock back and make a different approach to the building. By climbing the wall at two points, his men had successfully gotten inside the first line of defense. But in doing so they had placed themselves on different sides of the roadway entering the building.

Nelson spoke into his microphone. "Jeff, can you get your guys over on this side of the road?"

"Yeah, we'll patrol down there and sneak across."

Bonior moved his squad down the lava slope toward the building and then across to the edge of the road. They found themselves atop a ledge eight feet above the road.

The first two men lowered themselves carefully down the

wall and dashed across the road. One man boosted the other up the wall on the other side. From the top of the wall, the first man lowered the muzzle of his rifle and used it to pull his buddy to the top.

The second two men quickly followed.

As the last man clambered up the wall after crossing the road, a chunk of lava broke loose and clattered to the roadway.

The men dropped to the ground and lay motionless for more than a minute. Then, just as they were preparing to move out and join up with the other squad, a bank of lights along the top of the building flashed on. As a loud siren sounded, the doors to the building swung open and a dozen members of the guard force ran out onto the roadway, swinging their weapons from side to side, looking for the intruders.

The squads headed by Nelson and Bonior were still separated by about thirty feet, but the two squad leaders acted instinctively at the same moment, shouting: "Lights!"

Within seconds the commandos had shot out all the lights atop the building. Swiftly they pulled night vision goggles down over their eyes.

When the lights went out, the members of the guard force were suddenly at a serious disadvantage. Without night vision goggles and with their pupils still contracted, they found themselves groping in the dark. They were also hemmed in by the walls of lava on both sides of the roadway.

Nelson and Bonior quickly deployed their commandos along the edge of the wall and began picking off the men milling about below them. A couple of the guards tried firing back at the muzzle flashes, but then those who were still standing turned and ran back toward the safety of the building.

As suddenly as it had started, the firefight was over. But Nelson knew their advantage was fleeting. A reinforced guard force would soon be coming through the doors looking for them.

"Jack, let's get their power supply," Nelson said, grasping SEAL Chief Jack Berryman by the elbow.

Turning to the other men, he instructed them to remove their goggles.

On a rise to the right side of the building, a large tank sat on a platform. From their intelligence briefing, Nelson knew it contained natural gas, piped in from the gas field at Kapuni, a dozen miles away on the south slope of Mount Taranaki. The gas was used to run a large generator that supplied power for the entire complex.

Berryman fitted a steel-tipped shell into his .50-caliber sniper rifle and fired a single shot at the tank. Then, slipping an incendiary round into the chamber, he drew a bead on the spot where gas was now leaking from the tank.

There was a small flash where the shell struck before the tank erupted in a boiling fireball streaked with exotic colors. The commandos threw themselves to the ground and buried their heads in their arms as the initial waves of intense heat swept over them.

"Okay, let's go," Nelson commanded a moment later, rising from the ground and running, in a crouch, toward the building. He could feel the heat burning the exposed skin of his face and hands.

With the butt of his rifle, he smashed a large plate glass window, knocked loose the glass around the edges, and jumped into a large room filled with laboratory benches covered with beakers and other chemical paraphernalia.

Back in Hawaii, training for the mission, Nelson and his men had carefully memorized the layout of the compound they now found themselves in—or at least, the best description they could put together from a variety of intelligence sources. Nelson only hoped that the blueprint was reasonably accurate.

Nelson slipped his night vision goggles back down over his eyes and crossed the room to a door that swung into the room. Slowly, he inched it open until he could peer out into an internal corridor. Another door on the other side of the room, he knew, led into the large central hallway that the guards had emerged from. He didn't want to go that way.

Seeing no one in the corridor, Nelson signaled his men to follow him, moving slowly, cautiously, their backs against the wall and their weapons at the ready.

Nelson led his men along the corridor until it was intersected by another hallway. Turning right, he worked his way down the new corridor. After proceeding twenty yards, he stopped.

If his intelligence was correct, the hostages should be behind the second door on the right. Nelson was surprised to find there was no guard at the door. If there was a guard, and he was inside, that complicated his task.

Silently Nelson deployed his men on both sides of the door. They had all spent hours practicing this very maneuver over and over until every movement was automatic: break open the door, enter quickly, identify anyone with a weapon, and kill quickly with a shot to the head.

Nelson thought of the alternative they had often practiced: break in the door and then toss in a flash-stun grenade that would temporarily blind and disable everyone in the room. It might be the safer way to go, but Nelson wasn't going to do that to *these* hostages.

At a signal from Nelson, Jeff Bonior, the largest member of the team, kicked in the door and went right on through. Three other members of the team were right behind him.

Bonior swept the right side of the room. The man behind him covered the left side, his finger on the trigger of his rifle.

Then the two men strode slowly across the floor as other members of the team moved in behind him.

Bonior turned. "There's no one here, boss."

Scanning the room, Bonior could see scattered items of clothing. On a large table to one side of the room were plates with the leavings of a recent meal.

One of the men dropped to a knee on the other side of the room from the dining table.

"Look at this, Chief." He pushed up his night vision goggles and shined the beam of a small flashlight on the floor. Bonior and Nelson joined him, looking down over his shoulder.

On the floor was a large reddish-brown stain.

Nelson reached down, touched the stain with an index finger, and then brought the finger up into the light of his flashlight.

"Blood. And it's still wet."

The direct line to the White House on Adm. McKay's desk had not even completed the first ring when McKay picked up the receiver. "Admiral McKay here, sir."

"Any word yet, Mac?" The admiral could sense the tense weariness in the voice of President Maynard Walker.

"No, sir. I don't expect any for at least a few more minutes. The force has a total blackout on transmissions until the mission is wrapped up."

McKay heard a long sigh. "Yes, I understand. Please let me know as soon as you hear anything."

He put the phone back in its cradle and stared into the distance. He was the most powerful man in the world. He had at his fingertips nuclear weapons, billion-dollar attack crafts and small, elite commando units. Yet he felt totally helpless.

For it had been twenty-eight days now since the president's wife and son had been kidnapped during a state visit to New Zealand and spirited away to a mysterious compound on the slopes of Mount Taranaki.

SEALS
THE
WARRIOR BREED

Do you have what it takes to be a
NAVY SEAL?

Test your knowledge and your readiness at
www.AvonBooks.com/seals

- Learn more about the history and the traditions of the elite force.
- Sign up for e-mail notification of the next Avon SEALS book.
- Browse through our list of SEALS books.

SEALS
WARRIOR BREED

by H. Jay Riker

The face of war is rapidly changing, calling
America's soldiers into hellish regions where
conventional warriors dare not go.
This is the world of the SEALs.

SILVER STAR
76967-0/$5.99 US/$7.99 Can

PURPLE HEART
76969-7/$5.99 US/$7.99 Can

BRONZE STAR
76970-0/$5.99 US/$6.99 Can

NAVY CROSS
78555-2/$5.99 US/$7.99 Can

MEDAL OF HONOR
78556-0/$5.99 US/$7.99 Can